Ian Watson invented Warhammer 40,000 fiction for the Black Library of Games Workshop twenty years ago with his novel *Inquisitor*, not to mention his notorious *Space Marine*. His highly successful *Inquisition War* trilogy omnibus edition was recently reprinted, and *Space Marine* itself, often hailed as the best ever 40,000 novel, has just been released by the Black Library of Games Workshop as print-on-demand through their website due to overwhelming reader demand. He lives in Northamptonshire, England.

Ian Whates is the author of two novel sequences: the Noise Books (space opera) and The City of a Hundred Rows (urban fantasy with steampunk overtones and SF underpinning). He has also edited several anthologies, including *Solaris Rising* (Solaris, 2011) and two that specifically feature conflict within SF: *Conflicts* (2010) and *Further Conflicts* (2011), both via his own NewCon Press. He lives in Cambridgeshire, England.

Together they edited *The Mammoth Book of Alternate Histories*.

THE MAMMOTH BOOK OF SF WARS

EDITED BY
IAN WATSON AND
IAN WHATES

RUNNING PRESS
PHILADELPHIA · LONDON

Constable & Robinson Ltd
55–56 Russell Square
London WC1B 4HP
www.constablerobinson.com

First published in the UK by Robinson,
an imprint of Constable & Robinson Ltd, 2012

A copy of the British Library Cataloguing in Publication
Data is available from the British Library

UK ISBN 978-1-78033-040-2 (paperback)
UK ISBN 978 1 78033 546 9 (ebook)

1 3 5 7 9 10 8 6 4 2

First published in the United States in 2012 by Running Press Book Publishers,
A Member of the Perseus Books Group

Books published by Running Press are available at special discounts for bulk purchases in the
United States by corporations, institutions, and other organizations. For more information,
please contact the Special Markets Department at the Perseus Books Group,
2300 Chestnut Street, Suite 200, Philadelphia, PA 19103, or call (800) 810-4145, ext. 5000,
or e-mail special.markets@perseusbooks.com.

US ISBN: 978-0-7624-4592-9
US Library of Congress Control Number: 2011939121

9 8 7 6 5 4 3 2 1
Digit on the right indicates the number of this printing

Running Press Book Publishers
2300 Chestnut Street
Philadelphia, PA 19103-4371

Visit us on the web!
www.runningpress.com

Printed and bound in the UK

CONTENTS

ACKNOWLEDGEMENTS

INTRODUCTION by Ian Whates and Ian Watson, © 2012 Ian Whates and Ian Watson.

PEACEKEEPER by Mike Resnick and Brad R. Torgersen, © 2012 Mike Resnick and Brad R. Torgersen. First publication, original to this anthology. Printed by permission of the authors.

FROM OUT OF THE SUN, ENDLESSLY SINGING by Simon R. Green, © 2012 by Simon R. Green. First publication, original to this anthology. Printed by permission of the author.

ALL FOR LOVE by Algis Budrys, © Algis Budrys 1962. Printed by permission of the Estate of Algis Budrys.

THE WAR ARTIST by Tony Ballantyne, © Tony Ballantyne 2011. Published by permission of the author.

THE WAR MEMORIAL by Allen Steele, © 1995 Allen Steele. Printed by permission of the author.

POLITICS by Elizabeth Moon, © Elizabeth Moon 1990. Reprinted by permission of the author.

ARENA by Fredric Brown, © 1944, by Street & Smith Publications, copyright © 1974 by Fredric Brown. Originally appeared in *Astounding Science Fiction*. Reprinted by permission of the Estate and its agent, Barry N. Malzberg.

PEACEKEEPING MISSION by Laura Resnick, © 2008 Laura Resnick.

THE PEACEMAKER by Fred Saberhagen, originally published as "The Lifehater", © 1964 Fred Saberhagen. Printed by permission of the JSS Literary Productions.

JUNKED by Andy Remic, © 2009 Andy Remic. Published by permission of the author.

THE LIBERATION OF EARTH by William Tenn, © 1953, 1981 by William Tenn; first appeared in *Future Science Fiction*; reprinted by permission of the author's Estate and the Estate's agents, the Virginia Kidd Agency, Inc.

A CLEAN ESCAPE by John Kessel, © 1985 John Kessel. Published by permission of the author.

STORMING HELL by John Lambshead, © 2009 John Lambshead. Published by permission of the author.

SOLIDARITY by Walter Jon Williams, © 2005 Walter Jon Williams. Published by permission of the author.

THE PRICE by Michael Z. Williamson, © 2010 Michael Z. Williamson. Reprinted by permission of the author.

THE HORARS OF WAR by Gene Wolfe, © 1970 Gene Wolfe. Reprinted by permission of the author and the author's agents, the Virginia Kidd Agency, Inc.

THE TRAITOR by David Weber, © 1997 David Weber. Reprinted by permission of the author.

THE GAME OF RAT AND DRAGON by Cordwainer Smith, © 1955. Every effort has been made to contact the agent for the Estate.

CAUGHT IN THE CROSSFIRE by David Drake, © 1978 David Drake. Published by permission of the author.

THE RHINE'S WORLD INCIDENT by Neal Asher, © 2008 Neal Asher.

WINNING PEACE by Paul McAuley, © 2007 Paul McAuley. First published in *Postscripts 15*, PS Publishing.

TIME PIECE by Joe Haldeman, © 1970 Joe Haldeman. Printed by permission of the author.

THE WAKE by Dan Abnett, © 2011 Dan Abnett. Printed by permission of the author.

THE PYRE OF NEW DAY by Catherine Asaro, © Catherine Asaro 2012. First publication, original to this anthology. Printed by permission of the author.

INTRODUCTION

THE ABILITY TO make war appears to have been in mankind's blood from the moment we first began to evolve, violence being an integral part of our heritage. Picture a caveman and invariably we imagine him holding a spear or a club. Yet we call our species Homo sapiens, Intelligent Man, while some have even suggested that Homo faber, Man the Maker (of everything from ploughs to radiotelescopes) might be more appropriate. Perhaps both are misguided. Glance at our history, taking in the past few thousand years right up to the present day, and it would be hard to argue that Man the Warmaker isn't the most fitting designation of all. Have we outgrown war? Have we left it behind? No, and it's doubtful we ever will.

Some of the stories in this collection suggest that our warlike tendencies (which of course we all regret, don't we?) might come in rather useful in the future, supposing we encounter non-benevolent aliens. Just to be on the safe side, of course. After all, it's perfectly feasible that only general-purpose predators become fully sentient and claw their way to the stars.

As if to demonstrate that even this coin has a flipside, four of our twenty-four tales feature peace or peacekeeping in their titles – fittingly, since this is surely what we *really* want, or so we like to tell ourselves.

The truth is that there is something about warfare, about conflict, about violence, that sets the heart racing and the blood singing. Our genre has been responsible for some of the most thought-provoking, challenging, edifying and intelligent fiction of the past century, and doubtless it will continue to be so; but there is another side to science fiction. The tang of weapon-oil, the sleek slide or the grind of metal on metal, the sizzle of an energy beam, the raw ferocity of explosion, and the cunning of a black ops specialist, are just as important an aspect of science fiction as the virtual futures, cybernetic implants, and the nature of the multiverse. The brilliance of a ship's commander who triumphs against all odds (despite being heavily outgunned and tactically disadvantaged) will raise a cheer as surely as the flash of insight that casts light on a puzzling aspect of the human condition. In fact, the chances are that it was just such stories of bravery and derring-do that drew many of us into science fiction in the first place. We *like* big explosions and impossible missions, men and women pitted against aliens or against other men and women. We *like* to read of nobility, treachery, and sacrifice, of triumph and loss. And that's what this particular Mammoth is all about. Humankind pushed to the limits in every conceivable way.

A problem with tackling a subject as vast as "war" in a genre that has been fascinated by the subject for many, many decades is that there are a whole lot of stories to choose from. No single collection can ever encompass all that merit inclusion and no anthology can hope to satisfy everyone. There are bound to be those who glance down the contents list and think, but what about this story or that one? If we've missed out your favourite we apologize, but hope you'll take a look in any case and discover a few new favourites in the process. As with any anthology, not everything has gone absolutely to plan. Some of the stories we had hoped to include proved to be unavailable, while, despite initially promising signs, Games Workshop's Warhammer 40,000 proved one universe that was closed to us; alas, the company lawyers declined any reprinting in a non-GW publication.

Thankfully, our successes have far outweighed our disappointments, and we are delighted with both the quality and diversity of tale we have gathered together in *The Mammoth Book of SF Wars*. We only hope that you, the reader, are too.

Ian Whates and Ian Watson, 2012

PEACEKEEPER

Mike Resnick and
Brad R. Torgersen

Suppose that soldiers of our present day are drafted by advanced aliens as peace enforcers on a distant world in exchange for technology…

In this first of the three original stories commissioned for this book, Mike Resnick teams up with Brad Torgersen, a Writers of the Future finalist in 2009 who then speedily sold stories to Analog, *and who has been in the army reserves for twenty years. The amazingly energetic Mike Resnick has collaborated with a bushel of other authors (which turns out not to be a big sheaf but is actually eight gallons; nevertheless we'll leave this), as well as authoring a library of books by himself and being expert on horseracing, purebred collies, Africa and who knows what else. As of 2009 at least he has the unique distinction (ahem, there can only be one) of being the all-time top award winner for short fiction.*

IT WAS A normal duty day in the city until the Earth limo showed up. It glided through the chaotic *s'ndar* traffic that bustled across my assigned six-way intersection. Flow control was provided by a single *s'ndar* of the city's provisional constabulary, who jerked his brightly coloured paddles to and fro over his bug's head, herding his people this way and that.

Since the ceasefire, my squad and I didn't mess with the locals unless we had to. We kept out of the way, as backup for the traffic cop in case of real trouble.

I exchanged glances with Corporal Kent, who'd seen the limo. Her facial expression said, *You're the boss; you figure it out.*

I sighed, then got up out of my sandbagged security position and began walking towards the vehicle as it ground to a halt a few metres away.

The *s'ndar* traffic cop watched me, decided it was none of his business, and went back to waving his paddles.

Low-rise commercial and residential structures sprouted around the intersection like mushrooms, their hemispherical roofs designed to shelter pedestrians from the daily monsoon. Along the boulevards poles rose up from the pavement at regular intervals to support endless rows of electrical conduit, phone conduit and fibre optics.

A slight haze of smog hung over the *s'ndar* city. It was impossible to ignore how similar, and yet also totally different, the scene was from the average urban centre on Earth. Humans and *s'ndar* had reached roughly equivalent technology levels.

Then the Interstellar Conglomerate intervened.

The smooth hum of the limo's twin engines quit, and the man who stepped out of the car was someone I was familiar with only from the news feeds. Senator Jeff Petersen had played football in college, and still kept reasonably fit. Tall and broad-chested, his full head of pepper-tinged hair was trimmed close. He had on a khaki field vest – one of the Earth embassy models that contained ballistic armour plating in addition to being festooned with pouches and pockets. He also wore neatly pressed khaki shorts and high-topped boots.

Given the oppressive humidity, I envied his wardrobe.

Two similarly dressed Secret Service personnel – one male, with a pistol on his hip, the other female, with a sub-machine gun in her hands – flanked the senator as he strode towards me. Other Secret Service agents stepped from the car and scanned the surroundings cautiously, their mirror sunglasses and straight faces making them seem somehow robotic.

I saluted the senator when he drew near.

"Sergeant Colford!" yelled Petersen over the din of traffic as he extended his hand. He'd obviously read my name tape on my armour. Good politician's reflex. Made it seem like he really gave a damn who I was.

I rapidly chow-slung my rifle and shook Petersen's hand. He had a surprisingly strong grip. Well, maybe not so surprising, given his profession. His smile was amiable, and his nicely capped teeth sparkled in the oppressive sunlight.

I strongly resisted the urge to like him.

"Senator," I said formally, "I wish I'd known you were coming."

"You guys always say that," Petersen said, continuing to smile. "But how am I supposed to talk to you candidly if your commander or first sergeant is warning you at morning briefing?"

It was a good point. But if I knew my corporal, she was already calling in to the Tactical Operations Centre. Headquarters would have our asses if we didn't report the senator's arrival asap.

Petersen surveyed my semi-hardened position.

"A bunker and eleven troops. Kind of overkill, don't you think? The *s'ndar* in this city are pro-Conglomerate now. They're our friends."

"Maybe, sir," I replied. "But you weren't here six months ago."

"I read about that. Did you see a lot of fighting, son?"

Son? Hell, I was almost thirty.

"I saw my share," I said evenly. "My rifle company trained en route. Our Conglomerate transports already had mock-ups of *s'ndar* urban terrain on-board. We *thought* we'd be ready."

"But you thought wrong," the senator said.

"Yah," I replied, grimacing at the memory.

Petersen waited, as if expecting me to say something more. When I didn't, he ran a hand over his scalp and then folded his arms across his chest.

"So, you've seen some rough fighting. OK. Do you at least feel like it was worth it?"

"Worth *what*, sir?"

"Earth's involvement in *S'ndar-khk*'s civil war. *America*'s involvement in the CEMEF – the Combined Earth Military Expeditionary Force."

"I don't make policy, sir," I told him non-committally. "I just follow orders."

"Fair enough. But the UN's bargain with the Conglomerate is costing American lives. Do you think it's worth it?"

I frowned, remembering my sister Karen. She'd been an officer in the Air Force, and had wanted to be an astronaut too, before the Conglomerate established their first contact with Earth. The interstellar robotic transports the Conglomerate sent to us made Earth's space stations look like toys. We'd not even put a man on Mars yet, and the Conglomerate was picking us up and hauling us off in whole battalions – over 300 light years to this obscure little planet, where my sister had been thrilled as hell to see actual aliens.

Now she was buried back home, her skull split by a *s'ndar* bullet. It had been a closed-casket affair, given the damage. Mom and Dad still weren't over it.

"I've lost some friends here," I said. "And family too. Things were a mess on this planet when we showed up. Lots of killing all over the place. Now there's not so much. But only because we're still alert every hour of every day. You ask me if it's worth it … I sure as hell hope so."

Petersen's brow furrowed. He reached out and put a hand on my shoulder, his face turning empathetic.

"I'm sorry for your friends, and whoever else you lost in your family, too. Part of the reason I'm here is to assure you and the other troops that you're doing truly important work. You're saving lives. *Human* lives. We help the *s'ndar* establish and keep the peace, and the Conglomerate helps Earth. We *need* the Conglomerate's clean fusion technology to reverse the economic and political damage from the Oil Crash. You're standing guard on this intersection so that you – or someone like you – doesn't have to stand guard over a few barrels of crude in the Person Gulf or Venezuela."

"Militia coming!" yelled one of my privates.

Senator Petersen and I turned our heads to see a small patrol of *s'ndaran*-made armoured personnel carriers manoeuvring towards us through the hubbub. The large-wheeled, tank-like vehicles took a few minutes to reach our position, and when they did, several armed *s'ndar* climbed from the hatch on an aerial-spiked APC, and approached my squad.

The *s'ndar* in the lead looked older than the rest. It was a female. Hell, *all* the authority figures in the insectoid race from sergeant on up were females, just like the ants and bees back on Earth. Her chitin was greyed at the edges and had several wounds that had been puttied over with artificial quick-cure ceramic, now weathered. Her thorax bore the militia equivalent of a non-commissioned officer, and it didn't take a genius to figure out she'd seen her share of combat.

Sergeant to sergeant, we saluted, the *s'ndar* in its form, me in mine.

As I lowered my rifle from the vertical, my Conglomerate-manufactured Translation Application Device – TAD – began speaking into my helmet's earphones. Emotionless metallic English filled my ears as the *s'ndar*'s mandibles clicked and scratched consonants in between flute-like vowels.

"Good morning, Staff Sergeant," she said.

"Good morning, Primary Sergeant," I replied, my TAD turning my English into *s'ndar* words.

"My soldiers and I arrive in coordination with the senator's visit," said the primary sergeant.

I studied her. You could never really be sure about the militia. They worked for the provisional government, who worked with the Expeditionary Force. But that didn't mean much on the street. I'd learned that first-hand. A few of the militia were quality. Many of them were either incompetently hazardous or deceitfully dangerous. It was best to be cautious.

Petersen turned back to me. "Do you mind if I go talk with your people?"

"Feel free, sir," I said.

I watched Petersen navigate away from my fighting position, chatting briefly with privates, specialists and my corporal.

Finally the *s'ndar* sergeant spoke. "I apologize for this nuisance," she said.

"Not a problem," I answered, grateful my TAD didn't translate my distaste. We'd come to *S'ndar-khk* to help, and the various *s'ndar* hives had fought us tooth and nail – in the middle of their own stupid hive-on-hive war. They might have gone nuclear on each other if the Conglomerate hadn't established first contact, and intervened for humanitarian reasons.

I heard some loud, rumbling engines, and turned to see a series of large trucks manoeuvring into the intersection. They were flatbeds of *s'ndar* construction, weighed down with large, square containers. I frowned. Any kind of large-scale commercial traffic like this should have been cleared with the Tactical Operations Centre well beforehand. The native traffic cop out in the intersection knew it too, and began waving his paddles furiously, signalling for the trucks to stop.

Their drivers obeyed…

…and the traffic cop exploded in a spray of barking rifle fire.

After that everything became a blur.

I remember the sides of the shipping containers splitting open and a small swarm of *s'ndar* pouring out. Civilians on foot began to scatter while vehicles attempted to either halt, or speed off. The air buzzed with countless *s'ndar* voices which overwhelmed my TAD. I switched over to the squad channel as I brought my weapon from off my back and pulled the charging handle.

The turrets on the *s'ndar* APCs – armoured personnel carriers – rotated and began hammering heavy rounds towards the flatbeds, only to be hit by rocket-propelled grenades.

The APCs burned.

I couldn't determine which of the attacking *s'ndar* had fired. In the panicked crowd, it was impossible to tell the attackers apart from the civilians. I saw the primary sergeant hunched and firing her rifle, so I got down on one knee and began firing likewise. Whoever she shot at, I could shoot at, at least according to the rules of engagement – *s'ndar* being better able to tell one another apart.

Corporal Kent was taking care of the squad. Her bellowing voice was comforting through the speakers in my headset.

Using the laser sight on my weapon, I drew a bead on a *s'ndar* moving hurriedly towards me, while the crowd scrambled in the opposite direction. My finger gave a near-motionless trigger pull and my target's carapace cracked hideously as the jacketed round tore through its thorax.

I fired at another one, also moving against the crowd. And another. And another.

There were so many trying to converge on us at once!

The senator! I thought. They're after the senator!

His armoured car was in flames along with the militia's APCs, and I heard the popping of the Secret Service's pistols, punctuated by the occasional rip of their sub-machine guns.

From somewhere in the chaos of the crowd, numerous small objects catapulted. For an instant they looked like opaque mason jars, then one was smashing onto the pavement two metres from me.

Grenades?

I stopped firing and turned to see other such objects cascading across our sandbagged position.

I crouched down and began to move towards my people when I caught a deep whiff of a sickly sweet chemical. The contents of the mason jars had spilled wetly on the ground, vapours pluming, and I suddenly found myself rolling helplessly onto my side, arms and legs twitching sporadically.

The *s'ndar* had never used chemical weapons against us before. Neural agents which were effective against *s'ndar* didn't work against humans, and vice versa.

Until now, anyway.

My instinct was to reach for the unused protective mask in my thigh pouch, but the pouch was pinned under my bodyweight and I didn't have the strength to roll over. It was as if all the signals travelling from my brain to my body had been roadblocked.

Darkness began closing in on me from all sides, and I thought about how stupid it was to be snuffed like this.

The screams of my squad fell quickly silent, and the last thing I remembered was the murky shape of a *s'ndar* leaning over me.

It was not a member of the militia.

* * *

"Staff Sergeant?"

I didn't move.

"Staff Sergeant!"

I still didn't move. The neutered voice did not compute.

Something like a tree branch raked my face.

That computed.

I reflexively opened my eyes and tried to bring my arms forwards in self-defence, only to find them shackled over my head. Short, rusted iron chains kept me pinned against a cold wall. A single hole in the high ceiling allowed a broad-based shaft of sunlight to penetrate, forming a too bright circle on the cracked cement floor, and leaving the perimeter of the room in near darkness.

A sudden wave of nausea hit, and I coughed violently, my nose and eyes running – doubtless a final reaction to the residue of the chemical attack.

For a second I thought I was going to pass out again, but the nausea slowly subsided and I began blinking the tears from my eyes.

"He is alert," said the mechanical voice. "Go inform the others."

I kept blinking until a *s'ndar* silhouette took shape before me. The rotund, beetle-like being was resting on its lower motile legs with one utensil arm poised, ready to strike. The stiff hairs along that arm had stung mightily when it swiped me the first time. I'd have been happy to swing back, if only I wasn't chained.

"Who the hell are you?" I demanded.

My TAD scratched out a translation. I was thankful that both the device and its requisite headset were still on my person. That meant my captors wanted to talk, not just kill me.

"I am not authorized to tell you," answered the *s'ndar*, its own TAD turning clickety-clackety mandible movements into human speech.

"The timing of your ambush couldn't have been accidental."

"You are correct."

"What has happened to Senator Petersen and my squad?"

"No one has been harmed," the creature said. "You must realize that if we'd wanted to we could have killed you where you stood."

"OK, you could have killed us and you didn't," I said. "What now?"

The *s'ndar* turned and left my cell for a moment, the crude iron door hanging wide open, then returned with several others, including a larger, older female who wore the colourful cloth raiment of a priestess.

Great, I thought. Someone who knows God is on her side.

Among the usual squabbling of the various hives, there was a particularly absolutist sect of *s'ndar* fanatics who considered the human presence on their world to be a literal desecration. They were the ones still fighting guerrilla-style even when most of the other resistors had been bought off at the bargaining table, or beaten down into submission by the Expeditionary Force.

"We are holding your senator," said the priestess. "Do you understand what this means?"

"Yes," I said. Capture or assassination of the leader of a rival hive was a time-honoured tradition among the *s'ndar*. Kill or incapacitate the queen bee, and the hive falls apart. A simple yet effective strategy – if you grew up in a hive. "But I don't think *you* understand what it means."

The *s'ndar* remained silent, watching me with alien incomprehension.

"When word gets back to Earth that the senator has been taken hostage or, worse yet, killed, there will be a demand for justice."

"Justice," the priestess repeated. "By whose definition? How many thousands of innocent *s'ndar* are dead because of humans?"

"The Conglomerate seems to think that if we hadn't been sent in to stop your civil war for you, there'd be *millions* dead."

"The human presence on *S'ndar-khk* is immoral," she replied. "By intervening in our affairs, you deny us our divine right to order our own lives and our world according to *s'ndaran* destiny."

"You won't get any argument from me," I said. "I couldn't care less about you *or* your fucking planet. But seizing the senator won't get the Expeditionary Force to budge. They'll come after you with everything they've got."

My own words surprised me. I didn't owe the senator anything.

But he'd seemed an earnest man, and I'd already seen too many friends die. Somebody had to pay.

As if sensing my rising anger, the two *s'ndar* flanking the priestess suddenly exposed and charged their weapons.

"Are you threatening me, Staff Sergeant?" said the priestess.

"I'm in no position to threaten you," I told her. "I'm just stating a fact."

The priestess stared at me for several seconds then turned and left the cell, guards in tow.

They locked the cell door behind them, and I was left alone.

My left arm ached. It wasn't from the chains. There was a scabbed set of fresh stitches directly over where my Conglomerate-made ID chip had been implanted before leaving Earth. Every member of the military had one, to prevent us from going Missing-in-Action. But these *s'ndar* had been smart enough to cut the device out of me, lest it give my position away to the Conglomerate satellites in orbit.

I sighed. No hope of a quick rescue now.

Minutes crept by in silence. I shouted, hoping to get a response from any other human that might hear me.

No response.

It's amazing how long an hour becomes when you are deprived of typical sensory input. The cell became deathly quiet. There was no noise from beyond the iron door, no music, no human or alien speech, nothing to look at except the circle of light that slowly inched across the cement floor as the day dragged on and turned into night.

I grew thirsty. Only a prolonged and significant amount of clanging with my chains attracted the attention of the guards, who brought me a portable light and two buckets: one to fill up, and one to empty.

Guards removed the manacles from my wrists and ankles, and then brought an even longer chain, which they connected to a collar they placed around my neck. The other end of the long chain was attached to a cleat in the floor, and I was able to walk and move for the first time in almost twenty-four hours.

They left me in the dark again. When the sun came up the priestess reappeared, only this time without her escorts. She kept well away from me, but her posture expressed curiosity.

"What now?" I said.

"If seizing or killing your senator yields an effect opposite of what we desire, consideration must be taken as to how to proceed next. We do not ordinarily keep prisoners."

"What's *this* for then?" I demanded, yanking the chain on my collar.

"*Human* prisoners," she replied.

"You have the senator," I said, "so what happens to the rest of us?"

"We used forbearance during the ambush, at the cost of many *s'ndaran* lives. Your squad still lives because *I* wish it, in spite of the feelings of many others who would just as soon see you all dead. After all, you are *aliens*. Everything about you is alien. You have no business being here. We want you off our planet, but before that can happen there are a few of us who believe we must understand you first. The better we understand you, the better we will be able to determine by what leverage you are moved."

I stared at her. "Seizing hostages won't do it, that's for damned sure. We'll have every available troop scouring this planet for Senator Petersen. Once they find him, it won't be very pleasant for his captors."

"We will make your masters understand us," the priestess said, advancing close to me. She stabbed a foreleg into my chest. "You do not belong here."

"Tell that to the Conglomerate," I said.

"You *are* the Conglomerate!"

"No, we're just humans from Earth."

She stared intently at me. "Explain."

"It's simple enough," I said. "Earth's government cut a deal with the Conglomerate."

"What does that mean?"

I explained the essentials of the situation. Earth needed what the Conglomerate had to offer, and as long as that remained true, the United Nations would keep the Expeditionary Force on *S'ndar-khk*.

"We never knew any of this," the priestess said.

"You never asked," I said.

The next day of incarceration passed with numbing sameness. As did the next. And the one after that.

Then the priestess reappeared, only this time she had several other *s'ndar* with her. None of them were armed, though they hardly needed their weapons against a chained and defenceless prisoner. They all stood near the door, well out of the radius of the chain that kept me anchored to the cell floor.

"You were right," the priestess informed me. "News of the senator's abduction has caused human activity on *S'ndar-khk* to increase precipitously."

"That's hardly a surprise," I said. "They'll be looking for Petersen, me, and my whole squad. The Army doesn't leave its men and women behind."

"You are *that* valuable?"

"*Every* soldier is valuable," I said.

"Even those who are inferior?"

"*Subordinate*, not *inferior*," I said. "There's a big difference."

"We wish to know more of this deal humans have with the Conglomerate," said one of the priestess's companions. "At what point will it be satisfied?"

"I don't know," I answered. "Until someone in the Conglomerate decides the job is done, I suppose."

The *s'ndar* began skittering and scratching excitedly, and my TAD muted due to overload.

"If you really want humans gone," I said, "you could do yourselves a favour by not acting like such a bunch of bloodthirsty animals."

"I do not expect you to understand the complexities of inter-hive politics," she said, "nor do I expect you to grasp the richness and depth of my people. To us it is *you* who are the animals. You come without being invited or wanted, and enforce your version of 'peace'."

"Agreed," said a different *s'ndar*.

"Like I said before," I replied, "tell it to the Conglomerate."

The priestess circled me, her forelimbs folded thoughtfully. "Our history with the Conglomerate is complicated," she said. "When the Conglomerate made its first contact with us, many hives spurned its overtures, declaring that we have the right to live without alien interference. When its overtures became demands, we destroyed their probe ship in orbit. An additional series of probe ships were sent, and we destroyed them too. Then, a few years later, your human armies arrived."

"But not by our own means," I pointed out. "The Conglomerate *brought* us here to do a job. When they think it's done, they'll take us back home and you'll never have to see another human again. If you weren't so intent on slaughtering each other – and slaughtering humans in the process – we'd be gone by now."

The group chattered and clacked, and the priestess faced me squarely.

"So strange," she said. "You repulse and fascinate me at the same time."

"The feeling is mutual," I said.

She waited while we glared at one another, my human eyes and her multifaceted insect's eyes. Then she clacked her mandibles once, very sharply. Suddenly the entire lot of them fell silent, and began filing out of the cell.

"Hey!" I said to the priestess as she was leaving. "You want to start proving how civilized you really are, give me something to clean up with." I was over four days out of a shower. I stank.

The priestess paused, then waved a forelimb at me and left. A minute later the guards brought me cold water in a ten-gallon-sized tub, with a brick of industrial soap. There was no towel.

I scrubbed happily, ignoring the chill.

Repeated requests to see Senator Petersen, or anyone from my squad, were flatly denied. I began to wonder whether any of them had really made it. There was no reason to believe that the priestess, or any of the others, had been telling the truth, though why they'd keep me alive and kill the others just didn't make any sense.

Time dragged on. Week one became week two. Then three. Then

a month. For the first time in my life, I had a full beard. I did body-weight exercises in my cell to try to keep myself fit, and to keep from going insane with inactivity.

At night, when the dark closed in and I had to curl up on the hard floor, I hummed all my favourite songs until slumber finally overtook me and gave me an illusory form of freedom. I dreamed of all the neat places I'd ever been as a kid, all the neat and interesting people I'd ever met. I dreamed of all my favourite shows and movies, and especially of my favourite foods: mashed potatoes, buttered green beans, crisp corn on the cob, fried chicken, broiled T-bone steak. Anything but the damned half-rotten vegfruit the *s'ndar* – being a herbivorous race – preferred.

I also dreamed of home, and family. Of my sister Karen and me when we'd been kids, playing in our grandparents' backyard. A few times those dreams seemed so real that when I woke up I had tears in my eyes.

I grew to greatly resent the moments when I was awake.

I also began to cinch my belt tighter and tighter. The lack of protein in my eager diet was costing me muscle as well as fat.

My requests to see the priestess or any other authority figure were alternately denied or ignored. My TAD battery ran out of charge and wasn't replaced, so I was reduced to yelling at my guards, who neither understood nor cared.

I'd lost count of the weeks when the attack came.

A concussion lifted me up off the floor. I'd been fast asleep. I screamed and rolled onto my back, observing rivulets of dust spewing from cracks in the ceiling – cracks I was positive hadn't been there before, because I'd already memorized the existing cracks.

THUD.

More cracks shot across the ceiling, and a hunk broke loose and smacked into the ground near my head.

I leaped up from where I'd been lying and crouched in the circle of sunlight, hoping to get out from under any additional debris.

THUD – THUD – WHAM.

I couldn't tell if the explosions were coming from beyond the hole in the ceiling or outside the iron door. I *felt* them as much as I heard them.

The door to my cell burst open. A horde of *s'ndar* rushed in, snapped the collar off my neck and shoved me outside at gunpoint. The corridor beyond was crawling with *s'ndar* and humans. There were faces I recognized, far gaunter than I remembered them.

"Sergeant Colford!" said a desperate voice.

I turned and found myself face to face with Senator Petersen.

He looked like a shaggy ghost of his former self. His gleaming teeth had yellowed, his breath smelled and his face was a hollowed-out, grey-haired mask that barely resembled the confident politician who'd visited my intersection…who knew how long ago.

"Move!" commanded a *s'ndar*, its TAD dialled up to shouting volume. The Senator and I were roughly shoved down the corridor with the other humans. I saw Corporal Kent up at the front of the line, and tried to shout for her, but was silenced by another barrage of concussions that almost knocked us off our feet.

"What's happening?" Petersen said in my ear.

"Ours," I replied. "Air strike."

"They'll kill us!"

"They probably don't even know we're here," I said. "Something or someone must have tipped off the Expeditionary Force that there was a resistance stronghold in this area."

"Silence!" snapped an armed guard.

We twisted and turned our way frantically down a further series of corridors. I couldn't quite tell, but the floor seemed slanted. We could have been going up or down, I wasn't really sure.

Then we suddenly emptied out into the blindingly bright sunlight, all of us cringing and raising our hands to shield our eyes.

A quick look around revealed the rubble of what had once been a *s'ndar* industrial district. I actually laughed as I realized we'd been prisoners right under the Expeditionary Force's nose the whole time. The district had been levelled in the first month of the occupation, and declared off-limits. Barring occasional patrols, no human or *s'ndar* went in or out, except for these resistance fanatics, who'd obviously found a way to operate without being detected.

Until today.

A flight of jets screamed overhead – wide-winged ground attack planes with their payload doors hanging open. A cluster of bombs released and carpeted across the crushed factory complex from which we'd just exited. The blasts were deafening and the ground bucked hard under our feet.

I wondered if we could attempt an escape, and decided there were too many *s'ndar* for us to make it. Our duty hadn't changed: we had to keep the senator alive until we could transfer him to friendly hands.

We passed wrecked and burned-out vehicles, and the dried shells of *s'ndar* who'd been left where they'd fallen – their silenced mandibles hanging slackly by threads of dry tissue.

Then we were being herded down into a dry sewer, crouched and shuffling, while the round sewer pipe was somewhat more accommodating to the shorter, squatter *s'ndar*.

After twenty minutes the *s'ndar* ordered a rest, and we stopped.

I tried to push up to where Kent was, but was shoved back and ordered not to move.

Petersen was doubled over, gasping.

"Sir," I said. "Are you hurt?"

"No," he said. "Just out of shape. It was the cell…the damned cell…nothing to do but go crazy."

He looked into my eyes, and I realized the senator might not have been speaking metaphorically. His gaze was awful. Stricken. Not quite *there* somehow. It occurred to me that, for all his slick, football-player toughness, Petersen had probably never endured real deprivation before. Certainly not on the scale we'd been suffering since our capture.

I turned to the *s'ndar*. My TAD was gone, but theirs worked. "That air strike was just the first phase," I told them. "They're softening up the target before our rifle platoons get sent in to clean up. They know you're here, and they won't stop until they find you."

A single *s'ndar* shape pushed its way back towards me. I recognized her torn raiment; it was the priestess.

"We will move forward rapidly now," she said.

"Look at us," I told her, waving my hand at Petersen for emphasis. "We're in no condition to keep up the pace. In another hundred metres you'd be dragging us. So we'll have to go slow. I hope that doesn't scare you too much, but that's the way it is."

The priestess appeared to sag in on herself, if only a bit. "Yes," she said. "We are scared."

She studied my face. "You hide it well, but my fear makes you happy."

"Only because you're the enemy," I answered. Then I sighed deeply. "The shame of it is, you didn't have to be. There was no reason for it."

"I agree," she said. "But of course I would: *you* invaded *us*. It is you who are the enemy."

And suddenly I knew who the *real* enemy was.

"My sister died here," I said, as the low rumble of more bombs filled the sewer pipe, then fell silent. "She was excited by the idea of your alien culture, and she was killed for her enthusiasm. But she wouldn't have been here at all – none of us would be here – if not for the Conglomerate playing us off against each other."

"The 'deal' you spoke of," said the priestess.

"Yes," I said. "Back on Earth we treat the Conglomerate like saviours. You know something interesting? We've never even seen them."

Her eyes widened. "Never?"

"Just radio transmissions and text messages, and those robotic transport ships that show up in orbit. If they're so advanced, it should be an easy thing for them to pacify a planet with or without human help. So what's in it for them, using us like this? And why couldn't they just leave your world alone? Why do they care if you're at war?"

"Our particular hive has never known these answers," she said. "And since the arrival of humans, we've never cared to know. We want you gone. That is the sole thing that concerns us."

"Have you ever stopped to ask why humans would even want to be on your planet in the first place?"

The priestess was silent. As were every other *s'ndar* and human in the sewer. Petersen just looked at me, his limbs slightly shaking as the adrenaline from exertion began to wear off.

"*We're* here because of them," I said. "*You're* fighting an invading force because of them. Maybe it's time for both sides to take a deep breath and think about that."

She stared at me. "Go on," she said at last.

"If you stop fighting, *my* people have no reason to be here."

"A truce?"

"It would give us time to find out what the Conglomerate *really* wants," I said.

"And to prevent them from getting it," added the senator, who was quick on the uptake despite his condition.

She turned to the senator. "Do you have the power to order a ceasefire?"

He nodded his head. "I outrank every general officer on this planet," Petersen said, seeming to regain some of his former stature. "I'm sure I can convince our side to enter a temporary ceasefire."

"What good is temporary?" she asked.

"It gives us breathing space while we each try to talk our superiors into making it permanent."

"My superiors will assume you are lying to us," said the priestess.

Suddenly Petersen smiled. "When we stop talking war and start talking negotiations, now we *are* in my bailiwick," he said. "I propose a trade."

"A trade?"

"I want you to come back to Earth with me as a goodwill ambassador of your race, someone who can confirm what I have to tell them. View it as a public display of friendship and mutual trust." He turned to me. "And Sergeant Colford here will stay behind in the same capacity and speak to your people."

"Why me?" I demanded.

"Because you lost a sister in this war, and were incarcerated for some months. If *you* can forgive them and point to the real enemy, I think it will bolster the arguments of whatever *s'ndar* is speaking to his people on our behalf."

I considered. Could a ceasefire agreement – made in a sewer pipe between a staff sergeant, a priestess and a senator who were light years from Washington – actually have any legs?

We're now in the process of finding out.

I hope my sister didn't die for nothing. I hope my months of being chained in solitary served some purpose. I hope the priestess can sway her people and the senator can sway his. I even hope that someday I find out what the Conglomerate wants, and that I stop thinking of *them* as the enemy.

Mostly, though, I hope I can stop being a peacekeeper…

…and start being a peacemaker.

FROM OUT OF THE SUN, ENDLESSLY SINGING

Simon R. Green

The second of our stories original to this volume is cosmi-cally lyrical and legendary in the way, perhaps, of Cord-wainer Smith, while it deals death lavishly, as might be expected from the author of eight novels in a Deathstalker series, not to mention twelve Nightside books and other series; "trilogies are for wimps," says Simon R. Green. Born and based in Britain, which explains his devotion to tea and his acting in open-air productions of Shakespeare, to which he travels by motorbike, his novelization of the film Robin Hood: Prince of Thieves *sold a third of a million copies.*

THIS IS THE story. It is an old, old story, and most of the true details are lost to us. But this is how the story has always been told, down the many years. Of our greatest loss and our greatest triumph; of three who were sent down into Hell for ever, that the rest of Humanity might know safety, and revenge. This is the story of the Weeping Woman, the Man With the Golden Voice, and the Rogue Mind. If the story upsets you, pretend it never happened. It was a very long time ago, after all.

This goes back to the days of the Great Up and Out, when we left our mother world to go out into the stars; to explore the Galaxy and take her fertile planets for our own. All those silver ships, dancing through the dark, blazing bright in the jungle of the night. We met no opposition we couldn't handle, colonized every suitable world we came to and terraformed the rest, remaking them in our image. It was a glorious time, by all accounts, building our glittering cities and proud civilizations, in defiance of all that endless empty Space. We should have known better. We should have sent ahead, to say we were coming. Because it turned out we were trespassing, and not at all welcome.

They came to us from out of the Deep, from out of the darkest part of Deep Space, from far beyond the realms we knew, or could ever hope to comprehend. Without warning they came, aliens as big as starships, bigger than anything we had ever built, and far more powerful. Endless numbers of them, a hoard, a swarm, deadly things of horrid shape and terrible intent, blocking out the stars where they passed. They were each of them huge and awful, unknown and unknowable, utterly alien things moving inexorably through open Space on great shimmering wings. They came from where nothing comes from, and they thrived in conditions where nothing should live. Their shapes made no sense to human eyes, to human aesthetics. They were nightmares given shape and form, our darkest fears made flesh. We called them the Medusae, because wherever they looked, things died.

They destroyed the first colonized planets they came to, without hesitation, without warning. They paused in orbit just long enough to look down on the civilizations we had built there, and just their terrible gaze was enough to kill everything that lived. We still have recorded images from that time, of the dead worlds. Cities full of corpses, towns where nothing moved. Wildlife lying unmoving, rotting in the open, and fish of all kinds bobbing unseeing on the surfaces of the oceans. The Medusae moved on, from planet to planet, system to system, leaving only dead worlds in their wake.

We sent the Fleet out to meet them, hundreds and hundreds of our marvellous and mighty Dreadnaughts, armed to the teeth with disrupters and force shields, planet-buster bombs and reality invertors. The Fleet closed with the Medusae, singing our songs of glory, ravening energies flashing across open Space, and all of it was for nothing. We could not touch the Medusae. They passed over the Fleet like a storm in the night, and left behind them mile-long starships cracked open from stem to stern, with streams of dead bodies issuing out of broken hulls, scattering slowly across the dark. Occasionally some would tumble down through the atmosphere of a dead world, like so many shooting stars with no one to see them.

The Medusae moved on through the colonized systems, wiping clean every world we'd colonized or changed, as though just our presence on their planets had contaminated those beyond saving. One by one, the planetary comm systems fell silent, voices crying out for help that never came, fading into static ghosts. Some colonists got away, fleeing ahead of the Medusae on desperate, overcrowded ships; most didn't. There is no number big enough that the human mind can accept to sum up our losses. All the men, women and children lost in those long months of silent slaughter. All the proudly named cities, all the wonders and marvels we built out of nothing; gone, all gone. And finally, when they'd run out of planets to cleanse, and people to kill, the Medusae came looking for us. All that great swarm, hideous beyond bearing, complex beyond our comprehension, beyond reason or reasoning with…they followed the fleeing ships back to us, back to the home of Mankind.

Back to Old Earth.

We sent up every ship we had, everything that would fly, loaded with every weapon we had, and we met the Medusae at the very edge of our solar system. And there, we stopped them. The aliens looked upon our worlds, but came no closer. And for a while we rejoiced, because we thought we had won a great victory. We should have known better. The Medusae had stopped because they didn't need to come any closer. Hanging there in open Space, silent and huge and monstrous, out beyond the great gas-giant planets, they looked on Old Earth, and reached out with their incomprehensible energies to touch our world. They poisoned our planet. Changed her essential nature, so that our world would no longer support human life. They turned our home against Humanity. A fitting punishment, from the Medusae; they terraformed us.

And that … that was when we got really angry, and contemplated revenge.

The Lords and Ladies of Old Earth came together in Convocation, for the first time in centuries. They met at Siege Perilous, that wonderful ancient monument to past glories, shaped like a massive hourglass, towering high and high over the bustling starport of New Damascus. Immortal and powerful, relentless and implacable, the Lords and Ladies represented Concepts, not Countries. They spoke for all the various aspects of Humanity, and their word was Law. Made immortal, so that they could take the long view. Denied peace or rest, because they were needed. Cursed with conscience and damned with duty, because that's how we always reward the best of us.

Only the Lords and Ladies knew the secret truth of our poisoned estate; that we would have to leave Old Earth and find a new home somewhere else. The continuance of Humanity itself was at threat, but only the Lords and Ladies knew. Because only they could be trusted to know everything. The Lords and Ladies of Old Earth were given dominion to do anything and everything necessary to serve and preserve Humanity. In an acknowledged Emergency, the Lords and Ladies were authorized and enjoined to call upon any human being, anyone anywhere, for any necessary purpose. Humanity gave them this power, and trusted them to use it well and wisely. Because only they could take the truly long view; and because everyone else was just too busy.

There were checks and balances in place, of course. And truly terrible punishments.

They came to Convocation in the last hours of evening, their personal ships drifting down like so many falling leaves, settling easily onto the crystal landing pads set out on top of Siege Perilous. And then they made their way down to the single reserved meeting hall, a bare and sparse chamber, isolated from the world. They had no use for seats of state, for the trappings of power or the comforts of privilege. Exactly one hundred Lords and Ladies stood in a great circle, looking openly upon each other, in their traditional peacock robes of vivid colours. Their faces were naked and unmasked, so that everyone could see and be seen. Outside, combat androids programmed with the deposited memories of rabid wolves patrolled the perimeter, ready and eager to kill any living thing they encountered.

There were other, less noticeable protections in place, of course.

The Lord Ravensguard spoke for War, so he spoke first. Tall and grave he was, with cool, thoughtful eyes. He spoke of the horrors the Medusae had committed, of what they had done and might do yet. And then he spoke of possible responses and tactics.

"There are always the Forbidden Weapons," he said calmly. "Those ancient and detestable devices locked away for centuries, because they were deemed too terrible for Man to use upon Man. I speak of the Time Hammer, and the Despicable Childe. The Nightmare Engines and the Hour From Beyond."

"Could we use such things, and still call ourselves human?" said the Lord Zodiac, representing Culture. "You cannot defeat evil with evil methods. You cannot stop monsters by becoming monsters."

"The enemy we face has no understanding of such concepts," the Lord Ravensguard said firmly. "They do not seek to destroy us because they are Good or Evil. They do not think like us. They see us only as … an infestation."

"Have we exhausted all means of communicating with them?" said the Lady Benefice, who spoke for Communications.

"We have tried everything, from all the many forms of technology, to the most extreme reaches of psi," said the Lord Ravensguard. "They do not hear us. Or, more likely, they choose not to."

"Weapons are not the answer," said the Lady Subtle, who represented Security. Small she was, compact, determined. "We have tried weapons, and they have failed us. We must sink lower than that. We shall fight the Medusae with guile and betrayal, and they will not see it coming. Because they would never stoop so low."

"You have a plan?" said the Lord Ravensguard.

And everyone smiled, politely. Because the Lady Subtle always had a plan. She spoke to them at length, of a trap, and a punishment, and Humanity's final revenge. The Convocation then deliberated.

They did not have the luxury of being shocked, or offended; their duty demanded. Only was this awful plan practical? There was much discussion, which ended when the Lord DeMeter, who spoke for the soul of Humanity, raised the only question that mattered.

"Do we have the right," he asked, "to make such a sacrifice, and place such a stain upon the collective conscience of Humanity?"

"We can do this; we must do this," said the Lady Shard, who represented Duty. Vivacious, she was, full of life, and deadly in her focused malice. "We will do this because we have no other choice. Humanity will be saved, and avenged, and that is all that matters."

And so the decision was made, and the order given. The Lord Ravensguard and the Ladies Subtle and Shard went out from Convocation to cross the world and acquire the three necessary elements for Humanity's last blow at the Medusae.

The Lord Ravensguard went to the Grand Old Opera House, set among the gleaming spires and shimmering towers of the city Sydney, in Australia. Samuel DeClare was singing there that night. There was no greater singer among all Humanity at that time. They called him the Man With the Golden Voice. When he sang, everyone listened. He could break your heart and mend it, all in a single song. Make you cry and make you cheer; weigh you down and lift you up; and make you love every moment of it. His audiences adored him, and beat their hands bloody in applause at the end of every concert. And this night was his greatest appearance, before his biggest audience. Afterwards, everyone there said it was his finest moment. They were wrong, but they couldn't know that. The Lord Ravensguard stood at the very back of the massive concert hall, and listened, and was moved like everyone else. Perhaps more so, because he alone knew what Samuel DeClare's final performance would entail.

He went backstage to meet with DeClare after the concert was over. The greatest singer of all time sat slumped, unseeing, before his dressing-room mirror, surrounded by flowers and gifts, and messages of congratulation from everyone who mattered. He was big and broad-shouldered, and classically handsome, like some god of ancient times come down to walk among his worshippers. He sat slumped in his chair, tired, depressed, lost. He could barely find the energy to bow his head respectfully to the Lord Ravensguard.

"What is wrong?" said the Lord. "Your audience loved you. Listen; they're still cheering, still applauding. You sang magnificently."

"Yes," said DeClare. "But how can I ever follow that? There will be other songs, other performances, but nothing to match tonight. It hits hard, to reach the peak of your career and know there's nowhere left to go, but down."

"Ah," said the Lord Ravensguard. "But what if I were to offer you the chance for an even greater performance? One last song, of magnificent scope and consequence, before an audience greater than any singer has ever known?"

DeClare raised his heavy head, and looked at the Lord Ravensguard. "How long would this performance last?"

"Just the one song," said the Lord Ravensguard. Because he was allowed, and even encouraged, to lie when necessary.

The Lady Subtle went to meet the infamous Weeping Woman in that most ancient of prisons, the Blue Vaults. That wasn't her real name, of course. She was Christina Valdez, just another face in the crowd, until she did what she did, and the media called her La Llorona, the Weeping Woman. The authorities put her in the Blue Vaults for the murder of many children. She wept endlessly because she had lost her own children in an awful accident, which might or might not have been of her own making. And then she went out into the night, every night, drifting through the back streets of dimly lit cities, to abduct the children of others, to compensate her for her loss. None of these children ever went home again.

The Lady Subtle went down into the Blue Vaults, those great stone caverns set deep and deep under the Sahara Desert, and there she gave orders that one particular door be opened. Inside, Christina Valdez crouched naked in the small stone cell, covered in her own filth, blinking dazedly into the sudden and unexpected light. Because normally, when criminals came to the Blue Vaults, they were locked away for ever. No clothes, no windows, no light; food and water through a slot, and a grille in the floor. The door only opened again when they came to take out the body. The Lady Subtle dismissed the guard, and spoke, and the Weeping Woman listened.

"You have a chance to redeem yourself, Christina," said the Lady Subtle. "You have the opportunity to save all Humanity."

Valdez laughed in the Lady's face. "Let them all die! Where were they when my children died? Did any of them weep for my lost babies?"

"The Medusae have murdered millions of children," said the Lady Subtle. "You could weep for them, and avenge them, too."

The argument went round and round for some time, because the Lady Subtle was patient and wise, and Christina Valdez was distracted and quite mad. But eventually an agreement was reached, and the Lady Subtle led La Llorona out of her cell and into the light. And if the Lady Subtle felt any guilt at what was going to happen to Christina Valdez, she kept it to herself.

The Lady Shard tracked down that most dangerous of fugitives, Damnation Rue, to a sleazy bar in that maze of criss-crossing corridors called the Maul, deep in the slums of Under Rio. The media called him the Rogue Mind, because he was the most powerful telepath Humanity had ever produced, and because he would not be bound by Humanity's rules, or the psionic community's rules, or even the rules of polite conduct. He went where he would, did what he wanted, and no one could stop him. He built things up and tore them down, he owed money everywhere, and left broken hearts and minds in his wake, always escaping one step ahead of the consequences, or retribution.

The Lady Shard watched him cautiously from the shadows at the back of the packed bar, a foul and loathsome watering hole for the kind of people who needed somewhere to hide from a world that had had enough of them. The Rogue Mind was there to enjoy the barbaric customs and the madder music, the illegal drugs and the extremely dangerous drinks … and to enjoy the emotions of others, second-hand. For Damnation Rue, there was nothing more intoxicating than just a taste of other people's heavens and hells. He could always stir things up a little if things looked like getting too peaceful.

The air was full of drifting smoke, and the general gloom was broken only by the sudden flares of discharging energy guns or flashing blades. There was blood and slaughter and much rough laughter. The Rogue Mind loved it. The Lady Shard watched it all, hidden behind a psionic shield.

She brought Damnation Rue to book through the use of a pre-programmed pleasure droid, with a patina of artificially overlaid memories. She was beautiful to look at, this droid, in a suitably foul and sluttish way and, when Damnation Rue persuaded her to sit at his table, and watched what he thought were her thoughts, she drugged his drink.

When he finally woke up, he had a mind trap fastened tight to his brow, holding his thoughts securely inside his own head. He was strapped down, very securely, in a very secure airship, taking him directly to the Blue Vaults. The Lady Shard sat opposite him, told him where he was going, and observed the panic in his eyes.

"You do have another option," she said. "Save all of Humanity by performing a telepathic task no other could, and have all your many sins forgiven. Or you could spend the rest of your life in a small stone cell, with your mind trap bolted to your skull, alone with your own thoughts until you die. It's up to you."

"Money," said Damnation Rue. "I want money. Stick your forgiveness. I want lots and lots of money and a full pardon. How much is it worth to you, to save all Humanity?"

"You shall have as much money as you can spend," said the Lady Shard. "Once the mission is over."

The Rogue Mind laughed. He didn't trust the deal, and was already planning his escape. But no one escaped the clutches of the Lords and Ladies of Old Earth. The Lady Shard hid her smile. She hadn't actually lied to him, as such.

And so the three parts of Humanity's revenge on the Medusae came together at Siege Perilous, brought there by the Lord Ravensguard and the Ladies Subtle and Shard. Samuel DeClare, the very soul of song, looking fine and noble in his pure white robes, and only just a little disturbed, like a god who had come down to mix with men but could no longer quite remember why. And Christina Valdez, mostly hidden inside voluminous black robes, the hood pulled well forward to hide her face. Constantly wringing her hands, and never meeting anyone's gaze. Now and again a tear would fall, to splash on the marble floor. And Damnation Rue, wrapped in new robes that already appeared a little shabby; a sneaky sleazy little rat of a man, picking nervously with one fingertip at the mind trap still firmly fixed to his brow. Still looking for a way out, the fool.

The Lords and Ladies of Old Earth were not cruel. They praised all three of them as though they were volunteers, and promised them that their names would be remembered for ever. Which was true enough.

"You will sing," the Lord Ravensguard said to Samuel DeClare. "The greatest, most moving song you know."

"You will mourn," the Lady Subtle said to Christina Valdez. "The most tragic, heartbreaking weeping of all time."

"And you will broadcast it all telepathically," the Lady Shard said to Damnation Rue. "You will project it across all the open reaches of Space."

"Just one song?" said the Man With the Golden Voice.

"I only have to mourn?" said La Llorona, the Weeping Woman.

"And after I've broadcast this, I get my money?" said the Rogue Mind.

"Yes and yes and yes," said the Lords and Ladies of Old Earth. Who were not cruel, but knew all there was to know about duty and responsibility.

The three of them were taken immediately to the landing pads on top of Siege Perilous, where the starship was waiting for them. Specially adapted, with powerful force shields and a pre-programmed AI pilot. The ship was called *Sundiver*. The three of them stepped aboard, all unknowing, and strapped themselves in, and the AI pilot threw the ship up off the pads and into the sky, and then away from Old Earth and straight into the heart of the Sun.

The three inside knew nothing of this. They couldn't see out, and the force shields protected them. The pilot told them that the time had come, and one of them sang, and one of them mourned, and one of them broadcast it all telepathically. That was a terribly sad song, reaching out from inside the heart of the Sun. Earth did not hear it. Humanity did not hear it; the Lords and Ladies saw to that. Because it really was an unbearably sad song. But the Medusae heard it. The telepathic broadcast shot out of the Sun and spread across the whole planetary system, to the outer ranges of Space where the Medusae heard it. That marvellous, telepathically broadcast, siren song.

The aliens moved forward to investigate. The Fleet fell back on all sides, to let them pass. The Medusae came to the Sun, our Sun, Old Earth's Sun, drawn on by the siren song like so many moths to the flame. And then they plunged into the Sun, every last one of them, and it swallowed them all up without a murmur. Because as big as the swarm of the Medusae was, the Sun was so much bigger.

They never came out again.

The *Sundiver*'s force shields weren't strong enough to last long in the terrible heat of the heart of the Sun, but they didn't have to. The ship also carried that ancient horror, the Time Hammer. The weapon that could break Time. The AI pilot set it to repeat one moment of Time for all eternity. So that the siren song would never end. The Man With the Golden Voice sang, and the Weeping Woman mourned, and the Rogue Mind mixed them together and broadcast it, for ever and ever and ever. They're in there now, deep in the heart of the Sun, and always will be.

We never saw the Medusae again. It could be that they died, that not even they could withstand the fierce fires of the Sun. Or it might be that they are still in there, still listening, to a song that will never end. Either way we are safe, and we have had our revenge upon them, and that is all that matters.

That is the story. Afterwards, we left Old Earth, that poor poisoned planet, our ancient home which could no longer support us. Humanity set forth in our marvellous Fleet of Dreadnaughts, looking for new worlds to settle, hopefully this time without alien masters. We keep looking. The last of Humanity, moving ever on through open Space, on the wings of a song, for ever.

ALL FOR LOVE

Algis Budrys

What if the military effort to overthrow a single alien ship should completely obsess what remains of civilization on Earth, giving a new twist to "total war"?

Algirdas Jonas Budrys was son of the representative in the USA of the Lithuanian government-in-exile, a strange political limbo which perhaps reflects in his second novel Who?, *filmed eighteen years later, about whether a prosthetically rebuilt, and necessarily masked, man is the person whom he claims to be. Also outstanding as a novel of identity and obsession is his classic* Rogue Moon, *about successive attempts by identical teleported suicide volunteers to penetrate a lethal alien labyrinth, learning just a little more each time.* "All For Love" *is one of the most mordant and memorable of all his stories.*

I

MALACHI RUNNER DIDN'T like to look at General Compton. Compton the lean, keen, slash-gesturing semi-demagogue of a few years ago had been much easier to live with than Compton as he was now, and Runner had never had much stomach for him even then. So Runner kept his eyes firmly fixed on the device he was showing.

Keeping his eyes where they were was not as easy as it might have been. The speckled, bulbous distortion in front of him was what Headquarters, several hundred miles away under The Great Salt Lake, was pleased to refer to as an Invisible Weapons Carrier. It was hard to see because it was designed to be hard to see.

But Malachi Runner was going to have to take this thing up across several hundred miles of terrain, and he was standing too close to it not to see it. The Invisible Weapons Carrier was, in fact, a half-tone of reality. It was large enough to contain a man and a fusion bomb, together with the power for its engine and its light amplifiers. It bristled with a stiff mat of flexible-plastic light-conducing rods, whose stub ends, clustered together in a tight mosaic pointing outward in every conceivable direction, contrived to bend light around its bulk. It was presently conducting, towards Runner, a picture of the carved rock directly behind it.

The rock, here in this chamber cut under the eastern face of the Medicine Bow Mountains, was reasonable featureless; and the light-amplifiers carefully controlled the intensity of the picture. So the illusion was marred by only two things: the improbable angle of the pictured floor it was also showing him, and the fact that for every rod conducting light from the wall, another rod was conducting light from Runner's direction, so that to his eyes the ends of half the rods were dead black.

"Invisibility," Compton said scornfully from behind and to one side of Runner. Or, rather, he whispered and an amplifier took up the strain in raising his voice to a normal level. "But it's not bad camouflage. You might make it, Colonel."

"I have orders to try." Runner would not give Compton the satisfaction of knowing that his impatience was with the means provided, not with the opportunity. The war could not possibly be permitted to continue the thirty years more given to it by Compton's schedule. Compton himself was proof of that.

Not that proof required Compton. He was only one. There were many.

Runner glanced aside at the cadet officer who had guided him from the tramway stop to this chamber here, in one of the side passages of the siege bore that was being driven under the Medicine Bows in the direction of the alien spaceship that had dominated the world for fifty years. The boy – none of these underofficers were older than seventeen – had a face that looked as if it had been made from wet paper and then baked dry. His eyesockets were black pits from which his red eyes stared, and his hands were like chickens' feet. His bloated stomach pushed against the wide white plastic of his sidearm belt.

He looked, in short, like most of the other people Runner had seen here since getting off the tram. As he was only seventeen, he had probably been born underground, somewhere along the advancing bore, and had never so much as seen sunlight, much less eaten anything grown under it. He had been bred and educated – or mis-educated; show him something not printed in Military Alphabet and you showed him the Mayan Codex – trained and assigned to duty in a tunnel in the rock; and never in his life had he been away from the sound of the biting drills.

"You're not eager to go, Colonel?" Compton's amplified whisper said. "You're Special Division, so of course this isn't quite your line of work. I know your ideas, you Special Division men. Find some way to keep the race from dehumanizing itself." And now he chose to make a laugh, remembering to whisper it. "One way to do that would be to end the war before another generation goes by."

Runner wondered, not for the first time, if Compton would find some way to stop him without actually disobeying the Headquarters directive ordering him to cooperate. Runner wondered, too, what Compton would say if he knew just how eager he was for the mission – and why. Runner could answer the questions for himself by getting to know Compton better, or course. There was the rub.

Runner did not think he could ever have felt particularly civilized towards anyone who had married his fiancée. That was understandable. It was even welcome. Runner perversely cherished his failings. Not too perversely, at that – Runner consciously cherished every human thing remaining to the race.

Runner could understand why a woman would choose to marry the famous Corps of Engineers general who had already chivvied and bullied the Army – the organizing force of the world – into devoting its major resources to this project he had fostered. There was no difficulty in seeing why Norma Brand might turn away from Malachi Runner in favour of a man who was not only the picture of efficiency and successful intellect but also was thought likely to be the saviour of Humanity.

But Compton several years later was—

Runner turned and looked; he couldn't spend the rest of the day avoiding it. Compton, several years later, was precisely what a man of his time could become if he was engaged in pushing a three hundred mile tunnel through the rock of a mountain chain, never knowing how much his enemy might know about it, and if he proposed to continue that excavation to its end, thirty years from now, whether the flesh was willing to meet his schedules or not.

Compton's leonine head protruded from what was very like a steam cabinet on wheels. In that cabinet were devices to assist his silicotic lungs, his sclerotic blood vessels, and a nervous system so badly deranged that even several years ago Runner had detected the great man in fits of spastic trembling. And God knew what else might be going wrong with Compton's body that Compton's will would not admit.

Compton grinned at him. Almost simultaneously, a bell chimed softly in the control panel on the back of the cabinet. The cadet aide sprang forward, read the warning in some dial or other and made an adjustment in the settings of the control knobs. Compton craned his neck in its collar of loose grey plastic sheeting and extended his grin to the boy. "Thank you, Cadet. I thought I was starting to feel a little dizzy."

"Yes, sir." The aide went back to his rest position.

"All right, Colonel," Compton said to Runner as though nothing had happened. "I've been curious to see this gimmick of yours in operation ever since it was delivered here. Thank you. You can turn it off now. And after that, I'll show *you* something you've never seen."

Runner frowned for a moment. Then he nodded to himself. He crawled under the weapons carrier. From that close it was no longer "invisible", only vaguely dizzying to the eye. He opened the hatch and turned off the main switch.

Compton could only have meant he was going to show him the ship.

Of course, he had seen films of it often enough. Who had not? The Army had managed to keep spy-drones flying above the Mississippi plain. The ship ignored them unless they took on aggressive trajectories.

Presumably there was some limit to the power the ship felt able to expend. Or perhaps the ship simply did not care what Earthmen might learn from watching it; perhaps it underestimated them.

This latest in the long chain of Compton's command bunkers, creeping mole-like towards the ship, was lighted a sickly orange-yellow. Runner seemed to recall a minor scandal in the Quartermaster Corps. Something about a contractor who had bribed or cozened a Corps officer into believing that yellow light duplicated natural sunlight. Contractor and misled officer were no doubt long dead in one of the labour battalions at the bore face, but some use for the useless lights had had to be found. And so here they were, casting their pall, just as if two lives and two careers had not already gone towards settling the account.

But, of course, nothing settles an account as derelict as Earth's was.

In that light, Compton's cabinet rolled forward to the bank of hooded television screens jury-rigged against a somewhat water-proofed wall. A row of technicians perched on stools watched what the drones were showing them.

"Lights," Compton said, and the aide made the room dark. "Here, Colonel – try this one." He pointed his chin towards a particular screen, and Runner stepped closer. For the first time in his life, he saw something only a few hundred people of his time had seen in an undelayed picture; he saw the ship. It was two hundred miles away from his present location, and two hundred and fifty miles high.

II

Fifty years ago, the alien ship landed butt-down in the northwest quadrant of the central plain of the United States. Stern-first, she had put one of her four landing jacks straight down to bedrock through the town of Scott's Bluff, Nebraska, and the diagonally opposite leg seventy-five miles away near Julesburg, Colorado. Her shadow swept fifty thousand square miles.

A tower of pitted dull green and brown-gold metal, her forepeak narrowing in perspective into a needle raking unseen through the thinnest last margins of the atmosphere, she had neither parleyed nor even communicated with anything on or of Earth. No one had ever seen anything of what her crew might look like. To this day, she still neither spoke to Earth nor listened to whatever Terrestrials might want to say to her. She was neither an embassy nor an invader.

For fifty years she had been broadcasting the same code group into space, hour after hour, but she had neither made nor received any beam transmissions along any portion of the electromagnetic spectrum. The presumption was she had a distress beacon out on general principles, but had no hope of communicating with a particular source of rescue.

She had come down a little erratically; there was some suggestion of jury-rigging in the plates over an apparently buckled section of the hull shrouding her stern tubes; there seemed to be some abnormal erosion at one segment of the lip around the main jet. Over the years, Headquarters Intelligence had reached the decision that she was down on Earth for a self-refit.

Landing, she had immediately put out surface parties and air patrols – there were turret-mounted weapons all along her flanks; she was clearly a warship of some kind – in a display of resources that badly upset the Terrestrial military forces observing her. The surface parties were squat-profiled, tracked, armoured amphibious machines with sixteen-foot bogeys and a track-to-turtledeck height of seventy-five feet. They had fanned out over the surrounding states and, without regard to road, river, fence or farmhouse, had foraged for minerals. It had finally been concluded that the vehicles, equipped with power shovels, claws, drills, ore buckets and whatever other mining tools were necessary, were remote-controlled from the ship on the basis of local topography but not with any reference to the works of Man. Or to the presence of Man. The undeviating tracks made as much of a hayrick as they did of a company of anti-tank infantry or a battalion of what the Army in those days was pleased to call "armour".

Whatever had hurt her, there was no point in Earthmen speculating on it. No missile could reach her. She had antimissile missiles and barrage patterns that, in operation, had made the Mississippi plain uninhabitable. An attempt was made to strike her foraging parties, with some immediate success. She then extended her air cover to the entire civilized world, and began methodically smashing down every military installation and every industrial complex capable of supporting one.

It was a tribute to the energy and perseverance of Twentieth Century Man. And it was the cause of Twenty-First Century man's finding himself broken into isolated enclaves, almost all of them either underground or so geographically remote as to be valueless, and each also nearly incapable of physical communication with any other.

It did not take a great deal of Terrestrial surface activity to attract one of the ship's nearly invulnerable aircraft. Runner's journey between Salt Lake and the tunnel pit head had been long, complicated by the need to establish no beaten path, and anxious. Only the broken terrain, full of hiding places, had made it possible at all.

But the balance between birth and death rates was once more favourable, and things were no longer going all the ship's way – whether the ship knew it or not. Still, it would be another thirty years before this siege bore Compton was driving could reach, undermine and finally topple the ship.

Thirty years from now, Runner and the other members of Special Division knew, the biped, spindling, red-eyed creatures emerging from the ground to loot that broken ship and repay themselves for this nightmare campaign would be only externally human – some of them. Some would be far less. Special Division's hope – its prospects were not good enough to call it a task – was to attempt to shorten that time while Humanity was still human.

And if the human race did not topple the ship, or if the ship completed its refit and left before they could reach it, then all this fifty years of incalculable material and psychic expenditure was irretrievably lost. Humanity would be bankrupt. They were all living now on the physical and emotional credit embodied in that tower of alien resources. From it, they could strip a technology to make the world new again – nothing less could accomplish that; in its conquest, there was a triumph to renew the most exhausted heart. Or almost any such heart. Runner could only speculate on how many of the victors would be, like Compton, unable to dance upon the broken corpse.

If anyone on Earth doubted, no one dared to dwell aloud on the enfeebling thought.

They had to have the ship.

"She's got some kind of force field running over her structure," Compton remarked, looking at the image on the screen. "We know that much. Something that keeps the crystals in her metal from deforming and sliding. She'd collapse. If we had something like that field, we could build to her size, too."

"Is there that much metal in the world?"

Compton looked sideward at Runner. "A damned sight more. But if we had her, we wouldn't need it."

Yes, Runner thought, keeping himself from looking at the screen now as faithfully as he had prevented himself from looking at Compton earlier. Yes, if we had the ship we wouldn't need this, and we wouldn't need that, or the other thing. We could even engineer such wonderful cabinets like the one in which Compton dwells that none of us would have to fear a stop to our ambitions, and we could roll along in glory on the wonderfully smooth corridor floors we could carve, away from the places where storms and lightning strike.

For how could you live, Compton, out there where I have to go tomorrow?

Compton, looking up at him, shrewdly said: "Do you know I approve of the Special Division? I think you people serve a very necessary function. I need the pressure of rivals."

Runner thought: You are ugly.

"I have to go to sleep," he had said and left Compton to his screens and schedules. But he did not take the lift down to the Bachelor Officers' Quarters where had been given an accommodation – a two-man cubicle for himself alone; the aide, never having experienced solitude, as Runner had, had been envious. Instead, he puzzled his way through another of the branching temporary passageways that were crudely chopped out for living space near the advancing bore.

He searched until he found the proper door. The letter Norma had sent him did not contain the most exact directions. It had spoken in local terms: "Follow the first parallel until you reach the fourth gallery," and so forth.

He knocked, and the gas-tight door opened.

"I heard you would be here today," Norma said in a choked voice, and there was much for him to read in the waxiness of her skin and the deep wrinkles that ran from the corners of her nose to the corners of her bloodless mouth.

He took the hands she offered, and stepped inside.

There was one large room; that is, a room large enough for a free-standing single cot, rather than a bunk, and a cleared area, faintly marked by black rubber wheelmarks, large enough for a cabinet to turn around in.

"How are you, Norma?" he said as if he could not guess, and she did not trouble to answer him. She shut the door and leaned against it as if they had both just fled in here.

"Are you going out in the morning?"

Runner nodded. It seemed to him he had time at least to say a few conventional things to the girl who had been his fiancée, and then Compton's wife. But she apparently thought otherwise.

"Are you going to make it?"

"I don't know. It's a gamble."

"Do you think you'll make it?"

"No."

It had never seemed reasonable that he would. In the Technical Section of the Special Division there were men – fully his equals – who were convinced he could succeed. They said they had calculated the ship's weaknesses, and he believed they had figures and evaluations, right enough. He in his own turn believed there were things a man had to be willing to do whether they seemed reasonable or not, simply because they seemed necessary. So neither fact nor opinion could modify his taking the weapons carrier out against the ship tomorrow. "But I *hope* I'll make it," he said.

"You hope you'll make it," Norma said tonelessly. She reached quickly and took his hands again. "What a forlorn thing to tell me! You know I won't be able to stand it down here much longer. How do we know the ship doesn't have seismic detectors? How do we know it isn't just letting us concentrate ourselves here so it can smash us before we become dangerous?"

"Well, we don't know, but it seems unlikely. They have geological probes, of course. The gamble is that they're only probes and not detectors."

"If they don't smash us, there's only one reason – they know they'll be finished and gone before we can reach them!"

This was all wrong; he could not talk to her about anything important before he had calmed her. He said, searching for some way to reach her: "But we have to go on as if they won't. Nothing else we've tried has worked. At least Compton's project hasn't failed."

"Now you're on his side! You!"

She was nothing like the way she had been with him. She would never have been like this. The way she was now, she and Malachi Runner could not meet. He understood, now, that in the years since she had left Headquarters with Compton she had come to think back on Malachi Runner not as a man but as an embodiment of that safe life. It was not him she was shouting out to. It was to all those days gone for ever.

And so I must be those days of life in a place where shafts lead to the wine-rich air of the surface, and there is no sound of metal twisting in the rock. I am not Malachi Runner now. I hoped I could be. I should have read that letter as it was, not as I hoped it was. Goodbye, Runner, you aren't needed here.

"No, I'm not on his side. But I wouldn't dare stop him if I could. I wouldn't dare shut off any hope that things will end and the world can go back to living."

"End? Where can they end? He goes on; he can't move an arm or a finger, but he goes on. He doesn't need anything but that box that keeps him alive and this tunnel and that ship. Where can I touch him?"

They stood separated by their outstretched hands, and Runner watched her as intently as though he had been ordered to make a report on her.

"I thought I could help him, but now he's in that box!"

Yes, Runner thought, now he's in that box. He will not let death rob him of seeing the end of his plans. And you love him, but he's gone where you can't follow. Can you?

He considered what he saw in her now, and he knew she was lost. But he thought that if the war would only end, there would be ways to reach her. He could not reach her now; nothing could reach her. He knew insanity was incurable, but he thought that perhaps she was not yet insane; if he could at least keep her within this world's bounds, there might be time, and ways, to bring her back. If not to him, then at least to the remembered days of Headquarters.

"Norma!" he said, driven by what he foresaw and feared. He pulled her close and caught her eyes in his own. "Norma, you have got to promise me that no matter what happens, you won't get into another one of those boxes so you can be with him."

The thought was entirely new to her. Her voice was much lower. She frowned as if to see him better and said: "Get into one of those boxes? Oh, no – no, I'm not sick, yet. I only have to have shots for my nerves. A corpsman comes and gives them to me. He'll be here soon. It's only if you can't not-care; I mean, if you have to stay involved, like he does, that you need the interrupter circuits instead of the tranquilizer shots. You don't get into one of those boxes just for fear," she said.

He had forgotten that; he had more than forgotten it – there were apparently things in the world that had made him be sure, for a moment, that it really was fear.

He did not like hallucinating. He did not have any way of depending on himself if he had lapses like that.

"Norma, how do I look to you?" he said rapidly.

She was still frowning at him in that way. "You look about the same as always," she said.

He left her quickly – he had never thought, in conniving for this assignment with the letter crackling in his pocket, that he would leave her so quickly. And he went to his accommodation, crossing the raw, still untracked and unsheathed echoing shaft of the tunnel this near the face, with the labour battalion squads filing back and forth and the rubble carts rumbling. And in the morning he set out. He crawled into the weapons carrier, and was lifted up to a hidden opening that had been made for it during the night. He started the engine and, lying flat on his stomach in the tiny cockpit, peering through the cat's-eye viewports, he slid out onto the surface of the mountain and so became the first of his generation to advance into this territory that did not any more belong to Man.

When he was three days out, he passed within a hundred yards of a cluster of mining-machines. They paid him no attention, and he laughed, cackling inside his egg. He knew that if he had safely come so close to an extension of the ship – an extension that could have stepped over and crushed him with almost no extra expenditure – then his chances were very good. He knew he cackled. But he knew the Army's drones were watching, unobtrusively, for signs of his extinction or breakdown. Not finding them, they were therefore giving Compton and Headquarters the negative good news that he had not yet failed. At Headquarters, other Special Division personnel would be beginning to hope. They had been the minority party in the conflicts there for as long as they had been in existence at all.

But it did not matter, he thought as he lay up that night and sipped warm water from the carrier's tank. It didn't matter what party was winning. Surely even Compton would not be infuriated by a premature end to the war. And there were plenty of people at Headquarters who had fought for Compton not because they were convinced his was the only way, but only because his was a way that seemed sure. If slow. Or as sure as any way could be.

It came to Runner, for the first time in his life, that any race, in whatever straits, willing to expend so much of its resources on what was really not a surety at all, must be desperate beyond all reason.

He cackled again. He knew he cackled. He smiled at himself for it.

III

The interior of the weapons carrier was padded to protect him from the inevitable jounces and collisions. So it was hot. And the controls were crude; the carrier moved from one foot to another, like a turtle, and there were levers for each of his hands and feet to control. He sweated and panted for breath.

No other machine could possibly have climbed down the face of that mountain and then begun its heaving, staggering progress towards the spaceship's nearest leg. It could not afford to leave tracks. And it would, when it had covered the long miles of open country that separated it from its first destination, have to begin another inching, creeping journey of fifty-five miles, diagonally up the broadening, extensible pillar of the leg.

It stumbled forward on pseudopods – enormous hollow pads of tough, transparent plastic, moulded full of stress-channels that curled them to fit the terrain, when they were stiffened in turn by compressed colourless fluid. Shifting its weight from one of the these to another, the carrier duck-walked from one shadow to another as Runner, writhing with muscle cramps, guided it at approximately the pace of a drunken man.

But it moved forward.

After the first day Runner was ready to believe that the ship's radar systems were not designed to track something that moved so close to the ground and so slowly. The optical detection system – which Intelligence respected far more than it did radar; there were dozens of countered radar-proof missiles to confirm them – also did not seem to have picked him up.

He began to feel he might see Norma again. Thinking of that babbling stranger in Compton's accommodation, he began to feel he might someday see *Norma* again.

The ship's leg was sunken through the ground down to its anchorage among the deep rock layers sloping away from the mountains. It was, at ground level, so far across that he could not see past it. It was a wall of streaked and overgrown metal curving away from him, and only by shifting to one of the side viewports could he make out its apparent limits from where he now was.

Looking overhead, he saw it rise away from him, an inverted pylon thrust into the ground at an angle, and far, far above him, in the air towards which that angle pointed, something large and vague rested on that pylon. Obscured by mist and cloud, distorted by the curvature of the tiny lens though which he was forced to look at it, it was nothing meaningful. He reasoned the pylon led up to the ship. He could not see the ship; he concentrated on the pylon.

Gingerly, he extended a pseudopod. It touched the metal of the ship, through which the stabilizing field ran. There was an unknown danger here, but it hadn't seemed likely to Intelligence that the field would affect non-metallic substances.

It didn't. The pseudopod touched the metal of the ship, and nothing untoward happened. He drew it back, and cycled an entirely new fluid through the pseudopods. Hairline excretory channels opened on their soles, blown clean by the pressure. The pads flattened and increased in area. He moved forward towards the pylon again, and this time he began to climb it, held by air pressure on the pads and the surface tension on their wet soles. He began, then, at the end of a week's journey, to climb upon the ship no other aggression of Man's had ever reached. By the time he was a thousand feet up, he dared look only through the fore ports.

Now he moved in a universe of sound. The leg thrummed and quivered, so gently that he doubted anyone in the ship could feel it. But he was not in the ship; he was where the thrumming was. It invaded his gritted teeth and put an intolerable itching deep into his ears. This fifty-five miles had to be made without stop for rest; he could not, in fact, take his hands from the controls. He was not sure that he shouldn't be grateful – he would have gouged his ears with his nails, surely, if he had been free to work at them.

He was past laughter of any kind now – but exultation sustained him even when, near the very peak of his climb, he came to the rat guard.

He had studied this problem with a model. No one had tried to tell him what it might be like to solve it at this altitude, with the wind and mist upon him.

The rat guard was a collar of metal, cone-shaped and inverted downward, circling the leg. The leg here was several miles in diameter; the rat guard was a canopy several yards thick and several hundred feet wide from its joining at the leg to its lip. It was designed to prevent exactly what was happening – the attempted entry of a pest.

Runner extended the carrier's pseudopods as far and wide as they would go. He pumped more coagulant into the fluid that leaked almost imperceptibly out of their soles, and began to make his way, head downward, along the descending slope of the rat guard's outer face. The carrier swayed and stretched at the plastic membranes. He neutralized the coagulant in each foot in turn, slid it forward, fastened it again, and proceeded. After three hours he was at the lip, and dangling by the carrier's forelegs until he had succeeded in billowing one of the rear pads onto the lip as well.

And when he had, by this patient trial and error, scrambled successfully onto the rat guard's welcome upward face, he found that he was not past laughing after all. He shouted it; the carrier's interior frothed with it, and even the itching in his ears was lost. Then he began to move upward again.

Not too far away, the leg entered the ship's hull. There was an opening at least as large as the carrier needed. It was only a well; up here, the gleaming pistons that controlled the extension of the leg hung burnished in the gloom, but there was no entry to the ship itself. Nor did he need or want it.

He had reasoned long ago that whatever inhabited this ship must be as tired, as anxious, as beset any human being. He needed no new miseries to borrow. He wanted only to find a good place to attach his bomb, set the fuse and go. Before the leg, its muscles cut, collapsed upon the aliens' hope of ever returning to whatever peace they dreamed of.

When he climbed out of the carrier, as he had to, to attach the bomb, he heard one noise that was not wind-thrum or the throb of internal machinery. It was a persistent, nerve-torn ululation, faint but clear, deep inside the ship and with a chilling quality of endurance.

He hurried back down the leg; he had only four days to get clear – that is, to have a hope of getting clear – and he hurried too much. At the rat guard's lip, he had to hang on by his heels and cast the fore pads under. He though he had a grip, but he had only half a one. The carrier slipped, jerked and hung dangling by the pad. It began to slide back down the short distance to the lip of the guard, rippling and twisting as parts of its sole lost contact and other parts had to take up the sudden drag.

He poured coagulant into the pad, and stopped the awful series of sticks and slips. He slapped the other pads up into place and levered forward, forgetting how firmly that one pad had been set in his panic. He felt resistance, and then remembered, but by then the pull of the other three pads had torn the carrier forward and there was a long rip through which stress fluid and coagulant dripped in a turgid stream.

He came down the last ten miles of the leg like a runaway toboggan on a poorly surfaced slide, the almost flaccid pads turning brown and burnt, their plastic soft as jelly. He left behind him a long, slowly evaporating smear of fluid and, since no one had thought to put individual shut-offs in the cross-valving system between the pads, he came down with no hope of ever using the carrier to get back to the mountains.

It was worse than that. In the end, he crashed into the indented ground at the base of the leg, and, for all the interior padding, the drive levers bludgeoned him and broke bones for him. He lay in the wreck with only a faint awareness of anything but his pain. He could not even know whether the carrier, with its silent power supply, still as much as half hid him or whether that had broken, too.

It hadn't broken, but he was still there when the bomb exploded; it was only a few hours afterward that he came out of his latest delirium and found that the ground had been stirred and the carrier was lying in a new position.

He pried open the hatch – not easily or painlessly – and looked out.

The ship hadn't fallen. The leg had twitched in the ground – it was displaced by several thousand yards, and raw earth clung to it far overhead. It had changed its angle several degrees towards vertical and was much less deeply sunken into the ground. But the ship had not fallen.

He fell back into the carrier and cried because the ship hadn't come down and crushed him.

IV

The carrier had to be abandoned. Even if the pads had been usable, it was three-quarters buried in the upheaval the leg had made when it stirred. The machine, Runner thought contemptuously, had failed, while a man could be holed and broken and heal himself nevertheless.

He had very good proof of that, creeping back towards the mountains. Broken badly enough, a man might not heal himself into what he had been. But he would heal into something.

For a time he had to be very wary of the mining machines, for there had been a frenzied increase in their activity. And there was the problem of food and water. But he was in well-watered country. The comings and goings of the machines had churned the banks of the Platte River into a series of sinks and swamps without making it impossible for a thirsty, crawling man to drink. And he had his rations from the carrier while the worst of the healing took place. After that, when he could already scuttle on his hands and one knee, he was able to range about. In crawling, he had discovered the great variety of burrowing animals that lived beneath the eye of ordinary man; once he had learned which one made bolt-holes and which could be scooped out of the traps of their own burrows he began to supply himself with a fair amount of protein.

The ship, and its extensions, did him no harm. Some of this was luck, when he was in the zones traversed by the machines as they went to and from the ship. But after he had taken up a systematic trek back along the North Platte, and presumably ought to have stopped being registered in the ship's detectors as an aimless animal, he was apparently protected by his colouration, which was that of the ground, and again by his slow speed and ability to hug the terrain. Even without pseudopods and a fusion bomb to carry, his speed was no better than that.

When several months had passed he was able to move in a half-upright walk that was an unrelenting parody of a skip and a jump, and he was making fair time. But by then he was well up into the beginnings of the Medicine Bows.

He thought that even though the ship still stood, if he could reach Norma soon enough she might still not be too lost.

Not only the ship but the Army drones had missed him, until he was almost back to the now refilled exit from which he and the carrier had launched themselves. The passages were hurriedly unblocked – every cubic yard of rubble that did not have to be dispersed and camouflaged at the pithead represented an enormous saving of expenditure – and he was hauled back into the company of his fellow creatures.

His rescue was nearly unendurable. He lay on a bed in the Aid Station and listened to Compton's delight.

"They went wild when I told them at Headquarters, Colonel. You'd already been given a posthumous Medal of Honour. I don't know what they'll do now you're available for parades. And you certainly deserve them. I had never had such a moment in my life as when I saw what you'd done to the ship."

And while Compton talked, Norma – Norma with no attention to spare for Runner; a Norma bent forward, peering at the dials of Compton's cabinet, one hand continually twitching towards the controls – that Norma reached with her free hand, took a photograph out of a file folder clipped to the side of the cabinet and held the picture, unseeing, for Runner to look at while she continued her stewardship of Compton's dials. The cadet had been replaced. The wife was homemaking in the only way she could.

The ship no longer pointed directly away from the ground, nor was she equally balanced on the quadruped of her landing jacks. The bombed leg dangled useless, its end trailing in the ground, and the ship leaned away from it.

"When the bomb went off," Compton was explaining, "she did the only thing she could to save herself for the time being. She partially retracted the opposite leg to balance herself."

Norma reached out and adjusted one of the controls. The flush paled out of Compton's face, and his voice sank towards the toneless whisper Runner remembered.

"I was always afraid she would do that. But the way she is now, I know – I *know* that when I undermine another leg, she'll fall! And she can't get away from me. She'll never take off with the leg dragging. I never had a moment in my life like the moment I had when I saw her tilt. Now I know there's an end in sight. All of us here know there's an end in sight, don't you, Norma? The ship'll puzzle out how you did it, Runner, and she'll defend against another such attempt, but she can't defend against the ground opening up under. We'll run the tunnel right through the rock layers she rests on, get underneath, mine out a pit for the leg to stumble into and blow the rock – she'll go down like a tree in the wind, Runner. Thirty years – well, possibly forty, now that we've got to reach a further leg – and we'll have her! We'll swallow her up, Runner!"

Runner was watching Norma. Her eyes darted over the dials and not once, though most of the gestures were abortive, did her hands stop their twitching towards the controls. When she did touch them, her hands were sure; she seemed quite practised; Runner could calculate that she had probably displaced the cadet very soon after he had bombed the ship.

Runner comforted himself with the thought that the aliens in the ship had also gone mad. And he thought it was a very human thing to do – he thought, with some pride, that it was perhaps the last human thing – for him to refuse the doctors who offered to give him artificial replacements for the hopelessly twisted legs he had come back with.

"You will *not*!" he snapped, while up in the bunker, all unimaginable to him, Norma kissed Compton's face and said: "You *will* get her – you *will*!"

THE WAR ARTIST

Tony Ballantyne

Artists participating in and recording battle go back to the Napoleonic Wars and the American Revolutionary War, if not earlier. What might be the lot of the war artist in times to come?

A British master of IT, to Ballantyne code is poetry as he demonstrates in his blog, "Robots and Accordions", by implementing in Java the poem of a friend who challenged him. His debut SF trilogy of Recursion, Capacity *and* Divergence *led on to* Blood and Iron *and* Twisted Metal.

MY NAME IS Brian Garlick and I carry an easel into battle. Well, in reality I carry a sketchbook and several cameras, but I like to give people a picture of me they can understand.

The sergeant doesn't understand me, though. He's been staring since we boarded the flier in Marseilles. Amongst the nervous conversation of the troops, their high-pitched laughter like spumes of spray on a restless sea, he is a half-submerged rock. He's focusing on me with dark eyes and staring, staring, staring. As the voices fade to leave no sound but the whistle of the wind and the creak of the pink high-visibility straps binding the equipment bundles, he's still staring, and I know he's going to undermine me. I've seen that look before, though less often than you might expect. Most soldiers are interested in what I do, but there are always those who seem to take my presence as an insult to their profession. Here it comes...

"I don't get it," he says. "Why do we need a war artist?"

The other soldiers are watching. Eyes wide, their breath fast and shallow, but they've just found something to distract them from the coming fight. Well, I have my audience; it's time to make my pitch to try and get them on my side for the duration of the coming action.

"That's a good question," I reply. I smile, and I start to paint a picture. A picture of the experienced old hand, the unruffled professional.

"Someone once said a good artist paints what can't be painted. Well, that's what a war artist is supposed to do."

"You paint what can't be painted," says the sergeant. It's to his credit he doesn't make the obvious joke. For the moment he's intrigued, and I take advantage of the fact.

"They said Breughel could paint the thunder," I say. "You can paint lightning, sure, but can you make the viewer *hear* the thunder? Can you make them *feel* that rumble, deep in their stomach? That's the job of a war artist, to paint what can't be painted. You can photograph the battle, you can show the blood and the explosions, but does that picture tell the full story? I try to capture the excitement, the fear, the terror." I look around the rows of pinched faces, eyes shiny. "I try to show the heroism."

I've composed my picture; now, I surreptitiously snap it. That veneer of pride that overlays the hollow fear filling the flier as it travels through the skies.

The sergeant sneers; the mood evaporates. "What do *you* know about all that?"

I see the bitter smiles of the other soldiers. So I paint another picture. I lean forward and speak in a low voice.

"I've been doing this for six years. I was in Tangiers after the first Denial of Service attack. I was in Barcelona when the entire Spanish banking system was wiped out; I was in Geneva when the Swiss Government network locked. I know what we're flying into; I know what it's like to visit a state targeted by hackers."

There are some approving nods at this. Or is it just the swaying of the craft as we jump an air pocket? Either way, the sergeant isn't going to be convinced.

"Maybe you've seen some action," he concedes. "Maybe you've been shot at. That doesn't make you one of us. You take off the fatigues and you're just another civilian. You won't get jostled in the street back home, or refused service in shops. You won't have people calling you a butcher, when all you've tried to do is defend their country."

This gets the troops right back on his side. I see the memory of the taunts and the insults written on their faces. Too many people were against us getting involved in the Eurasian war, numbers that have only grown since the fighting started. There's a cold look in the troops' eyes. But I can calm them; I know what to say.

"That's why the government sent me here. A war artist communicates the emotions their patron chooses. That's why war artists are nearly always to be found acting in an official capacity. I'm here to tell *your* side of the story, to counteract those images you see on the web."

That's the truth, too. Well, almost the truth. It's enough to calm them down. They're on my side. Nearly all of them, anyway. The sergeant is still not convinced, but I don't think he ever will be.

"I don't like it," he says. "You've said it yourself, what you're painting isn't real war ..."

All that's academic now as the warning lights start to flash: orange sheets of fire engulfing the flier's interior. I photograph the scene, dark bodies lost in the background, faces like flame in the foreground, serious, stern, brave faces, awaiting the coming battle. That's the image I will create, anyway.

"Get ready!" calls the sergeant.

There's a sick feeling in my stomach as we drop towards the battle and I wonder, How can I show that?

A shriek of engines, a surge of deceleration and a jolt and we're down and the rear ramp is falling...

We land in a city somewhere in southern Europe. Part of what used to be Italy, I guess. Red bricks, white plaster, green tiles. I hear gunfire, but it's some distance away. I smell smoke; I hear the sound of feet on the metal ramp, the rising howl of the flier's engines as it prepares to lift off again. I see buildings, a narrow road leading uphill to a blue sky and a yellow sun. I smell something amidst the smoke, something that seems incongruous in this battle scene. Something that reminds me of parties and dinners and dates with women. It takes me a moment in all the confusion of movement to realize what it is.

Red wine. It's running down the street. Not a euphemism, there's a lorry at the top of the hill, on its side, the front smashed where it's run into a wall, the driver's arm drooping from the open window, the silver clasp of his watch popped open so it hangs like a bracelet ... Jewels of broken glass are scattered on the road, diamonds from the windshield, rubies from the truck's lights and emeralds from the broken bottles that are spilling red blood down the street. It's such a striking image that, instinctively, I begin snapping.

The soldiers are flattening themselves against the vine-clad walls that border the street, the chameleon material of their suits changing to dusty white, their guns humming as they autoscan the surrounding area. Their half-seen figures are edging their way up and down the hill, changing colour, becoming the red of doors and the dusty dark of windows. They're sizing up the area, doing their job, just like me, cameras in my hand, in my helmet, at my belt. Sizing up the scene.

The peacefulness of the street is at odds with the tension we feel, and I need to capture that. The lazy smell of the midday heat mixed with wine. Lemons hanging waxy from the trees leaning over the white walls, paint peeling from window frames. A soldier pauses to touch the petals trailing from a hanging basket and I photograph that.

As if in response to my action, someone opens fire from up the street and there is a whipsnap of movement all around. The sergeant shouts something into a communicator; the flier whines into the air, guns rattling. I see thin wisps of cloud emerge from the doorway of a house up the hill. Someone fired upon us, and now the flier's returned the compliment. Incendiaries, I guess, seeing the orange-white sheets that ripple and flicker up the plaster walls of the building.

I snap the picture, but it's not what I'm after: it's too insubstantial.

If I were to paint this, the explosion would be much bigger and blooming and orange. It would burst upon the viewer: a heroic response to a cowardly attack.

Then I see the children, and the image I'm forming collapses. Children and women are tumbling from the house. The sound of the flier, the crackle of the flames, they paint a picture in my mind that doesn't involve children. But the truth is unfolding. There were civilians in there! The camera captures their terrified, wide-eyed stares, but it can't capture that weeping, keening noise they make. It can't capture the lurching realization that someone just made a huge mistake.

I see the look on the sergeant's face, that sheer animal joy, and I turn the camera away. That's not what I'm after, but my hand turns back of its own accord. If I had time, I'd try to sketch it right here and now. There is something about the feelings of the moment, getting them down in pencil.

The sergeant sees me looking at him, and he laughs. "So? Innocents get hurt. That's what happens in war."

I make to answer him, but he's concentrating on his console. The green light of the computer screen illuminates his face.

"That's St Mark's church at the top of the hill," he says. "There's a square beyond it with a town hall facing it. We occupy those two buildings, we have the high ground." He runs his finger across the screen. "Big rooms in there, wide corridors. A good place to make our base."

A woman screams. She's pleading for something. I see a child; I see a lot of blood. A medic is running up, and I photograph that. The gallant liberators, aiding the poor civilians. That's the problem with a simple snap. Taken out of context, it can mean anything.

But that's why I'm here. To choose the context.

We make it to the top of the hill without further incident. The cries of pain are receding from my ears and memory. I focus on the scene at hand.

A wide square, littered with the torn canvas and broken bodies of umbrellas that once shaded café patrons. Upturned tables and chairs. Panic spreads fast when people find their mobile phones and computers have stopped working. They've seen the news from other countries; they know that the rioting is not far behind. Across the square, a classic picture: the signs of money and authority, targeted by the mobs. Two banks, their plate-glass fronts smashed open, their interiors peeled inside out in streamers of plastic and trampled circuitry.

The town hall is even worse. It looks like a hollow shell; the anger of the mob has torn the guts out of this place, eviscerated it.

This is what happens when a Denial of Service attack hits, wiping out every last byte of data attached to a country, smoothing the memory stores to an endless sequence of 1s.

Everything – pay, bank accounts, mortgages – wiped out completely. The rule of law breaks down, and armies are sent in to help restore order.

That was the official line, anyway.

"Funny," says the woman at my side. "We seem to be more intent on securing militarily advantageous positions than in helping the population."

"Shut up, Friis," snaps the sergeant.

"Just making an observation, Sergeant." The woman winks at me.

"Tell you what, Friis, you like making observations so much, why don't you head in there and check it out?"

"Sure," she says, and she looks at me with clear blue eyes. "You coming, painter boy?"

"Call me Brian."

"Aren't you afraid he might get hurt?" laughs the sergeant.

"I'll look after him."

I pat my pockets, checking my cameras, and follow her through the doorway, the glass crunching beneath my feet.

A large entrance hall, the floor strewn with broken chairs. The rioters haven't been able to get at the ceiling though, and I snap the colourful frescoes that look down upon us. The soldier notices none of this; she's scanning the room, calm and professional. She speaks without looking at me.

"I'm Agnetha."

"Pleased to meet you."

She has such a delightful accent. Vaguely Scandinavian.

I've heard it before.

I see strands of blonde hair curling from beneath her helmet. Her face is slightly smudged, which makes her look incredibly sexy.

We move from room to room. Everything is in disarray – this place has been stripped and gutted. There's paper and glass everywhere. Everything that could be broken has been broken.

"Always the same," says Agnetha. "The data goes, and people panic. They have no money to buy food; they can't use the phone. They think only of themselves, looting what they can and then barricading themselves into their houses. They steal from themselves, and then we come in and take their country from them."

"I thought we were here to help!"

She laughs at that, and we continue our reconnaissance.

Eventually, it's done. Agnetha speaks into her radio. "This place is clear."

I recognize the sergeant's voice. "Good. We'll move in at once. There are reports of guerrilla activity down at the Via Baciadonne."

"Baciadonne." Agnetha smiles at me. "That means 'kisses women'."

She's clever as well as pretty. I like that.

The area is quickly secured, which is good because outside the random sound of gunfire is becoming more frequent. I feel the excitement of the approaching battle building in my stomach. The flier comes buzzing up over the roofs, turning this way and that, and I watch the soldiers as they go through the building, filling it with equipment bundled in pink tape.

We find a room with two doors that open out on to a balcony with a view over the city beyond. Agnetha opens the doors to get a better field of fire, then leans against the wall opposite, her rifle slung across her knees. She smiles coquettishly at me.

"Why aren't you taking my picture?" she asks.

I point the camera at her and hear it click.

"Are you going to use that?"

"I don't know."

"Keeping it for your private collection?" She stretches her legs and yawns.

"You don't mind me being attached to your group, then," I say, "not like your sergeant."

She wrinkles her nose. "He doesn't speak for all of us. I don't agree with everything the government says, either. We're sent out here with insufficient equipment and even less backup, and when we get home we're forgotten about at best. I think it's good that we have people like you here." She frowns. "So tell me, what *are* you going to paint?"

"Actually, I don't just paint. I use computers, software, all those things. It's all about the final image."

"I understand that. But what *are* you going to paint?"

I can't keep evading the issue. For all my fine words about reflecting the war as it really is, the sergeant had it right. I'll paint whatever Command wants me to. I like to paint a picture of myself as a bit of a rogue, but, at heart, I know the establishment has me, body and soul.

"I don't know yet. That's why I'm here. I need to experience this place, and then I can try to convey some emotion."

"What emotion?"

"I don't know that, either."

There's a crackle of gunfire, sharp silver, like tins rattling on the floor. I ignore it.

"You're very pretty," I say.

"Thank you." She lowers her eyes in acknowledgement. I like that. She doesn't pretend she isn't pretty; she takes the compliment on its own terms.

"How did you end up in the Army?" I ask.

She yawns and stretches. "I worked in insurance," she says, and that seems all wrong. So drab and everyday. She should have been a model, or a mountaineer, or an artist or something. "I lost my job when Jutland got hit by the DoS attack. Everything was lost, policies, claims, payroll. The hackers had been feeding us the same worm for months; the backups were totally screwed."

"I'm sorry," I say, and I am. Really sorry. So that's why her accent sounded so familiar. Fortunately, she doesn't seem to notice my reaction.

"Other people had it worse." She shrugs. "We had a garden; we had plenty of canned goods in the house. My mother had the bath filled with water, all the pans and the dishes. We managed OK until your Army moved in to restore order."

She seems remarkably unperturbed by the affair.

"So you joined us out of gratitude?" I suggest.

She laughs. "No, I joined you for security. This way I get to eat and I'm pretty sure that my salary won't be wiped out at the touch of a button. If your Army's servers aren't secure, then whose are?"

"Fair enough."

"No, it's not fair. It's just life. Your Army wiped out Jutland's data. Just like it did this country's."

I try to look shocked. "You think that we are responsible for the trouble here?"

"It's an old trick. Create civil unrest and then send in your troops to sort out the problem. You've swallowed up half of Europe that way."

"I don't think it's that well planned," I said, honestly. "I just think that everyone takes whatever opportunity they can when a DoS hits."

As if to underline the point, the staccato rattle of gunfire sounds in the distance.

"Aren't you worried that I will report you?" I ask. "Have you charged with sedition?"

She rises easily to her feet and walks towards me. "No. I trust you. You have nice eyes."

She's laughing at me.

"Come here," she says. I lean down and she kisses me on the lips. Gently, she pushes my face away. "You're a very handsome man. Maybe later on we can talk properly."

"I'd like that."

She looks back out of the window, checking the area. Little white puffs of cloud drift across the blue sky.

"So, what are you going to paint?" she asks. "The heroic rescuers, making the country safe once more?"

"You're being sarcastic."

"No," she says, and she pushes a strand of blonde hair back up into her helmet. "No. We all do what we must to get by. Tell me, what will you paint?"

"I honestly don't know yet. I'll know it when I see it." I look down into the square, searching for inspiration. "Look at your flier."

She comes to my side. We look at the concrete-grey craft, a brutalist piece of architecture set amongst the elegant buildings of this city.

"Suppose I were to paint that?" I say. "I have plenty of photos, but I need a context, a setting. I could have it swooping down on the enemy! The smoke, the explosions, the bullets whizzing past."

"That's what the Army would like …"

"Maybe. How about I paint it with you all seated around the back? That could send a message to the people back home: that even soldiers are human; they sit and chat and relax. Or should I evoke sympathy? Draw the flier all shot up. The mechanics around it, trying to fix it up. One of you being led from the scene, blood seeping from the bandages."

She nods. She understands. Then her radio crackles, and I hear the sergeant's voice. "Friis! Get down to the flier! We need help bringing equipment inside."

"Coming!"

"I'll tag along," I say.

The whine of the flier is a constant theme; the engines are never turned off. We join the bustle of soldiers around the rear ramp, all busy unloading the pink-bound boxes and carrying them into the surrounding buildings.

"What is all that?" I wonder aloud.

"Servers, terminals, NAS boxes," says Agnetha. "I saw this in

Jutland. We're establishing a new government in this place."

"Keep it down, Friis," says the sergeant, but without heat. I notice that no one seems to be denying the charge. The head of the soldier behind him suddenly spouts red blood. I'm photographing the scene before I realize what's happening.

"Sniper!"

Everyone is dropping, looking this way and that.

"Up there," shouts someone.

The sergeant is looking at his console, the green light of the screen illuminating his face.

"That's the Palazzo Egizio. The Via Fossano runs behind it…" He's thinking. "Friis, Delgado, Kenton. Head to the far end of the street. See if you can get into that white building there…"

I raise my head to get a better look and feel someone push me back down. At the same time there are more shots and I hear a scream. I feel a thud of fear inside me.

Agnetha has been shot.

Shot protecting me.

She's coughing up blood.

"Agnetha…" I begin.

"Get back," yells the sergeant. "You've caused enough trouble as it is."

Agnetha's trying to speak, but there is too much blood. She holds out her hand and I reach for it, but the sergeant knocks it away.

"Let the medic deal with it," he says. "Let someone who should be here deal with it," he adds, nastily.

The other soldiers have located the sniper now, and I'm left to watch as a man kneels next to Agnetha and takes hold of her arm. She looks at me with those brilliant blue eyes, and I don't see her. For a brief moment I see another picture. Blues and greens. Two soldiers: a man and a woman, standing in front of a flier just like the one behind us. They're surrounded by cheering, smiling civilians. A young child comes forward, carrying a bunch of flowers. A thank you from the grateful liberated.

The picture I painted of Jutland.

I push it from my mind, and I see those brilliant blue eyes are already clouding over.

"We all do what we have to do," I whisper. But is that so true? She joined the Army so her family could eat. I'm here simply to build a reputation as an artist.

The medic injects her with something. She closes her eyes. The medic shakes his head. I know what that means. The sergeant looks at me.

"I'm sorry," I say.

"So?" he says. "How's that going to help?" He turns away. The others are already doing the same. Dismissing me.

I take hold of Agnetha's hand, feel the pulse fading.

The picture.

I wonder if Agnetha would approve of what I have done. I suspect not. She was too much of a realist.

I included the flier after all. But not taking off, not swooping down from the skies.

No, this was a different picture.

The point of view is from just outside the cockpit, looking in at the pilot of the craft. And here is where we move beyond the subject matter to the artistic vision, because the person flying the craft is not the pilot, but the sergeant.

His face is there, centred on the picture. He's looking out at the viewer, looking beyond the cockpit.

What can he see? The dead children in the square, sheltered by the bodies of their dead parents? We don't know. But that doesn't matter, because there is a clue in the picture. A clue to the truth. One that I saw all the time, but never noticed. It's written across the sergeant's face. Literally.

A reflection in green from the light of the monitor screen, a tracery of roads and buildings, all picked out in pale-green letters. Look closely at his cheek and you can just make out the words *St Mark's Church*. All those names that were supposedly wiped for good by the DoS attack, and yet there they were, still resident in the sergeant's computer. And none of us found that odd at the time. We could have fed that country's data back to it all along, but we chose not to.

They say a picture paints a thousand words.

For once, those words will be mostly speaking the truth.

THE WAR MEMORIAL

Allen Steele

Where there's no air, a battle may leave reminders for ever...

Restless visionary Allen Steele, originally a native of Nashville, has a BA in Communication and an MA in Journalism. He's a prolific author of short stories and essays, as well as novels, several concerned with the habitable moon Coyote in a solar system to which freedom-seeking pioneers flee in a stolen starship. His work has won and been nominated for several awards.

THE FIRST-WAVE ASSAULT is jinxed from the very beginning. Even before the dropship touches down, its pilot shouts over the comlink that a Pax missile battery seven klicks away has locked in on their position, despite the ECM buffer set up by the lunarsats. So it's going to be a dust-off; the pilot has done his job by getting the men down to the surface, and he doesn't want to be splattered across Mare Tranquillitatis.

It doesn't matter anyway. Baker Company has been deployed for less than two minutes before the Pax heatseekers pummel the ground around them and take out the dropship even as it begins its ascent.

Giordano hears the pilot scream one last obscenity before his ugly spacecraft is reduced to metal rain, then something slams against his back and everything within the suit goes black. For an instant he believes he's dead, that he's been nailed by one of the heatseekers, but it's just debris from the dropship. The half-ton ceramic-polymer shell of the Mark III Valkyrie Combat Armour Suit has absorbed the brunt of the impact.

When the lights flicker back on within his soft cocoon and the flatscreen directly in front of his face stops fuzzing, he sees that not everyone has been so lucky. A few dozen metres away at three o'clock, there's a new crater that used to be Robinson. The only thing left of Baker Company's resident card cheat is the severed rifle arm of his CAS.

He doesn't have time to contemplate Robinson's fate. He's in the midst of battle. Sgt Boyle's voice comes through the comlink, shouting orders. Travelling overwatch, due west, head for Marker One-Eight-Five. Kemp, take Robinson's position. Cortez, you're point. Stop staring, Giordano (yes sir). Move, move, move…

So they move, seven soldiers in semi-robotic heavy armour, bounding across the flat silver-grey landscape. Tin men trying to outrun the missiles plummeting down around them, the soundless explosions they make when they hit. For several kilometres around them, everywhere they look, there are scores of other tin men doing the same, each trying to survive a silent hell called the Sea of Tranquillity.

Giordano is sweating hard, his breath coming in ragged gasps. He tells himself that if he can just make Marker One-Eight-Five – crater Arago, or so the map overlay tells him – then everything will be OK. The crater walls will protect them. Once Baker Company sets up its guns and erects a new ECM buffer, they can dig in nice and tight and wait it out; the beachhead will have been established by then and the hard part of Operation Monkey Wrench will be over.

But the crater is five-and-a-half klicks away, across plains as flat and wide open as Missouri pasture, and between here and there a lot of shitfire is coming down. The Pax Astra guns in the foothills of the lunar highlands due west of their position can see them coming; the enemy has the high ground, and they're throwing everything they can at the invading force.

Sgt Boyle knows his platoon is in trouble. He orders everyone to use their jumpjets. Screw formation; it's time to run like hell.

Giordano couldn't agree more wholeheartedly. He tells the

Valkyrie to engage the twin miniature rockets mounted on the back of his carapace.

Nothing happens.

Once again, he tells the voice-activated computer mounted against the back of his neck to fire the jumpjets. When there's still no response, he goes to manual, using the tiny controls nestled within the palm of his right hand inside the suit's artificial arm.

At that instant, everything goes dark again, just like it did when the shrapnel from the dropship hit the back of his suit.

This time, though, it stays dark.

A red LCD lights above his forehead, telling him that there's been a total system crash.

Cursing, he finds the manual override button and stabs it with his little finger. As anticipated, it causes the computer to completely reboot itself; he hears servomotors grind within the carapace as its limbs move into neutral position, until his boots are planted firmly on the ground and his arms are next to his sides, his rifle pointed uselessly at the ground.

There is a dull click from somewhere deep within the armour, then silence.

Except for the red LCD, everything remains dark.

He stabs frantically at the palm buttons, but there's no power to any of the suit's major subsystems. He tries to move his arms and legs, but finds them frozen in place.

Limbs, jumpjets, weapons, ECM, comlink … nothing works.

Now he's sweating more than ever. The impact of that little bit of debris from the dropship must have been worse than he thought. Something must have shorted out, badly, within the Valkyrie's onboard computer.

He twists his head to the left so he can gaze through the eyepiece of the optical periscope, the only instrument within the suit that isn't dependent upon computer control. What he sees, terrifies him: the rest of his platoon jumpjetting for the security of the distant crater, while missiles continue to explode all around him.

Abandoning him. Leaving him behind.

He screams at the top of his lungs, yelling for Boyle and Kemp and Cortez and the rest, calling them foul names, demanding that they wait or come back for him, knowing that it's futile. They can't hear him. For whatever reason, they've already determined that he's out of action; they cannot afford to risk their lives by coming back to lug an inert CAS across a battlefield.

He tries again to move his legs, but it's pointless. Without direct interface from the main computer, the limbs of his suit are immobile. He might as well be wearing a concrete block.

The suit contains three hours of oxygen, fed through pumps controlled by another computer tucked against his belly, along with rest of its life-support systems. So at least he won't suffocate or fry...

For the next three hours, at any rate.

Probably less. The digital chronometer and life-support gauge are dead, so there's no way of knowing for sure.

As he watches, even the red coal of the LCD warning lamp grows dim until it finally goes cold, leaving him in the dark.

He has become a living statue. Fully erect, boots firmly placed upon the dusty regolith, arms held rigid at his sides, he is in absolute stasis.

For three hours. Certainly less.

For all intents and purposes, he is dead.

In the smothering darkness of his suit, Giordano prays to a god in which he has never really believed. Then, for lack of anything else to do, he raises his eyes to the periscope eyepiece and watches as the battle rages on around him.

He fully expects – and, after a time, even hopes – for a Pax missile to relieve him of his ordeal, but this small mercy never occurs. Without an active infrared or electromagnetic target to lock in upon, the heatseekers miss the small spot of ground he occupies, instead decimating everything around him.

Giordano becomes a mute witness to the horror of the worst conflict of the Moon War, what historians will later call the Battle of Mare Tranquillitatis. Loyalty, duty, honour, patriotism... all the things in which he once believed are soon rendered null and void as he watches countless lives being lost.

Dropships touch down near and distant, depositing soldiers in suits similar to his own. Some don't even make it to the ground before they become miniature supernovas.

Men and women like himself fly apart even as they charge across the wasteland for the deceptive security of distant craters and rills.

An assault rover bearing three lightsuited soldiers rushes past him, only to be hit by fire from the hills. It is thrown upside down, crushing two of the soldiers beneath it. The third man, his legs broken and his suit punctured, manages to crawl from the wreckage. He dies at Giordano's feet, his arms reaching out to him.

He has no idea whether Baker Company has survived, but he suspects it hasn't, since he soon sees a bright flash from the general direction of the crater it was supposed to occupy and hold.

In the confines of his suit, he weeps and screams and howls against the madness erupting around him. In the end, he goes mad himself, cursing the same god to whom he prayed earlier for the role to which he has been damned.

If God cares, it doesn't matter. By then, the last of Giordano's oxygen reserves have been exhausted; he asphyxiates long before his three hours are up, his body still held upright by the Mark III Valkyrie Combat Armour Suit.

When he is finally found, sixty-eight hours later, by a patrol from the victorious Pax Astra Free Militia, they are astonished that anything was left standing on the killing ground. This sole combat suit, damaged only by a small steel pipe wedged into its CPU housing, with a dead man inexplicably sealed inside, is the only thing left intact. All else has been reduced to scorched dust and shredded metal.

So they leave him standing.

They do not remove the CAS from its place, nor do they attempt to prise the man from his armour. Instead, they erect a circle of stones around the Valkyrie. Later, when peace has been negotiated and lunar independence has been achieved, a small plaque is placed at his feet.

The marker bears no name. Because so many lives were lost during the battle, nobody can be precisely certain of who was wearing that particular CAS on that particular day.

An eternal flame might have been placed at his feet, but it wasn't, because nothing burns on the Moon.

POLITICS

Elizabeth Moon

There's an art to writing military SF well, an art at which Elizabeth Moon is an acknowledged master. Moon, whose novel The Speed of Dark *won a Nebula Award in 2004 and was shortlisted for the Arthur C. Clarke Award the previous year, attempted her first novel at the age of six and started writing science fiction in her teens. "Politics" is a prime example of Moon at her best: the military aspects infused with a sense of authenticity that few can match, no doubt aided by her time as a US Marine – she achieved the rank of 1st Lieutenant. This is more than simply an "action" piece, however, and it's the added dimensions that help Moon's work stand out.*

POLITICS IS ALWAYS lousy in these things. Some guy with rank wants something done, and whether it makes any sense or not, some poor slob with no high-powered friends gets pushed out front to do it. Like Mac... he wants a fuzzball spit-polished, some guy like me will have to shave it bare naked and work it to a shine. Not that all his ideas are stupid, you understand, but there's this thing about admirals – and maybe especially *that* admiral – no one tells 'em when their ideas have gone off the screen. That landing on Caedmon was right out of somebody's old tape files, and whoever thought it up, Mac or somebody more local, should've had to be there. In person, in the shuttles, for instance.

You know why we didn't use tanks downside... right. No shields. Nothing short of a cruiser could generate 'em, and tanks are big enough to make good targets for anyone toting a tank-bashing missile. Some dumbass should have thought of shuttles and thought again, but the idea was the cruisers have to stay aloft. No risking their precious tails downside, stuck in a gravity well if something pops up. Tradition, you know? Marines have been landed in landing craft since somebody had to row the boat ashore. Marines have died that way just about as long.

Now on Caedmon, the Gerin knew we were coming. Had to know. The easy way would've been to blast their base from orbit, but that wouldn't do. Brass said we needed it, or something. I thought myself it was just because humans had had it first, and lost it; a propaganda move, something like that. There was some kind of garbage about how we had this new stealth technology that let the cruisers get in real close, and we'd drop and be groundside before they knew we were there, but we'd heard that before, and I don't suppose anyone but the last wetears in from training believed it. I didn't, and the captain for sure didn't.

He didn't say so, being the hardnosed old bastard he is, but we knew it anyway, from the expression in his eyes, and that fold of his lip. He read us what we had to know – not much – and then we got loaded into the shuttles like so many cubes of cargo. This fussy little squirt from the cruiser pushed and prodded and damn nearly got his head taken off at the shoulders, 'cept I knew we'd need all that rage later. Rolly even grinned at me, his crooked eyebrows disappearing into the scars he carries, and made a rude sign behind the sailor's back. We'd been in the same unit long enough to trust each other at everything but poker and women. Maybe even women. Jammed in like we were, packs scraping the bulkheads and helmets smack onto the overhead, we had to listen to another little speech – this one from the cruiser captain, who should ought to've known better, only them naval officers always think they got to give Marines a hard time. Rolly puckered his face up, then grinned again, and this time I made a couple of rude gestures that couldn't be confused with comsign, but we didn't say anything. The Navy puts audio pickups in the shuttles, and frowns on Marines saying what they think of a cruiser captain's speechifying.

So then they dropped us, and the shuttle pilot hit the retros, taking us in on the fast lane. 'Course he didn't care that he had us crammed flat against each other, hardly breath-room, and if it'd worked I'd have said fine, that's the way to go. Better a little squashing in the shuttle than taking fire. Only it didn't work.

Nobody thinks dumb Marines need to know anything, so of course the shuttles don't have viewports. Not even the computer-generated videos that commercial shuttles have, with a map-marker tracing the drop. All we knew was that the shuttle suddenly went ass over teakettle, not anything like normal re-entry vibration or kickup, and stuff started ringing on the hull, like somebody dropped a toolshed on us.

Pilot's voice came over the com, then, just, "Hostile fire." Rolly said, "Shut up and fly, stupid; I could figure out that much." The pilot wouldn't hear, but that's how we all felt. We ended up in some kind of stable attitude, or at least we weren't being thrown every which way, and another minute or two passed in silence. If you call the massed breathing of a hundred-man drop team silence. I craned my neck until I could see the captain. He was staring at nothing in particular, absolutely still, listening to whatever came through his comunit. It gave me the shivers. Our lieutenant was a wetears, a butterbar from some planet I never heard of, and all I could see was the back of his head anyway.

Now we felt re-entry vibration, and the troop compartment squeaked and trembled like it was being tickled. We've all seen the pictures; we know the outer hull gets hot, and in some atmospheres bright hot, glowing. You can't feel it, really, but you always think you can. One of the wetears gulped, audible even over the noise, and I heard Cashin, his corporal, growl at him. We don't get motion sickness; that's cause for selection out. If you toss your lunch on a drop, it's fear and nothing else. And fear is only worth-while when it does you some good – when it dredges up that last bit of strength or speed that we mostly can't touch without it. The rest of the time fear's useless, or harmful, and you have to learn to ignore it. That's what you can't teach the wetears. They have to learn for themselves. Those that don't learn mostly don't live to disagree with me.

We were well into the atmosphere, and dropping faster than my stomach liked, when the shuttle bucked again. Not a direct hit, but something transmitted by the atmosphere outside into a walloping thump that knocked us sideways and halfover. The pilot corrected – and I will say this about the Navy shuttle pilots, that while they're arrogant bastards and impossible to live with, they can pretty well fly these shuttles into hell and back. This time he didn't give us a progress report, and he didn't say anything after the next two, either.

What he did say, a minute or so later, was "Landing zone compromised."

Landing zone compromised can mean any of several things, but none of them good. If someone's nuked the site, say, or someone's got recognizable artillery sitting around pointing at the strip, or someone's captured it whole (not common, but it does happen) and hostile aircraft are using it. What landing zone compromised means to us is that we're going to lose a lot of Marines. We're going to be landing on an unimproved or improvised strip, or we're going to be jumping at low level and high speed. I looked for the captain again. This time he was linked to the shuttle com system, probably talking to whatever idiot designed this mission. I hoped. We might abort – we'd aborted a landing once before – but even that didn't look good, not with whatever it was shooting at us all the way back up. The best we could hope for was an alternate designated landing zone – which meant someone had at least looked at it on the upside scanners. The worst—

"Listen up, Marines!" The captain sounded angry, but then he always did before a landing. "We're landing at alternate Alpha, that's Alpha, six minutes from now. Sergeants, pop your alt codes…" That meant me, and I thumbed the control that dropped a screen from my helmet and turned on the display. Alternate Alpha was, to put it plainly, a bitch of a site. A short strip, partly overgrown with whatever scraggly green stuff grew on this planet, down in a little valley between hills that looked like the perfect place for the Gerin to have artillery set up. Little coloured lines scrawled across the display, pointing out where some jackass in the cruiser thought we ought to assemble, which hill we were supposed to take command of (that's what it said), and all the details that delight someone playing sandbox war instead of getting his guts shot out for real. I looked twice at the contour lines and values. Ten-metre contours, not five...those weren't just little bitty hills; those were going to give us trouble. Right there where the lines were packed together was just about an eighty-metre cliff, too much for a backpack booster to hop us over. Easy enough for someone on top to toss any old kind of explosive back down.

And no site preparation. On a stealth assault, there's minimal site preparation even on the main landing zones – just a fast first-wave flyover dropping screamers and gas canisters (supposed to make the Gerin itch all over, and not affect us). Alternate strips didn't get any prep at all. If the Gerin guessed where alternate Alpha was, they'd be meeting us without having to duck from any preparatory fire. That's what alternate landing sites were like: you take what you get and are grateful it doesn't mean trailing a chute out a shuttle hatch. That's the worst. We aren't really paratroops, and the shuttles sure as hell aren't paratroop carriers. Although maybe the worst is being blown up in the shuttle, and about then the shuttle lurched again, then bounced violently as something blew entirely too close.

Then we went down. I suppose it was a controlled landing, sort of, or none of us would have made it. But it felt, with all the pitching and yawing, like we were on our way to a crash. We could hear the tyres blow on contact, and then the gear folded, and the shuttle pitched forward one last time to plough along the strip with its heatshield nose. We were all in one tangled pile against the forward bulkhead by then, making almost as much noise as the shuttle itself until the captain bellowed over it. With one final lurch, the craft was motionless, and for an instant silent.

"Pop that hatch, Gunny." The captain's voice held that tone that no one argues with – no one smart, anyway – and Rolly and I started undogging the main hatch. The men were untangling them-selves now, with muttered curses. One of the wetears hadn't stayed up, and had a broken ankle; he bleated once and then fell silent when he realized no one cared. I yanked on the last locking lever, which had jammed in the crash, just as we heard the first explosions outside. I glanced at the captain. He shrugged. What else could we do? We sure didn't have a chance in this nicely marked coffin we were in. Rolly put his shoulders into it, and the hatch slid aside to let in a cool, damp breath of local air.

Later I decided that Caedmon didn't smell as bad as most planets, but right then all I noticed was the exhaust trails of a couple of Gerin fighters who had left their calling cards on the runway. A lucky wind blew the dust away from us, but the craters were impressive. I looked at the radiation counter on the display – nothing more than background, so it hadn't been nukes. Now all we had to do was get out before the fighters came back.

Normally we unload down ramps, four abreast – but with the shuttle sitting on its nose and the port wing, the starboard landing ramp was useless. The portside hatch wouldn't open at all. This, of course, is why we carry those old-fashioned cargo nets everyone teases us about. We had those deployed in seconds (we *practise* that, in the cruisers' docking bays, and that's why the sailorboys laugh at us). Unloading the shuttle – all men and materiel, including the pilot (who had a broken arm) and the wetear with the bad ankle – went faster than I'd have thought. Our lieutenant, Pascoe, had the forward team, and had already pushed into the scraggly stuff that passed for brush at the base of the nearest hill. At least he seemed to know how to do that. Then Courtney climbed back and placed the charges, wired them up, and came out. When he cleared the red zone, the captain pushed the button. The shuttle went up in a roiling storm of light, and we all blinked. That shuttle wasn't going anywhere, but even so I felt bad when we blew it…it was our ticket home. Not to mention the announcement the explosion made. We had to have had survivors to blow it that long after the crash.

What everyone sees, in the videos of Marine landings, is the frontline stuff – the helmeted troops with the best weapons, the bright bars of laser fire – or some asshole reporter's idea of a human interest shot (a Marine looking pensively at a dead dog, or something). But there's the practical stuff, which sergeants always have to deal with. Food, for instance. Medical supplies, not to mention the medics, who half the time don't have the sense to keep their fool heads out of someone's sights. Water, weapons, ammunition, spare parts, comunits, satellite comm bases, spare socks... whatever we use has to come with us. On a good op, we're resupplied inside twenty-four hours, but that's about as common as an honest dockside joint. So the shuttle had supplies for a standard week (Navy week: Old Terra standard – it doesn't matter what the local rotational day or year is), and every damn kilo had to be offloaded and hauled off. By hand. When the regular ground troops get here, they'll have floaters and trucks, and their enlisted mess will get fresh veggies and home-made pies... and that's another thing that's gone all the way back, near as I can tell. Marines slog through the mud, hump their stuff uphill and down, eat compressed bricks commonly called – well, you can imagine. And the next folks in, whoever they are, have the choppers and all-terrain vehicles and then make bad jokes about us. But not in the same joint, or not for long.

What bothered me, and I could see it bothered the captain, was that the fighters didn't come back and blow us all to shreds while all this unloading went on. We weren't slow about it; we were humping stuff into cover as fast as we could. But it wasn't natural for those fighters to make that one pass over the strip and then leave a downed shuttle alone. They had to know they'd missed – that the shuttle was intact and might have live Marines inside. All they'd done was blow a couple of holes in the strip, making it tough for anyone else to land there until it was fixed. They had to be either stupid or overconfident, and no one yet had accused the Gerin of being stupid. Or of going out of their way to save human lives. I had to wonder what else they had ready for us.

Whatever it was, they let us alone for the next couple of standard hours, and we got everything moved away from the strip, into a little sort of cleft between two of the hills. I wasn't there: I was working my way to the summit, as quietly as possible, with a five-man team. We'd been told the air was breathable, which probably meant the green stuff was photosynthetic, although it was hard to tell stems from leaves on the scrub. I remember wondering why anything a soldier has to squirm through is full of thorns, or stings on contact, or has sharp edges ... a biological rule no one yet has published a book on, I'll bet. Caedmon's scrub ran to man-high rounded mounds, densely covered with prickly stiff leaves that rustled loudly if we brushed against them. Bigger stuff sprouted from some of the mounds, treelike shapes with a crown of dense foliage and smooth blackish bark. Between the mounds a fine, grey-green fuzz covered the rocky soil, not quite as lush as grass but more linear than lichens. It made my nose itch, and my eyes run, and I'd *had* my shots. I popped a broad-spectrum anti-allergen pill and hoped I wouldn't sneeze.

Some people say hills are the same size all the time, but anyone who's ever gone up a hill with hostiles at the top of it knows better. It's twice as high going uphill into trouble. If I hadn't had the time readout, I'd have sworn we crawled through that miserable prickly stuff for hours. Actually it was less than half a standard when I heard something click, metal on stone, ahead of us. Above and ahead, invisible through the scrub, but definitely something metallic, and therefore – in this situation – hostile. Besides, after DuQuesne, we knew the Gerin would've wiped out any humans from the colony. I tongued the comcontrol and clicked a warning signal to my squad. They say a click sounds less human – maybe. We relied on it, anyhow, in that sort of situation. I heard answering clicks in my earplug. Lonnie had heard the noise, too (double-click, then one, in his response) which figured. Lonnie had the longest ears in our company.

This is where your average civilian would either panic and go dashing downhill through the brush to tell the captain there were nasties up there, or get all video-hero and run screaming at the Gerin, right into a beam or a slug. What else is there to do? you ask. Well, for one thing you can lie there quietly and think for a moment. If they've seen you, they've shot you – the Gerin aren't given to patience – and if they haven't shot you they don't know you're there. Usually.

It was already strange that the Gerin fighters hadn't come back. And if Gerin held the top of this hill – which seemed reasonable even before we went up it, and downright likely at the moment – they'd have to know we got out, and how many, and roughly where we were. And since Gerin aren't stupid, at least at war, they'd guess someone was coming up to check out the hilltop. So they'd have some way to detect us on the way up, and they'd have held off blowing us away because they didn't think we were a threat. Neither of those thoughts made me feel comfortable.

Detection systems, though … detection systems are a bitch. Some things work anywhere: motion detectors, for instance, or optical beams that you can interrupt and it sets off a signal somewhere. But that stuff's easy enough to counter. If you know what you're doing, if you've got any sort of counterhunt tech yourself, you'll spot it and disarm it. The really good detection systems are hard to spot, very specific, and also – being that good – very likely to misbehave in combat situations.

The first thing was to let the captain know we'd spotted something. I did that with another set of tongue-flicks and clicks, switching to his channel and clicking my message. He didn't reply; he didn't need to. Then I had us all switch on our own counterhunt units. I hate the things, once a fight actually starts: they weigh an extra kilo, and unless you need them it's a useless extra kilo. But watching the flicking needles on the dials, the blips of light on the readouts, I was glad enough then. Two metres uphill, for instance, a fine wire carried an electrical current. Could have been any of several kinds of detectors, but my unit located its controls and identified them. And countered them: we could crawl right over that wire, and its readout boxes wouldn't show a thing. That wasn't all, naturally: the Gerin aren't stupid. But none of it was new to our units, and all of it could fail – and would fail, with a little help from us.

Which left the Gerin. I lay there a moment longer wondering how many Gerin triads we were facing. Vain as they are, it might be just one warrior and his helpers, or whatever you want to call them. Gerin think they're the best fighters in the universe, and they can be snookered into a fight that way. Admiral Mac did it once, and probably will again. It would be just like their warrior pride to assign a single Gerin triad to each summit. Then again, the Gerin don't think like humans, and they could have a regiment up there. One triad we might take out; two would be iffy; and any more than that we wouldn't have a chance against.

Whatever it was, though, we needed high ground, and we needed it damn fast. I clicked again, leaned into the nearest bush, and saw Lonnie's hand beyond the next one. He flicked me a hand signal, caught mine, and inched forward. We were, in one sense, lucky. It was a single triad, and all they had was the Gerin equivalent of our infantry weapons: single-beam lasers and something a lot like a rifle. We got the boss, the warrior, with several rounds of rifle fire. I don't care what they say, there's a place for slug-throwers, and downside combat is that place. You can hit what you can't see, which lasers can't, and the power's already in the ammo. No worry about a discharged powerpack, or those mirrored shields some of the Gerin have used. Some Navy types keep wanting to switch all Marine forces away from slug weapons, because they're afraid we'll go bonkers and put a hole in a cruiser hull, but the day they take my good old Belter special away from me, I'm gone. I've done my twenty already; there's no way they can hold me.

Davies took a burn from one of the warrior's helpers, but they weren't too aggressive with the big number one writhing on the ground, and we dropped them without any more trouble. Some noise, but no real trouble. Lonnie got a coldpak on Davies, which might limit the damage. It wasn't that bad a burn, anyway. If he died down here, it wouldn't be from that, though without some time in a good hospital, he might lose the use of those fingers. Davies being Davies, he'd probably skin-graft himself as soon as the painkiller cut in...he made a religion out of being tough. I called back to our command post to report, as I took a look around to see what we'd bought.

From up here, maybe seventy metres above the strip, the scattered remains of the shuttle glittered in the sun. I could see the two craters, one about halfway along, and another maybe a third of the way from the far end. Across the little valley, less than a klick, the hills rose slightly higher than the one we lay on. The cliffs on one were just as impressive as I'd thought. The others rose more gently from the valley floor. All were covered with the same green scrub, thick enough to hide an army. Either army.

I told the captain all this, and nodded when Skip held up the control box the Gerin had used with their detectors. We could use the stuff once we figured out the controls, and if they were dumb enough to give us an hour, we'd have no problems. No problems other than being a single drop team sitting beside a useless strip, with the Gerin perfectly aware of our location and identity.

Brightness bloomed in the zenith, and I glanced up. Something big had taken a hit – another shuttle? We were supposed to have 200 shuttle flights on this mission, coming out of five cruisers – a full-scale assault landing, straight onto a defended planet. If that sounds impossibly stupid, you haven't read much military history – there are some commanders that have this thing about butting heads with an enemy strength, and all too many of them have political connections. Thunder fell out of the sky, and I added up the seconds I'd been counting. Ten thousand metres when they'd been blown – no one was going to float down from that one.

"What kind of an *idiot*…?" Lonnie began; I waved him to silence. Things were bad enough without starting that – we could place the blame later. With a knifeblade, if necessary.

"Vargas…" The captain's voice in my earplug drowned out the whisper of the breeze through stiff leaves. I pushed the subvoc microphone against my throat and barely murmured an answer. "Drop command says we lost thirty cents on the dollar. Beta-site took in four shuttles before it was shut out." Double normal losses on a hostile landing, then, and it sounded like we didn't have a secure strip. I tried to remember exactly where Beta-site was. "We're supposed to clear this strip, get it ready for the next wave—"

I must have made some sound, without meaning to, because there was a long pause before he went on. If the original idea had been stupid, this one was stupid plus. Even a lowly enlisted man knows it's stupid to reinforce failure, why can't the brass learn it? We weren't engineers; we didn't have the machinery to fill those craters, or the manpower to clear the surrounding hills of Gerin and keep the fighters off.

"They're gonna do a flyby drop of machinery," he went on. I knew better than to say what I thought. No way I could stop them if they wanted to mash their machinery on these hills. "We're going to put up the flyspy – you got a good view from there?"

"Yessir." I looked across the valley, around at all the green-clad slopes. The flyspy was another one of those things that you hated having to take care of until it saved your life. "By wire, or by remote?"

"Wire first." That was smart; that way they wouldn't have a radio source to lock onto. "I'm sending up the flyspy team, and some rockers. Send Davies back down." Rockers: rocket men, who could take out those Gerin fighters, always assuming they saw them in time, which they would if we got our detection set up.

Soon I could hear them crashing through the scrub, enough noise to alert anyone within half a klick. The rockers made it up first, four of them. I had two of them drag the Gerin corpses over to the edge and bounce 'em over, then they took up positions around the summit. Now we could knock off the Gerin fighters, if they came back: whatever's wrong with the rest of Supply, those little ground-air missiles we've got can do the job. Then the flyspy crew arrived, with the critter's wing folded back along its body. When they got to the clearing, they snapped the wings back into place, checked that the control wire was coiled ready to release without snagging, and turned on the scanners.

The flyspy is really nothing but a toy aeroplane, wings spanning about a metre, powered by a very quiet little motor. It can hold an amazing amount of spygear, and when it's designed for stealth use it's almost impossible to see in the air. On wire control, it'll go up maybe 100 metres, circle around, and send us video and IR scans of anything it can see; on remote, we can fly it anywhere within line-of-sight, limited only by its fuel capacity.

Soon it was circling above us, its soft drone hardly audible even on our hilltop, certainly too quiet to be heard even down on the strip. We didn't know whether the Gerin *did* hear, the way we hear, but we had to think about that. (We know they hear big noises, explosions, but I've heard a theory that they can't hear high-pitched noises in atmosphere.) The videos we were getting back looked surprisingly peaceful. Nothing seemed to be moving, and there was only one overgrown road leading away from the strip. Garrond punched a channel selector, and the normal-colour view turned into a mosaic of brilliant false colours: sulphur yellow, turquoise, magenta, orange. He pointed to the orange. "That's vegetation, like this scrub. Yellow is rock outcrops—"

The cliff across from us was a broad splash of yellow that even I could pick out. "Turquoise is disturbed soil: compacted or torn up, either one." The strip was turquoise, speckled with orange where plants had encroached on it. So was the nearly invisible road winding away from the strip between the hills. So also the summit of the hill which ended in cliffs above the strip ... and the summit of our own hill. Another outpost, certainly.

But nothing moved in the broad daylight of Caedmon's sun. According to briefing, we'd have another nine standard hours of light. None of our scanners showed motion, heat, anything that could be a Gerin force coming to take us out. And why not?

It bothered the captain, I could see, when he came up to look for himself. Our butterbars was clearly relieved, far too trusting an attitude if you want to survive very long. Things aren't supposed to go smoothly; any time an enemy isn't shooting at you, he's up to something even worse.

"An hour to the equipment drop," said the captain. "They're sending a squad of engineers, too." Great. Somebody else to look after, a bunch of dirtpushers. I didn't say it aloud; I didn't have to. Back before he saved Admiral Mac's life and got that chance at OCS, the captain and me were close, real buddies. Fact is, it was my fault he joined up – back then they didn't have the draft. Wasn't till he started running with me, Tinker Vargas, what everyone called gypsy boy – gambler and horsethief and general hothead – that Carl Dietz the farmer's son got into any trouble bigger than spilled milk. He was innocent as cornsilk back then, didn't even know when I was setting him up – and then we both got caught, and had the choice between joining the offworld Marines or going to prison. Yet he's never said a word of blame, and he's still the straightest man I know after all these years. He's one I *would* trust at poker, unlike Rolly who can't seem to remember friendship when the cards come out.

And no, I'm not jealous. It hasn't been easy for him, a mustang brought up from the ranks, knowing he'll never make promotions like the fast-track boys that went to the Academy or some fancy-pants university. He's had enough trouble, some of it when I was around to carefully not hear what the other guy said. So never mind the pay, and the commission: I'm happy with my life, and I'm still his friend. We both know the rules, and we play a fair game with the hand dealt us – no politics, just friends.

In that hour, we had things laid out more like they should be. Thanks to the flyspy, we knew that no Gerin triads lurked on the nearest two hilltops, and we got dug in well on all three hills that faced the strip on the near side. There was still that patch of turquoise to worry about on the facing hill, above the cliffs, but the flyspy showed no movement there, just the clear trace of disturbed soil. Our lieutenant had learned something in OCS after all; he'd picked a very good spot in a sort of ravine between the hills, out of sight beneath taller growth, for the headquarters dugout, meds and so on.

Then the equipment carrier lumbered into view. I know, it's a shuttle same as the troop shuttle, but that's a term for anything that goes from cruiser to ground. Equipment carriers are fatter, squatty, with huge cargo doors aft, and they have all the graceful ease of a grand piano dumped off a clifftop. This one had all engines howling loudly, and the flaps and stuffhanging down from the wings, trying to be slow and steady as it dropped its load. First ten little para-chutes (little at that distance), then a dark blob – it had to be really big if I could see it from here – trailing two chutes, and then a couple more, and a final large lumpy mass with one parachute.

"I don't believe it!" said the captain, stung for once into commentary. But it was – a netful of spare tyres for the vehicles, wrapped around a huge flexible fuel pod. Relieved of all this load, the shuttle retracted its flaps, and soared away, its engines returning to their normal roar.

Already the lieutenant had a squad moving, in cover, toward the landing parachutists. I watched the equipment itself come down, cushioned somewhat by airbags that inflated as it hit. Still nothing moved on the hilltop across from us. I felt the back of my neck prickle. It simply isn't natural for an enemy to chase you down, shooting all the while, then ignore you once you've landed. We know Gerin use air attack on ground forces: that's how they cleaned up those colonists on Duquesne.

Yet ignore us they did, all the rest of that day as the engineers got themselves down to the strip from where they'd landed, and their equipment unstowed from its drop configuration and ready for use. One grader, what we called back on my homeworld a maintainer, and two earth-movers. The whole time the engineers were out there getting them ready, I was sure some Gerin fighter was going to do a low pass and blow us all away … but it didn't happen. I'd thought it was crazy, dropping equipment that had to be prepped and then used in the open, but for once high command had guessed right.

By late afternoon, the engineers had their machines ready to work. They started pushing stuff around at the far end of the strip, gouging long scars in the dirt and making mounds of gravelly dirt. The captain sent Kittrick and one platoon over to take a hill on the far side; they got up it with no trouble, and I began to think there weren't any Gerin left there at all. Half that group climbed the hill with the cliff, and found evidence that someone had had an outpost there, but no recent occupation.

We were spread out pretty thin by this time, maybe thirty on the far side of the strip, the rest on the near side, but stretched out. We'd rigged our own detection systems, and had both flyspys up, high up, where they could see over the hills behind us. What they saw was more of the same, just like on the topo maps: lots of hills covered with thick green scrub, some creeks winding among the hills, traces of the road that began at the landing strip. Some klicks east of us (east is whatever direction the sun rises, on any world), the tumbled hills subsided into a broad river basin. The higher flyspy showed the edge of the hills, but no real detail on the plain.

Meanwhile the engineers went to work on that strip just as if they *were* being shot at. Dust went up in clouds, blown away from our side of the strip by a light breeze. Under that dust, the craters and humps and leftover chunks of our troop shuttle disappeared, and a smooth, level landing strip emerged. There's nothing engineers like better than pushing dirt around, and these guys pushed it fast.

By dark they had it roughed in pretty well, and showed us another surprise. Lights. Those tyres we'd laughed at each held a couple of lamps and reflectors, and the coiled wiring that connected them all into a set of proper landing lights controlled by a master-board and powered from the earthmover engine. By the time everyone had had chow, the first replacement shuttle was coming in, easing down to the lighted strip as if this were practice on a safe, peaceful planet far from the war.

None of us veterans could relax and enjoy it, though. The new arrivals had heard the same thing I had – 30 per cent losses on the initial drop, sixty shuttles blown. No report from anyone on what we'd done to the Gerin, which meant that the Navy hadn't done a damn thing...they tripled their figures when they did, but triple zilch is still zilch. So how come we weren't being overrun by Gerin infantry? Or bombed by their fighters? What were the miserable slimes up to? They sure weren't beat, and they don't surrender.

During the night, five more shuttles landed, unloaded and took off again. Besides the additional troops and supplies, we also had a new commanding officer, a mean-looking freckle-faced major named Sewell. I know it's not fair to judge someone by his looks, but he had one of those narrow faces set in a permanent scowl, with tight-bunched muscles along his jaw. He probably looked angry sound asleep, and I'd bet his wife (he had a wide gold ring on the correct finger) had learned to hop on cue. His voice fitted the rest of him, edged and ready to bite deep at any resistance. The captain had a wary look; I'd never served with Sewell, or known anyone who had, but evidently the captain knew something.

Major Sewell seemed to know what he was doing, though, and his first orders made sense, in a textbook sense. If you wanted to try something as impossible as defending a shuttle strip without enough troops or supplies, his way was better than most. Soon we had established a perimeter that was secure enough, dug into each of the main hills around the strip, each with its own supply of ammo, food and water. Besides the original headquarters and med dugout, he'd established another on the far side of the strip. All this looked pretty good, with no Gerin actually challenging it, but I wasn't convinced. It takes more than a few hundred Marines to secure an airstrip if the enemy has a lot of troops.

Shortly after sundown, one of the squads from the first replacement shuttle found ruins of a human settlement at the base of a hill near the end of the strip, and had to get their noses slapped on the comm for making so much noise about it. Not long after, the squad up on that clifftop put two and two together and made their own find. Having heard the first ruckus, they didn't go on the comm with it, but sent a runner down to Major Sewell.

There's a certain art to getting information, another version of politics you might call it. It so happened that someone I knew had a buddy who knew someone, and so on, and I knew the details before the runner got to Major Sewell.

We'd known the strip itself was human-made, from the beginning. What we hadn't known was that it had been privately owned, adjacent to the owner's private residence. It takes a fair bit of money to build a shuttle strip, though not as much as it takes to have a shuttle and *need* a shuttle strip. The same class of money can take a chunk of rock looking out over a little valley, and carve into it a luxurious residence and personal fortress. It can afford to install the best quality automated strip electronics to make landing its fancy little shuttle easier, and disguise all the installations as chunks of native stone or trees or whatever. The Gerin had missed it, being unfamiliar with both the world and the way that humans think of disguise. But to a bored squad sitting up on a hilltop with no enemy in sight, and the knowledge that someone might have hidden something…to them it was easy. Easy to find, that is, not easy to get into, at least not without blasting a way in ... which, of course, they were immediately and firmly told not to do.

Think for a little what it takes to do something like this. We're not talking here about ordinary dress-up-in-silk-everyday rich, you understand, not the kind of rich that satisfies your every whim for enough booze and fancy food. I can't even imagine the sort of sum that would own a whole world, hollow out a cliff for a home, operate a private shuttle, and still have enough clout left to bribe the Navy in the middle of a desperate war. This was the sort of wealth that people thought of the military-industrial complex having, the kind that the big commercial consortia do have (whether the military get any or not), the kind where one man's whim, barely expressed, sends ten thousand other men into a death-filled sky.

Or that's the way I read it. We were here to protect – to get back – some rich man's estate, his private playground, that the Gerin had taken away. Not because of colonists (did I see any colonists? Did anyone see any evidence of colonists?) but because of a rich old fart who had kept this whole world to himself, and then couldn't protect it. That's why we couldn't do the safe, reasonable thing and bomb the Gerin into dust, why we hadn't had adequate site preparation, why we hadn't brought down the tactical nukes. Politics.

I did sort of wonder why the Gerin wanted it. Maybe they had their own politics. I also wondered if anyone was hiding out in there, safe behind the disguising rock, watching us fight ... lounging at ease, maybe, with a drink in his hand, enjoying the show. We could take care of that later, too. If we were here.

Sometime before dawn – still dark, but over half the night gone – the higher flyby reported distant activity. Lights and non-visible heat sources over at the edge of the hills, moving slowly but steadily towards us. They didn't follow the old road trace, but kept to the low ground. According to the best guess of the instruments, the wettest low ground. I guess that makes sense, if you're an amphib. It still didn't make sense that they moved so slow, and that they hadn't come to hit us while we were setting up.

The next bad news came from above. Whatever the Navy had

thought they'd done to get the Gerin ships out of the way, it hadn't held, and the next thing we knew our guys boosted out of orbit and told us to hold the fort while they fought off the Gerin. Sure. The way things were going, they weren't coming back, and we wouldn't be here if they did. Nobody *said* that, which made it all the clearer that we were all thinking it.

During that long day we made radio contact with the survivors at Beta-site. They were about eighty klicks away to our north, trying to move their way through the broken hills and thick scrub. Nobody'd bothered them yet, and they hadn't found any sign of human habitation. Surprise. The major didn't tell them what we'd found, seeing as it wouldn't do them any good. Neither would linking up with us, probably.

The smart thing to do, if anyone had asked me, was for us to boogie on out of there and link with the Beta-site survivors, and see what we could do as a mobile strike force. Nobody asked me, at least nobody up top, where the orders came from. We were supposed to hold the strip, so there we stuck, berries on a branch ready for picking. I know a lot of the guys thought the same way I did, but hardly anyone mentioned it, seeing it would do no good and we'd have a lot more to bitch about later.

Slow as the Gerin were moving, we had time to set up several surprises, fill every available container with water, all that sort of thing. They ignored our flyspy, so we could tell where they were, what they had with them, estimate when they'd arrive. It was spooky...but then they didn't need to bother shooting down our toy; they only outnumbered us maybe a hundred to one. If every one of our ambushes worked, we might cut it down to ninety to one.

Gerin ground troops might be slow to arrive, but once they were there you had no doubt about it. Just out of range of our knuckle-knockers, the column paused and set up some tubing that had to be artillery of some sort. Sure enough, we heard a sort of warbling whoosh, and then a vast *whump* as the first shells burst over our heads and spit shards of steel down on us. After a couple or three shots, fairly well separated, they sent up a whole tanker load, and the concussion shuddered the hills themselves.

We watched them advance through the smoke and haze of their initial barrage. They were in easy missile range, but we had to save the missiles for their air support. Everyone's seen the news clips – that strange, undulating way they move. They may be true amphibians, but they're clearly more at home in water or space than walking around on the ground. Not that it's walking, really. Their weapons fire slower on automatic than ours, but they can carry two of them – an advantage of having all those extra appendages. And in close, hand-to-hand combat, their two metal-tipped tentacles are lethal.

They came closer, advancing in little bobbing runs that were similar to our own tactics, but not the same. It's hard to explain, but watching them come I felt how alien they were – they could not have been humans in alien suits, for instance. The very fact that I had trouble picking out the logic of their movements – why they chose to go *this* way up a draw, and not that – emphasized the differences.

Now they were passing the first marker. Rolly tapped me on the shoulder, and I nodded. He hit the switch, and a stormcloud rolled under them, tumbling them in the explosion. Those in the first rank let off a burst, virtually unaimed; the smack of their slugs on the rocks was drowned in the roar and clatter of the explosion, and the dust of it rolled forward to hide them all. Chunks of rock splattered all around; a secondary roar had to mean that the blast had triggered a rockslide, just as we'd hoped. When the dust cleared a little, we couldn't see any of the live ones, only a few wet messes just beyond a mound of broken stone and uprooted brush.

One of the wetears down at the far end of the trench stood up to peer out. Before anyone could yank him back, Gerin slugs took his face and the back of his head, and he toppled over. Then a storm of fire rang along the rocks nearby while we all ducked. Stupid kid should have known they wouldn't all be dead: we'd told them and told them. Our flyspy crew concentrated on their screens; at the moment the critter was reading infrared, and the enemy fire showed clearly. Garrond gave us the coordinates; our return fire got a few more (or so the flyspy showed – we didn't stand up to see).

But that was only the first wave. All too soon we could see the next Gerin working their way past the rockslide towards our positions. And although I'd been listening for it, I hadn't heard an explosion from the other side of the strip. Had they been overrun, or had the Gerin failed to attempt an envelopment?

Suddenly the sky was full of light and noise: the Gerin had launched another barrage. Oddly, the weapons seemed to be intended to cause noise as much as actual damage. And they were noisy: my ears rang painfully and I saw others shaking their heads. Under cover of that noise, Gerin leaped out, hardly ten metres away. Someone to my left screamed; their slugs slammed all around us. We fired back, and saw their protective suits ripple and split, their innards gushing out to stain the ground. But there were too many, and some of them made it to us, stabbing wildly with those metal-tipped tentacles. One of them smashed into Rolly's chest; his eyes bulged, and pink froth erupted from his mouth. I fired point-blank at that one. It collapsed with a gasping wheeze, but it was too late for Rolly.

Even in all the noise, I was aware that the Gerin themselves fought almost silently. I'd heard they had speech, of a sort – audible sounds, that is – but they didn't yell at each other, or cry out when injured. It was almost like fighting machines. And like machines, they kept coming. Even in the dark.

It was sometime in that first night when I heard the row between the captain and the major. I don't know when it started, maybe in private before the Gerin even got to us, but in the noise of combat, they'd both raised their voices. I was going along, checking ammo levels, making sure everyone had water, and passed them just close enough to hear.

"You can't do that," Major Sewell was saying. "They said, hold the strip."

"Because it's that bastard Ifleta's," said the captain. He'd figured it out too, of course; he didn't turn stupid when he got his promotion. I should have gone on, but instead I hunkered down a little and listened. If he talked the major around, I'd need to know. "So no heavy artillery, no tactical nukes, no damage to his art collection or whatever he thinks it is. And it's crazy... listen, the Gerin are amphibs; they even have swim tanks in their ships."

"So? Dammit, Carl, it's the middle of a battle, not a lecture room."

"So they're territorial." I could hear the expletive he didn't say at the end of that... Sewell was a senior officer, however dense. "It's part of that honour stuff: where you are determines your role in the dominance hierarchy. If we move, we're no threat; if we stay in one place they'll attack."

"They *are* attacking, in case you hadn't noticed, *Captain*. We're dug in here; if we move they can take us easily. Or were you suggesting that we just run for it?" The contempt in Sewell's voice was audible, even through the gunfire.

The captain made one more try. I knew, from our years together, what it took for him to hold his temper at the major's tone; the effort came through in his voice. "Sir, with all due respect, after the massacre on Duquesne, there was a study of Gerin psychology in the *Military Topics Review*, and that study indicated that the Gerin would choose to assault stationary, defended positions over a force in movement. Something about defending certain rock formations in the tidal zone, important for amphibians..."

"Yeah, well, what some egghead scientist thinks the slimes do and what the slimes out here in combat do is two different things. And our orders, Captain, say stand and defend this shuttle strip. It doesn't matter a truckful of chicken shit whether the strip is Ifleta's personal private hideaway or was built by the Gerin: I was told to defend it, and I'm going to defend it. Is that clear?"

"Sir." I heard boots scrape on the broken rock and got myself out of there in a hurry. Another time that I'd heard more than I should have, at least more than it would be comfortable to admit. Not long after, the captain met me as I worked my way back down the line. He leaned over and said in my ear, "I know you heard that, Gunny. Keep it to yourself."

"You got eyes in the dark?" I asked. It meant more than that; we'd used it as a code a long time ago. I didn't think he'd choose that way, but I'd let him decide.

"No," he said. A shell burst nearby, deafening us both for a moment; I could see, in the brief glare, his unshaken determination. "No," he said again after we could hear. "It's too late anyway."

"Ifleta's the owner?" I asked.

"Yeah. Senior counsellor – like a president – in Hamny's Consortium, and boss of Sigma Combine. This is his little hideaway – should have been a colony but he got here first. What I figure is this is his price for bringing Hamny's in free: three human-settled worlds, two of 'em industrial. Worth it, that's one way of looking at it. Trade a couple thousand Marines for three allied planets, populations to draft, industrial plants in place, and probably a good chunk of money as well."

I grunted, because there's nothing to say to that kind of argument. Not in words, anyway. Then I asked, "Does the major know?"

The captain shrugged. "You heard me – I told him. I told him yesterday, when they found the house. He doesn't care. Rich man wants the aliens out of his property, that's just fine – treat Marines like mercs, he doesn't give a damn, and *that*, Tinker, is what they call an officer and a gentleman. *His* father's a retired admiral; he's looking for stars of his own." It was a measure of his resentment that he called me by that old nickname…the others that had used it were all dead. I wondered if he resented his own lost patrimony… the rich bottomland farm that would have been his, the wife and many children. He had been a farmer's son, in a long line of farmers, as proud of their heritage as any admiral.

"Best watch him, Captain," I said, certain that I would. "He's likely to use your advice all wrong."

"I know. He backstabbed Tio, got him shipped over to the Second with a bad rep—" He stopped suddenly, and his voice changed. "Well, Gunny, let me know how that number three post is loaded." I took that hint, and went on; we'd talked too long as it was.

So now I knew the whole story – for one thing about Captain Carl Dietz, he never in his life made accusations without the information to back them up. He hadn't accused me when it might have got him a lighter sentence, all those years ago. If he said it was

Ifleta's place, if he was sure that our losses bought Ifleta's support, and three planets, then I was sure. I didn't like it, but I believed it.

The pressure was constant. We had no time to think, no time to rest, taking only the briefest catnaps one by one, with the others alert. We knew we were inflicting heavy losses, but the Gerin kept coming. Again and again, singly and in triads and larger groups, they appeared, struggling up the hills, firing steadily until they were cut down to ooze aqua fluid on the scarred slopes. Our losses were less, but irreparable.

It was dawn again – which dawn, how many days since landing, I wasn't at all sure. I glanced at the rising sun, irrationally angry because it hurt my eyes. What I could see of the others looked as bad as I felt: filthy, stinking, their eyes sunken in drawn faces, dirty bandages on too many wounds. The line of motionless mounds behind our position was longer, again. No time for burial, no time to drag the dead further away: they were here, with us, and they stank in their own way. We had covered their faces; that was all we could do.

Major Sewell crawled along our line, doing his best to be encouraging, but everyone was too tired and too depressed to be cheered. When he got to me, I could tell that he didn't feel much better. One thing about him, he hadn't been taking it easy or hiding out.

"We've got a problem," he said. I just nodded. Speech took too much energy, and besides it was obvious. "There's only one thing to do, and that's hit 'em with a mobile unit. I've been in contact with the Beta-site survivors, but they don't have a flyspy or good linkage to ours, and besides their only officer is a kid just out of OCS. The others died at the drop. They're about four hours away now. I'm gonna take a squad, find 'em, and go after the Gerin commander."

I still didn't say anything. That might have made sense, before the Gerin arrived. Now it looked to me like more politics – Sewell figured to leave the captain holding an indefensible position, while he took his chance at the Gerin commander. He might get killed, but if he didn't he'd get his medals … and staying here was going to get us all killed. Some of that must have shown in my face, because his darkened.

"Dammit, Gunny, I know what Captain Deitz said made sense, but our *orders* said defend this strip. The last flyspy image gave me a lock on what may be the Gerin commander's module, and that unit from Beta-site may give me the firepower I need. Now you find me—" My mind filled in "a few good men" but he actually asked for a squad of unwounded. We had that many, barely, and I got them back to the cleft between the first and second hills just in time to see that last confrontation with the captain.

If I hadn't known him that long, I'd have thought he didn't care. Sewell had a good excuse, as if he needed one, for leaving the captain behind: Deitz had been hit, though that wound wouldn't kill him. He couldn't have moved fast for long, not without a trip through Med or some stim-tabs. But they both knew that had nothing to do with it. The captain got his orders from Sewell in terse phrases; he merely nodded in reply. Then his eyes met mine.

I'd planned to duck away once we were beyond the Gerin lines – assuming we made it that far, and since the other side of the strip hadn't been so heavily attacked, we probably would. I had better things to do than babysit a major playing politics with the captain's life. But the captain's gaze had the same wide-blue-sky openness it had always had, barring a few times he was whacked out on bootleg whiskey.

"I'm glad you've got Gunny Vargas with you," the captain said. "He's got eyes in the dark."

"If it takes us that long, we're in trouble again," said the major gruffly. I smiled at the captain, and followed Sewell away down the trail, thinking of the years since I'd been in that stuffy little courtroom back on that miserable backwater colony planet. The captain played fair, on the whole; he never asked for more than his due, and usually got less. If he wanted me to babysit the major, I would. It was the least I could do for him.

We lost only three on the way to meet the Beta-site survivors, and I saved the major's life twice. The second time, the Gerin tentacle I stopped shattered my arm just as thoroughly as a bullet.

The major thanked me, in the way that officers are taught to do, but the thought behind his narrow forehead was that my heroism didn't do him a bit of good unless he could win something. The medic we had along slapped a field splint on the arm, and shot me up with something that took all the sharp edges off. That worried me, but I knew it would wear off in a few hours. I'd have time enough.

Then we walked on, and on, and damn near ran headlong into our own people. They looked a lot better than we did, not having been shot up by Gerin for several days; in fact, they looked downright smart. The butterbar had an expression somewhere between serious and smug – he figured he'd done a better than decent job with his people, and the glance I got from his senior sergeant said the kid was OK. Sewell took over without explaining much, except that we'd been attacked and were now going to counterattack; I was glad he didn't go further. It could have created a problem for me.

Caedmon's an official record, now. You've seen the tapes, maybe, or the famous shot of the final Gerin assault up the hills above the shuttle strip, the one that survived in someone's personal vicam to be stripped later by Naval Intelligence after we took the hills back, and had time to retrieve personal effects. You know that our cruisers came back, launched fighters that tore the Gerin fighters out of the sky, and then more shuttles, with more troops, enough to finish the job on the surface. You know that the "gallant forces" of the first landing (yeah, I heard that speech, too) are credited with *almost* winning against fearful odds, even wiping out the Gerin commander and its staff, thanks to the brilliant tactic of one Marine captain, unfortunately himself a casualty of that last day of battle. You've seen his picture, with those summer-sky-blue eyes and that steadfast expression, a stranger to envy and fear alike.

But I know what happened to Major Sewell, who is listed simply as "killed in action". I know how come the captain got his posthumous medals and promotion, something for his family back home to put up on their wall. I know exactly how the Gerin commander died, and who died of Gerin weapons and who of human steel. And I don't think I have to tell you every little detail, do I? It all comes down to politics, after all. An honest politician, as the saying goes, is the one who stays bought. I was bought a long time ago, with the only coin that buys any gypsy's soul, and with that death (you know which death) I was freed.

ARENA

Fredric Brown

Suppose single combat might decide the fate of interstellar empires…

One of us editors still vividly remembers reading Fredric Brown's collection of brief witty stories, Nightmares and Geezenstacks, *then newly published, while hitchhiking across Germany in 1961; "Arena" has stuck in the mind for a long time too. Brown also wrote many detective stories, and solving clues is a key to the outcome of what happens in a place beyond space and time.*

CARSON OPENED HIS eyes, and found himself looking upwards into a flickering blue dimness.

It was hot, and he was lying on sand, and a rock embedded in the sand was hurting his back. He rolled over to his side, off the rock, and then pushed himself up to a sitting position.

I'm crazy, he thought. Crazy – or dead – or something. The sand was blue, bright blue. And there wasn't any such thing as bright blue sand on Earth or any of the planets. Blue sand under a blue dome that wasn't the sky nor yet a room, but a circumscribed area – somehow he knew it was circumscribed and finite even though he couldn't see to the top of it.

He picked up some of the sand in his hand and let it run through his fingers. It trickled down on to his bare leg. Bare?

He was stark naked, and already his body was dripping perspiration from the enervating heat, coated blue wherever sand had touched it. Elsewhere his body was white.

He thought: then this sand is really blue. If it seemed blue only because of the blue light, then I'd be blue also. But I'm white, so the sand is blue. Blue sand: there isn't any blue sand. There isn't any place like this place I'm in.

Sweat was running down in his eyes. It was hot, hotter than hell. Only hell – the hell of the ancients – was supposed to be red and not blue.

But if this place wasn't hell, what was it? Only Mercury, among the planets, had heat like this and this wasn't Mercury. And Mercury was some four billion miles from … From?

It came back to him then, where he'd been: in the little one-man scouter, outside the orbit of Pluto, scouting a scant million miles to one side of the Earth Armada drawn up in battle array there to intercept the Outsiders.

That sudden strident ringing of the alarm bell when the rival scouter – the Outsider ship – had come within range of his detectors!

No one knew who the Outsiders were, what they looked like, or from what far galaxy they came, other than that it was in the general direction of the Pleiades.

First, there had been sporadic raids on Earth colonies and outposts; isolated battles between Earth patrols and small groups of Outsider spaceships; battles sometimes won and sometimes lost, but never resulting in the capture of an alien vessel. Nor had any member of a raided colony ever survived to describe the Outsiders who had left the ships, if indeed they had left them.

Not too serious a menace, at first, for the raids had not been numerous or destructive. And, individually, the ships had proved slightly inferior in armament to the best of Earth's fighters, although somewhat superior in speed and manoeuvrability. A sufficient edge in speed, in fact, to give the Outsiders their choice of running or fighting, unless surrounded.

Nevertheless, Earth had prepared for serious trouble, building the mightiest armada of all time. It had been waiting now, that armada, for a long time. Now the showdown was coming.

Scouts twenty billion miles out had detected the approach of a mighty fleet of the Outsiders. Those scouts had never come back, but their radiotronic messages had. And now Earth's armada, all ten thousand ships and half-million fighting spacemen, was out there, outside Pluto's orbit, waiting to intercept and battle to the death.

And an even battle it was going to be, judging by the advance reports of the men of the far picket line who had given their lives to report – before they had died – on the size and strength of the alien fleet.

Anybody's battle, with the mastery of the solar system hanging in the balance, on an even chance. A last and only chance for Earth and all her colonies lay at the utter mercy of the Outsiders if they ran that gauntlet. Oh yes. Bob Carson remembered now. He remembered that strident bell and his leap for the control panel. His frenzied fumbling as he strapped himself into the seat. The dot in the visiplate that grew larger. The dryness of his mouth. The awful knowledge that this was it for him, at least, although the main fleets were still out of range of one another.

This, his first taste of battle! Within three seconds or less he'd be victorious, or a charred cinder. One hit completely took care of a lightly armed and armoured one-man craft like a scouter.

Frantically – as his lips shaped the word "one" – he worked at the controls to keep that growing dot centred on the crossed spiderwebs of the visiplate. His hands doing that, while his right foot hovered over the pedal that would fire the bolt. The single bolt of concentrated hell that had to hit – or else. There wouldn't be time for any second shot.

"Two." He didn't know he'd said that, either. The dot in the visiplate wasn't a dot now. Only a few thousand miles away, it showed up in the magnification of the plate as though it were only a few hundred yards off. It was a fast little scouter, about the size of his.

An alien ship, all right!

"Thr—" His foot touched the bolt-release pedal.

And then the Outsider had swerved suddenly and was off the crosshairs. Carson punched keys frantically to follow.

For a tenth of a second, it was out of the visiplate entirely, and then as the nose of his scouter swung after it, he saw it again, diving straight towards the ground.

The ground?

It was an optical illusion of some sort. It had to be: that planet – or whatever it was – that now covered the visiplate couldn't be there. Couldn't possibly! There wasn't any planet nearer than Neptune three billion miles away – with Pluto on the opposite side of the distant pinpoint sun.

His detectors! They hadn't shown any object of planetary dimensions, even of asteroid dimensions, and still didn't.

It couldn't be there, that whatever-it-was he was diving into, only a few hundred miles below him.

In his sudden anxiety to keep from crashing, he forgot the Outsider ship. He fired the front breaking rockets and, even as the sudden change of speed slammed him forward against the seat straps, fired full right for an emergency turn. Pushed them down and held them down, knowing that he needed everything the ship had to keep from crashing and that a turn that sudden would black him out for a moment.

It did black him out.

And that was all. Now he was sitting in hot blue sand, stark naked but otherwise unhurt. No sign of his spaceship and – for that matter – no sign of space. That curve overhead wasn't a sky, whatever else it was.

He scrambled to his feet.

Gravity seemed a little more than Earth-normal. Not much more.

Flat sand stretching away, a few scrawny bushes in clumps here and there. The bushes were blue, too, but in varying shades, some lighter than the blue of the sand, some darker.

Out from under the nearest bush ran a little thing that was like a lizard, except that it had more than four legs. It was blue, too. Bright blue. It saw him and ran back again under the bush.

He looked up again, trying to decide what was overhead. It wasn't exactly a roof, but it was dome-shaped. It flickered and was hard to look at. But, definitely, it curved down to the ground, to the blue sand, all around him.

He wasn't far from being under the centre of the dome. At a guess, it was a hundred yards to the nearest wall, if it was a wall. It was as though a blue hemisphere of something about two hundred and fifty yards in circumference was inverted over the flat expanse of the sand.

And everything blue, except one object. Over near a far curving wall there was a red object. Roughly spherical, it seemed to be about a yard in diameter. Too far for him to see clearly through the flickering blueness.

But, unaccountably, he shuddered.

He wiped sweat from his forehead, or tried to, with the back of his hand.

Was this a dream, a nightmare? This heat, this sand, that vague feeling of horror he felt when he looked towards that red thing?

A dream? No, one didn't go to sleep and dream in the midst of a battle in space.

Death? No, never. If there were immortality, it wouldn't be a senseless thing like this, a thing of blue heat and blue sand and a red horror.

Then he heard the voice.

Inside his head he heard it, not with his ears. It came from nowhere or everywhere.

"Through spaces and dimensions wandering," rang the words in his mind, "and in this space and this time, I find two peoples about to exterminate one and so weaken the other that it would retrogress and never fulfil its destiny, but decay and return to mindless dust whence it came. And I say this must not happen."

"Who … What are you?" Carson didn't say it aloud, but the question formed itself in his brain.

"You would not understand completely. I am—" There was a pause as though the voice sought – in Carson's brain – for a word that wasn't there, a word he didn't know. "I am the end of evolution of a race so old the time cannot be expressed in words that have meaning to your mind. A race fused into a single entity, eternal.

"An entity such as your primitive race might become—" again the groping for a word "—time from now. So might the race you call, in your mind, the Outsiders. So I intervene in the battle to come, the battle between fleets so evenly matched that destruction of both races will result. One must survive. One must progress and evolve."

One? thought Carson. Mine or ...

"It is in my power to stop the war, to send the Outsiders back to their galaxy. But they would return, or your race would sooner or later follow them there. Only by remaining in this space and time to intervene constantly could I prevent you from destroying one another, and I cannot remain.

"So I shall intervene now. I shall destroy one fleet completely without loss to the other. One civilization shall thus survive."

Nightmare. This had to be nightmare, Carson thought. But he knew it wasn't.

It was too mad, too impossible, to be anything but real.

He didn't dare ask the question – which? But his thoughts asked it for him.

"The stronger shall survive," said the voice. "That I cannot – and would not – change. I merely intervene to make it a complete victory, not—" groping again "—not Pyrrhic victory to a broken race.

"From the outskirts of the not-yet battle I plucked two individuals, you and an Outsider. I see from your mind that, in your early history of nationalisms, battles between champions to decide issues between races were not unknown.

"You and your opponent are here pitted against one another, naked and unarmed, under conditions equally unfamiliar to you both, equally unpleasant to you both. There is no time limit, for here there is no time. The survivor is the champion of his race. That race survives."

"But—" Carson's protest was too inarticulate for expression, but the voice answered it.

"It is fair. The conditions are such that the accident of physical strength will not completely decide the issue. There is a barrier. You will understand. Brain-power and courage will be more important than strength. Most especially courage, which is the will to survive."

"But while this goes on, the fleets will—"

"No, you are in another space, another time. For as long as you are here, time stands still in the universe you know. I see you wonder whether this place is real. It is, and it is not. As I – to your limited understanding – am and am not real. My existence is mental and not physical. You saw me as a planet; it could have been as a dust-mote or a sun. But to you this place is now real. What you suffer here will be real. And if you die here, your death will be real. If you die, your failure will be the end of your race. That is enough for you to know."

And then the voice was gone.

Again he was alone, but not alone. For as Carson looked up, he saw that the red thing, the sphere of horror that he now knew was the Outsider, was rolling towards him.

Rolling.

It seemed to have no legs or arms that he could see, no features. It rolled across the sand with the fluid quickness of a drop of mercury. And before it, in some manner he could not understand, came a wave of nauseating hatred.

Carson looked about him frantically. A stone, lying in the sand a few feet away, was the nearest thing to a weapon. It wasn't large, but it had sharp edges, like a slab of flint. It looked a bit like blue flint.

He picked it up, and crouched to receive the attack. It was coming fast, faster than he could run.

No time to think out how he was going to fight it; how anyway could he plan to battle a creature whose strength, whose character-istics, whose method of fighting he did not know? Rolling so fast, it looked more than ever like a perfect sphere.

Ten yards away. Five. And then it stopped.

Rather, it was stopped. Abruptly the near side of it flattened as though it had run up against an invisible wall. It bounced, actually bounced back.

Then it rolled forward again, but more cautiously. It stopped again, at the same place. it tried again, a few yards to one side.

Then it rolled forward again, but more cautiously. It stopped again, at the same place. It tried again, a few yards to one side.

There was a barrier there of some sort. It clicked, then, in Carson's mind, that thought projected by the Entity who had brought them there: "... accident of physical strength will not completely decide the issue. There is a barrier."

A force field, of course. Not the Netzian Field, known to Earth science, for that glowed and emitted a crackling sound. This one was invisible, silent.

It was a wall that ran from side to side of the inverted hemisphere; Carson didn't have to verify that himself. The Roller was doing that, rolling sideways along the barrier, seeking a break in it that wasn't there.

Carson took half a dozen steps forward, his left hand groping out before him, and touched the barrier. It felt smooth, yielding, like a sheet of rubber rather than glass, warm to his touch, but no warmer than the sand underfoot. And it was completely invisible, even at close range.

He dropped the stone and put both hands against it, pushing. It seemed to yield, just a trifle, but no further than that trifle, even when he pushed with all his weight. It felt like a sheet of rubber backed up by steel. Limited resiliency, and then firm strength.

He stood on tiptoe and reached as high as he could and the barrier was still there.

He saw the Roller coming back, having reached one side of the arena. That feeling of nausea hit Carson again, and he stepped back from the barrier as it went by. It didn't stop.

But did the barrier stop at ground level? Carson knelt down and burrowed in the sand; it was soft, light, easy to dig in. And two feet down the barrier was still there.

The Roller was coming back again. Obviously, it couldn't find a way through at either side.

There must be a way through, Carson thought, or else this duel is meaningless.

The Roller was back now, and it stopped just across the barrier, only six feet away. It seemed to be studying him although, for the life of him, Carson couldn't find external evidence of sense organs on the thing. Nothing that looked like eyes or ears, or even a mouth. There was though, he observed, a series of grooves, perhaps a dozen of them altogether, and he saw two tentacles push out from two of the grooves and dip into the sand as though testing its consistency. These were about an inch in diameter and perhaps a foot and a half long.

The tentacles were retractable into the grooves and were kept there except when in use. They retracted when the thing rolled and seemed to have nothing to do with its method of locomotion; that, as far as Carson could judge, seemed to be accomplished by some shifting – just how he couldn't imagine – of its centre of gravity.

He shuddered as he looked at the thing. It was alien, horribly different from anything on Earth or any of the life forms found on the other solar planets. Instinctively, he knew its mind was as alien as its body.

If it could project that almost tangible wave of hatred, perhaps it could read his mind as well, sufficiently for his purpose.

Deliberately, Carson picked up the rock that had been his only weapon, then tossed it down again in a gesture of relinquishment and raised his empty hands, palms up, before him.

He spoke aloud, knowing that although the words would be meaningless to the creature before him, speaking them would focus his own thoughts more completely upon the message. "Can we not have peace between us?" he said, his voice strange in the stillness. "The Entity who brought us here has told us what must happen if our races fight – extinction of one and weakening and retrogression of the other. The battle between them, said the Entity, depends upon what we do here. Why cannot we agree to an eternal peace – your race to its galaxy, we to ours?"

Carson blanked out his mind to receive a reply.

It came, and it staggered him back, physically. He recoiled several steps in sheer horror at the intensity of the lust to kill of the red images projected at him. For a moment that seemed eternity he had to struggle against the impact of that hatred, fighting to clear his mind of it and drive out the alien thoughts to which he had given admittance. He wanted to retch.

His mind cleared slowly. He was breathing hard and he felt weaker, but he could think.

He stood studying the Roller. It had been motionless during the mental duel it had so nearly won. Now it rolled a few feet to one side, to the nearest of the blue bushes. Three tentacles whipped out of their grooves and began to investigate the bush.

"OK," Carson said, "so it's war then." He managed a grin. "If I got your answer straight, peace doesn't appeal to you." And, because he was, after all, a young man and couldn't resist the impulse to be dramatic, he added, "To the death!"

But his voice, in that utter silence, sounded silly even to himself. It came to him, then, that this was to the death, not only his own death or that of the red spherical thing, which he thought of as the Roller, but death to the entire race of one or the other of them: the end of the human race, if he failed.

It made him suddenly very humble and very afraid to think that. With a knowledge that was above even faith, he knew that the Entity who had arranged this duel had told the truth about its intentions and its powers. The future of humanity depended upon him. It was an awful thing to realize. He had to concentrate on the situation at hand.

There had to be some way of getting through the barrier, or of killing through the barrier.

Mentally? He hoped that wasn't all, for the Roller obviously had stronger telepathic powers than the undeveloped ones of the human race. Or did it?

He had been able to drive the thoughts of the Roller out of his own mind; could it drive out his? If its ability to project were stronger, might not its receptivity mechanism be more vulnerable?

He stared at it and endeavoured to concentrate and focus all his thought upon it.

Die, he thought. You are going to die. You are dying. You are—

He tried variations on it, and mental pictures. Sweat stood out on his forehead and he found himself trembling with the intensity of the effort. But the Roller went ahead with its investigation of the bush, as utterly unaffected as though Carson had been reciting the multiplication table.

So that was no good.

He felt dizzy from the heat and his strenuous effort at concentration. He sat down on the blue sand and gave his full attention to studying the Roller. By study, perhaps, he could judge its strength and detect its weaknesses, learn things that would be valuable to know when and if they should come to grips.

It was breaking off twigs. Carson watched carefully, trying to judge just how hard it worked to do that. Later, he thought, he could find a similar bush on his own side, break off twigs of equal thickness himself, and gain a comparison of physical strength between his own arms and hands and those tentacles.

The twigs broke off hard; the Roller was having to struggle with each one. Each tentacle, he saw, bifurcated at the tip into two fingers, each tipped by a nail or claw. The claws didn't seem to be particularly long or dangerous, or no more so than his own fingernails, if they were left to grow a bit.

No, on the whole, it didn't look too hard to handle physically. Unless, of course, that bush was made of pretty tough stuff. Carson looked round; within reach was another bush of identically the same type.

He snapped off a twig. It was brittle, easy to break. Of course, the Roller might have been faking deliberately but he didn't think so. On the other hand, where was it vulnerable? How would he go about killing it if he got the chance? He went back to studying it. The outer hide looked pretty tough; he'd need a sharp weapon of some sort. He picked up the piece of rock again. It was about twelve inches long, narrow and fairly sharp on one end. If it chipped like flint, he could make a serviceable knife out of it.

The Roller was continuing its investigations of the bushes. It rolled again, to the nearest one of another type. A little blue lizard, many-legged like the one Carson had seen on his side of the barrier, darted out from under the bush.

A tentacle of the Roller lashed out and caught it, picked it up. Another tentacle whipped over and began to pull legs off the lizard, as coldly as it had pulled twigs off the bush. The creature struggled frantically and emitted a shrill squealing that was the first sound Carson had heard here, other than the sound of his own voice.

Carson made himself continue to watch; anything he could learn about his opponent might prove valuable, even knowledge of its unnecessary cruelty – particularly, he thought with sudden emotion, knowledge of its unnecessary cruelty. It would make it a pleasure to kill the thing, if and when the chance came.

With half its legs gone, the lizard stopped squealing and lay limp in the Roller's grasp.

It didn't continue with the rest of the legs. Contemptuously it tossed the dead lizard away from it, in Carson's direction. The lizard arced through the air between them and landed at his feet.

It had come through the barrier! The barrier wasn't there any more! Carson was on his feet in a flash, the knife gripped tightly in his hand, leaping forward. He'd settle this thing here and now! With the barrier gone... but it wasn't gone. He found that out the hard way, running head on into it and nearly knocking himself silly. He bounced back and fell.

As he sat up, shaking his head to clear it, he saw something coming through the air towards him, and threw himself flat again on the sand, to one side. He got his body out of the way, but there was a sudden sharp pain in the calf of his left leg.

He rolled backwards, ignoring the pain, and scrambled to his feet. It was a rock, he saw now, that had struck him. And the Roller was picking up another, swinging it back gripped between two tentacles, ready to throw again.

It sailed through the air towards him, but he was able to step out of its way. The Roller, apparently, could throw straight, but neither hard nor far. The first rock had struck him only because he had been sitting down and had not seen it coming until it was almost upon him.

Even as he stepped aside from that weak second throw Carson drew back his right arm and let fly with the rock that was still in his hand. If missiles, he thought with elation, can cross the barrier, then two can play at the game of throwing them.

He couldn't miss a three-foot sphere at only four-yard range, and he didn't miss. The rock whizzed straight, and with a speed several times that of the missiles the Roller had thrown. It hit dead centre, but hit flat instead of point first. But it hit with a resounding thump, and obviously hurt. The Roller had been reaching for another rock, but changed its mind and got out of there instead. By the time Carson could pick up and throw another rock, the Roller was forty yards back from the barrier and going strong.

His second throw missed by feet, and his third throw was short. The Roller was out of range of any missile heavy enough to be damaging.

Carson grinned. That round had been his.

He stopped grinning as he bent over to examine the calf of his leg. A jagged edge of the stone had made a cut several inches long. It was bleeding pretty freely, but he didn't think it had gone deep enough to hit an artery. If it stopped bleeding of its own accord, well and good. If not, he was in for trouble.

Finding out one thing, though, took precedence over that cut: the nature of the barrier.

He went forward to it again, this time groping with his hands before him. Holding one hand against it, he tossed a handful of sand at it with the other hand. The sand went right through; his hand didn't.

Organic matter versus inorganic? No, because the dead lizard had gone through it, and a lizard, alive or dead, was certainly organic. Plant life? He broke off a twig and poked it at the barrier. The twig went through, with no resistance, but when his fingers gripping the twig came to the barrier, they were stopped.

He couldn't get through it, nor could the Roller. But rocks and sand and a dead lizard... How about a live lizard?

He went hunting under bushes until he found one, and caught it. He tossed it against the barrier and it bounced back and scurried away across the blue sand.

That gave him the answer, so far as he could determine it now. The screen was a barrier to living things. Dead or inorganic matter could cross it.

With that off his mind, Carson looked at his injured leg again. The bleeding was lessening, which meant he wouldn't need to worry about making a tourniquet. But he should find some water, if any was available, to clean the wound.

Water – the thought of it made him realize that he was getting awfully thirsty. He'd have to find water, in case this contest turned out to be a protracted one.

Limping slightly now, he started off to make a circuit of his half of the arena. Guiding himself with one hand along the barrier, he walked to his right until he came to the curving sidewall. It was visible, a dull blue-grey at close range, and the surface of it felt just like the central barrier.

He experimented by tossing a handful of sand at it, and the sand reached the wall and disappeared as it went through. The hemispherical shell was a force field, too, but an opaque one, instead of transparent like the barrier.

He followed it round until he came back to the barrier, and walked back along the barrier to the point from which he'd started.

No sign of water.

Worried now, he started a series of zigzags back and forth between the barrier and the wall, covering the intervening space thoroughly.

No water. Blue sand, blue bushes and intolerable heat. Nothing else.

It must be his imagination, he told himself, that he was suffering that much from thirst. How long had he been there? Of course, no time at all, according to his own space-time frame. The Entity had told him time stood still out there, while he was here. But his body processes went on here, just the same. According to his body's reckoning, how long had he been here? Three or four hours, perhaps. Certainly not long enough to be suffering from thirst.

Yet he was suffering from it; his throat was dry and parched. Probably the intense heat was the cause. It was hot, 130° Fahrenheit, at a guess. A dry, still heatwithout the slightest movement of air.

He was limping rather badly and utterly fagged when he finished the futile exploration of his domain.

He stared across at the motionless Roller and hoped it was as miserable as he was. The Entity had said the conditions here were equally unfamiliar and uncomfortable for both of them. Maybe the Roller came from a planet where 200° heat was the norm; maybe it was freezing while he was roasting. Maybe the air was as much too thick for it as it was too thin for him. For the exertion of his explorations had left him panting. The atmosphere here, he realized, was not much thicker than on Mars.

No water. That meant a deadline, for him at any rate. Unless he could find a way to cross that barrier or to kill his enemy from this side of it, thirst would kill him eventually.

It gave him a feeling of desperate urgency, but he made himself sit down a moment to rest, to think.

What was there to do? Nothing, and yet so many things. The several varieties of bushes, for example; they didn't look promising, but he'd have to examine them for possibilities. And his leg – he'd have to do something about that, even without water to clean it; gather ammunition in the form of rocks; find a rock that would make a good knife.

His leg hurt rather badly now, and he decided that came first. One type of bush had leaves – or things rather similar to leaves. He pulled off a handful of them and decided, after examination, to take a chance on them. He used them to clean off the sand and dirt and caked blood, then made a pad of fresh leaves and tied it over the wound with tendrils from the same bush.

The tendrils proved unexpectedly tough and strong.

They were slender and pliable, yet he couldn't break them at all, and had to saw them off the bush with the sharp edge of blue flint. Some of the thicker ones were over a foot long, and he filed away in his memory, for future reference, the fact that a bunch of the thick ones, tied together, would make a pretty serviceable rope. Maybe he'd be able to think of a use for rope.

Next, he made himself a knife. The blue flint did chip. From a foot-long splinter of it, he fashioned himself a crude but lethal weapon. And of tendrils from the bush, he made himself a rope-belt through which he could thrust the flint knife, to keep it with him all the time and yet have his hands free.

He went back to studying the bushes. There were three other types. One was leafless, dry, brittle, rather like a dried tumbleweed. Another was of soft, crumbly wood, almost like punk. It looked and felt as though it would make excellent tinder for a fire. The third type was the most nearly woodlike. It had fragile leaves that wilted at the touch, but the stalks, although short, were straight and strong.

It was horribly, unbearably hot.

He limped up to the barrier, felt to make sure that it was still there. It was. He stood watching the Roller for a while; it was keeping a safe distance from the barrier, out of effective stone-throwing range. It was moving around back there, doing something. He couldn't tell what it was doing.

Once it stopped moving, came a little closer, and seemed to concentrate its attention on him. Again Carson had to fight off a wave of nausea. He threw a stone at it; the Roller retreated and went back to whatever it had been doing before.

At least he could make it keep its distance. And, he thought bitterly, a lot of good that did him. Just the same, he spent the next hour or two gathering stones of suitable size for throwing, and making several piles of them near his side of the barrier.

His throat burned now. It was difficult for him to think about anything except water. But he had to think about other things: about getting through that barrier, under or over it, getting at that red sphere and killing it before this place of heat and thirst killed him.

The barrier went to the wall upon either side, but how high, and how far under the sand?

For a moment, Carson's mind was too fuzzy to think out how he could find out either of those things. Idly, sitting there in the hot sand – and he didn't remember sitting down – he watched a blue lizard crawl from the shelter of one bush to the shelter of another.

From under the second bush, it looked out at him.

Carson grinned at it, recalling the old story of the desert-colonists on Mars, taken from an older story of Earth – "Pretty soon you get so lonesome you find yourself talking to the lizards, and then not so long after that you find the lizards talking back to you..."

He should have been concentrating, of course, on how to kill the Roller, but instead he grinned at the lizard and said, "Hello there."

The lizard took a few steps towards him. "Hello," it said.

Carson was stunned for a moment, and then he put back his head and roared with laughter. It didn't hurt his throat to do so, either; he hadn't been that thirsty.

Why not? Why should the Entity who thought up this nightmare of a place not have a sense of humour, along with the other powers he had? Talking lizards, equipped to talk back in my own language, if I talk to them – it's a nice touch.

He grinned at the lizard and said, "Come on over." But the lizard turned and ran away, scurrying from bush to bush until it was out of sight.

He had to get past the barrier. He couldn't get through it, or over it, but was he certain he couldn't get under it? And come to think of it, didn't one sometimes find water by digging?

Painfully now, Carson limped up to the barrier and started digging, scooping up sand a double handful at a time. It was slow work because the sand ran in at the edges and the deeper he got the bigger in diameter the hole had to be. How many hours it took him, he didn't know, but he hit bedrock four feet down: dry bedrock with no sign of water.

The force field of the barrier went down clear to the bedrock.

He crawled out of the hole and lay there panting, then raised his head to look across and see what the Roller was doing.

It was making something out of wood from the bushes, tied together with tendrils, a queerly shaped framework about four feet high and roughly square. To see it better, Carson climbed onto the mound of sand he had excavated and stood there staring.

There were two long levers sticking out of the back of it, one with a cup-shaped affair on the end. Seemed to be some sort of a catapult, Carson thought.

Sure enough, the Roller was lifting a sizable rock into the cup-shape. One of his tentacles moved the other lever up and down for a while, and then he turned the machine slightly, aiming it, and the lever with the stone flew up and forward.

The stone curved several yards over Carson's head, so far away that he didn't have to duck, but he judged the distance it had travelled, and whistled softly. He couldn't throw a rock that weight more than half that distance. And even retreating to the rear of his domain wouldn't put him out of range of that machine if the Roller pushed it forward to the barrier.

Another rock whizzed over, not quite so far away this time.

Moving from side to side along the barrier, so the catapult couldn't bracket him, he hurled a dozen rocks at it. But that wasn't going to be any good, he saw. They had to be light rocks, or he couldn't throw them that far. If they hit the framework, they bounced off harmlessly. The Roller had no difficulty, at that distance, in moving aside from those that came near it.

Besides, his arm was tiring badly. He ached all over.

He stumbled to the rear of the arena. Even that wasn't any good; the rocks reached back there, too, only there were longer intervals between them, as though it took longer to wind up the mechanism, whatever it was, of the catapult.

Wearily he dragged himself back to the barrier again. Several times he fell and could barely rise to his feet to go on. He was, he knew, near the limit of his endurance. Yet he didn't dare stop moving now, until and unless he could put that catapult out of action. If he fell asleep, he'd never wake up.

One of the stones from it gave him the glimmer of an idea. It hit one of the piles of stones he'd gathered near the barrier to use as ammunition and struck sparks.

Sparks! Fire! Primitive man had made fire by striking sparks, and with some of those dry crumbly bushes as tinder…

A bush of that type grew near him. He uprooted it, took it over to the pile of stones, then patiently hit one stone against another until a spark touched the punklike wood of the bush. It went up in flames so fast that it singed his eyebrows and was burned to an ash within seconds.

But he had the idea now, and within minutes had a little fire going in the lee of the mound of sand he'd made. The tinder bushes started it, and other bushes which burned more slowly kept it a steady flame.

The tough tendrils didn't burn readily; that made the fire-bombs easy to rig and throw; a bundle of faggots tied about a small stone to give it weight and a loop of the tendril to swing it by.

He made half a dozen of them before he lighted and threw the first. It went wide, and the Roller started a quick retreat, pulling the catapult after him. But Carson had the others ready and threw them in rapid succession. The fourth wedged in the catapult's framework and did the trick. The Roller tried desperately to put out the spreading blaze by throwing sand, but its clawed tentacles would take only a spoonful at a time and its efforts were ineffectual. The catapult burned.

The Roller moved safely away from the fire and seemed to concentrate its attention on Carson. Again he felt that wave of hatred and nausea – but more weakly; either the Roller itself was weakening or Carson had learned how to protect himself against the mental attack.

He thumbed his nose at it and then sent it scuttling back to safety with a stone. The Roller went to the back of its half of the arena and started pulling up bushes again. Probably it was going to make another catapult.

Carson verified that the barrier was still operating, and then found himself sitting in the sand beside it, suddenly too weak to stand up.

His leg throbbed steadily now and the pangs of thirst were severe. But those things paled beside the physical exhaustion that gripped his entire body.

Hell must be like this, he thought, the hell that the ancients had believed in. He fought to stay awake, and yet staying awake seemed futile, for there was nothing he could do while the barrier remained impregnable and the Roller stayed back out of range.

He tried to remember what he had read in books of archaeology about the methods of fighting used back in the days before metal and plastic. The stone missile had come first, he thought. Well, that he already had.

Bow and arrow? No; he'd tried archery once and knew his own ineptness even with a modern sportsman's dura-steel weapon, made for accuracy. With only the crude, pieced-together outfit he could make here, he doubted if he could shoot as far as he could throw a rock.

Spear? Well, he could make that. It would be useless at any distance, but would be a handy thing at close range, if he ever got to close range. Making one would help keep his mind from wandering, as it was beginning to do.

He was still beside one of the piles of stones. He sorted through it until he found one shaped roughly like a spearhead. With a smaller stone he began to chip it into shape, fashioning sharp shoulders on the sides so that if it penetrated it would not pull out again like a harpoon. A harpoon was better than a spear, maybe, for this crazy contest. If he could once get it into the Roller, and had a rope on it, he could pull the Roller up against the barrier and the stone blade of his knife would reach through that barrier, even if his hands wouldn't.

The shaft was harder to make than the head, but by splitting and joining the main stems of four of the bushes, and wrapping the joints with the tough but thin tendrils, he got a strong shaft about four feet long, and tied the stone head in a notch cut in one end. It was crude, but strong.

With the tendrils he made himself twenty feet of line. It was light and didn't look strong, but he knew it would hold his weight and to spare. He tied one end of it to the shaft of the harpoon and the other end about his right wrist. At least, if he threw his harpoon across the barrier, he'd be able to pull it back if he missed.

He tried to stand up, to see what the Roller was doing, and found he couldn't get to his feet. On the third try, he got as far as his knees and then fell flat again.

I've got to sleep, he thought. If a showdown came now, I'd be helpless. He could come up here and kill me, if he knew. I've got to regain some strength.

Slowly, painfully, he crawled back from the barrier.

The jar of something thudding against the sand near him wakened him from a confused and horrible dream to a more confused and horrible reality, and he opened his eyes again to blue radiance over blue sand.

How long had he slept? A minute? A day?

Another stone thudded nearer and threw sand on him. He got his arms under him and sat up. He turned round and saw the Roller twenty yards away, at the barrier.

It rolled off hastily as he sat up, not stopping until it was as far away as it could get.

He'd fallen asleep too soon, he realized, while he was still in range of the Roller's throwing. Seeing him lying motionless, it had dared come up to the barrier. Luckily, it didn't realize how weak he was, or it could have stayed there and kept on throwing stones.

He started crawling again, this time forcing himself to keep going until he was as far as he could go, until the opaque wall of the arena's outer shell was only a yard away.

Then things slipped away again ...

When he awoke, nothing about him was changed, but this time he knew that he had slept a long while. The first thing he became aware of was the inside of his mouth; it was dry, caked. His tongue was swollen.

Something was wrong, he knew, as he returned slowly to full awareness. He felt less tired, the stage of utter exhaustion had passed. But there was pain, agonizing pain. It wasn't until he tried to move that he knew that it came from his leg.

He raised his head and looked down at it. It was swollen below the knee, and the swelling showed even halfway up his thigh. The plant tendrils he had tied round the protective pad of leaves now cut deeply into his flesh.

To get his knife under that imbedded lashing would have been impossible. Fortunately, the final knot was over the shin bone where the vine cut in less deeply than elsewhere. He was able, after an effort, to untie the knot.

A look under the pad of leaves showed him the worst: infection and blood poisoning. Without drugs, without even water, there wasn't a thing he could do about it, except die when the poison spread through his system.

He knew it was hopeless, then, and that he'd lost, and with him humanity. When he died here, out there in the universe he knew, all his friends, everybody, would die too. Earth and the colonized planets would become the home of the red, rolling, alien Outsiders.

It was that thought which gave him courage to start crawling, almost blindly, towards the barrier again, pulling himself along by his arms and hands.

There was a chance in a million that he'd have strength left when he got there to throw his harpoon-spear just once, and with deadly effect, if the Roller would come up to the barrier, or if the barrier was gone.

It took him years, it seemed, to get there. The barrier wasn't gone. It was as impassable as when he'd first felt it.

The Roller wasn't at the barrier. By raising himself up on his elbows, he could see it at the back of its part of the arena, working on a wooden framework that was a half-completed duplicate of the catapult he'd destroyed.

It was moving slowly now. Undoubtedly it had weakened, too.

Carson doubted that it would ever need that second catapult. He'd be dead, he thought, before it was finished.

His mind must have slipped for a moment, for he found himself beating his fists against the barrier in futile rage, and made himself stop. He closed his eyes, tried to make himself calm.

"Hello," said a voice.

It was a small, thin voice. He opened his eyes and turned his head. It was a lizard.

"Go away," Carson wanted to say. "Go away; you're not really there, or you're there but not really talking. I'm imagining things again."

But he couldn't talk; his throat and tongue were past all speech with the dryness. He closed his eyes again.

"Hurt," said the voice. "Kill. Hurt – kill. Come."

He opened his eyes again. The blue ten-legged lizard was still there. It ran a little way along the barrier, came back, started off again, and came back.

"Hurt," it said. "Kill. Come."

Again it started off, and came back. Obviously, it wanted Carson to follow it along the barrier.

He closed his eyes again. The voice kept on. The same three meaningless words. Each time he opened his eyes, it ran off and came back.

"Hurt. Kill. Come."

Carson groaned. Since there would be no peace unless he followed the thing, he crawled after it.

Another sound, a high-pitched squealing, came to his ears. There was something lying in the sand, writhing, squealing. Something small, blue, that looked like a lizard.

He saw it was the lizard whose legs the Roller had pulled off, so long ago. It wasn't dead; it had come back to life and was wriggling and screaming in agony.

"Hurt," said the other lizard. "Hurt. Kill. Kill."

Carson understood. He took the flint knife from his belt and killed the tortured creature. The live lizard scurried off.

Carson turned back to the barrier. He leaned his hands and head against it and watched the Roller, far back, working on the new catapult.

I could get that far, he thought, if I could get through. If I could get through, I might win yet. It looks weak, too. I might…

And then there was another reaction of hopelessness, when pain sapped his will and he wished that he were dead, envying the lizard he'd just killed. It didn't have to live on and suffer.

He was pushing on the barrier with the flat of his hands when he noticed his arms, how thin and scrawny they were. He must really have been here a long time, for days, to get as thin as that.

For a while he was almost hysterical again, and then came a time of deep calm and thought.

The lizard he had just killed had crossed the barrier, still alive. It had come from the Roller's side; the Roller had pulled off its legs and then tossed it contemptuously at him and it had come through the barrier.

It hadn't been dead, merely unconscious. A live lizard couldn't go through the barrier, but an unconscious one could. The barrier was not a barrier, then, to living flesh, but to conscious flesh. It was a mental protection, a mental hazard.

With that thought, Carson started crawling along the barrier to make his last desperate gamble, a hope so forlorn that only a dying man would have dared try it.

He moved along the barrier to the mound of sand, about four feet high, which he'd scooped out while trying – how many days ago? – to dig under the barrier or to reach water. That mound lay right at the barrier, its farther slope half on one side of the barrier, half on the other.

Taking with him a rock from the pile nearby, he climbed up to the top of the dune and lay there against the barrier, so that if the barrier were taken away he'd roll on down the short slope, into the enemy territory.

He checked to be sure that the knife was safely in his rope belt, that the harpoon was in the crook of his left arm and that the twenty-foot rope was fastened to it and to his wrist. Then with his right hand he raised the rock with which he would hit himself on the head. Luck would have to be with him on that blow; it would have to be hard enough to knock him out, but not hard enough to knock him out for long.

He had a hunch that the Roller was watching him, and would see him roll down through the barrier, and come to investigate. It would believe he was dead, he hoped – he thought it had probably drawn the same deduction about the nature of the barrier that he had. But it would come cautiously; he would have a little time … He struck himself.

Pain brought him back to consciousness, a sudden, sharp pain in his hip that was different from the pain in his head and leg. He had, thinking things out before he had struck himself, anticipated that very pain, even hoped for it, and had steeled himself against awakening with a sudden movement.

He opened his eyes just a slit, and saw that he had guessed rightly. The Roller was coming closer. It was twenty feet away; the pain that had awakened him was the stone it had tossed to see whether he was alive or dead. He lay still. It came closer, fifteen feet away, and stopped again. Carson scarcely breathed.

As nearly as possible, he was keeping his mind a blank, lest its telepathic ability detect consciousness in him. And with his mind blanked out that way, the impact of its thoughts upon his mind was shattering.

He felt sheer horror at the alienness, the differentness of those thoughts, conveying things that he felt but could not understand or express, because no terrestrial language had words, no terrestrial brain had images to fit them. The mind of a spider, he thought, or the mind of a praying mantis or a Martian sand-serpent, raised to intelligence and put in telepathic rapport with human minds, would be a homely familiar thing, compared to this.

He understood now that the Entity had been right: Man or Roller, the universe was not a place that could hold them both.

Closer. Carson waited until it was only feet away, until its clawed tentacles reached out... Oblivious to agony now, he sat up, raised and flung the harpoon with all the strength that remained to him. As the Roller, deeply stabbed by the harpoon, rolled away, Carson tried to get to his feet to run after it. He couldn't do that; he fell, but kept crawling.

It reached the end of the rope, and he was jerked forward by the pull on his wrist. It dragged him a few feet and then stopped. Carson kept going, pulling himself towards it hand over hand along the rope. It stopped there, tentacles trying in vain to pull out the harpoon. It seemed to shudder and quiver, and then realized that it couldn't get away, for it rolled back towards him, clawed tentacles reaching out.

Stone knife in hand, he met it. He stabbed, again and again, while those horrid claws ripped skin and flesh and muscle from his body.

He stabbed and slashed, and at last it was still.

A bell was ringing, and it took him a while after he'd opened his eyes to tell where he was and what it was. He was strapped into the seat of his scouter, and the visiplate before him showed only empty space. No Outsider ship and no impossible planet.

The bell was the communications plate signal; someone wanted him to switch power into the receiver. Purely reflex action enabled him to reach forward and throw the lever.

The face of Brander, Captain of the *Magellan*, mothership of his group of scouters, flashed into the screen. His face was pale and his black eyes glowing with excitement.

"*Magellan* to Carson," he snapped. "Come on in. The fight's over. We've won!"

The screen went blank; Brander would be signalling the other scouters of his command.

Slowly, Carson set the controls for the return. Slowly, unbelievingly, he unstrapped himself from the seat and went back to get a drink at the cold-water tank. For some reason, he was unbelievably thirsty. He drank six glasses.

He leaned there against the wall, trying to think.

Had it happened? He was in good health, sound, uninjured. His thirst had been mental rather than physical; his throat hadn't been dry.

He pulled up his trouser leg and looked at the calf. There was a long white scar there, but a perfectly healed scar; it hadn't been there before. He zipped open the front of his shirt and saw that his chest and abdomen were criss-crossed with tiny, almost unnoticeable, perfectly healed scars.

It had happened!

The scouter, under automatic control, was already entering the hatch of the mothership. The grapples pulled it into its individual lock and, a moment later, a buzzer indicated that the lock was airfilled. Carson opened the hatch and stepped outside, went through the double door of the lock.

He went right to Brander's office, entered, and saluted.

Brander still looked dazed. "Hi, Carson," he said. "What you missed; what a show!"

"What happened, sir?"

"Don't know, exactly. We fired one salvo, and their whole fleet went up in dust! Whatever it was jumped from ship to ship in a flash, even the ones we hadn't aimed at and that were out of range! The whole fleet disintegrated before our eyes, and we didn't get the paint of a single ship scratched!

"We can't even claim credit for it. Must have been some unstable component in the metal they used, and our sighting shot just set it off. Man, too bad you missed all the excitement!'

Carson managed a sickly ghost of a grin, for it would be days before he'd be over the impact of his experience, but the captain wasn't watching.

"Yes, sir," he said. Common sense, more than modesty, told him he'd be branded as the worst liar in space if he ever said any more than that. "Yes, sir, too bad I missed all the excitement…"

PEACEKEEPING MISSION

Laura Resnick

What if North America needs peacekeeping, in a satiric alternity…?

Father and daughter in the same volume! Laura Resnick is the author of the popular Esther Diamond series, whose releases include Unsympathetic Magic, Doppelgangster, Disappearing Nightly *and the upcoming* Vamparazzi. *She has also written traditional fantasy novels such as* In Legend Born, The Destroyer Goddess *and* The White Dragon, *which made the "Year's Best" lists of* Publishers Weekly *and* Voya. *An opinion columnist, frequent public speaker, award-winning former romance writer and the Campbell Award-winning author of many short stories, she is on the Web at* www.LauraResnick.com.

THE WAR BETWEEN Canada and the United States had dragged on for more than twenty years by the time peacekeepers parachuted into Ohio – though sending troops to keep the "peace" in a crazy hellhole like North America was like sending forces to the South Pacific to keep the ocean dry.

Much of the world had already forgotten (or, in fact, never knew) the origins of this costly war. All that most people knew was that those crazy Canadians and Americans hated each other with a rabid passion that defied all reason. Most of the international community had given up believing there would ever be anything friendlier between them than the occasional brief ceasefire. And, as all the world knew after two decades of watching this insane conflict, all a ceasefire really accomplished was to give those nutty North Americans a chance to rest up enough to begin another round of all-out fighting. War and chaos just seemed to be their default setting.

We in the Middle East couldn't understand it.

As an intelligence officer, my mission was to liaise with local militia leaders in an attempt to end the latest round of senseless strikes and retaliations. So on 6 June, I parachuted into Ohio with the Mohammed–Moses Brigade a.k.a. the Perilous Prophets, an elite unit of the best-trained peacekeepers in the Israeli–Palestinian Army. The original company had been formed forty years ago, shortly after Israel and Palestine realized how silly it was to have *two* countries crammed in such a tiny place and decided to unite as one nation and share the land fairly, in peace and brotherhood.

Why couldn't those crazy North Americans, who had something like five hundred times as much land, do the same?

"That's just how Americans and Canadians are," said the Druze military-intelligence colonel who had prepared me for my first mission here three years ago. "Incapable of reason."

On that occasion, I had been assigned to infiltrate the embattled district of Hollywood, in the decimated wasteland of southern California, in an attempt to help the underground movement there, Filmmakers For Freedom, re-establish communications with their comrades in New York, known as the Thespian Peaceniks. My predecessor on this assignment, a much-decorated intelligence officer from Ramallah, had stepped down a few weeks earlier, reporting that the powerbrokers of the Hollywood community would be more receptive to a Jewish liaison officer. I was sickened by that kind of intolerance, but I put my feelings aside for the sake of the mission and accepted the assignment.

The Middle East League hoped that the combined pressure of (what little remained of) the coastal American entertainment communities could convince Washington to sit down at the negotiating table. My job was to do whatever it took to bring this about.

Thousands of miles away, my colleague Khalil Bouhabib was trying to convince the now-impoverished TV community in Toronto to pressure Ottawa to do the same.

Those goddamn Canadians. They sent Khalil back to Jerusalem in twelve different boxes. Each one with a maple leaf stamped on it. Bastards.

No one is meaner than a Canadian.

Except maybe an American. It turned out that the Hollywood community was just using me to get locations on the hideouts of Canadian actors who'd been long-time US residents and were still living there secretly, unwilling to go back to their native land. Thanks to the war, there was no film work in Canada. Also, any Canadian who'd ever worked in American films, TV, or theatre was a "traitor" in Canada by then. (Hence the notorious Stratford-Ontario Festival massacres, a few years ago – a whole generation of classically trained actors wiped out in a single season. What a goddamn waste.) According to our intel, there are still several thousand Canadian actors living in hiding or under false identities in the US – although the paranoid Actors Equity Association wildly inflates the likely numbers.

Anyhow, what can I say? I'd spent most of my life in Gaza before being sent to America. So, despite my training, I was naive. I had no idea how depraved people can be. When the Hollywood underground asked for my help, I agreed to put them in touch with William Shatner.

I'll never forgive myself for what they did to him. His acting wasn't *that* bad.

It was a cruel lesson in the ways of North Americans, and I never forgot it.

A lot of people believe the war began with a bloody incident twenty-one years ago, known as the Puck Riot, when Montreal attacked Syracuse over the disputed outcome of a hockey game. But the conflict's true origin goes back even further.

A few years ago, Iraqi human rights workers came across a cache of documents hidden in an old sushi joint in Detroit. Suspecting these were important, they turned them over to Lebanese intelligence – a long-time ally who, in turn, shared them with us. The newly discovered documents turned out to be top-secret correspondence that told the whole story of how the war *really* began.

Twenty-two years ago, a geographer in Moose Jaw, Saskatchewan, discovered that the US border, unbeknownst to anyone until then, illegally extended into Canadian territory by 217 metres.

Representatives from both countries met in Bismarck, North Dakota, to discuss the situation.

Rather than move the official border, the US State Department proposed that the Canadians cede the disputed land to the United States. Canada's minister of International Cooperation refused to agree to this. The governor of North Dakota remarked that, with this refusal, the minister was failing to live up to her all-too-Canadian title.

According to reports relayed to Washington at the time, the Canadian minister replied, "What do you mean by that, you rube?"

(However, some historians think that since Minister Michelle Bouvier was a francophone Canadian, she may actually have called the governor a *rue*, which is French for "street". But it remains unclear to this day why she would have called Governor Williams a street, so this theory has never gained significant support.)

The subsequent exchange of insults between the two parties is too culturally specific to make much sense, but the upshot was that the American governor shot the Canadian minister. (Governor Williams was killed four years later by a direct missile strike. His personal journal was recently found by Pakistani peacekeepers patrolling house to house in what's left of Bismarck. In his private writings, his long-standing bigotry against Canadians is detailed in shockingly specific language. Among other things, he firmly believed you could detect any Canadian, no matter how cleverly disguised, by smell.)

In an attempt at damage control after this disastrous summit, the Americans bribed the Canadians to hush up the minister's murder by giving them Detroit. We think a key piece of documentation must have been destroyed, because no one can figure out why Canada agreed to such a bad exchange. Meanwhile, the

Americans kept their North Dakota border right where it was. And more than a few Canadians went home fuming with wounded pride and a burning sense of injustice – a dangerous combination in the frozen north.

Indeed, many staffers on *both* sides resented the infamous Bismarck Capitulation, as it came to be known in the cache of secret documents that were uncovered in Detroit decades later. Some Americans believed their government should never have ceded an inch of territory to "those smelly moose-huggers" from across the border. Meanwhile, a number of Canadians were bitterly disappointed in their prime minister, who they thought should have held out for Silicon Valley or the Big Apple rather than settling for the Motor City.

These malcontents on both sides of the secret Bismarck agreement began sowing discontent among the masses of both nations. Canadians grew to resent America's economic imperialism and bad daytime television. Americans began to hate being the butt of so many Canadian jokes. So, next thing you know, rebel movements intent on destabilizing both governments turned a rather dull hockey game between Montreal and Syracuse into the war's first battlefield.

After that, things just kept escalating. The Pentagon ordered missile strikes in Quebec. Ottawa retaliated by invading Washington state and pushing all the way south to Oregon. North Dakota invaded Saskatchewan, but it was years before anyone noticed. Montana went up in flames as brother fought brother.

There was a brief period of hope after the Negev Peace Agreement, when the Israel–Palestine government forced the North Americans to sit down and negotiate a ceasefire. But the IP diplomats really had no idea what they were dealing with. They walked away from the Bedouin tent where the accords had been signed and celebrated a job well done. Within days, though, there were riots in Calgary, Vancouver, Orlando and Kansas City protesting the terms of the agreement. And within weeks, Des Moines, Savannah, San Diego, Toronto, Victoria and Whitehorse were rioting, too.

The Middle East tried to ignore these violent, isolated outbursts as the usual sabre-rattling of the rabid citizens of those two famously infantile nations. We all hoped that if we just pretended not to see their tantrums, they'd get tired of throwing them. And for almost a full year, the tense ceasefire still held.

But then a splinter rebel faction of lunatic Canadians slipped into New York and burned down Yankee Stadium. Then the Boston Tea Martyrs, a motley but massive underground militia of Americans, retaliated by dumping seventeen tons of mercury into Lake Ontario, as close to the Canadian shoreline as they could. (Were they too ignorant to understand the toxic water would damage their own ecosystem, too? Or were they just too bloodthirsty to care? In North America, you never really know.)

That was when Israel–Palestine, Lebanon, Iran, Iraq, Egypt, Jordan and Syria created a join task force, the Middle East League, to try to prevent all-out war from breaking out again in North America. (Oman, Yemen and Saudi Arabia would have joined the League, too, but they were too busy trying to establish a lasting peace between England, Wales and Scotland.) Our diplomats hastened to Washington and Ottawa to see what could be accomplished. (I hear that talking to the US president was like trying to reason with the sea. And some of our diplomats confided upon their return home that they believed the Canadian prime minister was suffering some form of psychosis. Consequently, some of the Middle East's best psychiatrists joined the next few peace missions to Canada, disguised as junior diplomatic aids. Unfortunately, no diagnosis was ever reached. Doctors thought the PM's condition could be anything from syphilis to schizophrenia to just being a power-hungry jackass.)

However, the League's hope of negotiating a renewed ceasefire, never mind real peace in the region, was shattered when a gang of radical senior citizens in Miami, armed with light artillery, began attacking Canadian cruise ships that docked there under the terms of the Negev Agreement. In response, the Maple Leaf Brigade began firing home-made missiles across the border at Maine, Vermont and New Hampshire. When his boyhood home was destroyed in one of these strikes, the US president ordered carpet bombing in Nova Scotia.

And so the war was back on again.

Maybe it's the climate that drives men mad here?

By the time I dropped into Ohio with the Perilous Prophets, I was well into my second tour in Nam, as we called North America, and the senseless rage of this continent was eating away at me. I needed to get out. Get out *soon*.

My initial recon of the volatile southern Ohio Valley revealed that the inhabitants had burned down every maple tree in their region. This senseless destruction of life was just another way, in their view, of attacking Canada symbolically. Some of the younger Prophets were disturbed by such wanton waste.

In this bastion of hyper-patriotism, Ohioans had renamed Canadian bacon as "freedom bacon". Canada's maple syrup products had been banned here for years; they weren't even available on the black market in Ohio, as they were in New York and New Jersey. Clothing merchants had to show proof that their wares contained no Canadian wool. No one bought furniture any more made of maple wood, and people burned their old maple furniture by night in communal bonfires.

In northern Ohio, various factions were lobbing a deadly assortment of home-made rockets, expired Soviet ordinance, and heat-seeking missiles across the border into Ontario. Most of their artillery couldn't clear Lake Erie, though, and wound up in the drink. The environmental consequences were increasingly dire, but neither the Middle East League nor the Peace in Our Time triumvirate on the Saudi peninsula could get permission for our experts to assess the damage to the lake's marine life.

My mission here was to facilitate a key step in a multi-stage process designed to get Canada and the US to withdraw to their original pre-war borders and come back to the negotiating table. The Middle East League knew better than even to *mention* the subject of the North Dakota–Saskatchewan border that had, as top-level officials inside both North American governments knew, led to the start of the war in the first place. That dispute was so sensitive, so volatile, so seemingly irresolvable, the first parameter established for a new wave of proposed peace talks was that the subject wouldn't even be put on the table. It would be postponed until a later, indefinite set of talks.

I thought this was a doomed strategy. How could we *ever* get these two nations to stop fighting if we didn't force them to discuss and resolve the issue that had led to twenty-one years of war in the first place?

This strategy was the idea of the Mexicans, who were desperate. Their once-thriving economy was in trouble because of the flood of American refugees pouring across their border after most of California was occupied four years ago. Canada had vowed to bomb Mexico if they didn't turn over American refugees involved in cross-border raids against Canadian occupiers; and the US had vowed to blockade all Mexico's Gulf ports if they complied with the Canadians.

So Mexico had begged the Middle East League to try once again to end the war. And I had been sent to Ohio, one of the hottest fronts in the war these days. My assignment was to establish contact with the chiefs of the most active fighting forces here – whether official-military, rebel, splinter, or counter-revolutionary – and convince them to cooperate with a call from Washington for a ceasefire. The federal government was by now so weak and ineffectual that it would topple altogether if it tried to end the war *without* the full political support of the country's various militia.

"But we're not *at* war," said Herb Neiheisel, leader of the Battling Ohioans, soon after I located his base camp near the lakefront town of Sandusky.

"You're kidding me," I said to Neiheisel. "You and Ontario exchange heavy artillery fire almost every day. Civilians in both countries – women and children – are killed by direct strikes, as well as by enemy raids, on a weekly basis. It's illegal for Canadians to travel to the US, and vice versa. It's illegal for an American to marry a Canadian, and vice versa. American forces are occupying Saskatchewan—"

"They are?" said Neiheisel in surprise.

"—and Canadians have occupied Washington, Oregon and California. So tell me—" I spread my hands as I asked "—in what way are you *not* at war?"

"We *won* the war," Neiheisel said smugly. "Those goddamn Canadians just don't accept it yet."

After three years in this place, I should have known better than to ask a logical question.

"OK, fine, you won the war," I said, "but since the Canadians don't accept that yet, and your life would be easier if they *would* acc—"

"I ain't interested in no *Canadian* making my life no easier."

Trying to untangle the double negatives, I said, "But what about your children?"

"They fight Canadians with pride, just like their daddy."

Neiheisel looked about thirty-five, surely not old enough to have kids of military age. "How old are they?"

"My son is twelve and carries light ammunition to combat units under fire. My daughter'll be fifteen in October. She can already take apart and reassemble an AK-47 in the dark."

"But don't you want them to be able to finish school?" I said, searching for an argument that might open this man's mind to the possibility of a ceasefire. "Go to college? Get married and have kids of their own?"

"I want them to *kill Canadians*!"

Since this was the most important combat leader in northwestern Ohio, I tried once more. If there was any possible way Neiheisel might consider peace, I had to find that crack in his stony exterior.

So I said, "Are you sure you're taking the best position?"

"Of course I am!"

"Because I've talked with 'General' Joe Johnson of the Columbus Defense Forces, and he—"

"You've talked with the General?" Neiheisel's eyes brightened. "Now *there's* a patriot! A great leader! A true soldier of the people!"

In fact, Johnson was an opportunistic thug who used a totally fictitious military title and had probably killed his first wife. But he was the single most powerful man in Ohio. Even the governor – no, *especially* the corrupt, spineless governor – took orders from Joe Johnson, the so-called general of Ohio.

"Yes, I've been in talks with him," I told Neiheisel. "And General Joe favours peace."

Neiheisel's eyes bulged. "*What?*"

"General Joe says twenty-one years of war are enough; it's time to end the fighting, start rebuilding the country, and raise American children in peace and prosperity."

Neiheisel frowned thoughtfully. "General Joe said that?"

"Yes," I lied. "The general favours peace talks."

In fact, General Joe had threatened to cut out my tongue just for suggesting a ceasefire. But maybe I could go back to Columbus and work on him some more after I gathered support elsewhere for the idea. And, as per my training and my instructions, I would do whatever it took to *get* that support, if it was at all possible.

I suddenly heard the high-pitched whine of a missile approaching its target, and I was on the ground with my arms covering my head even before Neiheisel shouted, "Incoming!"

The missile exploded about two hundred yards from us.

As I got up and started brushing myself off, I said to Neiheisel, "General Joe knows that ongoing hostilities could jeopardize peace talks. The president needs a ceasefire. This can only work if Ohio will cooperate."

I heard another whining missile coming towards us. But Neiheisel, also rising from the ground, shook his head. "No, that one won't make it this far." He listened a moment longer, then nodded as the noise disappeared. "Went down in the lake."

"So what do you think?" I prodded. "Will the Battling Ohioans cooperate in a ceasefire?"

"What I think is, those two missiles are the start of a full-scale barrage, and you'd better get the hell out of here if you don't want to violate your status as a peacekeeper and help us kill some Canadians today."

"But—"

"I have to think about it, and today's not a good day for thinking," Neiheisel said, as another missile flew overhead, confirming that this was indeed the start of a battle. "Where can I get a message to you?"

"The Israeli–Palestinian peacekeeper base at Columbus."

"Expect to hear from me soon," Neiheisel said.

Well, he wasn't kidding. Two days after I slipped out of Neiheisel's embattled base camp and returned to Columbus to report my findings to date, I got his message. He sent me General Joe's severed head in a box. The enclosed note said, "Death to all traitors."

This goddamn continent.

I decided I'd had enough of this insane war. The next morning, I applied for a transfer.

After taking a mental-health leave back in Gaza, I'll be headed for the peacekeeping mission in Lichtenstein. Maybe I can do some good there. At any rate, after three years in North America, I'm just sure I can't do any good in *this* crazy hellhole.

THE PEACEMAKER

Fred Saberhagen

What if intelligences mightier than ourselves are on the lookout for organic life in our galaxy, just as we ourselves are, but to exterminate it wherever found...?

Fred Saberhagen first forged this influential theme in the 1960s, and his interstellar killing machines make him, as it were, Mr Berserker, although he also wrote much varied and energetic fiction ranging from sword and sorcery and riffs upon Dracula to time-travel to extraordinary solo SF novels such as The Veils of Azlaroc. *Besides, he was an editor of the* Encyclopedia Britannica *and wrote the original entry there on science fiction.*

CARR SWALLOWED A pain pill and tried to find a less uncomfortable position in the combat chair. He keyed his radio transmitter, and spoke:

"I come in peace. I have no weapons. I come to talk to you."

He waited. The cabin of his little one-man ship was silent. His radar screen showed the berserker machine still many light-seconds ahead of him. There was no reaction from it, but he knew that it had heard him.

Behind Carr was the Sol-type star he called sun, and his home planet, colonized from Earth a century before. It was a lonely settlement, out near the rim of the galaxy; until now, the berserker war had been no more than a remote horror in news stories. The colony's only real fighting ship had recently gone to join Karlsen's fleet in the defence of Earth, when the berserkers were said to be massing there. But now the enemy was here. The people of Carr's planet were readying two more warships as fast as they could – they were a small colony, and not wealthy in resources. Even if the two ships could be made ready in time, they would hardly be a match for a berserker.

When Carr had taken his plan to the leaders of his planet, they had thought him mad. Go out and talk to it of peace and love? *Argue* with it? There might be some hope of converting the most depraved human to the cause of goodness and mercy, but what appeal cold alter the built-in purpose of a machine?

"Why not talk to it of peace?" Carr had demanded. "Have you a better plan? I'm willing to go. I've nothing to lose."

They had looked at him, across the gulf that separates healthy planners from those who know they are dying. They knew his scheme would not work, but they could think of nothing that would. It would be at least ten days until the warships were ready. The little one-man ship was expendable, being unarmed. Armed, it would be no more than a provocation to a berserker. In the end, they let Carr take it, hoping there was a chance his arguments might delay the inevitable attack.

When Carr came within a million miles of the berserker, it stopped its own unhurried motion and seemed to wait for him, hanging in space in the orbital track of an airless planetoid, at a point from which the planetoid was still several days away.

"I am unarmed," he radioed again. "I come to talk with you, not to damage you. If those who built you were here, I would try to talk to them of peace and love. Do you understand?" He was serious about talking love to the unknown builders; things like hatred and vengeance were not worth Carr's time now.

Suddenly it answered him: "Little ship, maintain your present speed and course towards me. Be ready to stop when ordered."

"I...I will." He had thought himself ready to face it, but he stuttered and shook at the mere sound of its voice. Now the weapons which could sterilize a planet would be trained on him alone. And there was worse than destruction to be feared, if one tenth of the stories about berserkers' prisoners were true. Carr did not let himself think about that.

When he was within ten thousand miles it ordered: "Stop. Wait where you are, relative to me."

Carr obeyed instantly. Soon he saw that it had launched towards him something about the size of his own ship – a little moving dot on his video screen, coming out of the vast fortress-shape that floated against the stars.

Even at this range he could see how scarred and battered that fortress was. He had heard that all of these ancient machines were damaged, from their long senseless campaign across the galaxy; but surely such apparent ruin as this must be exceptional.

The berserker's launch slowed and drew up beside his ship. Soon there came a clanging at the airlock.

"Open!" demanded the radio voice. "I must search you."

"Then will you listen to me?"

"Then I will listen."

He opened the lock, and stood aside for the half-dozen machines that entered. They looked not unlike robot valets and workers to Carr, except these were limping and worn, like their great master. Here and there a new part gleamed, but the machines' movements were often unsteady as they searched Carr, searched his cabin, probed everywhere on the little ship. When the search was completed one of the boarding machines had to be half-carried out by its fellows.

Another one of the machines, a thing with arms and hands like a man's, stayed behind. As soon as the airlock had closed behind the others, it settle itself in the combat chair and began to drive the ship towards the berserker.

"Wait!" Carr heard himself protesting. "I didn't mean I was surrendering!" The ridiculous words hung in the air, seeming to deserve no reply. Sudden panic made Carr move without thinking; he stepped forward and grabbed at the mechanical pilot, trying to pull it from the chair. It put one metal hand against his chest and shoved him across the cabin, so that he staggered and fell in the artificial gravity, thumping his head painfully against a bulkhead.

"In a matter of minutes we will talk about love and peace," said the radio.

***

Looking out through a port as his ship neared the immense berserker, Carr saw the scars of battle become plainer and plainer, even to his untaught eye. There were holes in the berserker's hull, there were square miles of bendings and swellings, and pits where the metal had once flowed molten. Rubbing his bumped head, Carr felt a faint thrill of pride. We've done that to it, he thought, we soft little living things. The martial feeling annoyed him in a way. He had always been something of a pacifist.

After some delay, a hatch opened in the berserker's side, and the ship followed the berserker's launch into darkness.

Now there was nothing to be seen through the port. Soon there came a gentle bump, as of docking. The mechanical pilot shut off the drive, and turned towards Carr and started to rise from its chair.

Something in it failed. Instead of rising smoothly, the pilot reared up, flailed for a moment with arms that sought a grip or balance, and then fell heavily to the deck. For half a minute it moved one arm, and made a grinding noise. Then it was still.

In the half-minute of silence which followed, Carr realized that he was again master of his cabin; chance had given him that. If there was only something he could do—

"Leave your ship," said the berserker's calm voice. "There is an air-filled tube fitted to your airlock. It will lead you to a place where we can talk of peace and love."

Carr's eyes had focused on the engine switch, and then had looked beyond that, to the C-plus activator. In such proximity as this to a mass the size of the surrounding berserker, the C-plus effect was not a drive but a weapon – one of tremendous potential power.

Carr did not – or thought he did not – any longer fear sudden death. But now he found that with all his heart and soul he feared what might be prepared for him outside his airlock. All the horror stories came back. The thought of going out through that airlock now was unendurable. It was less terrifying for him to step carefully around the fallen pilot, to reach the controls and turn the engine back on.

"I can talk to you from here," he said, his voice quavering in spite of an effort to keep it steady.

After about ten seconds, the berserker said: "Your C-plus drive has safety devices. You will not be able to kamikaze me."

"You may be right," said Carr after a moment's thought. "But if a safety device does function, it might hurl my ship away from your centre of mass, right through your hull. And your hull is in bad shape now; you don't want any more damage."

"You would die."

"I'll have to die sometime. But I didn't come out here to die, or to fight, but to talk to you, to try to reach some agreement."

"What kind of agreement?"

At last. Carr took a deep breath, and marshalled the arguments he had so often rehearsed. He kept his fingers resting gently on the C-plus activator, and his eyes alert on the instruments that normally monitored the hull for micrometeorite damage.

"I've had the feeling," he began, "that your attacks upon humanity may be only some ghastly mistake. Certainly we were not your original enemy."

"Life is my enemy. Life is evil." Pause. "Do you want to become goodlife?"

Carr closed his eyes for a moment; some of the horror stories were coming to life. But then he went firmly on with his argument. "From our point of view, it is you who are bad. We would like you to become a good machine, one that helps men instead of killing them. Is not building a higher purpose than destroying?"

There was a longer pause. "What evidence can you offer that I should change my purpose?"

"For one thing, helping us will be a purpose easier of achievement. No one will damage you and oppose you."

"What is it to me, if I am damaged and opposed?"

Carr tried again. "Life is basically superior to non-life; and man is the highest form of life."

"What evidence do you offer?"

"Man has a spirit."

"I have learned that many men claim that. But do you not define this spirit as something beyond the perception of any machine? And are there not many men who deny that this spirit exists?"

"Spirit is so defined. And there are such men."

"Then I do not accept the argument of spirit."

Carr dug out a pain pill and swallowed it. "Still, you have no evidence that spirit does not exist. You must consider it as a possibility."

"That is correct."

"But leaving spirit out of the argument for now, consider the physical and chemical organization of life. Do you know anything of the delicacy and intricacy of organization in even a single living cell? And surely you must admit we humans carry wonderful computers inside our few cubic inches of skull."

"I have never had an intelligent captive to dissect," the mechanical voice informed him blandly, "though I have received some relevant data from other machines. But you admit that your form is the determined result of the operation of physical and chemical laws?"

"Have you ever thought that those laws may have been designed to do just that – produce brains capable of intelligent action?"

There was a pause that stretched on and on. Carr's throat felt dry and rough, as if he had been speaking for hours.

"I have never tried to use that hypothesis," it answered suddenly. "But if the construction of intelligent life is indeed so intricate, so dependent upon the laws of physics being as they are and not otherwise – then to serve life may be the highest purpose of a machine."

"You may be sure, our physical construction is intricate." Carr wasn't sure he could follow the machine's line of reasoning, but that hardly mattered if he could somehow win the game for life. He kept his fingers on the C-plus activator.

The berserker said: "If I am able to study some living cells—"

Like a hot iron on a nerve, the meteorite-damage indicator moved; something was at the hull. "Stop that!" he screamed, without thought. "The first thing you try, I'll kill you!"

Its voice was unevenly calm, as always. "There may have been some accidental contact with your hull. I am damaged and many of my commensal machines are unreliable. I mean to land on this approaching planetoid to mine for metals and repair myself as far as possible." The indicator was quiet again.

The berserker resumed its argument. "If I am able to study some living cells from an intelligent life-unit for a few hours, I expect I will find strong evidence for or against your claims. Will you provide me with cells?"

"You must have had prisoners, sometime." He said it as a suspicion; he really knew no reason why it must have had human captives. It could have learned the language from another berserker.

"No. I have never taken a prisoner."

It waited. The question it had asked still hung in the air.

"The only human cells on this ship are my own. Possible I could give you a few of them."

"Half a cubic centimetre should be enough. Not a dangerous loss for you, I believe. I will not demand part of your brain. Also I understand that you wish to avoid the situation called pain. I am willing to help you avoid it, if possible."

Did it want to drug him? That seemed too simple. Always unpredictability, the stories said, and sometimes a subtlety out of hell.

He went on with the game. "I have all that is necessary. Be warned that my attention will hardly waver from my control panel. Soon I will place a tissue sample in the airlock for you."

He opened the ship's medical kit, took two painkillers, and set very carefully to work with a sterile scalpel. He had some biological training.

When the small wound was bandaged, he cleansed the tissue sample of blood and lymph and with unsteady fingers sealed it into a little tube. Without letting down his guard, he thought, for an instant, he dragged the fallen pilot to the airlock and left it there with the tissue sample. Utterly weary, he got back to the combat chair. When he switched the outer door open, he heard something come into the lock and leave again.

He took a pep pill. It would activate some pain, but he had to stay alert. Two hours passed. Carr forced himself to eat some emergency rations, watched the panel, and waited.

He gave a startled jump when the berserker spoke again; nearly six hours had gone by.

"You are free to leave," it was saying. "Tell the leading life-units of your planet that when I have refitted, I will be their ally. The study of your cells has convinced me that the human body is the highest creation of the universe, and that I should make it my purpose to help you. Do you understand?"

Carr felt numb. "Yes. Yes. I have convinced you. After you have refitted, you will fight on our side."

Something shoved hugely and gently at his hull. Through a port he saw stars, and he realized that the great hatch that had swallowed his ship was swinging open.

This far within the system, Carr necessarily kept his ship in normal space to travel. His last sight of the berserker showed it moving as if indeed about to let down upon the airless planetoid. Certainly it was not following him.

A couple of hours after being freed, he roused himself from contemplation of the radar screen, and went to spend a full minute considering the inner airlock door. At last he shook his head, dialled air into the lock, and entered it. The pilot-machine was gone, and the tissue sample. There was nothing out of the ordinary to be seen. Carr took a deep breath, as if relieved, closed up the lock again, and went to a port to spend some time watching the stars.

After a day he began to decelerate, so that when hours had added into another day, he was still a good distance from home. He ate, and slept, and watched his face in a mirror. He weighed himself, and watched the stars some more, with interest, like a man re-examining something long forgotten.

In two more days, gravity bent his course into a hairpin ellipse around his home planet. With it bulking between him and the berserker's rock, Carr began to use his radio.

"Ho, on the ground, good news."

The answer came almost instantly. "We've been tracking you, Carr. What's going on? What's happened?"

He told them. "So that's the story up to now," he finished. "I expect the thing really needs to refit. Two warships attacking it now should win."

"Yes." There was excited talk in the background. Then the voice was back, sounding uneasy. "Carr – you haven't started a landing approach yet, so may you understand. The thing was probably lying to you."

"Oh, I know. Even that pilot-machine's collapse might have been staged. I guess the berserker was too badly shot up to want to risk a battle, so it tried another way. Must have sneaked the stuff into my cabin air, just before it let me go – or maybe left it in my airlock."

"What kind of stuff?"

"I'd guess it's some freshly mutated virus, designed for specific virulence against the tissue I gave it. It expected me to hurry home and land before betting sick, and spread a plague. It must have thought it was inventing biological warfare, using life against life, as we use machines to fight machines. But it needed that tissue sample to blood its pet viruses; it must have been telling the truth about never having a human prisoner."

"Some kind of virus, you think? What's it doing to you Carr? Are you in pain? I mean, more than before?"

"No." Carr swivelled his chair to look at the little chart he had begun. It showed that in the last two days his weight loss had started to reverse itself. He looked down at his body, at the bandaged place near the centre of a discoloured unhuman-looking area. That area was smaller than it had been, and he saw a hint of new and healthy skin.

"What *is* the stuff doing to you?"

Carr allowed himself to smile, and to speak aloud his growing hope. "I think it's killing off my cancer."

JUNKED
A COMBAT K ADVENTURE

Andy Remic

Humans have to be tough in the big bad galaxy...

Andy Remic is the wonderfully vivacious wham-bang man of modern conflict SF whose vivid voicy prose delivers more whams per bang than most. Titles such as Biohell, Warhead, Vampire Warlords *and* Hardcore *have caused comparison with Tarantino, and indeed Remic makes some films too. "Wired and Weird" is the subtitle of his website at* www.andyremic.com.

THE SLAM CRUISER howled through the upper atmosphere of Ryzor, buffeted by an enraged storm. Lightning sparkled from armoured hull shells in crackles. Iron bruise clouds closed around the SLAM like a fist around a pebble, holding it tight for a frozen moment before flinging it down in a violent acceleration...

"We're gonna die," moaned Franco, curled foetal in his Crash-Couch, forehead touching his knees, beard rimed with droplets of sweat and vibrating vigorously. He clutched his Kekra quad-barrel machine pistol to his chest, as a mother would a weary child.

"Don't be such a pussy," snarled Pippa, glaring at Franco with cold eyes. The female member of this particular Combat K squad, Pippa was low on empathy and understanding, high on the twin goals of violence and destruction. "You knew we were breaching the storm, dickhead. What did you expect, sunshine?"

"I would have preferred a scanty-clad welcome party of thong-strapped, lap-dancing beauties," said Franco, without any hint of sarcasm. "Either that, or a good pub. Maybe a tastefully decorated brothel." He glanced up, making eye contact with Pippa, who was battling the SLAM cruiser's controls. "Hey, actually, now we're on the subject of sex, what about you and I..."

"No."

"You don't know what I was going to suggest?"

"Yeah, I do, Franco. You're a sexual deviant, and I've suffered enough depraved suggestions to last any woman, whore or gal-slacker a lifetime. Just stay in your couch, focus on the mission and keep your paws off my arse."

Franco mumbled, and closed his eyes as the SLAM rattled violently, huge shudders juddering corrugated walls, buffeted by Nature. Nature was in a foul mood. She was good and ready for a spot of fisticuffs.

"Coming in fast, Keenan. Bang goes our covert entry."

Keenan reclined, one army boot on the console, drawing on a home-rolled smoke filled with harsh Widow Maker tobacco. He gave a single nod, rubbed weary eyes. "They'll not scan shit in this storm," he drawled on an exhalation of diesel smoke. "Drop us vertical under the Beacon Scanners, an' we'll cruise up the river and go in light. I doubt General Zenab is hard to find; the junks will be treating the bastard like a king."

Combat K were elite, murderous combat squads trained by the Quad-Gal Military specializing in interrogation, infiltration, assassination and detonation. Their original game plan had been simple: to end the Helix War, which had raged for a thousand years. However, after QGM quelled one conflict, so another had taken its place – in the form of *junks*, a twisted hazardous species of deviated aliens, a toxic race intent on polluting the Quad-Gal with their infestation – and wiping out *all* species in the process.

Once believed extinct, the junks had reappeared on Galhari, a quiet fringe planet, with devastating suddenness... in a flood of *millions*. The planet had been taken in hours, and from that foothold the junks began a galaxy-wide conquest which had, in all honesty, gone *bad* for Quad-Gal Military. Recently, a series of freak coincidences led to military intelligence uncovering a source of the junks' expertise: a psychic general, capable of reading minds across the

Four Galaxies and uncovering QGM's secret plans. Named Zenab, the general was also rumoured to have invented a Nano-Bomb, a microscopic detonation device which could put QGM out of the game for good. Zenab was making it possible for the junks to extend their diseased and toxic empire, and had set up camp in his Nano-Bomb Factory. Now, it was Combat K's mission to take him out ... before millions more died.

"Tipping in now," said Pippa.

The SLAM's engines quietened, and it fell vertical, accelerating through high-altitude range towards the smash of jungle canopy below. Like a meteorite they plummeted, the ship's computers masking their profile and using a radioactive Doppelganger Shift to pre-empt rogue AI SAMs.

Without incident, the SLAM reached a half-klick above the rain-lashed jungle, and engines suddenly roared, energy *whumping* against trees and blasting a crater fifty metres wide. Every tree in the radius was shredded, instantly. The SLAM levelled out, stabilizers grunting, and settled into the crater. Engines died. Rain played drumbeats on the hull, and Franco uncurled from his CrashCouch and glared at Pippa with a teenage pout. "Not exactly what I'd call smooth," he said.

"Get to shit, Franco. I'd like to see you do better."

"Actually, they don't call me Franco 'Ace Pilot' Haggis for nothing, chipmunk."

Keenan placed a hand on Pippa's shoulder, and smiled into her blossoming wrath. Relax, said that smile. Chill. There are more important things than Franco's attitude.

Keenan stood, stretched and, removing his cigarette, which he stubbed into a whirring mechanical ashtray with six metal fingers which took the weed and crushed it into recyclable pulp, said, "Let's tool up."

The ramp hit the blasted jungle crater, and Combat K descended, guns primed, covering one another's arcs of fire with a practised finesse. Pippa held a PAD computer alongside her D5 shotgun. "All clear," she said, expert eyes reading the scanner.

They stepped into the rain and a cool wind, and were instantly drenched. In one fist Franco carried a small black ball, which appeared to be made from rubber. It gleamed in the rain.

They crossed the crater, climbed slick mud sides and moved efficiently into the jungle, a well-oiled military machine, Keenan walking point, Pippa scanning central and Franco, complaining as usual in a mumbling mutter, bringing up the rear. He had three D5 shotguns on his back, a military porcupine, a Kekra quad-barrel in one fist and a Bausch & Harris sniper rifle strapped to his pack. As was usual, Franco was terribly over-tooled for the mission, but he wouldn't have it any other way. He'd been in a savage fire-fight once and run out of ammo; it hadn't been a pleasant experience, and Franco spent many long hours, drunk, regaling people with an exaggeration of the tale.

The trees were eerie, silent. The rain danced. A strong aroma of rotting vegetation flooded the jungle like toxic gas.

It was too … still. Just too damn lifeless.

The squad halted in a vast swathe of curving jungle. Somewhere they could hear a raging waterfall. Keenan glanced at Pippa. "How far to the contact?"

Pippa smiled at that. Keenan could be so … clinical. The *contact*. The target. The assassination. The taking of a human life, and yeah, OK, that guy was responsible for the deaths of millions according to the unreliable monkeys of QGM military intelligence, but who's to say they were right? Who gave Combat K the right to play God?

"Twenty klicks. Northeast."

"How far to the Blood River?"

"Eight hundred and twenty seven metres. Give or take."

"Let's move out."

They eased through the enemy jungle. There had been no early ScoutBot Scan infiltrations or WebCloud relays, because QGM wanted to retain the element of surprise. In and out in three hours. A neat excision.

It was immensely dark in the jungle, and muted sounds echoed metallic between trees. The sounds were odd, unlike usual jungle noises. Keenan and Pippa exchanged glances, but continued, heightened senses alert to danger, guns rain-slick and slippery in gloved hands. Permatex WarSuits moderated body temperature and kept the stifling jungle humidity from biting…too much. Franco still mumbled curses as he brought up the rear, expertly scanning their back-trail, and expertly watching Pippa's arse. I wish, he thought sourly. Oh to get my paws on that ripe pair of peaches! But it would never happen, especially as Franco was currently married to an eight-foot mutated zombie super-soldier, once beautiful, now an abomination of pus. He frowned at the memory. It was a long story, a tale of violence and psychopathic *biohell*.

The river surprised them, despite electronic warnings. It slammed from the darkness, a muted roaring greeting them instantaneously from gloom. It was lighter here, out from under the tree canopy, and a rim of green moonlight crept from behind bruised copper clouds. Keenan gave Franco a nod, and the small ginger squaddie knelt in the mud by the side of the river.

"Do it."

"Yeah, boss."

Franco twisted the small rubber ball, and tossed it into the river on the end of a flexing TitaniumIII cord. The ball gave a *crack* of ignition, and a hiss, and inflated instantly into a special forces covert boat, nicknamed a Rubber Duck, or Sitting Duck by the more cynical members of the squads. Pippa and Keenan climbed in, guns tracking dark shorelines overhung with skeletal branches. The air crackled with strange, metallic creaking, not unlike the discharge of energy. Pippa gave a shudder.

"You OK?"

"I feel like we're being watched. The PAD states otherwise."

"Still no life?"

"No life," said Pippa. "By that, I mean *absolutely* no life. This jungle is deader than a crypt. There's no indigenous life forms; no birds, no insects. Nothing. I've seen more energy in a corpse."

Franco jumped in and fired stealth engines, a twin-set of Suzuki Whisper MkIVs. He eased them out into the strong tug of the river, and turned against the current. They were headed upriver; deeper into the jungle, deeper into nigritude, deeper into the heart of darkness.

Franco stared at the gloom. "I don't suppose there's any brothels up there?" he muttered.

"Don't be an idiot," snapped Pippa.

"Pubs? You reckon?" He sounded feebly hopeful.

"Dickhead."

"What about a casino or two? It's ages since I've had a flutter."

"Mate, the last time you gambled you lost your damn *house*. Haven't you learned your lesson?"

"'Twas a simple error of reading the cards. I'll do better next time, so I will."

"Well," said Pippa carefully, "I don't see how. After you shot the place up with that K7 shotgun, and dropped a BABE grenade in the manager's office. Fair blew the place to shit. You've been banned from every gambling franchise on The City."

"Rubbish! They know that was only little old me playing toy soldiers." He brightened. "Still. This guy is a king, right? This General Zenab? Showered in gold and jewels by the junks? Treated like royalty?" His eyes went suddenly crafty, as he guided the small submersible through dark channels of foaming river. Rainfall gleamed on his skin and, as green moonlight caught him, he looked quite demonic. Like a devil, sick of sin. Like a twice reanimated corpse. "We might even make a few dollars!" He beamed. "There might be dancing girls in the palace!" He beamed wider, showing his broken tooth from too many drunken bar brawls.

Pippa slapped his arm. "You're a muppet. You need to focus, Franco, and focus hard. This ain't no game we're playing. Kee. I told you he'd be a damn liability. I told you to choose somebody else."

"Well, charming!" stuttered Franco. "Thanks for your vote of confidence, sweetie."

"We might need his detonation skills," growled Keenan, with a shaded glance. "And you *know* there's nobody better with a Bausch & Harris. I'm hoping we can get this gig finished – *without* getting our hands dirty."

They cruised in silence through obsidian shadows. The jungle closed in as the river narrowed, became yet more violent, raging and pounding around black fists of ancient volcanic rock. Quietly, Pippa said, "Never in a million years."

They stopped in a small bay of calm water for navigation checks. Pippa was jagging the touch-dials of the PAD, and shook her head. "No good, Kee. There's something wrong – either with the PAD, or with the whole damn planet."

"Leave it," said Keenan. "We'll use our eyes and ears. Just like the old days on Molkrush Fed."

He glanced up, and there, at the edge of the jungle, perhaps five metres away, stood a squad of junks. Four of them. Heavily armed. For what seemed an eternity the two groups faced one another across the expanse of stagnant water, a platter of stinking glass ... then hell erupted ...

Keenan's Techrim 11 mm was out and pumping in his fist and he dived right, over the edge of the boat. Pippa dropped to one knee, D5 in her gloved hands, *booms* crashing through the jungle. Franco split left, a Kekra quad-barrel machine pistol in each hand slamming bullets at the squad. The junks were tall and powerful, wearing basic electronic leather armour, skin pitted like metal, eyes like pools of blood, short, forked silver tongues flickering in silver mouths like liquid metal – they split with equal skill and speed, their MPKs firing volleys of roaring bullets at Combat K. Everything was a deafening bellow of chaos and confusion. The jungle screamed with concussion and bullets, a distillation of confusion, as Keenan pumped rounds into a junk's face and watched him stumble back, blood spewing from destroyed eyes, his face a mash of chewed bone and gristle and flapping cheek skin. Franco, yelling, charged with Kekras roaring. Two bullets *thumped* his WarSuit like hammer blows, knocking the wind from him, slamming his heart with pounding fists, but he was on the junk, both guns screaming, aware like the others that junks were insanely tough, hard to kill, real *bastards* to put down. Their eyes were their Achilles' heel; shoot out their eyes and death would follow. Franco was on the junk, both boots slamming the stunned, eye-destroyed face and riding him to the ground to crouch beside the writhing figure. The two remaining junks charged Pippa, her D5 still cracking but they *absorbed* shells in primitive armour and skin and muscle, which rolled like melted wax, reforming, repairing even as it was decimated and Pippa felt panic well in her breast at this seemingly indestructible threat before her ... and closing fast. One reached out, took the D5 from her hands and bent it into two discrete parts with a *snap* and scatter of unspent shells. The junk screamed in her face, a toxic blast of poisonous air that made her weak at the knees, ingested toxins attacking her central nervous system as the second junk turned on Franco and fired a volley of MPK rounds...

And Keenan was there, Techrim against the junk's head. "Put her down, shitbag." The junk turned and grinned at Keenan, blood-red eyes narrowing as he pulled the trigger and the bullet whined through skull and brain, erupting in a mushroom shower of shards and mashed brain-slop. It rammed a fist into Keenan's chest, slamming him back over the boat in an acceleration of gasping pain and realization that the junk *could still operate with a bullet in the head*... The junk turned on Pippa, who smiled a nasty smile, and slammed her knife into one eye with a downwards punch. She ripped the blade sideways, cutting out the junk's second blood orb and it screamed, a sudden high-pitched shrill, flopping back in the Duck, thrashing as Pippa hurled the blade to embed in the final junk's armour. It turned from Franco, lying back on the rocks, stunned by bullet blasts in his Permatex. When it glanced at Pippa, Franco reached back and grabbed the first thing which came to hand. His Bausch & Harris sniper rifle, packing high velocity 8.98 medium calibre rounds. At that range, face to face, the weapon was devastating. The rifle gave a *thump* in Franco's gloved fists and the junk's head disintegrated. The body stood for a moment, jiggling, blood a fountain from the jagged neck, then fell flat and dead on the rocks. A thick, evil stench poured from the open neck. An aroma of rotten eternity. The perfume of the junk.

Franco coughed, and looked to Keenan, who struggled from the water clutching his chest. He felt like he'd suffered a heart attack. Felt like he'd died. "Get back on the boat," he wheezed, and they all scrambled aboard.

As they cruised into violent storm waters, wind howling, the heavens pounding their insignificant craft with needles of rain, Pippa gave Keenan and Franco a savage snarl. "We can assume the bastard PAD is compromised, yeah? We're on our own, boys."

"Just the way we like it," Franco smiled sardonically.

The storm died in a sudden rush of warm air, like a dragon blast. As if in response, or perhaps by coincidence, the river became a flat platter, glass, ice. Pippa, now pilot, slowed their cruise to a halt and they sat for a few moments, rocking, listening, peering at the over-hanging edges of uncompromising metallic-stinking jungle.

"Never get out of the boat," muttered Franco.

"What?" snapped Pippa.

"Just something I heard."

"How far?" said Keenan.

"Three klicks. We're getting close. That's why we met that little scouting party. Was it an accident, I wonder, or were the bastards looking for us? Maybe they saw the SLAM come in, thought they'd investigate."

"To all sensors it'd still look like a meteor strike."

"Still,' said Pippa. "I'd want to know what came down twenty klicks from *my* base of operations. Especially if this place *is* a Nano-Bomb Factory."

"Let's assume they know we're here," said Keenan, mind ticking. "What would General Zenab do? He can read minds, or so we're told. See through tangled paths of the future. Has he seen his own impending assassination?"

Pippa stared at Keenan. "That isn't even funny."

"Do you see me laughing? OK. So you've got patrols in the jungle, textbook. What about the river? Patrol boats? We've not seen anything here. What else could you use?"

"It's not deep enough for a sub," said Franco, frowning.

"When I went in the river before, this water, it's not normal. I know it's red because of mineral deposits, but it was also full of... oil, or something. A lubricant. It wasn't natural."

"Is that why we can smell metal?"

Keenan shrugged. "Not sure. But whatever it is, it may have a purpose. It reminded me of the Terminus5 Shell reactor; remember the bunker? Full of that insane AI bio-wire which ate through your bones and separated a person long-ways out?"

"I remember," said Franco, voice low. "You think they may have AI tech?"

"I always thought the junks low-tech, but...we should prepare for anything. This gig stinks like a dead cat."

"You want to ditch the boat?"

"Maybe. I'm considering it."

They paused, and something *slopped* in the river. They glanced at one other. "I saw something," said Pippa, carefully, hoisting her weapon, nervous now, gun tracking an invisible foe. The river seemed deeper, here, more stable; and yet more threatening at the same time. Like a motionless predator, a hunter waiting to pounce.

Ripples suddenly drifted away from the Rubber Duck, or at least, from something *near* it. Pippa stood, alongside Keenan, and they both aimed weapons at the flat surface.

"I don't like this," moaned Franco.

"Shut up. Pippa, get us out of here."

Pippa nodded, and eased them forward. They moved across the water, still as a lake, green-tinged from the moon. Ripples flowed, slapping shores. The engine purred, near silent, and Pippa angled towards the shore...

It was this that saved their lives.

The *thing* squirmed across the river, surfacing sideways like a sidewinder serpent, a long, bright silver eel as thick as a man's waist and perhaps thirty or forty feet long. Pippa gasped and Keenan started firing at the creature undulating towards them. Pippa joined him, but their bullets were absorbed with tiny *plops* as it accelerated, a massive eel that crashed into the Rubber Duck with stunning force, sending all three Combat K soldiers flipping into the river...

Keenan went under, felt something cold and metallic brush his WarSuit, recoil for an instant, then *slap* him with such force only his armour stopped immediate death through impact. He choked.

Everything, all wind and life, was knocked from him and yet he forced himself to swim, powerful strokes, towards the shore. He *felt* the eel's approach rather than saw it, and dived, twisting, by some miracle passing under the undulating body of thick muscle. He struck out, under the river, fighting strange currents until he clambered up the shore, dripping, panting, muscles screaming like irate fishmongers. Franco was already there, heaving, hands on knees, looking sorry for himself in a hangdog fashion.

"Where's Pippa?"

Franco stood upright, stared out, watched the mercury eel circle their Rubber Duck boat and suddenly ensnare it, its whole body flipping from the river to wrap around the boat again and again in huge circles, and with a sudden *pulse* and tug, crush the boat into a hissing, buckling, pulped oblivion.

Slowly, Franco pulled free his Bausch & Harris. "She's there. See. Pippa, Hey!" He waved. She seemed disorientated in the gloom, in the drizzle of light rain, but focused on his words and struck out towards him. However, the eel also heard Franco and turned, writhing in foam as Franco snarled a curse and aimed down the rifle's sight.

"You'll draw attention to us!" snapped Keenan, hoisting his own guns and casting about for enemy.

"I can't let her *die*," said Franco.

He fired, a muted *thump* and the bullet disappeared in the eel's mass. Pippa powered on, but the eel moved fast for something so big. It gained swiftly. If it caught her, it would crush her without doubt. Franco breathed deep, and fired off another three shots in quick succession. The thump of bullets echoed off, flesh slaps, muted by the jungle.

"It's going to kill her," said Keenan.

"Not on *my* watch," snapped Franco, and he began pumping shot after shot after shot into the silver eel, unaware if his bullets had effect, unaware if this *thing* was something they could *kill*. What was it? AI? A simpConstruct robot? Organic? Or a meld of all three?

"Come on!" urged Keenan.

Franco kept on firing, and the eel suddenly slowed, its sidewinder motion becoming erratic. Pippa reached the shore, but the eel's tail lunged from blood waters and wrapped around her chest. It dragged her back, and both Keenan and Franco leaped forward, guns thundering and howling into the thick silver body which twitched and pulsed. Pippa screamed, hands straining against the metallic surface. Then her fingers slipped inside, as if entering jelly, and came out, shocked, trailing umbilicals of silver eel strand...

Franco dropped to his knees on the rocks, in the mud, his eyes locked to Pippa's and reading the pain and suffering there. He pulled a BABE grenade from his belt, gave her a wide grin, pulled the pin and plunged his fist *inside* the eel's apparently semi-solid body. He pulled free his arm, rocked back on heels, and fell to his arse. He watched as there came a muffled *crack*. Ripples shuddered along the length of the eel, and it twitched, every molecule vibrating out of synchronization with every other. Then the creature was still.

Franco and Keenan dragged Pippa from the strange creature's embrace, Pippa coughing, holding her chest. Without her WarSuit she'd be a mashed pulp, a skin bag of crumbled bones. Even now, the armour was buzzing warnings; it was seriously damaged, and would fail if it took another serious impact.

"I'd say they know we're here," said Franco.

"Let's move out. The quicker we get this done, the quicker we go home."

"I'm beginning to hate this planet," said Franco, pulling his sulky lip.

Pippa coughed, and stood. She took several deep breaths. She looked annoyed. More than annoyed. She looked ready to *kill*. "Let's go assassinate this bastard," she said, and hoisted her shotgun with a scowl.

They moved like ghosts through the jungle. Up close, the trees were metallic, coated in a sheen of oil. They were not living, not organic, but simple machines designed to imitate life. A machine jungle. An army of sentry steel.

"What kind of freak creates such a place?" said Franco, frowning. It was the waste and pointlessness, more than anything, that offended him.

"Just keep your eye on the PAD."

For the last two klicks they'd evaded nine junk patrols, keeping low and quiet, going to ground at the first hint of enemy activity. But the fact still nagged Combat K – if the enemy knew they were there, on the planet, alertness would be increased. And the enemy may also now have discovered the SLAM cruiser. The last thing a soldier needed after a bad gig was a compromised ride home.

Franco, bringing up the rear, caught Keenan's signal and dropped instantly, silent. He carried the Bausch & Harris, now, in his big pugilist's paws. He was twitchy, on edge. A man on a high wire. A hairline trigger.

Franco dropped to his belly against the floppy, metallic leaves and commando-crawled forward. They were on a cliff top over-looking a bowl valley devoid of jungle, although with so many thick creepers it could happily be described as a bowel valley. To the left, the Blood River eased sluggish and wide. Boats were moored there, low alloy vessels with big guns. Several ornately carved stone buildings squatted at the centre of the cleared jungle, lights shining in windows. And yet the whole place was deserted, especially as this was supposed to be the Nano-Bomb Factory. It felt wrong, and much too small in scale. If this was a Nano-Bomb Factory, would General Zenab really surround himself with a mere handful of junk protectors? If this man really was as richly rewarded, highly prized and threatening to QGM as they claimed, wouldn't the security be far more aggressive?

"This stinks," said Pippa.

"Like a ten-week dead pig," added Franco.

"Let me think," said Keenan. "Is the PAD still dead?"

"Like a ten-week dead skunk," said Franco.

Keenan held up one fist. "Stop! I need to think. Pippa, is this the target?"

"Yeah."

"It's so wrong."

"I know that, Kee. This ain't no Nano-Bomb Factory."

Keenan bellied down, chin on his hands, and watched the modest activity which surrounded the small stone buildings. The carvings were ancient. Alien archaeology. He shuddered. It always filled him with a desolation, as if humans had only been kicking around the Quad-Gal for a few minutes – which in reality, they had. Aliens, sentient life-species as a matrix, had been around a billion times longer. This simple infancy made humanity feel quite insecure; something they made up for with aggression and a savage empire.

"Maybe," said Keenan, "this bastard is so tough he doesn't need protection. We're looking at this wrong. Maybe Zenab is an ancient alien creature, more powerful than any of us dreamed. After all, we're assuming he's human, because QGM *assumed* he was human. That was never confirmed."

"Shit intel, again," snapped Pippa. "The story of our lives."

"We need to make the best of it," said Keenan. "This is the gig. I'll head in alone; you two cover me, especially Franco with that lethal bastard rifle. OK?"

"I don't like it," said Pippa.

"I didn't ask whether you liked it."

Pippa took his arm, stared into his eyes. And he could read it there – the love, the need, the want, the lust, sexual desire but more than that, a deep and meaningful *connection*.

"Don't go, Kee," she said.

"We need to get this done."

And he was gone, easing down the slope, fingers digging in rock, eyes and senses alert for enemy activity. But the camp, or base, the supposed Nano-Bomb Factory was pretty much deserted. It was a ghost ship.

"He'll be OK," said Franco, grinning, and patting Pippa on the shoulder. "Let's keep him covered."

"If he's not back in ten minutes, I'm going in."

"That isn't what he said."

"It's what *I said*," she hissed, eyes an insane glare.

"OK, OK, don't take it out on poor old Franco."

"Just play with your gun."

Mumbling, Franco checked over his rifle, and tried not to look concerned.

Keenan touched down on moist soil. His eyes raked the jungle
perimeter. The stone buildings appeared inviting, warm, homely,
and for the first time in a long, *long* time he found himself thinking
of home. His old home. Before Galhari, and before the ... *murders*.
The word sat foul on his tongue, in his brain, like a diseased implant,
a toxic augmentation. His wife, Freya, and their children, Rachel
and Ally, had been killed. At first, it had been pinned on Pippa and
they had hated one another, tried to kill one another – after all,
hadn't Pippa been his lover? Hadn't he cast her aside? Hadn't she
had *motive* to murder his family? But as days fell into weeks fell into
months, it had blurred and become apparent that something far
more sinister was at work, so complex even Pippa herself wasn't
sure if she'd committed the evil deed. One thing was for sure,
however. Keenan's family were dead, slaughtered, and sometimes,
occasionally, more often now as months flowed like mercury, he
longed to join them.

He knew they were waiting.

Keenan descended the final section of rocky slope, boots digging
in, searching for targets. But the area was deserted and this worried
him more than any waiting army. Keeping a low profile, he crossed
the bare ground to the largest of the stone buildings, eyes taking in
ancient carvings which passed through several planes of reality.
They were deeply alien, twisted, some shifting from sight to scent to
aural expression, and dazzling Keenan with a form of sensual
confusion. "Alien shit," he muttered. "Bring back Picasso."

He stopped, back to the wall, gun against his cheek, and glanced
up to where Franco and Pippa were camouflaged, invisible, their
guns trained, protecting him like hot metal guardians. A robot dad.
He peered into the building, which was cool and inviting, a staggered tile floor, every inch of the walls lined with rich tapestries
hanging ceiling to floor.

Keenan stepped in, sounds muffled by the vibrant needlework.
He moved through rooms, realizing the building was much larger
than anticipated ... but there was no bomb-making equipment on

show, no advanced circuitry for the design and production of nano technology. It was primitive. Bare. A let-down. A cerebral retard.

He emerged on the edges of a modest room, circular, walls hung with green tapestries which shifted in a breeze. Sliding behind these convenient screens, he observed three figures, three huge junks with rippling muscles and holstered machine guns. Before them stood a child, a girl, six years old with fine blonde hair and blue eyes in a pretty, oval face. She wore a simple white robe, and clutched a low-profile wooden box in both hands. She was talking, words gentle, like whispers on the wind.

Keenan's gaze shifted back to the three junks and he wondered which one was General Zenab...

"Hello, Mr Keenan," said the child, turning, head tilting, just as Keenan was deciding which junk to kill first. He froze, aware he'd made no sound, had not compromised his position in the slightest. He relaxed. So. They knew he was coming and, more than that, they knew who he was.

Combat K. QGM. *Shit.*

He stepped from his tapestry-concealed hiding place, grinning wryly. He'd never made a good assassin. Hell, he thought, I'm barely a soldier these days, barely human. He expected a battle, but the junks failed to present arms. They stood, facing away like automatons, apparently oblivious to his existence. Drones in the hive.

"Come forward," said the little girl.

Keenan moved, D5 shotgun in his gloved hands, ready at a twitch to blow any living creature in half. He was watching the junks, eyes narrowed, senses screaming at him with his tainted alien blood, but he could *feel* no others. The five of them were alone...

"Which of you is Zenab?"

"Ahh," said the little girl, eyes sparkling, hands clutching the wooden box so tightly her knuckles were white. "You have come for murder. Assassination. Death. We will be sorry to disappoint you; sorry to send you away."

"So he's not here?"

"Assumptions by Quad-Gal Military are so refreshing." Something about the way she spoke the name made Keenan freeze, boots welded to floor tiles, eyes fixed on her and realizing, an instant too late, that she was more than the sum of her parts, and infinitely more dangerous than her simple image led him to believe…

He gazed into that face, and his heart melted, and he knew, knew in a blinding white hot intensity that this girl, this child, this pale innocent was the *general* he sought to exterminate. And he knew, knew deep in his soul that he could not kill this person.

That's what it wants you think… whispered the dark side of his soul.

No! She's a child, a puppet of the junks; I should kill them, her guards, the scourge which has imprisoned her! I should take her away from this place, this evil, take her away to a better life… a life with kindness, and family, a place filled with warmth and love.

She will kill you, Keenan. She will possess you! She is not human… she will usurp your flesh.

But that was impossible, he realized. She could not usurp him, or possess him, because he barely lived there himself.

"You are General Zenab." It was not a question.

"So very perceptive." She smiled, with small white teeth. And he knew; understood that her arrogance precluded an awesome power. She was no human, because *Keenan was no longer human*, and the alien blood from an earlier encounter had tainted his own blood, own soul, had somehow elevated him, somehow desecrated him, dropped him into another plane of existence.

"I have been sent to… to *kill* you." Keenan's voice was quiet. "But I will give you a choice. I will take you away from this place. Give you another life, a better life." He no longer saw Zenab. He saw Rachel and Ally. Their bloody corpses. It ate him like acid.

"Like you would have done for your girls?"

"Yes." Keenan's voice was strangled, neither human nor animal; an imitation of the organic. And a tidal wave of guilt and shame washed over him, flooded him inside out and he felt his knees go weak, his anger flee, any straggled remnants of hatred were torn and all he wanted, more than anything in this world, in this life, was to save this child...as he had failed to save his own.

He knelt, and placed his gun on the floor with a *clack*. "Come with me," he said.

She laughed. "I cannot. You do not understand."

"I understand you are prisoner, forced to use your talents for the junks, to aid their empire, to extend their evil."

She smiled, pretty face wrinkling, and Keenan's heart melted, his soul burned, and he only realized Pippa and Franco were behind him when he saw the barrel of Franco's Bausch & Harris rifle ease past his shoulder...

"Don't move, buddy," said Franco.

"What are you *doing?*" snapped Keenan.

"She's a witch, a changer, a junk-spawn. She's infested, mate. She's hooked into your brain, and into your spine. She's using you Kee. She'll kill you. Don't trust her." He grinned, but the smile looked wrong on his face. Twisted. Too much bone. Too much skull.

Keenan frowned, the whole world tumbling down. "Bullshit!" he snapped. "She's a prisoner. We have to rescue her...to free her! What's wrong with you, Franco? Can't you see?"

"He's right." Pippa's hand touched Keenan's shoulder, then her gun caressed the side of his head. "Sorry, Kee. It's time to die."

A feeling swept over Keenan, nausea, a violent bout of sickness worse than anything ever felt. Like a puzzle solved, everything clicked into place. The pulse of alien blood through his veins, the beat of his heart, all melded to show him the truth...he ducked as Pippa pulled the trigger, and her bullet whined, entered Franco's skull with a *slap*, blasting his head into ribbons of flesh and curled bone. Brain mushroomed out then paused, like elastic caught at the point of furthest trajectory, and ravelled swiftly back in as the head reformed itself disjointedly and for a moment, the briefest of instants, Keenan saw the face disintegrate into a cloud of particles... and rearrange as solid flesh.

Keenan whirled fast and the world kicked into guns and bullets, into action and reaction as Franco and Pippa leaped from a doorway with guns thundering, bullets scything into the fake forms of Franco and Pippa, into their *simulacrums*, created things, imitations of life.

Pippa killed herself with a shotgun blast to the head, and watched her own body curl in on itself, into a shower of silver powder that trickled down between cracks in the floor tiles. Franco had a short vicious fight with his own head-holed ganger, and shot himself in the stomach, then the throat, and finally the face. He watched himself die and, in dying, so the real Franco was born again.

"Shit," he panted, face bathed in sweat. "They nearly had you, Keenan!"

The three junks attacked, as Combat K attacked. Keenan was kicked out of his shock, grabbing the D5 shotgun and leaping forward, blasting a junk guard in the face with a burst of shells and removing his head. There was a whirlwind of violence which left Combat K crouched on the tiles, surrounded by blood and junk gore, limbs, chunks of flesh, as a cool wind blew through the chamber and they realized the little girl had gone.

"The General's fled," said Pippa. "What the fuck's going on?"

"Nano-technology," snarled Keenan. "And the box she carries. It's the Nano-Bomb Factory. I don't know why we thought it'd be an installation; it's something complex, something small, something incredibly advanced. We have to get it. It's too dangerous to let go."

They ran through corridors, through chambers, all writhing with ancient alien stonecraft. They emerged, saw the little girl sprinting towards the river and a sleek alloy craft.

"She's going to escape," snapped Pippa. "Shoot her! QGM rely on it! Millions rely on it."

Franco lifted his rifle, and caught Keenan's eye. Keenan looked as if he'd been hit by a hammer. How could he shoot his own daughter in the back? *How could he murder his little girl?*

Franco, also, was flooded with doubt. He lowered the gun, long barrel pointing at the churned mud floor. "I can't," he said. "I can't shoot a child in the back. It's just not right!"

"Give me the gun," snarled Pippa, dragging the rifle from Franco's scarred hands. She aimed, and with a *crack* took the back of the girl's head off. General Zenab toppled to the floor in a tangle of limbs, and did not move.

"I'm just mangled," said Franco. "What the hell actually happened? Why did I just kill myself?"

They moved to the girl, a destroyed form. Even as they watched, a tiny cloud, millions of silver particles, formed into a fist, then dissipated swiftly on the wind.

"Nanobots," said Keenan, mouthed twisted in a sour grin. "They imitated you. Imitated the girl. General Zenab doesn't exist; it's an AI construct, a very, very advanced machine."

Pippa stooped, picked up the wooden box. "But we got the Nano-Bomb equipment."

"Yeah. At least we got something."

"We didn't kill her, him ... *it*, did we?" said Pippa.

"We hurt it," said Keenan. "Whatever the hell it was. And we bought QGM some time."

"So we'll be back?"

Keenan, programming the PAD to bring in the SLAM, nodded. "Yeah, Pippa. The war ain't over. We'll be back. For people like us, this kind of shit never ends. The suffering never stops."

Pippa gave a nod and, clutching the small wooden box, waited for exit.

THE LIBERATION
OF EARTH

William Tenn

"It became necessary to destroy the town in order to save it," an American major notoriously said during the Vietnam War. What if the entire Earth similarly falls victim to the tactics of warring super-aliens?

William Tenn was the pen-name of Philip Klass, who appropriately taught classes at Pennsylvania State College in SF and writing. He served in World War Two and wrote darkly comic tales as well as one marvellous novel, Of Men and Monsters, *in which the human race only survive mice-like in the walls of the homes and starships of giant alien invaders, although thus we spread out to the stars, verminously.*

THIS, THEN, IS the story of our liberation. Suck air and grab clusters! Heigh-ho, here is the tale!

August was the month, a Tuesday in August. These words are meaningless now, so far have we progressed; but many things known and discussed by our primitive ancestors, our unliberated, unreconstructed forefathers, are devoid of sense to our free minds. Still the tale must be told, with all of its incredible place-names and vanished points of reference.

Why must it be told? Have any of you a *better* thing to do? We have had water and weeds and lie in a valley of gusts. So rest, relax and listen! And suck air, suck air!

On a Tuesday in August, the ship appeared in the sky over

France in a part of the world then known as Europe. Five miles long the ship was, and word has come down to us that it looked like an enormous silver cigar.

The tale goes on to tell of the panic and consternation among our forefathers when the ship abruptly materialized in the summer-blue sky. How they ran; how they shouted; how they pointed!

How they excitedly notified the United Nations, one of the chiefest institutions, that a strange metal craft of incredible size had materialized over their land. How they sent an order *here* to cause military aircraft to surround it with loaded weapons, gave instructions *there* for hastily grouped scientists, with signalling apparatus, to approach it with friendly gestures. How, under the great ship, men with cameras took pictures of it; men with typewriters wrote stories about it; and men with concessions sold models of it.

All these things did our ancestors, enslaved and unknowing, do.

Then a tremendous slab snapped up in the middle of the ship and the first of the aliens stepped out in the complex tripodal gait that all humans were shortly to know and love so well. He wore a metallic garment to protect him from the effects of our atmospheric peculiarities, a garment of the opaque, loosely folded type that these, the first of our liberators, wore throughout their stay on Earth.

Speaking in a language none could understand, but booming deafeningly through a huge mouth about halfway up his twenty-five feet of height, the alien discoursed for exactly one hour, waited politely for a response when he had finished, and, receiving none, retired into the ship.

That night, the first of our liberation! Or the first of our first liberation, should I say? *That* night, anyhow! Visualize our ancestors scurrying about their primitive intricacies: playing ice hockey, televising, smashing atoms, red-baiting, conducting give-away shows and signing affidavits – all the incredible minutiae that made the olden times such a frightful mass of cumulative detail in which to live – as compared with the breathless and majestic simplicity of the present.

The big question, of course, was – what had the alien said? Had he called on the human race to surrender? Had he announced that he was on a mission of peaceful trade and, having made what he considered a reasonable offer – for, let us say, the north polar ice cap – politely withdrawn so that we could discuss his terms among ourselves in relative privacy? Or, possibly, had he merely announced that he was the newly appointed ambassador to Earth from a friendly and intelligent race – and would we please direct him to the proper authority so that he might submit his credentials?

Not to know was quite maddening.

Since decision rested with the diplomats, it was the last possibility which was held, very late that night, to be most likely; and early the next morning, accordingly, a delegation from the United Nations waited under the belly of the motionless star-ship. The delegation had been instructed to welcome the aliens to the outermost limits of its collective linguistic ability. As an additional earnest of mankind's friendly intentions, all military craft patrolling the air about the great ship were ordered to carry no more than one atom bomb in their racks, and to fly a small white flag – along with the UN banner and their own national emblem. Thus did our ancestors face this, the ultimate challenge of history.

When the alien came forth a few hours later, the delegation stepped up to him, bowed, and, in the three official languages of the United Nations – English, French and Russian – asked him to consider this planet his home. He listened to them gravely, and then launched into his talk of the day before – which was evidently as highly charged with emotion and significance to him as it was completely incomprehensible to the representatives of world government.

Fortunately, a cultivated young Indian member of the secretariat detected a suspicious similarity between the speech of the alien and an obscure Bengali dialect whose anomalies he had once puzzled over. The reason, as we all know now, was that the last time Earth had been visited by aliens of this particular type, humanity's most advanced civilization lay in a moist valley in Bengal; extensive dictionaries of that language had been written, so that speech with the natives of Earth would present no problem to any subsequent exploring party.

However, I move ahead of my tale, as one who would munch on the succulent roots before the dryer stem. Let me rest and suck air for a moment! Heigh-ho, truly those were tremendous experiences for our kind!

You, sir, now you sit back and listen! You are not yet of an age to Tell the Tale. I remember, *well enough do I remember* how my father told it, and his father before him. You will wait your turn as I did; you will listen until too much high land between water holes blocks me off from life.

Then *you* may take your place in the juiciest weed patch and, reclining gracefully between sprints, recite the great epic of our liberation to the carelessly exercising young.

Pursuant to the young Hindu's suggestions, the one professor of comparative linguistics in the world capable of understanding and conversing in this peculiar version of the dead dialect was summoned from an academic convention in New York where he was reading a paper he had been working on for eighteen years: *An Initial Study of Apparent Relationships Between Several Past Participles in Ancient Sanskrit and an Equal Number of Noun Substantives in Modern Szechuanese.*

Yea, verily, all these things – and more, many more – did our ancestors in their besotted ignorance contrive to do. May we not count our freedoms indeed?

The disgruntled scholar, minus – as he kept insisting bitterly – some of his essential word lists, was flown by fastest jet to the area south of Nancy which, in those long-ago days, lay in the enormous black shadow of the alien spaceship.

Here he was acquainted with his task by the United Nations delegation, whose nervousness had not been allayed by a new and disconcerting development. Several more aliens had emerged from the ship carrying great quantities of immense, shimmering metal which they proceeded to assemble into something that was obviously a machine – though it was taller than any skyscraper man had ever built, and seemed to make noises to itself like a talkative and sentient creature. The first alien stood courteously in the neighbourhood of the profusely perspiring diplomats; ever and anon he would go through his little speech again, in a language that had been almost forgotten when the cornerstone of the library of Alexandria was laid. The men from the UN would reply, each one hoping desperately to make up for the alien's lack of familiarity with his own tongue by such devices as hand gestures and facial expressions. Much later, a commission of anthropologists and psychologists brilliantly pointed out the difficulties of such physical, gestural communication with creatures possessing – as these aliens did – five manual appendages and a single unwinking compound eye of the type the insects rejoice in.

The problems and agonies of the professor as he was trundled about the world in the wake of the aliens, trying to amass a usable vocabulary in a language whose peculiarities he could only extrapolate from the limited samples supplied him by one who must inevitably speak it with the most outlandish of foreign accents – these vexations were minor indeed compared to the disquiet felt by the representatives of world government. They beheld the extraterrestrial visitors move every day to a new site on their planet and proceed to assemble there a titanic structure of flickering metal which muttered nostalgically to itself, as if to keep alive the memory of those faraway factories which had given it birth.

True, there was always the alien who would pause in his evidently supervisory labours to release the set little speech; but not even the excellent manners he displayed, in listening to upward of fifty-six replies in as many languages, helped dispel the panic caused whenever a human scientist, investigating the shimmering machines, touched a projecting edge and promptly shrank into a disappearing pinpoint. This, while not a frequent occurrence, happened often enough to cause chronic indigestion and insomnia among human administrators.

Finally, having used up most of his nervous system as fuel, the professor collated enough of the language to make conversation possible. He – and, through him, the world – was thereupon told the following:

The aliens were members of a highly advanced civilization which had spread its culture throughout the entire galaxy. Cognizant of the limitations of the as-yet-under-developed animals who had latterly become dominant upon Earth, they had placed us in a sort of benevolent ostracism. Until either we or our institutions had evolved to a level permitting, say, at least *associate* membership in the galactic federation (under the sponsoring tutelage, for the first few millennia, of one of the older, more widespread and more important species in the federation) – until that time, all invasions of our privacy and ignorance – except for a few scientific expeditions conducted under conditions of great secrecy – had been strictly forbidden by universal agreement.

Several individuals who had violated this ruling – at great cost to our racial sanity, and enormous profit to our reigning religions – had been so promptly and severely punished that no known infringements had occurred for some time. Our recent growth curve had been satisfactory enough to cause hopes that a bare thirty or forty centuries more would suffice to place us on applicant status with the federation.

Unfortunately, the peoples of this stellar community were many, and varied as greatly in their ethical outlook as their biological composition. Quite a few species lagged a considerable distance behind the Dendi, as our visitors called themselves. One of these, a race of horrible, worm-like organisms known as the Troxxt – almost as advanced technologically as they were retarded in moral development – had suddenly volunteered for the position of sole and absolute ruler of the galaxy. They had seized control of several key suns, with their attendant planetary systems, and, after a calculated decimation of the races thus captured, had announced their intention of punishing with a merciless extinction all species unable to appreciate from these object lessons the value of unconditional surrender.

In despair, the galactic federation had turned to the Dendi, one of the oldest, most selfless, and yet most powerful of races in civilized space, and commissioned them – as the military arm of the federation – to hunt down the Troxxt, defeat them wherever they had gained illegal suzerainty, and destroy for ever their power to wage war.

This order had come almost too late. Everywhere the Troxxt had gained so much the advantage of attack, that the Dendi were able to contain them only by enormous sacrifice. For centuries now, the conflict had careered across our vast island universe. In the course of it, densely populated planets had been disintegrated; suns had been blasted into novae; and whole groups of stars ground into swirling cosmic dust.

A temporary stalemate had been reached a short while ago, and – reeling and breathless – both sides were using the lull to strengthen weak spots in their perimeter.

Thus, the Troxxt had finally moved into the till-then-peaceful section of space that contained our solar system – among others. They were thoroughly uninterested in our tiny planet with its meagre resources, nor did they care much for such celestial neighbours as Mars or Jupiter. They established their headquarters on a planet of Proxima Centaurus – the star nearest our own sun – and proceeded to consolidate their offensive–defensive network between Rigel and Aldebaran. At this point in their explanation, the Dendi pointed out, the exigencies of interstellar strategy tended to become too complicated for anything but three-dimensional maps; let us here accept the simple statement, they suggested, that it became immediately vital for them to strike rapidly, and make the Troxxt position on Proxima Centaurus untenable – to establish a base inside their lines of communication.

The most likely spot for such a base was Earth.

The Dendi apologized profusely for intruding on our development, an intrusion which might cost us dear in our delicate developmental state. But, as they explained – in impeccable pre-Bengali – before their arrival we had, in effect, become (all unknowingly) a satrapy of the awful Troxxt. We could now consider ourselves liberated.

We thanked them much for that.

Besides, their leader pointed out proudly, the Dendi were engaged in a war for the sake of civilization itself, against an enemy so horrible, so obscene in its nature, and so utterly filthy in its practices, that it was unworthy of the label of intelligent life. They were fighting not only for themselves, but also for every loyal member of the galactic federation; for every small and helpless species; for every obscure race too weak to defend itself against such a ravaging conqueror. Would humanity stand aloof from such a conflict?

There was just a slight bit of hesitation as the information was digested. Then – "No!" humanity roared back through such mass-communication media as television, newspapers, reverberating jungle drums, and mule-mounted backwoods messenger. *"We will not stand aloof. We help you destroy this menace to the very fabric of civilization. Just tell us what you want us to do."*

Well, nothing in particular, the aliens replied with some embarrassment. Possibly in a little while there might *be* something – *several* little things, in fact – which would be *quite* useful; but, for the moment, if we would concentrate on not getting in their way when they serviced their gun-mounts, they would be very grateful, really...

This reply tended to create a large amount of uncertainty among the two billion of Earth's human population. For several days afterwards, there was a planet-wide tendency – the legend has come down to us – of people failing to meet each other's eyes.

But then Man rallied from this substantial blow to his pride. He would be useful, be it ever so humbly, to the race which had liberated him from potential subjugation by the ineffably ugly Troxxt. For this, let us remember well our ancestors! Let us hymn their sincere efforts amid their ignorance!

All standing armies, all air and sea fleets, were reorganized into guard-patrols around the Dendi weapons: no human might approach within two miles of the murmuring machinery without a pass countersigned by the Dendi. Since they were never known to sign such a pass during the entire period of their stay on this planet, however, this loophole-provision was never exercised as far as is known; and the immediate neighbourhood of the extraterrestrial weapons became and remained henceforth wholesomely free of two-legged creatures.

Cooperation with our liberators took precedence over all other human activities. The order of the day slogan first given voice by a Harvard professor of government in a querulous radio round table on "Man's Place in a Somewhat Over-Civilized Universe".

"Let us forget our individual egos and collective conceits!" the professor cried at one point. "Let us subordinate everything – to the end that the freedom of the solar system in general, and Earth in particular, must and shall be preserved!"

Despite its mouth-filling qualities, this slogan was repeated everywhere. Still, it was difficult sometimes to know exactly what the Dendi wanted – partly because of the limited number of interpreters available to the heads of the various sovereign states, and partly because of their leader's tendency to vanish into his ship after ambiguous and equivocal statements – such as the curt admonition to "Evacuate Washington!"

On that occasion, both the secretary of state and the American president perspired fearfully though five hours of a July day in all the silk-hatted, stiff-collared, dark-suited diplomatic regalia that the barbaric past demanded of political leaders who would deal with the representatives of another people. They waited and wilted beneath the enormous ship – which no human had ever been invited to enter, despite the wistful hints constantly thrown out by university professors and aeronautical designers – they waited patiently and wetly for the Dendi leader to emerge and let them know whether he had meant the State of Washington or Washington, DC.

The tale comes down to us at this point as a tale of glory. The capitol building taken apart in a few days, and set up almost intact in the foothills of the Rocky Mountains; the missing Archives, that were later to turn up in the children's room of a public library in Duluth, Iowa; the bottles of Potomac River water carefully borne westward and ceremoniously poured into the circular concrete ditch built around the president's mansion (from which unfortunately it was to evaporate within a week because of the relatively low humidity of the region) – all these are proud moments in the galactic history of our species, from which not even the later knowledge that the Dendi wished to build no gun-site on the spot nor even an ammunition dump, but merely a recreation hall for their troops, could remove any of the grandeur of our determined cooperation and most willing sacrifice.

There is no denying, however, that the ego of our race was greatly damaged by the discovery, in the course of a routine journalistic interview, that the aliens totalled no more powerful a group than a squad; and that their leader, instead of the great scientist and key military strategist that we might justifiably have expected the Galactic Federation to furnish for the protection of Terra, ranked as the interstellar equivalent of a buck sergeant.

That the president of the United States, the commander-in-chief of the Army and the Navy, had waited in such obeisant fashion upon a mere non-commissioned officer was hard for us to swallow; but that the impending Battle of Earth was to have a historical dignity only slightly higher than that of a patrol action was impossibly humiliating.

And then there was the matter of "lendi".

The aliens, while installing or servicing their planet-wide weapon system, would occasionally fling aside an evidently unusable fragment of the talking metal. Separated from the machine of which it had been a component, the substance seemed to lose all those qualities which were deleterious to mankind and retain several which were quite useful indeed.

For example, if a portion of the strange material was attached to any terrestrial metal – and insulated carefully from contact with other substances – it would, in a few hours, itself become exactly the metal that it touched, whether that happened to be zinc, gold, or pure uranium.

This stuff – "lendi", men have heard the aliens call it – was shortly in frantic demand in an economy ruptured by constant and unexpected emptyings of its most important industrial centres.

Everywhere the aliens went, to and from their weapon sites, hordes of ragged humans stood chanting – well outside the two-mile limit – "Any lendi Dendi?" All attempts by law-enforcement agencies of the planet to put a stop to this shameless, wholesale begging were useless – especially since the Dendi themselves seemed to get some unexplainable pleasure out of scattering tiny pieces of lendi to the scrabbling multitude. When policemen and soldiery began to join the trampling murderous dash to the corner of the meadows wherein had fallen the highly versatile and garrulous metal, governments gave up.

Mankind almost began to hope for the attack to come, so that it would be relieved of the festering consideration of its own patent inferiorities. A few of the more fanatically conservative among our ancestors probably even began to regret liberation.

They did, children; they did. Let us hope that these would-be troglodytes were among the very first to be dissolved and melted down by the red flame-balls. One cannot, after all, turn one's back on progress.

Two days before the month of September was over, the aliens announced that they had detected activity upon one of the moons of Saturn. The Troxxt were evidently threading their treacherous way inward through the solar system. Considering their vicious and deceitful propensities, the Dendi warned, an attack from these worm-like monstrosities might be expected at any moment.

Few humans went to sleep as the night rolled up to and past the meridian on which they dwelt. Almost all eyes were lifted to a sky carefully denuded of clouds by watchful Dendi. There was a brisk trade in cheap telescopes and bits of smoked glass in some sections of the planet; while other portions experienced a substantial boom in spells and charms of the all-inclusive, or omnibus, variety.

The Troxxt attacked in three cylindrical black ships simultaneously; one in the Southern Hemisphere, and two in the Northern. Great gouts of green flame roared out of their tiny craft; and everything touched by this imploded into a translucent, glass-like sand. No Dendi was hurt by these, however, and from each of the now-writhing gun-mounts there bubbled forth a series of scarlet clouds which pursued the Troxxt hungrily, until forced by a dwindling velocity to fall back upon Earth.

Here they had an unhappy after-effect. Any populated area into which these pale pink cloudlets chanced to fall was rapidly transformed into a cemetery – a cemetery, if the truth be told as it has been handed down to us, that had more the odour of the kitchen than the grave. The inhabitants of these unfortunate localities were subjected to enormous increases of temperature. Their skin reddened, then blackened; their hair and nails shrivelled; their very flesh turned into liquid and boiled off their bones. Altogether a disagreeable way for one-tenth of the human race to die.

The only consolation was the capture of a black cylinder by one of the red clouds. When, as a result of this, it had turned white hot and poured its substance down in the form of a metallic rainstorm, the two ships assaulting the Northern Hemisphere abruptly retreated to the asteroids into which the Dendi – because of severely limited numbers – steadfastly refused to pursue them.

In the next twenty-four hours the aliens – *resident* aliens, let us say – held conferences, made repairs to their weapons and commiserated with us. Humanity buried its dead. This last was a custom of our forefathers that was most worthy of note; and one that has not, of course, survived into modern times.

By the time the Troxxt returned, Man was ready for them. He could not, unfortunately, stand to arms as he most ardently desired to do; but he could and did stand to optical instrument and conjurer's oration.

Once more the little red clouds burst joyfully into the upper reaches of the stratosphere; once more the green flames wailed and tore at the chattering spires of lendi; once more men died by the thousands in the boiling backwash of war. But this time, there was a slight difference: the green flames of the Troxxt abruptly changed colour after the engagement had lasted three hours; they became darker, more bluish. And, as they did so, Dendi after Dendi collapsed at his station and died in convulsions.

The call for retreat was evidently sounded. The survivors fought their way to the tremendous ship in which they had come. With an explosion from her stern jets that blasted a red-hot furrow southward through France, and kicked Marseilles into the Mediterranean, the ship roared into space and fled home ignominiously.

Humanity steeled itself for the coming ordeal of horror under the Troxxt.

They were truly worm-like in form. As soon as the two night-black cylinders had landed, they strode from their ships, their tiny segmented bodies held off the ground by a complex harness supported by long and slender metal crutches. They erected a dome-like fort around each ship – one in Australia and one in the Ukraine – captured a few courageous individuals who had ventured close to their landing site, and disappeared back into the dark craft with their squirming prizes.

While some men drilled about nervously in the ancient military patterns, others pored anxiously over scientific texts and records, pertaining to the visit of the Dendi – in the desperate hope of finding a way of preserving terrestrial independence against this ravening conqueror of the star-spattered galaxy.

And yet all this time, the human captives inside the artificially darkened spaceships (the Troxxt, having no eyes, not only had little use for light but the more sedentary individuals among them actually found such radiation disagreeable to their sensitive, unpigmented skins) were not being tortured for information – nor vivisected in the earnest quest of knowledge on a slightly higher level – but educated.

Educated in the Troxxtian language, that is.

True it was that a large number found themselves utterly inadequate for the task which the Troxxt had set them, and temporarily became servants to the more successful students. And another, albeit smaller, group developed various forms of frustration hysteria – ranging from mild unhappiness to complete catatonic depression – over the difficulties presented by a language whose every verb was irregular, and whose myriads of prepositions were formed by noun–adjective combinations derived from the subject of the previous sentence. But, eventually, eleven human beings

were released, to blink madly in the sunlight as certified interpreters of Troxxt.

These liberators, it seemed, had never visited Bengal in the
heyday of its millennia-past civilization.

Yes, these *liberators*. For the Troxxt had landed on the sixth day
of the ancient, almost mythical month of October. And October
the Sixth is, of course, the Holy Day of the Second Liberation. Let
us remember, let us revere. (If only we could figure out which day it
is on our calendar!)

The tale the interpreters told caused men to hang their heads in
shame and gnash their teeth at the deception they had allowed the
Dendi to practise upon them.

True, the Dendi had been commissioned by the Galactic Federation to hunt the Troxxt down and destroy them. This was largely
because the Dendi *were* the Galactic Federation. One of the first
intelligent arrivals on the interstellar scene, the huge creatures had
organized a vast police force to protect them and their power
against any contingency of revolt that might arise in the future.
This police force was ostensibly a congress of all thinking life forms
throughout the galaxy; actually, it was an efficient means of
keeping them under rigid control.

Most species thus-far discovered were docile and tractable,
however; the Dendi had been ruling from time immemorial, said
they – very well, then, let the Dendi continue to rule. Did it make
that much difference?

But throughout the centuries, opposition to the Dendi grew –
and the nuclei of the opposition were the protoplasm-based creatures. What, in fact, had become to be known as the Protoplasmic
League.

Though small in number, the creatures whose life cycles were
derived from the chemical and physical properties of protoplasm
varied greatly in size, structure and specialization. A galactic
community deriving the main wells of its power from them would
be a dynamic instead of a static place, where extra-galactic travel
would be encouraged, instead of being inhibited, as it was at
present because of Dendi fears of meeting a superior civilization. It

would be a true democracy of species – a real biological republic – where all creatures of adequate intelligence and cultural development would enjoy a control of their destinies at present experienced by the silicon-based Dendi alone.

To this end, the Troxxt – the only important race which had steadfastly refused the complete surrender of armaments demanded of all members of the Federation – had been implored by a minor member of the Protoplasmic League to rescue it from the devastation which the Dendi intended to visit upon it, as punishment for an unlawful exploratory excursion outside the boundaries of the galaxy.

Faced with the determination of the Troxxt to defend their cousins in organic chemistry, and the suddenly aroused hostility of at least two-thirds of the interstellar peoples, the Dendi had summoned a rump meeting of the Galactic Council; declared a state of revolt in being; and proceeded to cement their disintegrating rule with the blasted life-forces of a hundred worlds. The Troxxt, hopelessly outnumbered and out-equipped, had been able to continue the struggle only because of the great ingenuity and selflessness of other members of the Protoplasmic League, who had risked extinction to supply them with newly developed secret weapons.

Hadn't we guessed the nature of the beast from the enormous precautions it had taken to prevent the exposure of any part of its body to the intensely corrosive atmosphere of Earth? Surely the seamless, barely translucent suits which our recent visitors had worn for every moment of their stay on our world should have made us suspect a body chemistry developed from complex silicon compounds rather than those of carbon?

Humanity hung its collective head and admitted that the suspicion had never occurred to it.

Well, the Troxxt admitted generously, we were extremely inexperienced and possibly a little too trusting. Put it down to that. Our naivety, however costly to them – our liberators – would not be allowed to deprive us of that complete citizenship which the Troxxt were claiming as the birthright of all.

But as for our leaders, our probably corrupted, certainly irresponsible leaders...

The first executions of UN officials, heads of states and pre-Bengali interpreters as "Traitors to Protoplasm" – after some of the lengthiest and most nearly perfectly fair trials in the history of Earth – were held a week after G-J day, the inspiring occasion on which – amidst gorgeous ceremonies – Humanity was invited to join, first the Protoplasmic League and thence the New and Democratic Galactic Federation of All Species, All Races.

Nor was that all. Whereas the Dendi had contemptuously shoved us to one side as they went about their business of making our planet safe for tyranny, and had – in all probability – built special devices which made the very touch of their weapons fatal for us, the Troxxt – with the sincere friendliness which had made their name a byword for democracy and decency wherever living creatures came together among the stars – our Second Liberators, as we lovingly called them, actually *preferred* to have us help them with the intensive, accelerating labour of planetary defence.

So men's intestines dissolved under the invisible glare of the forces used to assemble the new, incredibly complex weapons; men sickened and died, in scrabbling hordes, inside the mines which the Troxxt had made deeper than any we had dug hitherto; men's bodies broke open and exploded in the undersea oil-drilling sites which the Troxxt had declared were essential.

Children's schooldays were requested, too, in such collecting drives as "Platinum Scrap for Procyon" and "Radioactive Debris for Deneb". Housewives were also implored to save on salt whenever possible – this substance being useful to the Troxxt in literally dozens of incomprehensible ways – and colourful posters reminded: "*Don't salinate – sugarfy!*"

And over all – courteously caring for us like an intelligent parent – were our mentors, taking their giant supervisory strides on metallic crutches, while their pale little bodies lay curled in the hammocks that swung from each paired length of shining leg.

Truly, even in the midst of a complete economic paralysis caused by the concentration of all major productive facilities on other-worldly armaments, and despite the anguished cries of those suffering from peculiar industrial injuries which our medical men were totally unequipped to handle, in the midst of all this mind-racking disorganization, it was yet very exhilarating to realize that we had taken our lawful place in the future government of the galaxy and were even now helping to make the Universe Safe for Democracy.

But the Dendi returned to smash this idyll. They came in their huge, silvery spaceships and the Troxxt, barely warned in time, just managed to rally under the blow and fight back in kind. Even so, the Troxxt ship in the Ukraine was almost immediately forced to flee to its base in the depths of space. After three days, the only Troxxt on Earth were the devoted members of a little band guarding the ship in Australia. They proved, in three or more months, to be as difficult to remove from the face of our planet as the continent itself; and since there was now a state of close and hostile siege, with the Dendi on one side of the globe and the Troxxt on the other, the battle assumed frightful proportions.

Seas boiled; whole steppes burned away; the climate itself shifted and changed under the gruelling pressure of the cataclysm. By the time the Dendi solved the problem, the planet Venus had been blasted from the skies in the course of a complicated battle manoeuvre, and Earth had wobbled over as orbital substitute.

The solution was simple: since the Troxxt were too firmly based on the small continent to be driven away, the numerically superior Dendi brought up enough firepower to disintegrate all Australia into an ash that muddied the Pacific. This occurred on the twenty-fourth of June, the Holy Day of First Reliberation. A day of reckoning for what remained of the human race, however.

How could we have been so naïve, the Dendi wanted to know, as to be taken in by the chauvinistic pro-protoplasm propaganda? Surely, if physical characteristics were to be the criteria of our racial empathy, we would not orient ourselves on a narrow chemical basis: the Dendi life-plasma was based on silicon instead of carbon, true, but did not vertebrates – *appendaged* vertebrates, at that, such as we and the Dendi – have infinitely more in common, in spite of a *minor* biochemical difference or two, than vertebrates and legless, armless, slime-crawling creatures who happened, quite accidentally, to possess an identical organic substance?

As for this fantastic picture of life in the galaxy... *Well!* The Dendi shrugged their quintuple shoulders as they went about the intricate business of erecting their noisy weapons all over the rubble of our planet. Had we ever seen a representative of these proto-plasmic races the Troxxt were supposedly protecting? No, nor would we. For as soon as a race – animal, vegetable or mineral – developed enough to constitute even a *potential* danger to the sinuous aggressors, its civilization was systematically dismantled by the watchful Troxxt. We were in so primitive a state that they had not considered it at all risky to allow us the outward seeming of full participation.

Could we say we had learned a single useful piece of information about Troxxt technology – for all of the work we had done on their machines, for all of the lives we had lost in the process? No, of course not. We had merely contributed our mite to the enslavement of far-off races who had done us no harm.

There was much that we had cause to feel guilty about, the Dendi told us gravely – once the few surviving interpreters of the pre-Bengali dialect had crawled out of hiding. But our collective onus was as nothing compared to that borne by "vermicular collaborationists" – those traitors who had supplanted our martyred former leaders. And then there were the unspeakable human interpreters who had had linguistic traffic with creatures destroying a two-million-year-old galactic peace. Why, killing was almost too good for them, the Dendi murmured as they killed them.

When the Troxxt ripped their way back into possession of Earth some eighteen months later, bringing us the sweet fruits of the Second Reliberation – as well as a complete and most convincing rebuttal of the Dendi – there were few humans found who were willing to accept with any real enthusiasm the responsibilities of newly opened and highly paid positions in language, science and government.

Of course, since the Troxxt, in order to reliberate Earth, had found it necessary to blast a tremendous chunk out of the northern hemisphere, there were very few humans to be found in the first place…

Even so, many of these committed suicide rather than assume the title of secretary-general of the United Nations when the Dendi came back for the glorious Re-Reliberation, a short time after that. This was the liberation, by the way, which swept the deep collar of matter off our planet, and gave it what our forefathers came to call a pear-shaped look.

Possibly it was at this time – possibly a liberation or so later – that the Troxxt and the Dendi discovered that the Earth had become far too eccentric in its orbit to possess the minimum safety conditions demanded of a Combat Zone. The battle, therefore, zigzagged coruscatingly and murderously away in the direction of Aldebaran.

That was nine generations ago, but the tale that has been handed down from parent to child, to child's child, has lost little in the telling. You hear it now from me almost exactly as I heard it. From my father I heard it as I ran with him from water puddle to distant water puddle, across the searing heat of yellow sand. From my mother I heard it as we sucked air and frantically grabbed at clusters of thick green weed, whenever the planet beneath us quivered in omen of a geological spasm that might bury us in its burned-out body, or a cosmic gyration threatened to fling us into empty space.

Yes, even as we do now did we do then, telling the same tale, running the same frantic race across miles of unendurable heat for food and water; fighting the same savage battles with the giant rabbits for each other's carrion – and always, ever and always, sucking desperately at the precious air, which leaves our world in greater quantities with every mad twist of its orbit.

Naked, hungry and thirsty came we into the world, and naked, hungry and thirsty do we scamper our lives out upon it, under the huge and never-changing sun.

The same tale it is, and the same traditional ending it has as that I had from my father and his father before him. Suck air, grab clusters and hear the last holy observation of our history!

"Looking about us, we can say with pardonable pride that we have been about as thoroughly liberated as it is possible for a race and a planet to be."

A CLEAN ESCAPE

John Kessel

To hint at what is in John Kessel's story would spoil the reading experience.

Shortly after publication in Asimov's, he turned the following story into a one-act play, then a decade later into a radio play performed by the online series Seeing Ear Theater, and then a TV version was adapted for a Masters of Science Fiction series. Among Kessel's feats is a marriage between Jane Austen's Pride and Prejudice and Mary Shelley's Frankenstein, namely the novelette "Pride and Prometheus", which won the 2008 Nebula Award. Other recent publications are The Baum Plan for Financial Independence and Other Stories and, with his friend James Patrick Kelly, an anthology of stories inspired and influenced by Franz Kafka.

"I've been thinking about devils. I mean, if there are devils in the world, if there are people in the world who represent evil, is it our duty to exterminate them?"

– John Cheever "The Five-Forty-Eight"

AS SHE SAT in her office, waiting – for exactly what she did not know – Dr Evans hoped that it wasn't going to be another bad day. She needed a cigarette and a drink. She swivelled the chair around to face the closed venetian blinds beside her desk, leaned back, and laced her hands behind her head. She closed her eyes and breathed deeply. The air wafting down from the ventilator in the ceiling smelled of machine oil. It was cold. Her face felt it, but the bulky sweater kept the rest of her warm. Her hair felt greasy. Several minutes passed in which she thought of nothing. There was a knock at the door.

"Come in," she said absently.

Havelmann entered. He had the large body of an athlete gone slightly soft, grey hair, and a lined face. At first glance he didn't look sixty. His well-tailored blue suit badly needed pressing.

"Doctor?"

Evans stared at him for a moment. She would kill him. She looked down at the desk, rubbed her forehead. "Sit down," she said.

She took the pack of cigarettes from her desk drawer. "Would you care to smoke?"

The old man accepted one. She watched him carefully. His brown eyes were rimmed with red; they looked apologetic.

"I smoke too much," he said. "But I can't quit."

She gave him a light. "More people around here are quitting every day."

Havelmann exhaled smoothly. "What can I do for you?"

What can I do for *you*, sir.

"First, I want to play a little game." Evans took a handkerchief out of her pocket. She moved a brass paperweight, a small model of the Lincoln Memorial, to the centre of the desk blotter. "I want you to watch what I'm doing now."

Havelmann smiled. "Don't tell me – you're going to make it disappear, right?"

She tried to ignore him. She covered the paperweight with the handkerchief. "What's under this handkerchief?"

"Can we put a little bet on it?"

"Not this time."

"A paperweight."

"That's wonderful." Evans leaned back. "Now I want you to answer a few questions."

The old man looked around the office curiously: at the closed blinds, at the computer terminal and keyboard against the wall, at the pad of switches in the corner of the desk. His eyes came to rest on the mirror high in the wall opposite the window. "That's a two-way mirror."

Evans sighed. "No kidding."

"Are you videotaping this?"

"Does it matter to you?"

"I'd like to know. Common courtesy."

"Yes, we're being recorded. Now answer the questions."

Havelmann seemed to shrink in the face of her hostility. "Sure."

"How do you like it here?"

"It's OK. A little boring. A man couldn't even catch a disease here, from the looks of it, if you know what I mean. I don't mean any offense, Doctor. I haven't been here long enough to get the feel of the place."

Evans rocked slowly back and forth. "How do you know I'm a doctor?"

"Aren't you a doctor? I thought you were. This is a hospital, isn't it? So I figured when they sent me in to see you, you must be a doctor."

"I am a doctor. My name is Evans."

"Pleased to meet you, Dr Evans."

She would kill him. "How long have you been here?"

The man tugged on his earlobe. "I must have just got here today. I don't think it was too long ago. A couple of hours. I've been talking to the nurses at their station."

What she wouldn't give for three fingers of Jack Daniel's. She looked at him over the steeple of her fingers. "Such talkative nurses."

"I'm sure they're doing their jobs."

"I'm sure. Tell me what you were doing before you came to this ... hospital."

"You mean right before?"

"Yes."

"I was working."

"Where do you work?"

"I've got my own company – ITG Computer Systems. We design programs for a lot of people. We're close to getting a big contract

with Ma Bell. We swing that and I can retire by the time I'm forty –
if Uncle Sam will take his hand out of my pocket long enough for
me to count my change."

Evans made a note on her pad. "Do you have a family?"

Havelmann looked at her steadily. His gaze was that of an earnest
young college student, incongruous on a man of his age. He stared
at her as if he could not imagine why she would ask him these
abrupt questions. She detested his weakness; it raised in her a fury
that pushed her to the edge of insanity. It was already a bad day,
and it would get worse.

"I don't understand what you're after," Havelmann said, with
considerable dignity. "But just so your record shows the facts: I've
got a wife, Helen, and two kids. Ronnie's nine and Susan's five. We
have a nice big house and a Lincoln and a Porsche. I follow the
Braves and I don't eat quiche. What else would you like to know?"

"Lots of things. Eventually I'll find them out." Evans tapped her
pencil on the edge of the desk. "Is there anything you'd like to ask
me? How you came to be here? How long you're going to have to
stay? Who you are?"

Havelmann's voice went cold. "I know who I am."

"Who are you, then?"

"My name is Robert Havelmann."

"That's right," Dr Evans said. "What year is it?"

Havelmann watched her warily, as if he were about to be tricked.
"What are you talking about? It's 1984."

"What time of year?"

"Spring."

"How old are you?"

"Thirty-five."

"What do I have under this handkerchief?"

Havelmann looked at the handkerchief on the desk as if noticing
it for the first time. His shoulders tightened and he looked suspi-
ciously at her.

"How should I know?"

He was back again that afternoon, just as rumpled, just as innocent. How could a person get old and remain innocent? She could not remember things ever being that easy. "Sit down," she said.

"Thanks. What can I do for you, Doctor?"

"I want to follow up on the argument we had this morning."

Havelmann smiled. "Argument? This morning?"

"Don't you remember talking to me this morning?"

"I never saw you before."

Evans watched him coldly. Havelmann shifted in his chair.

"How do you know I'm a doctor?"

"Aren't you a doctor? They told me I should go in to see Dr Evans in room 10."

"I see. If you weren't here this morning, where were you?"

Havelmann hesitated. "Let's see – I was at work. I remember telling Helen – my wife – that I'd try to get home early. She's always complaining because I stay late. The company's pretty busy right now: big contract in the works. Susan's in the school play, and we have to be there by eight. And I want to get home in time to do some yard work. It looked like a good day for it."

Evans made a note. "What season is it?"

Havelmann fidgeted like a child, looked at the window, where the blinds were still closed.

"Spring," he said. "Sunny, warm – very nice weather. The redbuds are just starting to come out."

Without a word Evans got out of her chair and opened the blinds, revealing a barren field swept with drifts of snow. Dead grass whipped in the strong wind, and clouds rolled in the sky.

"What about this?"

Havelmann stared. His back straightened. He tugged at his earlobe.

"Isn't that a bitch. If you don't like the weather here – wait ten minutes."

"What about the redbuds?"

"This weather will probably kill them. I hope Helen made the kids wear their jackets."

Evans looked out the window. Nothing had changed. She drew the blinds and sat down again.

"What year is it?"

Havelmann adjusted himself in his chair, calm again. "What do you mean? It's 1984."

"Did you ever read that book?"

"Slow down a minute. What book?"

Evans wondered what he would do if she got up and ground her thumbs into his eyes. "The book by George Orwell titled *Nineteen Eighty-Four*." She forced herself to speak slowly. "Are you familiar with it?"

"Sure. We had to read it in college." Was there a trace of irritation beneath Havelmann's innocence? Evans sat as still as she could.

"I remember it made quite an impression on me," Havelmann continued.

"What kind of impression?"

"I expected something different from the professor. He was a confessed liberal. I expected some kind of bleeding-heart book. It wasn't like that at all."

"Did it make you uncomfortable?"

"No. It didn't tell me anything I didn't know already. It just showed what was wrong with collectivism. You know – communism represses the individual, destroys initiative. It claims it has the interests of the majority at heart. And it denies all human values. That's what I got out of *Nineteen Eighty-Four*, though to hear that professor talk about it, it was all about Nixon and Vietnam."

Evans kept still. Havelmann went on.

"I've seen the same mentality at work in business. The large corporations, they're just like the government. Big, slow. You could show them a way to save a billion, and they'd squash you like a bug because it's too much trouble to change."

"You sound like you've got some resentments," said Evans.

The old man smiled. "I do, don't I. I admit it. I've thought lot about it. But I have faith in people. Someday I may just run for state assembly and see whether I can do some good."

Her pencil point snapped. She looked at Havelmann, who looked back at her. After a moment she focused her attention on the notebook. The broken point had left a black scar across her precise handwriting.

"That's a good idea," she said quietly, her eyes still lowered. "You still don't remember arguing with me this morning?"

"I never saw you before I walked in this door. What were we supposed to be fighting about?"

He was insane. Evans almost laughed aloud at the thought – of course he was insane – why else would he be here? The question, she forced herself to consider rationally, was the nature of his insanity. She picked up the paperweight and handed it across to him. "We were arguing about this paperweight," she said. "I showed it to you, and you said you'd never seen it before."

Havelmann examined the paperweight. "Looks ordinary to me. I could easily forget something like this. What's the big deal?"

"You'll note that it's a model of the Lincoln Memorial."

"You probably got it at some gift shop. DC is full of junk like that."

"I haven't been to Washington in a long time."

"I wish I could avoid it. I live there. Bethesda, anyway."

Evans closed her notebook. "I have a possible diagnosis of your condition," she said suddenly.

"What condition?"

This time the laughter was harder to repress. Tears almost came to her eyes. She caught her breath and continued. "You exhibit the symptoms of Korsakov's syndrome. Have you ever heard of that before?"

Havelmann looked as blank as a whitewashed wall. "No."

"Korsakov's syndrome is an unusual form of memory loss. Recorded cases go back to the late 1800s. There was a famous one in the 1970s – famous to doctors, I mean. A Marine sergeant named Arthur Briggs. He was in his fifties, in good health aside from the lingering effects of alcoholism, and had been a career noncom until his discharge in the mid-sixties after twenty years in the service. He functioned normally until the early seventies, when he lost his memory of any events that occurred to him after September 1944. He could remember in vivid detail, as if they had just happened, events up until that time. But of the rest of his life – nothing. Not only that, his continuing memory was affected so that he could remember events that occurred in the present only for a period of minutes, after which he would forget totally."

"I can remember what happened to me right up until I walked into this room."

"That's what Sergeant Briggs told his doctors. To prove it he told them that World War II was going strong, that he was stationed in San Francisco in preparation for being sent to the Philippines, that it looked like the St Louis Browns might finally win a pennant if they could hold on through September, and that he was twenty years old. He had the outlook and abilities of an intelligent twenty-year-old. He couldn't remember anything that happened to him longer than twenty minutes. The world had gone on, but he was permanently stuck in 1944."

"That's horrible."

"So it seemed to the doctor in charge – at first. Later he speculated that it might not be so bad. The man still had a current emotional life. He could still enjoy the present; it just didn't stick with him. He could remember his youth, and for him his youth had never ended. He never aged. He never saw his friends grow old and die; he never remembered that he himself had grown up to be a lonely alcoholic. His girlfriend was still waiting for him back in Columbia, Missouri. He was twenty years old forever. He had made a clean escape."

Evans opened a desk drawer and took out a hand mirror. "How old are you?" she asked.

Havelmann looked frightened. "Look, why are we doing—"

"How old are you?" Evans's voice was quiet but determined. Inside her a pang of joy threatened to break her heart.

"I'm thirty-five. What the hell—"

Shoving the mirror at him was as satisfying as firing a gun. Havelmann took it, glanced at her, then tentatively, like the most nervous of freshmen checking the grade on his final exam, looked at his reflection. "Jesus Christ," he said. He started to tremble.

"What happened? What did you do to me!" He got out of the chair, his expression contorted. "What did you do to me! I'm thirty-five! What happened?"

Dr Evans stood in front of the mirror in her office. She was wearing her uniform. It was as rumpled as Havelmann's suit. She had the tunic unbuttoned and was feeling her left breast. She lay down on the floor and continued the examination. The lump was undeniable. No pain yet.

She sat up, reached for the pack of cigarettes on the desk top, fished out the last one and lit it. She crumpled the pack and threw it at the wastebasket. Two points. She had been quite a basketball player in college, twenty years before. She lay back down and took a long drag on the cigarette, inhaling deeply, exhaling the smoke with force, with a sigh of exhaustion. She probably couldn't make it up and down the court a single time anymore.

She turned her head to look out the window. The blinds were open, revealing the same barren landscape that showed before. There was a knock at the door.

"Come in," she said.

Havelmann entered. He saw her lying on the floor, raised an eyebrow, grinned. "You're Dr Evans?"

"I am."

"Can I sit here, or should I lie down too?"

"Do whatever you fucking well please."

He sat in the chair. He had not taken offense. "So what did you want to see me about?"

Evans got up, buttoned her tunic, sat in the swivel chair. She stared at him. "Have we ever met before?" she asked.

"No. I'm sure I'd remember."

He was sure he would remember. She would fucking kill him. He would remember that.

She ground out the last inch of cigarette. She felt her jaw muscles tighten; she looked down at the ashtray in regret. "Now I have to quit."

"I should quit. I smoke too much myself."

"I want you to listen to me closely now," she said slowly. "Don't respond until I'm finished."

"My name is Major D. S. Evans, and I am a military psychologist. This office is in the infirmary of NECDEC, the National Emergency Center for Defense Communications, located one thousand feet below a hillside in West Virginia. As far as we know we are the only surviving governmental body in the continental United States. The scene you see through this window is being relayed from a surface monitor in central Nebraska; by computer command I can connect us with any of the twelve monitors still functioning on the surface."

Evans turned to her keyboard and typed in a command; the scene through the window snapped to a shot of broken masonry and twisted steel reinforcement rods. The view was obscured by dust caked on the camera lens and by a heavy snowfall. Evans typed in an additional command and touched one of the switches on her desk. A blast of static, a hiss like frying bacon, came from the speaker.

"That's Dallas. The sound is a reading of the background radiation registered by detectors at the site of this camera." She typed in another command and the image on the "window" flashed through a succession of equally desolate scenes, holding ten seconds on each before switching to the next. A desert in twilight, motionless under low clouds; a murky underwater shot in which the remains of a building were just visible; a denuded forest half-buried in snow; a deserted highway overpass. With each change of scene the loudspeaker stopped for a split second, then the hiss resumed.

Havelmann watched all of this soberly.

"This has been the state of the surface for a year now, ever since the last bombs fell. To our knowledge there are no human beings alive in North America – in the Northern Hemisphere, for that matter. Radio transmissions from South America, New Zealand, and Australia have one by one ceased in the past eight months. We have not observed a living creature above the level of an insect through any of our monitors since the beginning of the year. It is the summer of 2010. Although, considering the situation, counting years by the old system seems a little futile to me."

Dr Evans slid open a desk drawer and took out an automatic. She placed it in the middle of the desk blotter and leaned back, her right hand touching the edge of the desk near the gun.

"You are now going to tell me that you never heard of any of this, and that you've never seen me before in your life," she said. "Despite the fact that I have been speaking to you daily for two weeks and that you have had this explanation from me at least three times during that period. You are going to tell me that it is 1984 and that you are thirty-five years old, despite the absurdity of such a claim. You are going to feign amazement and confusion; the more I insist that you face these facts, the more you are going to become distressed. Eventually you will break down into tears and expect me to sympathize. You can go to hell."

Evans's voice had grown angrier as she spoke. She had to stop; it was almost more than she could do. When she resumed she was under control again. "If you persist in this sham, I may kill you. I assure you that no one will care if I do. You may speak now."

Havelmann stared at the window. His mouth opened and closed stupidly. How old he looked, how feeble. Evans felt a sudden surge of doubt. What if she were wrong? She had an image of herself as she might appear to him: arrogant, bitter, an incomprehensible inquisitor whose motives for tormenting him were a total mystery. She watched him. After a few minutes his mouth closed; the eyes blinked rapidly and were clear.

"Please. Tell me what you're talking about."

Evans shuddered. "The gun is loaded. Keep talking."

"What do you want me to say? I never heard of any of this. Only this morning I saw my wife and kids, and everything was all right. Now you give me this story about atomic war and 2010. What, have I been asleep for thirty years?"

"You didn't act very surprised to be here when you walked in. If you're so disoriented, how do you explain how you got here?"

The man sat heavily in the chair. "I don't remember. I guess I thought I came here – to the hospital, I thought – to get a checkup. I didn't think about it. You must know how I got here."

"I do. But I think you know too, and you're just playing a game with me – with all of us. The others are worried, but I'm sick of it. I can see through you, so you may as well quit the act. You were famous for your sincerity, but I always suspected that was an act, too, and I'm not falling for it. You didn't start this game soon enough for me to be persuaded you're crazy, despite what the others may think."

Evans played with the butt of her dead cigarette. "Or this could be a delusional system," she continued. "You think you're in a hospital, and your schizophrenia has progressed to the point where you deny all facts that don't go along with your attempts to evade responsibility. I suppose in some sense such an insanity would absolve you. If that's the case, I should be more objective.

"Well, I can't. I'm failing my profession. Too bad." Emotion had drained away from her until, by the end, she felt as if she were speaking from across a continent instead of a desk.

"I still don't know what you're talking about. Where are my wife and kids?"

"They're dead."

Havelmann sat rigidly. The only sound was the hiss of the radiation detector. "Let me have a cigarette."

"There are no cigarettes left. I just smoked my last one." Evans touched the ashtray. "I made two cartons last a year."

Havelmann's gaze dropped. "How old my hands are! Helen has lovely hands."

"Why are you going on with this charade?"

The old man's face reddened. "God damn you! Tell me what happened!"

"The famous Havelmann rage. Am I supposed to be frightened now?"

The hiss from the loudspeaker seemed to increase. Havelmann lunged for the gun. Evans snatched it and pushed back from the desk. The old man grabbed the paperweight and raised it to strike. She pointed the gun at him.

"Your wife didn't make the plane in time. She was at the western White House. I don't know where your damned kids were – probably vaporized with their own families. You, however, had Operation Kneecap to save you, Mr President. Now sit down and tell me why you've been playing games, or I'll kill you right here and now. Sit down!"

A light seemed to dawn on Havelmann. "You're insane."

"Put the paperweight back on the desk."

He did. He sat.

"But you can't simply be crazy," Havelmann continued. "There's no reason why you should take me away from my home and subject me to this. This is some kind of plot. The government. The CIA."

"And you're thirty-five years old?"

Havelmann examined his hands again. "You've done something to me."

"And the camps? Administrative Order 31?"

"If I'm the president, then why are you quizzing me here? Why can't I remember a thing about it?"

"Stop it. Stop it right now," Evans said. She heard her voice for the first time. It sounded more like that of an old man than Havelmann's. "I can't take any more lies. I swear that I'll kill you. First it was the commander-in-chief routine, calisthenics, stiff upper lips and discipline. Then the big brother, let's have a whiskey and talk it over, son. Yessir, Mr President."

Havelmann stared at her. He was going to make her kill him, and she knew she wouldn't be strong enough not to.

"Now you can't remember anything," she said. "Your boys are confused; they're fed up. Well, I'm fed up too."

"If this is true, you've got to help me."

"I don't give a rat's ass about helping you!" Evans shouted. "I'm interested in making you tell the truth! Don't you realize that we're dead? I don't care about your feeble sense of what's right and wrong; just tell me what's keeping you going. Who do you think you're going to impress? You think you've got an election to win? A place in history to protect? There isn't going to be any more history! History ended last August!

"So spare me the fantasy about the hospital and the nonexistent nurses' station. Someone with Korsakov's wouldn't make up that story. He would recognize the difference between a window and an HD screen. A dozen other slips. You're not a good enough actor."

Her hand trembled. The gun was heavy. Her voice trembled, too, and she despised herself for it. "Sometimes I think the only thing that's kept me alive is knowing I had half a pack of cigarettes left. That and the desire to make you crawl."

The old man sat looking at the gun in her hand. "I was the president?"

"No," said Evans. "I made it up."

His eyes seemed to sink farther back in the network of lines surrounding them.

"I started a war?"

Evans felt her heart race. "Stop lying! You sent the strike force; you ordered the preemptive launch."

"I'm old. How old am I?"

"You know how old—" She stopped. She could hardly catch her breath. She felt a sharp pain in her breast. "You're sixty-one."

"Jesus, Mary, Joseph."

"That's it? That's all you can say?"

Havelmann stared hollowly, then slowly, so slowly that at first it was not apparent what he was doing, lowered his head into his hands and began to cry. His sobs were almost inaudible over the hiss of the radiation detector. Evans watched him. She rested her elbows on the desk, steadying the gun with both hands. Havelmann's head shook in front of her. Despite his age, his grey hair was thick.

After a moment Evans reached over and switched off the loudspeaker. The hissing stopped.

Eventually Havelmann stopped crying. He raised his head. He looked dazed. His expression became unreadable. He looked at the doctor and the gun. "My name is Robert Havelmann," he said. "Why are you pointing that gun at me?"

"Don't do this," said Evans. "Please."

"Do what? Who are you?"

Evans watched his face blur. Through her tears he looked like a much younger man. The gun drooped. She tried to lift it, but it was as if she were made of smoke – there was no substance to her, and it was all she could do to keep from dissipating, let alone kill anyone as clean and innocent as Robert Havelmann.

He reached forward. He took the gun from her hand. "Are you all right?" he asked.

Dr Evans sat in her office, hoping that it wasn't going to be a bad day. The pain in her breast had not come that day, but she was out of cigarettes. She searched the desk on the odd chance she might have missed a pack, even a single butt, in the corner of one of the drawers. No luck.

She gave up and turned to face the window. The blinds were open, revealing the snow-covered field. She watched the clouds roll before the wind. It was dark. Winter. Nothing was alive.

"It's cold outside," she whispered.

There was a knock at the door. Dear god, leave me alone, she thought. Please leave me alone.

"Come in," she said.

The door opened and an old man in a rumpled suit entered. "Dr Evans? I'm Robert Havelmann. What did you want to talk about?"

STORMING HELL

John Lambshead

"Steampunk" applies Victorian technology, attitudes and scientific theories to a future that might have been, perhaps; in this case a sparkling yarn of interstellar naval combat...

John Lambshead is a semi-retired research scientist in the fields of ecology, evolution and biodiversity. He has always had another life designing computer games and writing fiction and military history. Married with two adult daughters, he lives on the North Kent coast of England. A lead story in Baen's Universe *magazine, this became a Best of the Year choice.*

THE SUN ROSE slowly on another long day. Crystal showers of frozen air fell gently, sublimed upwards under the sun's rays, only to refreeze and fall again. Fine snow littered the surface like baking sugar, lending the splintered landscape a surreal beauty. This was a place of dialectical extremes, of hot and cold, of light and dark and of stone and dust.

The only splash of colour came from Sarah's multiple reflections in the viewing port. Convention decreed that her long dress and tailored jacket be Royal Navy blue, her blouse cream, but she was allowed to express some individuality in a neck tie and the band around her straw hat. She elected to wear a defiant red.

Sarah was too keyed up to enjoy the bleak landscape. She gazed out of the porthole, lost in her thoughts, disinterested in the view.

"Ma'am?" a piping voice sounded behind her.

She turned, moving carefully so that her skirt would not fly up.

A boy in a midshipman's uniform half made a salute then thought better of it. "Is that your sea trunk, ma'am?"

She nodded in assent and he clicked his fingers at the porters. Two Selenites scuttled forward, sharp claws tapping on the stone floor. Like all lunar natives, they were six limbed but their exoskeleton was without the tripartite division that characterized the insect body. The size of a large dog, they stood mostly on four legs so that their front claws could be used as hands. The Queen Below bred them for Port Bedford's use as part of the Cooperation Pact with the British Empire. A not unpleasant wet-straw smell drifted off the creatures as they grappled with her luggage.

"The captain presents his compliments, ma'am, and asks you to accompany me to the ship."

"Thank you," she said. "Lead on."

They made a strange crocodile through the narrow corridors, the midshipman in front, her behind and the Selenites bringing up the rear. Convention decreed that they should walk in single file on the right. This necessitated one of the Selenites walking backwards, something that seemed to discommode him not at all. She thought of the Selenite as 'him', though 'it' was probably a more accurate pronoun for a sterile worker.

Sarah stepped over the lip of a double-doored hatchway into the aethership, revealing far too much ankle for her liking. The porters banged her trunk against the hatchway. She admonished them and they listened politely, clacking lateral mouth mandibles in reply before forcing her trunk through the narrow opening. The midshipman walked on without pausing, causing her to half run to catch up. It was so undignified; her instructors had impressed upon her the importance of comportment for a lady but what was one to do?

The air inside the aethership held a sharp tang of carbolic soap, like a newly scrubbed hospital. The ship had recently been refurbished so it did not yet smell of stale sweat seasoned with the aroma of ripe latrine but, given time, it would. Port Bedford's air was clean and natural in comparison, if a trifle musty, refreshed as it was from fungal forests below.

She was soon completely disorientated in the maze of cramped passageways and staircases. Sailors hurrying about their duties gave way when her party needed to pass. She ignored their interested glances. A final spiral staircase gave access to the bridge. The midshipman stopped in front of a man wearing a captain's uniform and smartly snapped to attention, saluting.

The captain, who was deep in discussion with one of his lieutenants, ignored them. She took the opportunity to study the man who would be in control of her life for the foreseeable future. He was about thirty-five, tall, slim and fair-haired – a typical member of the Anglo-Norman ruling families. She resigned herself to being patronized when he finally acknowledged her existence.

"My dear Miss Brown, welcome aboard Her Majesty's Aethership *Cassandra*." He pumped her hand vigorously and grinned. "I trust that they made you comfortable at Port Bedford while you waited for us. I am afraid we had a little trouble with our cavorite panels, which delayed our departure."

"Thank you, yes, I was quite comfortable," she said.

"Either I am getting older, or the pilots are getting younger and prettier," said the captain to the officer beside him.

She blushed: the interview was not going precisely to her expectations. "This is my first independent posting but I assure you that I am properly qualified, Captain Fitzwilliam," she said. She tried to sound brisk and efficient but it came out as pompous.

"I never doubted it, dear lady," he said. He cocked his head to one side and looked expectantly at her.

For a second Sarah's mind blanked and then she realized that she had unaccountably forgotten to carry out her first duty. Fumbling in her bag, she finally managed to remove the two critical pieces of paper. Why did everything take twice as long when one was flustered? "My posting and pilot's certificate, sir," she said, handing them to him.

He cast a quick eye over them as convention decreed before handing the certificate back.

"Show the lady to her room, Mister Chomondely," he said to the midshipman.

"Aye, aye, sir."

She made to go but the captain stopped her with a raised finger. "I hope to have the pleasure of your company at dinner tonight, Miss Brown, but in the meantime, stow your gear quickly and strap yourself in, as we shall be lifting shortly." He glared at the other officers as if defying them to contradict him.

The midshipman showed her aft to a small cabin, taking his leave of her without entering. The click-clack of Selenite claws disappeared down the corridor as she shut and locked the door. Pilots had a special status on Queen Mary's ships because the Royal Navy still struggled with the concept of a lady in the crew. Ruling queens were a long accepted tradition in Britain, ever since Queen Boudicca told her groom to sharpen the scythe blades on her chariot wheels while she looked up London on the map, but ladies on a Royal Navy bridge were anathema.

The Senior Service had settled for a typical British compromise. She was classed as an officer and so bunked aft and ate in the wardroom. However, it was strictly understood that she most assuredly had no place in the chain of command. One of her instructors had compared the position of Royal Navy pilots with that of the Army's regimental mascots – and not to the detriment of the latter.

Stowing her luggage took little time as there was very little storage space to put anything in. She left most of her possessions in her trunk, which she pushed with some difficulty under the bunk. Then she arranged herself on the narrow bed and fastened herself down with the safety webbing. She stared blankly at the featureless grey walls, trying to control her breathing. Terrors nibbled at the edges of her mind like hyenas around a wounded beast but she was determined not to give way to hysteria. She inhaled and held her breath for a count of two, then again to a count of three and so on. Slowly, she brought her rebellious body under control.

Sarah balanced a watercolour miniature on her stomach that depicted the likeness of a cavalier sitting upon a rearing horse. He waved his hat high over his head with one hand while the other pointed a pistol at a coach. A speech-bubble depicted him saying "Stand and deliver all enemies of the crown".

She composed herself and prayed, slipping gently into a trance, but she was nervous and could not quite achieve enthasis. When she opened her eyes, she saw nothing but featureless light grey haze, like sunlit fog.

"Captain, Captain, are you there?" she asked.

White rings formed cloud-like shapes, sharply defined on the outside edge but fading into mist in the centre. They developed, imploded, and were replaced in a repetitive moving pattern. She prayed harder and for a moment thought she saw the shadow of a figure but it drifted away when she reached out. Her stomach lurched and she disconnected, suddenly back in her cabin. She was upside down, hanging by the webbing, which alternatively pulled and relaxed at her body as she became lighter and heavier. The three coloured galvanic warning lights over the cabin door shone steadily; the ship was lifting from the lunar surface.

Her stomach lurched again as she first became weightless and then fell back into her bunk as down reasserted itself. Obviously the engineering problems had not been entirely addressed. She grabbed the bowl that a steward had thoughtfully clipped to her cabin wall and was violently and horribly sick.

She was a fashionable five minutes late, as befitted a lady. The gentlemen failed to stand when she entered the captain's cabin. Naval surgeons had become exasperated at patching up young officers injured while making ever more gallant gestures of respect to the ship's pilot, so the usual niceties were ignored.

"Sit opposite me, Miss Brown," said the captain, gesturing to an empty place at the table. "May I introduce my first lieutenant, Mister Brierly, my engineering officer, Mister Fadden, and Lieutenants Crowly and Smythe. Major Riley here is the commander of our marine contingent." He gestured at an officer dressed in red rather than the otherwise ubiquitous navy blue.

She exchanged polite greetings with the men. Brierly was a good ten years older than his captain and his accent suggested a modest north country background. He must be competent to rise to first lieutenant, but not quite good enough to be posted captain without patronage.

Fadden was a cheerful, round-faced character whose figure suggested that he was an accomplished trencherman. Engineering officers, like pilots, were a relatively new innovation in the Royal Navy. The complexity of operating aetherships demanded specialist skills, something only reluctantly conceded by the traditionalists who tended to regard any change as a source of potential ruin to the service.

One of the young lieutenants sprang up to seat her, his breeding as a gentleman momentarily overcoming official regulations. She was not sure which lieutenant was which, so she murmured vague thanks.

"May I congratulate you on your splendid gown, Miss Brown? It brings a welcome splash of colour to our grey existence," said the captain.

"Yes, top-hole," said a lieutenant, eyeing her enthusiastically. She thought it was the one called Smythe.

His captain quelled the young officer with a glance.

Actually, she was pleased that they had noticed how much effort she had expended in dressing for dinner. She had always considered that the maroon evening dress showed her modest figure off to best effect.

Now that the party was complete the steward served soup. She looked down at the complex array of cutlery and glasses in front of her and felt the familiar surge of panic. A woman in a Royal Navy wardroom had to look, behave and think like a lady – had to *be* a lady. She had been extensively trained at the Academy to play the role but deep down she feared that one day someone would point the finger and publicly denounce her as a fraud.

Inside, she was still the same fourteen-year-old daughter of a Bermondsey costermonger that she had been before the Spiritualist Church had selected her in the annual sweep. The sneers and gibes of the better-bred girls in the dormitory had cut deep and left permanent scars. She had been plucked out of one world and dropped into another, gilded like a fake antique in an auction. The most frightening thing of all was that she couldn't go back to her old life if she failed in the new one. She now lacked the social and practical skills to survive in Bermondsey. Sarah was not even her real name. Her parents had christened her Daisy but ladies did not have flower names. The better London houses were full of maids with names like Daisy, Rose, or Violet "below stairs" but such names were never found "above".

It took a moment to register that Captain Fitzwilliam was speaking.

"I was not sure that you would be joining us, Miss Brown. I was concerned that you might be indisposed." He grinned at her slyly.

He knew she had been sick! How had he known? She glared at the steward who avoided making eye contact. The little rat had dobbed her in to the captain. She was so angry that she forgot her anxieties, which on reflection might have been Fitzwilliam's intention all along. This one would merit watching carefully, as he might be a lot more subtle than he looked.

"Not at all, Captain," she said with a smile. "I have been looking forward to dinner."

"I'm impressed by your fortitude," said Fitzwilliam. "Personally, I found getting underway so disturbing that I nearly lost my lunch. I haven't experienced rolls like that since I rounded Cape Horn as a midshipman."

The engineer adopted a defensive expression and talked for some time on the difficulties involved in balancing galvanic flow through the various cavorite panels that repelled the moon. Sarah knew the basic theory, of course, the polarity of cavorite could be excited using galvanism, but she was uninterested in the practical details. The Navy called the composite ceramic-metal alloy "cavorite" in honour of the inventor of the first aethership. Cavorite was also used to maintain normal body weight in the ship once it was clear of the pull of a heavenly body. This was essential as early explorations had revealed that people weakened quickly when weightless.

Sarah let the conversation drift over her and gave the excellent dinner her full attention. She had gone hungry far too often as a child, so the habit of wolfing down food when it was available was hard to eradicate. She forced herself to toy fashionably with a potato, as befitted a lady. A word caught her attention.

"Let's hope we achieve metastasis more smoothly," said Fitzwilliam.

"I've never experienced metastasis," said Lieutenant Crowly, or maybe it was Smythe. "What's it like?"

The first lieutenant, Brierly, crooked a forefinger at the young man, summoning him closer. "You want to know what metastasis feels like? Well, I'll tell you. It's as if someone forces his fist down your throat and pulls you inside out."

Brierly snapped his hand at the young man's face, causing him to recoil back in his seat so hard that he almost went over backwards. The older officers laughed at the younger man's discomfort.

"Fortunately, the whole thing is over quickly," said Fadden.

"As short-lived as a young man's stamina," said Major Riley, eliciting another round of guffaws.

"Gentlemen, lady present," murmured Fitzwilliam. "Is metastasis equally fast and unpleasant for you, Miss Brown?"

"Pilots are rather busy at the time, finding our way and so on," she replied, vaguely.

The Pilot's Academy had firm views on what knowledge was suitable for general circulation and what was best restricted.

"But of course you have your spirit guide to help you," Fitzwilliam said.

"Can you pilot without a spirit?" asked Brierly.

"In theory," she replied. "But it is easier and safer if the pilot is in enthasis with a guide."

"And who is your guide?" asked Fitzwilliam.

"Captain James Hind, the highwayman and cavalier, who was hanged for high treason in 1652. It is said he tried to assassinate Cromwell himself on the London road from Huntingdon. The Lord Protector had seven guards and Hind but one accomplice so the attempt failed. Captain Hind barely escaped; his friend was taken and executed on the spot."

"Indeed!" Fitzwilliam raised an eyebrow. "Then we must drink a toast to the good Captain Hind, gentlemen, as we shall be entrusting ourselves to his care shortly."

The men raised their glasses and gave a ragged chorus of "Captain Hind". She raised her glass to her lips with them but did not drink. She had learned to pace herself very carefully with alcohol. The temptation to drown her social anxieties in the comfort blanket of intoxication was too strong.

"Do you think that the spirit guides really are the souls of dead people, Miss Brown, or something inhuman?" asked Lieutenant Crowly.

"The Spiritualist Church is certainly of the view that they are human. They believe that the soul passes through layers of heavenly spheres as it gains enlightenment, until it is holy enough to come back and guide the living," she replied.

"I have often wondered why spirit guides devote so much time to our needs," said Fitzwilliam. "What's in it for them?"

This was delicate and she felt the glow of a blush heating her cheeks. The captain's smile broadened. Bastard!

"Perhaps the Church is right and they help us because they are enlightened," she said, trotting out the official explanation.

"Ah, altruism, that explains it," said Fitzwilliam, with a cynical smile. "Nevertheless, it is interesting that pilots are drawn mostly from the ranks of young women."

"That can partly be explained by tradition," said Fadden, interrupting. "Von Reichenbach recruited girls from the poorer social classes to act as sensitives for his experiments into life energy and how to channel it for psychokinesis. I suspect that, initially, this was simply because they were cheaply hired and young women are malleable and suggestive."

"I have never found young women to be particularly malleable or suggestive," said Fitzwilliam, smiling at her.

She suspected that his boyish smile had made many young women very malleable to his suggestions indeed, perhaps too much so for their own good.

The engineer ploughed on pedantically, as if his captain had not spoken. "Of course, as the creators of new life, young women are particularly strong in universal life energy, what Von Reichenbach termed Odic Force."

"The kirks in Scotland think that spirit guides are daemons from Hell," said Crowly, stubbornly returning to his point.

"Oh, the Wee Free kirks. What would we do without them?" asked Fadden, sarcastically.

"Do you think you consort with daemons, Miss Brown? Are you dealing with Heaven or Hell?" asked Fitzwilliam.

"The Spiritualist Church would deny the existence of either," Sarah replied.

"Have you ever tried to check the veracity of your Captain Hind?" Fitzwilliam asked.

"There definitely was a real person called James Hind," said Sarah. "Sometimes what he tells me about his past agrees with the records and sometimes it is contradicted." She shrugged.

"That could simply mean that the records are wrong." Fitzwilliam laughed. "Who is naive enough to believe official documents?"

"Sometimes the contradictions are of a particular nature," said Sarah.

"Such as?" Fitzwilliam asked. He sounded genuinely interested.

"Well, for example, my Captain Hind says that he was the son of a gentleman but the parish register records his father as a butcher."

"Well, he wouldn't be the first man to embellish the truth to a pretty girl," said Fitzwilliam, with a smirk.

"According to last month's *Times*, the Wee Free want the Spiritualist Church banned throughout the Empire and the Royal Naval Pilot's Academy closed." Crowly would not be deflected.

"That's ridiculous. We would have problems reaching even Venus and Mars without pilots," said Fitzwilliam.

"Many books of the Bible warn against spiritualism, especially Leviticus," Crowly said.

"Oh, Leviticus," said Fitzwilliam, sniffing. "If we took Leviticus literally, we would have to stone half the aristocracy."

"This is all superstitious twaddle," said Fadden. "There is a simple scientific explanation for metastasis. We flood the ship with

Noetic radiation, which a pilot controls using her Odic Force and, hence, achieves psychokinesis."

"But what about spirit guides and the visions experienced by pilots?" asked Crowly.

"If you are surprised that young women have hysterical visions when under stress then you know nothing about the fairer sex, my boy," Fadden said. "The sooner science discovers how to control Noetic energies with machines then the sooner delightful young ladies, like Miss Brown here, can go back to fulfilling God's plan for them by marrying and having babies."

Fitzwilliam winked at Sarah. She could not decide which of the two men most deserved a slap.

Sarah adjusted the pilot's leather seat on the bridge into a semi-reclining position, which supported her body comfortably from head to toe, and fiddled with the straps that held her down.

"When you are ready, Miss Brown," said Fitzwilliam, clearly becoming impatient.

Sarah ignored him and gave everything one last check. Let the so-and-so wait – his mother had to. She also tried to ignore the revolver that she knew Brierly concealed behind his back. It was his duty to kill her if something went badly wrong. She closed her eyes.

"Captain Hind, are you there?" she asked.

Nothing happened so she repeated the phrase. A cold draught brushed her face. When she opened her eyes, Hind stood in front of her dressed in riding boots and a profusion of blue and red silk. He swept a feathered hat from his head and bowed in a single fluid motion. One of the petty officers on the bridge watched her, looking right through Hind. It had initially puzzled her that no one else could see her spirit guide. Now she just accepted the phenomenon. He appeared entirely corporal to her, not like a ghost at all.

"My dear Miss Brown, what a pleasure to be with you again," Hind said.

She knew that everyone else on the bridge would hear his words come out of her mouth, albeit in a masculine voice, but to her it seemed that Hind himself spoke.

Fadden signalled to a petty officer who pushed a long lever over with both hands. The engineer peered at a gauge. "Noetic radiation levels building up nicely."

Fitzwilliam gestured to her. "Very well, Pilot, you may..."

"I need your help, Captain," she prayed.

"Of course, my dear," Hind said, holding out his hand.

She reached upwards, touching him, and the world froze. She could see Fadden and Captain Fitzwilliam rigidly fixed in position and she knew that, if she turned around, she would find her body still reclining on the chair. She kept her eyes resolutely fixed on Captain Hind. Seeing yourself from outside was too much like dying.

She hung in cloud formations which dissolved in a haze of golden bubbles. They hosed up from somewhere below her, jostling and bursting on her. Little galvanic charges flashed from imploding bubbles, tickling where they encountered bare skin. She felt relaxed and contented, the anxieties that characterized her normal state draining from her. She could have stayed there forever, in blissful surrender, until the quiet peace of non-existence took her soul.

Mediums had been known to fall into comas. Some came round but many just slipped away into death.

A callused male hand slipped into hers and pulled gently. The spell broke and she dropped.

It was early morning on the moors so there was still a chill in the air despite the season. She stood in a valley carved out by a small stream that tumbled cheerfully down through the boulders and rocks strewn across the ground. Downstream, the valley opened into hedged fields and scattered clumps of trees. Smoke curled from a village sited where the stream combined with a larger cousin to form a modest river. Upstream, the valley narrowed as it climbed up to the moor.

"Come sit with me for a while, lass," said Hind, who was perched on a protruding wedge of granite.

Sarah wore a flouncy dress that parodied the costume of a seventeenth-century barmaid – a dress that was too tight and far, far too low-cut at the front. She concentrated hard, saying the prayer of metamorphosis, and her clothes became a more modest lady's split-skirt riding costume.

Hind grimaced. "I take it that you are in a hurry to start our journey. I was hoping—"

"It is my first independent posting," Sarah said, interrupting. "I can't concentrate on anything else until metastasis is complete."

"Very well, lass, but you have been neglecting me," said Hind, glumly, rising easily to his feet and brushing down his breeches. Hind was always most particular about his appearance.

"Yes, that's true," she said. "When this is out of the way, we will take a holiday together."

"I know just the place," Hind said, noticeably cheering up.

He walked to his black stallion, which grazed on some tough-looking grass nearby. She had not noticed the horse before but things did tend to arrive and disappear rather unexpectedly in the spirit world. Hind lifted his horse's reins off the ground and hauled himself into the dual saddle. He reached down and pulled Sarah effortlessly up into the rear seat.

Hind clicked his tongue and the horse moved off, following an unmetalled road that wound along by the stream. As they climbed into the wilderness, the road became narrower and more uneven. He put his hand on her knee and Sarah slapped it off. Her mind returned to the dinner table conversation. Did she think that Hind was truly the spirit of a man or some sort of daemon? Sometimes, it was difficult to tell the difference. He was certainly male, whatever else he was.

Sarah perceived the spirit world as English countryside, particularly the high moors. Every pilot experienced something different: a mighty city, jungles, deserts, treasure islands or even more exotic locations.

Routes in the spirit world were created by the passage of travellers, who were not necessarily human. The better the road, the more travelled the route. After some miles, they rode on an ancient highway surfaced with cracked and weathered cobblestones. It crumbled away at the edge and disappeared in places, vegetation intruding everywhere.

"This was once an important road," said Sarah. "But it looks as if it has been barely used for centuries. Who built it?"

"No idea; it must have been long before my time," said Hind.

A horseman appeared riding towards them with the unexpected suddenness that she associated with the spirit world. Hind cursed and pulled his horse off the road. As the stranger approached, she could see that he had the appearance of an ancient soldier. A highly polished bronze helmet and breastplate protected his head and chest, and a blood-red cloak fell around his shoulders.

Hind's stallion whinnied and shuffled its feet so he hushed it, patting the animal on the nose.

"Who is that?" Sarah asked.

"Quiet, girl, best not to speak of him – in fact, best not to even look at him."

Sarah lowered her eyes, obediently, but she could not resist a quick glance as the soldier passed. He seemed to feel Sarah's eyes and slowly turned his head to look at her. There was no face under the helmet, just a black void. A great cold penetrated her bones and emptiness sucked at her mind. She couldn't look away.

Hind grabbed the back of her head, forcing it down until she lost eye contact. The freezing cold disappeared, leaving her numb and tingling. Hind kept his hand warningly on the back of her head but she had learned her lesson and kept her eyes firmly shut until the tap of horse's hooves faded into the distance.

"What was that thing?" she asked.

"Nothing that concerns us," Hind replied. "I thought I told you to look away." He sighed. "I should have known that a maid's curiosity is stronger than her sense. Next time, I'll cover your eyes myself."

"Next time, I'll take your advice," Sarah promised.

"No, you won't," Hind said, grinning. He patted her thigh; this time she didn't object.

He guided the stallion off the road onto a path that was little more than an animal track. The ground became progressively waterlogged, small puddles of surface water giving way to pools. Bubbles intermittently rose to the surface and she smelt foetid marsh gas. The horse mistepped and one of its front legs sank into an innocuous-looking pool right up to the knee. The animal scrambled back onto firm ground dragging its leg from the black goo with a sucking noise. A sickly organic smell like rotting flesh filled the air and tiny flying things burst out of the mud before the hole filled with water.

"Shhh, shhh," said Hind, patting the animal's neck to calm it.

Sarah tied a scarf around her mouth and nose to keep the buzzing "flies" out.

A great lake stretched before them. Hind guided the horse along its shoreline without comment. Sarah amused herself by watching light play on the water ripples.

A small head on a long neck popped out of the lake near the shore, just behind them. It had a single eye, a cheerful grin and a bright yellow tuft of hair on top. A second and then a third popped up. Soon there were dozens all swaying hypnotically in patterns that rippled through the herd. They followed the travellers, sometimes submerging and resurfacing.

Sarah spotted the shadow of a large dark shape beneath the surface as if something was stalking the herd but it made no aggressive move. The snakes gradually caught up with the travellers, bobbing and weaving the whole time.

"Look at those water snakes! Aren't they just delightful?" Sarah said, pulling on Hind's arm.

Hind stiffened, glanced over his shoulder, and reacted instantly, pulling the wide-muzzled highwayman's blunderbuss from its leather scabbard.

The lake exploded; Sarah had an impression of stout leg-like flippers and a mouth the size of a cave entrance. Hind steadied the gun against his waist and discharged it with a loud crack. Billowing white smoke rolled across the water hiding the monster from view.

There was a scream like the hiss of a giant kettle-whistle and a mighty splash. When the smoke cleared, the lake was quiet again but dirty brown streaks of colour drifted up from below and spread out across the surface.

"What happened to the quaint little snakes?" said Sarah. Somehow, their fate seemed to matter to her.

"There were no quaint little snakes," said Hind. "They were lures on the beast's head to tempt the lack-witted close to the water."

"I don't think you should call yourself lack-witted," said Sarah, sympathetically. "You couldn't have known the monster was there."

"I meant you!" Hind said, indignantly. "'Look at those water snakes! Aren't they just delightful?'" He mimicked her voice in a mocking way that was most ungentlemanly. "I suppose you would have wanted to pat them if I hadn't intervened."

Hind recharged his blunderbuss as they rode, the wide muzzle allowing him to pour powder down the barrel despite the motion.

They left the marsh and entered grasslands with little copses of trees. The terrain was gentler now, somehow more civilized. Small furry animals grazed among low bushes, shooting down burrows if Hind's horse came too close.

"Please don't try to stroke the cute little bunnies," said Hind. "They have a nasty, diseased bite."

Sarah stuck her nose in the air, treating that remark with the disdain it merited. "How far now to New Isle of Wight?" she asked.

Hind pointed. "There it is, down in that bowl."

Sarah peered where he indicated. What she had thought was a fallen tree on closer inspection turned out to be a tumbledown rustic shepherd's hut, although she could see no sheep.

"Are you sure?" she asked, uncertainly.

"You were expecting St Paul's?" replied Hind.

"I will disconnect here, out of range of any sensitives in the colony," Sarah said. "Captain Fitzwilliam wants to arrive unannounced and has given me strict instructions."

Hind swung a leg over the horse's head and dismounted in one smooth athletic movement. He handed Sarah down, only releasing her waist reluctantly. She moved away, enthasizing, reaching out with her mind to locate her position in the living world. She picked up an emotion from Hind that made her look back.

Many of the girls from the Academy saw their interaction with the spirit guides as essentially a business relationship. Sarah had been particularly horrified by one aristocratic girl.

"It's like marriage, my dear, but more convenient. You do your duty to Queen and country on your back but at least you are spared the tedium of producing the heir and spare."

Sarah, the respectable Bermondsey Street girl, had been shocked.

Hind looked so lost and lonely that she impulsively ran back and kissed him on the lips.

"I will remember my promise," she said.

He grinned at her, clearly pleased, and patted her bottom as she walked away. The man was incorrigible. After ten or twelve steps, Sarah checked her position, enthasizing the hut for location. The living world flowed around her like an echo from a dream.

She dithered, wondering whether perhaps she should move a few steps further in, or perhaps to the left.

This is ridiculous, she thought. Just get it over with, girl.

Sarah closed her eyes and recited the prayer taught to her at the Naval Academy. She "pushed" with her mind, imagining a pair of scissors cutting a ribbon, and felt a tug at her body, gentle at first but fast becoming agonizing. Disconnection hit her like a tidal wave.

"...proceed," said Fitzwilliam.

Sarah gasped and flopped back in the chair, shaking with fatigue. The bridge was filled with swirling grey energy. Someone retched with a particularly unpleasant gargle.

The grey cleared and Sarah saw stars through the portholes, foreign stars arranged in novel patterns. Brick-red light filled the bridge from a foreign sun.

Mr Brierly ran up a staircase to a glass dome at the rear of the bridge and took sightings with his sextant, measuring the angles between various astronomical features with great care. Sarah lay back exhausted, a tight knot of anxiety forming in her stomach. Had she brought them anywhere near the right location or was she about to suffer more humiliation?

Brierly took his time, double checking the sightings and jotting the results down carefully in a leather-bound notebook. He consulted a navigational almanac, comparing the tables of figures with those he had measured.

His slow deliberation did nothing for Sarah's peace of mind. Why was he frowning and rechecking? What had gone wrong?

At last Brierly was ready to announce the results of his observations.

"Captain, we are in the vicinity of New Isle of Wight on the blind side of Lucifer. We're within a few hundred miles of where you wanted us."

The seamen on the bridge cheered.

"Silence!" A petty officer killed the spontaneous demonstration with a single word.

Fitzwilliam whistled. Arrival within two or three thousand miles of a far colony was considered proficient. Sometimes, an aethership had to use metastasis two or even three times to reach a suitable sailing point for the final journey in.

"Very well done, Pilot," Fitzwilliam said. "I fancy we can sail the rest of the way."

Sarah was absolutely horrified. Now they would expect miraculous piloting skills from her every time. All her anxieties flooded back like a tidal bore. She cursed the ill luck that had caused this.

"Carry on, Mr Brierly," said Fitzwilliam. "Mr Smythe – please get a seaman to clean up that awful mess you have made on my bridge deck."

The young lieutenant was a nasty greenish-yellow colour. "Aye, aye, sir," Smythe said, disappearing.

"All topmen on deck," Brierly yelled into a speaking tube.

Sarah heard the tramp of heavy boots clanging. Sound travelled easily through the steel-built vessel. The bridge was within an armoured tower on the back of the top deck. Sarah had a good view down the starboard side of the ship from the pilot's chair.

Seamen in aethersuits emerged from hatches onto the deck and climbed the thick steel masts. Within minutes, sails unfurled and filled, picking up the solar winds.

"Sailing skills had almost died out in the Navy when the first aetherships were launched," Fitzwilliam said from beside her chair. "We had to recruit old salts from merchant tramp ships to teach the new generation of topmen. That's why we all start our careers on saltwater sailing ships. Do you know how the ship navigates?"

"They teach us the basics," Sarah replied, shrugging. "The solar wind in the sails pushes against a keel of aetherium that runs down the centre of the ship. The resulting parallelogram of forces squeezes the ship in the desired direction."

"Very good," said Fitzwilliam, patronizingly, as if talking to a precocious child at a party.

Sarah glared at him. The man must think she was an idiot.

Fitzwilliam carried on as if she had not spoken. "Now we are under way, we will be turning onto a port tack. Lucifer will come into view to starboard."

Sarah peered out of the porthole, irritation forgotten. A huge red-brown ball slid out from under the bow. Yellow and orange bands streaked its surface, colouring great frozen whirlpools, each of which must be bigger than the Earth.

"New Isle of Wight is one of Lucifer's moons," Fitzwilliam said. "Tidal forces heat the world otherwise it would be colder than Mars. The sun here may be large but its fires are weak with age."

"Why is it called Lucifer?" Sarah asked. "It doesn't look especially hellish."

"I wondered that as well," Fitzwilliam replied. "Perhaps the dull red sun inspired the name, or maybe it's because Lucifer has unusually bad tidal disruptions in the aether, which is why the colony is called New Isle of Wight." He smiled at her blank expression. "The Isle of Wight off southern England has four tides a day and is surrounded by vicious rip currents. Drake's men used them to lure the Armada to destruction in Southampton waters."

"I have never stood on the soil of a far world," Sarah said, changing the subject as she knew little history. Academy training had been thorough but narrow in scope and she lacked the liberal school education of a real lady.

"And you won't on this cruise, either," said Fitzwilliam. "We are not going anywhere near the colony. Merchant ships are disappearing on the New Isle of Wight run. Ships do disappear but the Admiralty suspect that there's a pirate operating in this area. The City is berating the politicians over their losses and the politicians are leaning on the Navy. Not that they will vote us any more money, of course. My orders are to stop the attacks permanently and we won't do that by advertising our presence; pounds to peanuts the pirate has informers in the colony giving information about shipping. We want to catch the villains, not just scare them somewhere else."

Sarah was disappointed that they would not be docking at New Isle of Wight but she was cheered up by the news that the *Cassandra* would be chasing pirates. The Admiralty never told pilots why they were going somewhere; they only released destinations to pilots because they had no choice, but pirate hunting sounded exciting.

Sarah was so bored that she had taken to reading Admiralty regulations to while away the time. She was currently memorizing the range of buoy coloured bands used to indicate right of way exceptions. The only fun to be had was with Hind but there were practical limits to how often she could enthasize with him without exhaustion setting in. There were Admiralty regulations about even this – under enthasis, pilots for the use of, frequency per month.

A light coming on in her cabin indicated another alert; a ship must have been sighted. Regulations demanded that she be on the bridge during an engagement, not that there was much chance of finding anything to engage. For six long weeks, the *Cassandra* had tacked backwards and forwards across New Isle of Wight's shipping lanes. This was only the third vessel sighted and the other two had been harmless merchantmen.

Sarah took her place on the pilot's couch, ignored by the other crew. Mr Brierly had a long telescope trained through a forward porthole. "She's a Yankee sloop running straight towards us; nothing suspicious about her at all." Disappointment coloured his voice. "She's carrying a large spread of sail but she probably has degradable luxury foods aboard and her captain wants to get to market before they spoil."

"Very good, Mr Brierly. Bring us about before they spot us, assuming they have any lookouts at all," said Fitzwilliam, who clearly had no great regard for the merchant marine.

"An awful lot of sail," Brierly said, half to himself. He kept his telescope trained on the schooner. "Captain! I think I am looking at two ships, one directly behind the other. I think the Yankee is being chased."

"Thank you, Mr Brierly," said Fitzwilliam, calmly. "Signal action stations, if you please, Mr Crowly."

The ship became a whirl of organized activity. Sarah shrank back on her couch trying to keep out of the way. Her sole duty was to hold herself ready to take the ship into metastasis. She recited the prayer for calmness in her head. She couldn't enthasize with Hind unless she was reposed.

The ships crept together, mile by mile. Sarah had heard it said that a sea fight was like jousting in slow motion but the reality was excruciating. She fidgeted on her seat until she received an irritated glance from Fitzwilliam.

"The chaser is a large warship with the lines of a galleon," Brierly said.

Sarah opened her mouth to ask what a galleon was but thought better of disturbing the officers and left the question unasked.

"That's what we call a Spanish colonial battleship," Smythe said to her in an undertone. He had clearly noted her puzzlement.

"What's a Spaniard doing here chasing a Yankee?" Fitzwilliam asked, rhetorically. "Can you see any colours, Mr Brierly?"

"Not Spain's," Brierly replied. "There is some sort of odd device on the foresail."

"A mutineer, then," Fitzwilliam said. "Some governor of a Spanish colony has rebelled, or maybe the local militia leader has shot the governor and declared himself generalissimo."

"But why is he chasing a sloop?" Sarah asked, unable to contain herself further.

"Because he needs loot to reward his men; no pay and he will be the next up against the wall," said Fitzwilliam.

"We will engage?" asked Brierly.

"Of course," Fitzwilliam replied.

The captain opened the cover of a speaking tube. He couldn't address the whole crew but his words would be repeated on from man to man through the ship's compartments.

"This is the captain," Fitwilliam said, speaking slowly and clearly, pitching his voice to carry. "A Spanish battleship is attacking a Yankee in one of our colonies. That means that the Americans are under Queen Mary's protection. The Spaniard is three times our size, has four times our men and twice our number of guns but we are the Royal Navy…"

Whatever else Fitzwilliam intended to say was drowned by a cheer coming back up the tube. He gave up and recapped it.

"Don't be frightened, Miss Brown. Captain Fitzwilliam will best them," said Smythe.

"I am not frightened," Sarah said, crisply, rather surprised to find that it was true. All sorts of things scared her – being found out, being laughed at, failing – but dying wasn't one of them. Nevertheless, she knew bollocks when she heard it and Smythe was full of it. She accepted as a matter of course that the Royal Navy was superior to anything else in the aether but, nonetheless, a frigate against a battleship, even a third-rate battleship, was hopeless. Even she knew that much about naval tactics.

"Mr Brierly, if I fall your orders are to smash up the enemy badly enough that he can't escape whomsoever the Admiralty sends to replace us. That warship must not be allowed to get away unscathed."

"Aye, aye, sir." If Brierly was concerned about being ordered to commit suicide then he hid it well.

"Take personal command of the gun deck, Mr Brierly. I will try to position the ship so you can get both broadsides away. I intend to use our superior speed and manoeuvrability to hit and run."

"Aye, aye, sir." Brierly saluted and left the bridge.

"A point to starboard, Helmsman," Fitzwilliam said. "We will pass the sloop close on her port side, provided her master doesn't panic and ram us."

The *Cassandra* had two helmsmen behind large oak wheels. One operated vertical rudders of aetherium while the other controlled horizontal direction.

Aetherium was the only substance yet known opaque to aether. Before the secret of its manufacture had been learned from the Martians, aetherships had been spherical capsules covered in cavorite panels that were navigated by pushing and pulling against heavenly bodies. The death rate had been higher than even Germany's submersible steam boats.

The sloop's master showed admirable presence of mind by running straight as the *Cassandra* swept past. The frigate turned to present its port broadside to the pursuing battleship.

The Spanish ship failed to react for some minutes as if the commander could not quite believe the sudden appearance of the RN frigate and was wondering what to do. Then its bow tilted ever so slowly to port, trying to match the *Cassandra*'s turn to exchange broadsides on a parallel course. The battleship was far too slow and the *Cassandra* crossed her bow.

"Fire when ready, Mr Brierly," Fitzwilliam said down a speaking tube.

Brierly discharged the *Cassandra*'s port broadside battery by battery into the Spaniard's bow. The ship whipsawed under their recoil. Sarah had never experienced the detonation of naval artillery pieces. She had expected the noise but the shock waves set up in the hull surprised her. Dust rose from every surface and everything rattled. A pencil rolled off the navigational table and danced on the floor.

Sarah could see pieces flying off the enemy battleship as the shells struck home.

"Hard to port," Fitzwilliam ordered.

The helmsman spun the wheel and a rating frantically pulled levers that operated the signalling arms on top of the bridge's armoured roof. Topmen in aethersuits winched the sails around to put the ship on a new tack. It was hard gruelling work but the Royal Navy acknowledged few equals at the task.

The second helmsmen hauled on his wheel to counter the roll to starboard generated by *Cassandra*'s abrupt change in course. The Spaniard continued its turn to port so that the ships were momentarily side by side, passing closely on opposite courses. Brierly fired the starboard guns in a single broadside that rolled the *Cassandra* to port. The recoil on the ship's hull was enough to knock a man off his feet. Sarah fancied she saw the red dots streak away from the ships side. Strikes appeared all over the hull of the battleship.

"Good shooting, Mr Brierly," Fitzwilliam said, to no one in particular. "She'll be well armoured but that must have hurt."

A handful of ragged flashes on the battleship's upper decks gave notice that she was returning fire. A thump that Sarah felt more than heard indicated that at least one of the enemy's shots had struck home.

"Two broadsides with barely a shot in return," Fadden said, with great satisfaction. "Oh, well played, Captain!"

"The galleon is not well handled," Fitzwilliam said, mildly. "I suspect that she has no officers aboard."

"They probably went for a walk in the aether out of an access hatch if the crew mutinied," said Fadden.

"Without aethersuits?" asked Sarah, shocked.

"Oh, no. They will have been given aethersuits," said Fadden. "To prolong the agony, don't you see?"

Cassandra carried on her tack leaving the enemy to stern. The battleship continued in its turn until it was following the frigate.

"We seem to have gained their attention," said Fitzwilliam. "What is the sloop doing?"

Smythe trained a telescope astern. "She is getting clear of the battle, sir."

"Very wise," Fitzwilliam said. "Now, Pilot, I want you to take us into metastasis and position the *Cassandra* just behind the battleship. You understand what I require from you, Miss Brown?"

"Yes, Captain," she answered.

Her stomach contracted in a knot; this was exactly what she had feared might happen. Fitzwilliam had acquired an exaggerated idea of her capabilities from the lucky metastasis to Lucifer. Now he was placing the entire safety of his ship in her hands.

Something of what she felt must have shown on her face.

"It won't be easy but I have every confidence in your skills, Pilot," Fitzwilliam said, gently. "You can do it, Sarah."

It occurred to her that if she got it badly wrong and placed them under the battleship's guns then the frigate would be destroyed and all aboard killed – so she wouldn't have to face the consequences. This thought cheered her up. She felt so much better that she indulged herself in feeling indignation at Fitzwilliam's cavalier familiarity with her. She calmed herself and began enthasis, searching for Hind.

Nothing happened.

Alarmed, Sarah searched deeper, trying to reach into the spirit world. She slipped out of her body and hit a shining purple barrier, bouncing back. She tried again with the same result.

"Captain, I can't get us into metastasis. Something is blocking me," she said.

Fitzwilliam looked at her sharply. "Is this some natural phenomenon or a trick of the enemy?"

"I don't know," Sarah replied, nearly in tears. "I have never experienced anything like it. It's as if we are surrounded by a wall."

"That is inconvenient," said Fitzwilliam, with masterly English understatement. He opened a speaking tube. "Mr Brierly, there is a change of plan. We will lead the enemy into Lucifer's rip tides."

Fadden interrupted. "That will disrupt our control of the *Cassandra*'s cavorite panels and make it difficult to hold the ship steady. We will have a devil of a job training the guns."

"Quite true, Mr Fadden, but it will be a bloody sight more difficult for the battleship to use her primary weapons," said Fitzwilliam.

"True, Captain, her heavy guns will be muzzle loaders, hauled in on hydraulic rams."

"Badly maintained hydraulic rams," said Fitzwilliam.

"Which will jam solid on a rolling ship," said Fadden.

The two men grinned at each other.

"Of course she still has more light breach loaders than our entire armament," said Fitzwilliam.

"But we are the Royal Navy," Sarah said, quietly.

"Exactly so, Pilot," said Fitzwilliam.

Lucifer hung in front like a bloodshot eye growing ever larger until it filled the heavens. Sarah reconsidered her view that it didn't look hellish. The giant planet's surface looked like boiling multicoloured water that had been frozen in place. She could see where great arches of gas were in the process of ejection. The world was spinning so fast that she could actually detect a slow movement by eye.

Cassandra began to roll and pitch, like a seaship in a gale. Sarah tightened the straps on the pilot's couch. Fitzwilliam stood with bent knees, seemingly unconcerned, but even he, eventually, had to grasp a rail. The ship shuddered and vibrations passed down the hull.

"Having trouble balancing the cavorite panels again, Mr Fadden?" Fitzwilliam asked.

"Sorry, sir. I believe I have the measure of it now," replied Fadden, adjusting a bank of circular wooden knobs.

Sarah failed to notice any improvement, indeed the aethership shook all the more, but Fitzwilliam seemed satisfied. He trained a telescope aft, observing their pursuer.

The *Cassandra* shook again, whipsawing from stem to stern. Sarah saw topmen hanging desperately to the rolling masts. One slipped but his lifeline held and he was reeled in by a petty officer.

"We must turn back soon, sir. The panels won't take much more," said Fadden.

"Just a bit further, Mr Fadden. You want to see the Spaniard if you think we have it bad," said Fitzwilliam. "They lost a mast in that last wave."

Fadden gave him an agonized look as *Cassandra* corkscrewed.

"Oh, very well, Mr Fadden," said Fitzwilliam. "Signal the topmen to stand by for a new tack."

The petty officer manning the signal lever sprang to work. The *Cassandra* turned to starboard, Fitzwilliam skilfully timing the manoeuvre between aether waves.

Once again the battleship was slow to respond and its own turn was hesitant and choppy. The *Cassandra* managed to deliver a starboard broadside into the port bow of the Spaniard, reverse tack and discharge a port broadside before resuming course. The swirling aether currents made the frigate a poor firing platform so many of the shots missed, even at close range. As Fitzwilliam had predicted, the Spaniard could only reply with light cannon on its upper gun deck. Nevertheless, the *Cassandra* took some nasty knocks in return.

Fitzwilliam repeated the tactic, using the frigate's greater agility and its sailors' higher skills to score hits and then dance away before the battleship could return effective fire. All the time, he lured the Spaniard deeper into Lucifer's tidal drag.

This was Sarah's first sea fight and she was enthralled. She had been taught basic naval tactics but this was astonishing. The motto of a famous New York prizefighter went through her mind – float like a butterfly but sting like a wasp. The captain danced the frigate around the less agile battleship, avoiding an exchange of blows that they couldn't win but landing painful jabs all the while. She began to believe that they could win.

Fitzwilliam caught her gazing at him so she wiped the admiration off her face. The man was cocksure enough already without her adding to his ego.

"Any chance of getting us out of here, Pilot?" he asked.

"No, Captain," she replied. "I keep trying but something is still impeding me. In any case, it would be dangerous to go into metastasis this close to Lucifer." She felt idiotic even as she made the last remark. At the moment, all their options were dangerous.

"Ah well," Fitzwilliam said. "I had hoped that the enemy would have broken contact by now but he seems to be somewhat annoyed at us. We will just have to hope that Lucifer's tidal rips break him first, so that we can extricate ourselves."

"Your strategy does seem to be working," Sarah said, trying to demonstrate a proper naval insouciance in the face of the foe.

It was at that moment that chaos broke out.

A sailor spun away from his station as if he had been punched by a steam hammer. A pipe fractured, spewing hot water into a rating's face; his screams echoed from the metal walls. Navigational maps flew up in the air and the ship's deck lurched, throwing Sarah against her straps. The dial in from of the engineering officer shattered and Fadden uttered a most ungentlemanly oath.

"The galvanic coils," he said, before running down the spiral stair into the bowels of the ship.

Sarah noticed ghostly figures on the edge of her vision that vanished as soon as she looked at them directly, like trying to see a dim star at night. She enthasized and was horrified to see goblin-like forms lurching around the bridges like small boys who had got out of their governess's control. The spirit world was overflowing into the natural realm and something was psychically boarding the *Cassandra*.

Sarah slipped from her body and was sucked in to the otherworld.

She arrived in a large kitchen that must be part of some great house. The walls were brick, supported by heavy black wooden beams. The kitchen was full of ovens, cupboards, and tables littered with culinary equipment, spoons, ladles, pots, kettles, plates and cutlery. Sarah was dressed in a female version of a highwayman's outfit, with breeches and a thick leather jerkin.

Anthropoid creatures with short legs and overlong arms ran round the kitchen, smashing china and upturning anything loose. As she watched, two overturned a cupboard with a tremendous crash. They also struck out at ghostly servants who were trying to cook. These must be the shadows of the *Cassandra*'s crew into the spirit world. Sarah had never seen such a phenomenon before; non-sensitives usually left no impression here.

The nearest goblin turned to face her, a wide grin showing large upward-facing canines. It wore the tattered remains of clothes that were too small and the wrong shape. No, not clothes, she thought, but a uniform since other goblins showed the same colours. It ran towards her on bowed legs with a rolling gait that covered the ground surprisingly quickly. She pulled a pistol from a sash around her waist and levelled it. The creature stopped where she could stare into human-looking eyes. Sarah imagined that she could see fear and terror buried deep behind those eyes. She hesitated, unwilling to pull the trigger. She had never shot anything before, let alone something with sad brown eyes.

The goblin hit her hard over the left kidney. Its hand ended in vicious hooked claws that tore through the thick leather, into her body. She screamed and gripped the gun hard in shock, discharging it.

The blast blew a hole the size of her fist in the creature's chest, knocking it over backwards. Sarah doubled up in pain. She pushed her left hand hard against her side but it still hurt terribly. Get a grip, girl, she said to herself and willed the pain to subside. She was not entirely successful but at least she could now function.

Sarah focused her mind with the chronotic prayer to create an aeon, a bubble of time in which her life ran faster than the spirit world around her. This emergency measure was used only sparingly as it put great strain on the pilot. The world around her slowed down.

The goblins clawed slowly at each other, hindering themselves in their eagerness to get at her. She backed into a corner, firing the pistol as fast as she could reload. Sarah was not exactly a markswoman but she could hardly miss. One shot smashed a goblin's kneecap, another burst a head like a ripe pear hit with a mallet and a third clipped a goblin's shoulder, spinning him around into his fellows.

The blood drove the creatures mad and they tore into their fallen comrades. The goblin with the shattered leg tried to defend itself but another ripped his throat out with an upwards slash of the impressive canines. Red blood spurted across the floor causing increasing frenzy. Sarah began to hope that the goblins might kill each other off. She was tired now and finding it hard to concentrate. Half of her mind concentrated on maintaining the aeon through prayer, while the rest went through the ritual of load, aim, fire and back away.

She stumbled over the words of the prayer and the aeon flickered. A ridiculous-looking scrawny man in some sort of Native American kilt and headdress made the horned sign, the *mano cornuta*, at her. Her aeon collapsed and the world speeded up. The man was an unrestrained sensitive. Pilots called them sorcerers.

One of the unacknowledged reasons that the Navy only used girl mediums was that they were considered to be more controllable. Her instructors had drummed into her the safe limits of her talent beyond which she was forbidden to experiment. To do so would put her very soul into peril and for that there was the threat of the Church exorcists.

The "goblins" were sailors or soldiers, sacrificed in some dreadful ritual that had bound their souls to the sorcerer's service. The Academy could control what the girls did but they couldn't stop them gossiping. Sarah had heard of vile ceremonies that were rumoured to be carried out in the more backward territories.

The sorcerer screamed in anger and hopped from foot to foot, shaking a stick with a feather on the tip at the goblins. He slapped the nearest goblin with the stick and it whimpered as if lashed by a whip.

The magician gestured at Sarah and the goblins obediently charged towards her. She fired once into the crush without result. She felt the creatures' thoughts and their lust for hot, red blood. There was no time left to reload her weapon, no time for anything. In desperation, she cried for help, calling Hind's name.

The kitchen door flew off its hinges into the crush of goblins, knocking several over. This was followed by the sound and smell of a heavy gun firing. A tunnel of body parts showed where Hind had discharged his blunderbuss.

The goblins in front of Sarah hesitated. The sorcerer shouted more instructions. Most of the goblins attacked Hind leaving just two to finish her off, which was probably overkill.

Sara saw Hind drop the blunderbuss and draw a pistol with each hand. She saw him shoot a goblin in the face; it somersaulted onto its back. Then the two goblins were on her. Summoning the last of her strength, she hit one over the head with her gun, felling it. She heard the crash of Hind's pistol discharging and the howl of goblins. She leaned back against the wall, exhausted, the pain in her side flooding over her as her mind failed to maintain the block. Her hand unclenched, dropping her pistol to the floor with a clatter. She was spent with nothing left to give, but surely no one could criticize her for that? Hadn't she done enough?

The surviving goblin grabbed her by the shoulders, its claws drawing blood. This one's eyes showed nothing but savage pleasure. If there was anything human left in the goblin then it was the sort of man who took joy in a woman's pain. The goblin lifted her off the ground with its claws, pulling her slowly towards its fangs, savouring her fear like a connoisseur with a fine wine. It smelled of stale sweat and decay.

A steel point erupted from the goblin's throat, spraying Sarah with a fine mist of blood. The creature dropped and fell. Hind pulled his sword free and stamped hard on the goblin's neck. Sarah heard the sharp crack of breaking bones and the goblin went limp. She sank to her knees and closed her eyes, ineffectually putting her hands over her ears, trying shut out the terrible sounds. She did not want to see or hear Hind die.

A final scream and then silence caused her to open her eyes. There was only her, Hind and the sorcerer left in the kitchen, just them and a carpet of dead goblins that were already starting to decay. The sorcerer looked to be in shock and Sarah knew how he felt. Hind was covered in blood, some of it his, and his anger was terrible.

The sorcerer made a bolt for the doorway.

"Stop him," Sarah said, weakly.

Hind reversed his grip on the sword and threw it like a javelin. It struck the sorcerer point first in the back, slicing deep into his body. The man fell through the doorway out of her sight, arms splayed out as if he were worshiping a pagan god.

"You stupid, stupid girl," Hind said, angrily. "Whatever made you think you could do this unaided? You could have been killed and I would have lost you for ever."

It was not until much later that Sarah pondered over the significance of that remark.

Hind held her tight and kissed her hard on the lips. His grip caused the pain in her side to flare and she gasped.

"You're hurt," Hind said, concern replacing anger in his face. "You need to go back, now."

He looked at her intently, said something that she didn't catch, and the kitchen faded away.

The bridge was a shambles of broken equipment. Fitzwilliam and Crowly stared at her; there were just the three of them on the bridge, apart from bodies.

"You were screaming, Pilot," said Fitzwilliam in answer to her unasked question. "And stuff was streaming off you."

Ectoplasm leaked from Sarah's side where the goblin had clawed her. The white filmy material dissolved where it trailed into the oily liquids on the deck. The *Cassandra* corkscrewed in a violent motion that set off a metallic groaning from overstressed steel.

"Give me a few minutes to rest and I will take us through metastasis," Sarah said.

"It's too late for that," said Fitzwilliam. "We are falling towards Lucifer."

"And the battleship?" Sarah asked.

Fitzwilliam looked at her, head tilted to one side. "It exploded just after strange things stopped happening here, just after you stopped screaming. You wouldn't know why that was, would you?"

Sarah considered. The sorcerer was escaping back into the living world when Hind speared him. What would have happened if he had died at the point of disconnection? She thought it best not to speculate as it could be dangerous to reveal too much.

"I've no idea, Captain," she replied, complementing the lie with her most innocent expression.

"Hmpf," Fitzwilliam exclaimed, clearly unconvinced. "We are abandoning ship, so make your way to the boat deck."

Sarah tried to get up but she was utterly exhausted and every muscle in her torso ached. She sank back with a groan. "You will have to go without me. I don't think I can walk," she said.

"Don't be ridiculous, Pilot," said Fitzwilliam. "I don't have time for heroic posturing. Mr Crowly!"

"Sir."

"Escort the pilot to the rear boat deck. Carry her if necessary. I will join you as soon as I have destroyed the signal book in my cabin."

"Aye, aye, sir," said Crowly, saluting.

Captain Fitzwilliam ran down the spiral stairs, taking them two at a time.

Crowly watched him go.

Sarah waited for the lieutenant to help her but she was ignored. Crowly cocked his head, listening to the metallic clang of the Captain's footsteps fade.

"Mr Crowly?" she asked politely, holding out her hand so he could assist her up.

His face twisted in hatred. "Witch!" he said, spitting the word out as if it were a venomous bug.

Sarah recoiled in shock.

It took a visible effort for Crowly to regain control of himself.

"'Thou shall not suffer a witch to live,' Exodus, twenty-two eighteen," he said more calmly. "Goodbye, Miss Brown."

He turned and strode off the bridge, leaving her alone. The next roll of the ship turned a body over so that it was face up.

"Mr Smythe," she said, softly. "So now you know the answer to the great mystery. Have you a spirit guide, I wonder, or do you dwell with angels? Well, I'll soon join you and find out for myself."

She doubted that the young man had sinned sufficiently to go below but she was not so sure about her own ultimate destination. The ship rolled again and Smythe's head lolled until he stared straight at her with accusing eyes. Coward, Sarah, he seemed to say, taking the easy option again? I fought to the end, his eyes said. I did not just give up.

Sarah heaved herself upright and limped over to the spiral stairs. Her weight kept changing and a sudden tug nearly pitched her down the steps. She clutched the rail for support and fell to her knees.

The lieutenant was looking at her again. "I tried," she told him. "I really did, Mr Smythe, but I can't do it, so do stop reproaching me!"

"Miss Brown, is that you?" Fitzwilliam came up the stairs, taking them three at a time.

"Where's Crowly? I told him to help you."

"He has firm views on helping witches," said Sarah. "Exodus, you know."

Fitzwilliam swore. "I'll have his commission for this. I'm sorry, Sarah, this is my fault. I knew he was in some humourless sect but it never occurred to me that he would put religion before duty." Fitzwilliam swore again. "That's no excuse, of course."

A grinding shudder went through the hull.

"Perhaps we should go?" Sarah ventured to say.

"What? Yes, of course," Fitzwilliam said.

He put Sarah's arm around his neck and half carried her down the steps. The journey through the ship was nightmarish. It was hardly recognizable as the smart Royal Navy vessel of a few short hours ago. The corridors were erratically lit and sharp-edged wreckage lay in wait. Progress was painfully slow and Sarah was tempted to suggest Fitzwilliam go on alone, but she realized that it would be a waste of breath. He really was an insufferably arrogant man but he was also a brave one.

They had only gone about though two hatchways when the ship's hull rang like a steel drum hit by a hammer and there was a terrible tearing sound.

"Wait here," Fitzwilliam said. He ran to the next hatchway and peered through the porthole.

"The ship has broken her back. We cannot reach the aft boat deck so we will have to go back. This section will lose its air next."

Sarah groaned at the thought of reversing their steps but Fitzwilliam was adamant. She just wished the damn man would let her lie down and die in peace.

Fitzwilliam bullied and hauled her back to the deck below the bridge, where there was a small hatchway that Sarah had not noticed before. A yellow bar emphasized the legend LIFEBOAT.

Sarah stared at it open-mouthed. "But if this was here, why did we ..."

Fitzwilliam flung open the hatch. "Because it is for one person only," he said. "A last chance escape route for the captain."

"That was where you were going when you heard me?" asked Sarah. Then she realized the more relevant part of his comment. "But it's only for one person."

"Always enough space for a little'un," said Fitzwilliam, cheerfully, throwing her head first through the hatch.

Sarah found herself in a pitch black tube. Fitzwilliam dropped on top, knocking the breath from her. He had a hard muscular body.

"Sorry," he said, insincerely.

She was about to make some pithy and sarcastic comment to put him in his place when an elbow caught her in the stomach as he twisted around to shut the hatch. By the time she recovered, the devastatingly witty comment had slipped from her mind, which was a shame as she was sure that it had been jolly good and that it would have utterly crushed the insufferable man. Fitzwilliam grunted with effort, a lever moved and an explosive charge shot them away from the doomed ship with a thump.

"You really don't give a lady time to catch her breath," said Sarah.

There was a click and a dim light came on. They were nose to nose.

"Sorry about the accommodation," said Fitzwilliam, while focusing on adjusting some controls behind Sarah's head.

"I must look a frightful mess," she said and could have kicked herself. Why did she have this urge to babble inanities when she was anxious?

"I believe that I may just be able to survive looking at you for a while longer," said Fitzwilliam, with a smile. "I have a robust constitution so I'm willing to take the risk."

Sarah sniffed. He was far too glib for her liking although he did have a nice smile. Sarah looked out of a small porthole by her head. The boat was rotating around its axis every ten seconds or so. Lucifer dominated the heavens filling the boat with red light on every rotation. The remains of the rear hull of the *Cassandra* passed across the window. A great gout of flame blasted silently out of the wreckage, vanishing quickly as its air supply dissipated into the aether.

"Now we wait for rescue," Fitzwilliam said. "Do you know any good word games?"

"Rescue by whom?" Sarah asked, calmly. "We are going to die in here, aren't we?"

He looked at her and she could see that he was considering what to say. "Yes, I'm afraid that's likely," he eventually replied. "The boat will drop into Lucifer when the galvanic cell fails and the cavorite panels stop working but I fancy that we will be dead by then. The air supply is only intended for one person."

"I see," Sarah said. She was glad that he had enough respect for her intellect not to try to fob her off with a comforting lie.

"Back there in the ship, when everything went to hell. You were fighting some sort of magical battle, I suppose," he said, making the sentence a statement rather than a question.

The expression on her face must have shown her shock, because he hurried to reassure her.

"My father is in the Foreign Office, Miss Brown. I understand more than you might imagine about the duties and proscriptions of your profession."

"Magic is not a word I would like to be associated with," Sarah said. "I mean, with which I would like to be associated." All her anxieties flooded back; she would be talking in a south London accent next.

"Have no fear, Miss Brown. The Navy looks after its own, and I look after my people, especially those who have served faithfully. You have my personal guarantee of protection. My uncle is the Bishop of Bath and Wells, charming old chap who still has an eye for a well-turned ankle. He'll like you." He turned on that annoying grin.

"I see," said Sarah. "So you were making fun of me when you asked all those embarrassing questions on my first night aboard."

"Well, perhaps just teasing you a little," said Fitzwilliam. "You looked so nervous that that I thought you needed distracting."

"You obnoxious, arrogant...man!" Sarah said, unable to think of a worse name to call him. She tried to slap him, which was not easy in the cramped conditions and he caught her wrist without difficulty.

"Bad girl," he said. "Hitting your captain in a war zone could be construed as mutiny and I would have to shoot you."

She pulled her arm free angrily. A sharp insertion of pain reminded her that she was not entirely healed.

"Let's see where you are hurt," Fitzwilliam said, looking genuinely upset. "I'm sorry, I had quite forgot about your injury."

"You won't find a wound," Sarah said, mollified by his show of concern. "The damage was psychic. I feel much recovered already."

"Nevertheless, I think I should examine you," said Fitzwilliam.

His hands moved gently over her body, while she lay back and closed her eyes. His touch was comforting, more like caresses than a medical examination, so she relaxed. Actually, it was a lot like caresses.

"Captain Fitzwilliam," she said, eventually.

"Yes, Miss Brown."

"You wouldn't be the sort of cad who takes advantage of a helpless lady under your protection, would you?"

"I regret to say that I may well be just such a bounder, Miss Brown."

She opened her eyes and examined him. He was quite handsome in a rugged sort of way and he did have an engaging smile. He would have been safe if he had not come back to rescue her. Perhaps he deserved some compensation for the loss of his life. She considered her options and recalled that she really hated word games.

"Well, if I am to be ravished I suppose I must submit gracefully," she said, and kissed him.

It was some time before Sarah came up for air. When she did, she turned her head to look out of the porthole while he playfully nuzzled her neck.

"Captain Fitzwilliam," she said.

"What is it now, Miss Brown?" he asked, a faint edge of frustration colouring his tone.

She giggled, wondering if he would see the funny side. The poor man was in for more frustration.

"I think you should look out," she said. "I believe you may have, um, missed the boat, so to speak."

"What?"

Sarah pointed to where the American sloop headed straight for them, demonstrating the famous sailing qualities of the type by navigating easily through Lucifer's rip tides. Fitzwilliam clearly did not see the funny side. "Bloody Americans," he said. "They've been a perpetual nuisance since Boston Harbor."

SOLIDARITY

Walter Jon Williams

Resistance to a conqueror needn't be futile, but may need to be nudged along by an expert ...

A master of many subgenres of SF, including military SF in his Dread Empire's Fall series, as well as authoring historical adventure and crime, Walter Jon Williams is a multiple award nominee and winner who has "to write novels in order to afford to write shorter work" because "I really love writing short stories." Hooray. And who else's personal page of Frequently Asked Questions would include the info that "mataglap" is an Indonesian word, indicating that someone is about to go berserk and start killing at random?

SULA DRESSED IN fine Riverside low style for her meeting with Casimir. The wide, floppy collar of her blouse overhung a bright tight-waisted jacket with fractal patterns. Pants belled out around platform shoes. Cheap colourful plastic or ceramic jewellery. A tall velvet hat, crushed just so, with one side of the brim held up by a gold pin with an artificial diamond the size of a walnut.

"I don't like this," Macnamara said.

Sula peered at herself in the mirror, flipped her fingers through her dyed black hair.

"I wish there were other choices," she said, "but there aren't."

"My lady—" he began.

She turned to him.

"I'm going," she said. "We need allies."

And, because he was under military discipline, he said nothing more, just glowered in his petulant way.

The neighbourhood known as Riverside was still, and the pavement radiated the heat of the day as if it were exhaling a long, hot breath. Between bars of light, the long shadows of buildings striped the street like prison bars. She saw no sign of Naxid or police patrols.

The Cat Street Club was nearly deserted, inhabited only by a few people knocking back drinks on their way home from, or on their way to, their work. The hostess said that Casimir wasn't in yet. Sula sat at a back table and ordered sparkling water and transformed the tabletop into a video screen so that she could watch the news programme, the usual expressionless Daimong announcer with the usual bland tidings, all about the happy, content people of many species who worked productively and happily under their new Naxid overlords.

She didn't see Casimir arrive; there was only the hostess coming to her and saying that he was in. The hostess escorted Sula to the back of the club, up a staircase of black iron, and to a door glossy with polished black ceramic. Sula looked at her reflection in the door's lustrous surface and adjusted the tilt of her hat.

The next room featured a pair of Torminel guards, fierce in their grey fur and white fangs, and Sula concluded that Casimir must be nervous. Lamey had never gone around with guards, not until the very end, when the Legion of Diligence was after him.

The guards patted Sula down – she had left her pistol at home – and scanned her with a matt-black polycarbon wand intended to detect any listening devices. Then they waved her through another polished door to Casimir in his suite.

The suite was large and decorated in black and white, from the diamond-shaped floor tiles to the onyx pillars that supported a series of white marble Romanesque arches, impressive but non-structural, intended purely for decoration. The chairs featured cushions so soft they might tempt a sitter to sprawl. There was a video wall that enabled Casimir to watch the interior of the club, and several different scenes played there in silence. Sula saw that one of the cameras was focused on the table she'd just left.

"Were you watching me?" she asked.

"I hadn't seen you around," Casimir said. "I was curious."

He had come around his desk to greet her. He was a plain-featured young man a few years older than Sula, with longish dark hair combed across his forehead and tangled down his collar behind. He wore a charcoal-grey velvet jacket over a purple silk shirt, with gleaming black boots beneath fashionably wide-bottomed trousers. His hands were long and pale and delicate, with fragile-seeming wrists; the hands were posed self-consciously in front of his chest, the fingers tangled in a kind of knot. His voice was surprisingly deep and full of gravel, like a sudden flood over stony land.

She felt the heat of his dark eyes and knew at once that danger smouldered there, possibly for Sula, possibly for himself, possibly for the whole world. Possibly he himself didn't know; he would strike out at first one, then the other, as the mood struck him.

Sula felt a chord of danger chime deep in her nerves, and it was all she could do to keep her blood from thundering an answer.

"I'm new," she said. "I came down from the ring a few months ago, before they blew it up."

"Are you looking for work?" He tilted his head and affected to consider her. "For someone as attractive as you, I suppose something could be found."

"I already have work," Sula said. "What I'd like is steady pay." She took from an inner pocket of her vest a pair of identity cards, and offered them.

"What's this?" Casimir approached and took the cards. His eyes widened as he saw his own picture on both cards, each of which identified him as "Michael Saltillo".

"One's the primary identity," Sula said, "and the other's the special card that gets you up to the High City."

Casimir frowned, took the cards back to his desk, and held them up to the light. "Good work," he said. "Did you do these?"

"The government did them," Sula said. "They're genuine."

He pursed his lips and nodded. "You work in the Records Office?"

"No," Sula lied. "But I know someone who does."

He gave her a heavy-lidded look. "You'll have to tell me who that is."

Sula shook her head. "No. I can't."

He glided towards her. Menace flowed off him like an inky rain. "I'll need that name," he said.

She looked up at him and willed her muscles not to tremble beneath the tide of adrenaline that flooded her veins. "First," Sula said, speaking softly to keep a tremor from her voice, "she wouldn't work with you. Second—"

"I'm *very persuasive*," Casimir said. The deep, grating words seemed to rise from the earth. His humid breath warmed her cheek.

"Second," Sula continued, calmly as she could, "she doesn't live in Zanshaa, and if you turn up on her doorstep she'll call the police and turn you in. You don't have any protection where she is, no leverage at all."

A muscle pulsed in one half-lowered eyelid: Casimir didn't like being contradicted. Sula prepared herself for violence and wondered how she would deal with the Torminel.

"I don't believe I got your name," Casimir said.

She looked into the half-lidded eyes. "Gredel," she said.

He turned, took a step away, then swung back and with an abrupt motion thrust out the identity cards. "Take these," he said. "I'm not going to have them off someone I don't know. I could be killed for having them in my office."

Sula made certain her fingers weren't trembling before she took the cards. "You'll need them sooner or later," she said, "the way things are going under the Naxids."

She could see that he didn't like hearing that, either. He turned again and walked to the far side of his desk and stood there with his head down, his long fingers tidying papers.

"There's nothing I can do about the Naxids," he said.

"You can kill them," Sula said, "before they kill you."

He kept his eyes on his papers, but a smile touched his lips. "There are a lot more Naxids than there are of me."

"Start at the top and work your way down," Sula advised. "Sooner or later you'll reach equilibrium."

The smile still played about his lips. "You're quite the provocateur, aren't you?" he said.

"It's fifty for primary ID. Two hundred for the special pass to the High City."

He looked up at her in surprise. "*Two* hundred?"

"Most people won't need it. But the ones who'll need it will really need it."

His lips gave a sardonic twist. "Who would want to go to the High City now?"

"People who want to work for Naxids. Or steal from Naxids. Or kill Naxids." She smiled. "Actually, that last category gets the cards free."

He turned his head slightly to hide a grin. "You're a pistol, aren't you?"

Sula said nothing. Casimir stood for a moment in thought, then suddenly threw himself into his chair in a whoof of deflating cushions and surprised hydraulics, and then he put his feet on his desk, one gleaming boot crossed over the other.

"Can I see you again?" he said.

"To do what? Talk business? We can talk business *now*."

"Business, certainly," he said with a nod. "But I was thinking we could mainly entertain ourselves."

"Do you still think I'm a provocateur?"

He grinned and shook his head. "The police under the Naxids don't have to bother with evidence any more. Provocateurs are looking for work like everyone else."

"Yes," Sula said.

He blinked. "Yes what?"

"Yes. You can see me."

His grin broadened. He had even teeth, brilliantly white. Sula thought his dentist was to be congratulated.

"I'll give you my comm code. Set your display to receive."

They activated their sleeve displays, and Sula broadcast her electronic address. It was one she'd created strictly for this meeting, along with another of what were proving to be a dizzying series of false identities.

"See you then." Sula walked for the door, then stopped. "By the way," she said. "I'm also in the delivery business. If you need something moved from one place to another, let me know." She permitted herself a smile. "We have very good documents," she said. "We can move things wherever you need them."

She left, then, before glee got the better of her.

Once outside on the hot, dark streets, she used evasion procedures to make certain she wasn't followed home.

Casimir called after midnight. Sula groped her way from her bed to where she'd hung her blouse and told the sleeve to answer.

The chameleon fabric showed Casimir with a slapdash grin pasted to his face. There was blaring music in the background and the sound of laughter.

"Hey Gredel!" he said. "Come have some fun!"

Sula swiped sleep from her eyes. "I'm asleep. Call me tomorrow."

"Wake up! It's still early!"

"I work for a living! Call me tomorrow!"

As she told the sleeve to end her transmission and made her way back to the bed, she decided that she'd done a good job setting the hook.

The next day she had deliveries in the High City, the cocoa and tobacco and coffee that Sula had spent her modest fortune acquiring when she found out that Zanshaa's ring was going to be destroyed, and that there wouldn't be imports of anything for a long time. At each stop she talked to business owners and employees, a task which came under the heading of "intelligence gathering" even though there was no one left to report the intelligence *to* – all her superiors had been captured and tortured to death, their torments broadcast live to the planet as a lesson to anyone tempted by the idea of loyalty to the old regime. Sula survived by way of bombing her own apartment as the Naxid police crashed down the door, and then used her back door into the Records Office computer to give herself and her team clean identities.

Sula returned to her apartment weary and sweat-stained. Gredel's comm unit showed that Casimir had logged three calls asking her out for the night. She took a long, delicious bath in lilac-scented water while considering an answer, then picked up the comm, turned off the camera button that would transmit her image, then returned the last call.

"Why not?" she said at the sullen face that answered. "Unless you've made other plans, of course."

The sulky look vanished as Casimir peered into his sleeve display in failed search for an image. "Is this Gredel?" he asked. "Why can't I see you?"

"I'm in the tub."

A sly look crossed his features. "I could use a wash myself. How about I join you?"

"I'll meet you at the club," Sula said. "Just tell me what time."

He told her. Sula would have time to luxuriate in her bath for a while longer and then to nap for a couple hours before joining him.

"How should I dress?" Sula asked.

"What you're wearing now is fine."

"Ha ha. Will I be all right in the sort of thing I wore last night?"

"Yes. That'll do."

"See you then."

She ended the call, then ordered the hot water tap to open. The bathroom audio pickup wasn't reliable and she had to lean forward to open the tap manually. As the hot water raced from the tap and the steam rose, she sank into the tub and closed her eyes. She allowed herself to slowly relax, to let the scent of lilacs rise in her senses.

The day had started well. She thought it would only get better.

Sula adjusted her jacket as she gazed out the window of the apartment she shared with Macnamara and Spence, the two members of her team. Because of electricity shortages, only every third street lamp was lit. Most businesses were closed, and those remaining open had turned off their signs. The last of the street vendors were closing their stalls or driving away in their little three-wheeled vehicles with their business packed on the back. The near-blackout imposed by the Naxids – not to mention the hostage-taking, the round-ups that took place in public areas – had severely impacted their business, and there weren't enough people on the streets after dark to keep them at their work.

"I should be with you," Macnamara argued. He was a tall young man, a bushy-haired recruit who had been the star of the Fleet's combat course. He was from a mountain village on a backwater planet, and war was his way of seeing the worlds.

"You should be with me on a *date*?" Sula laughed.

Macnamara pushed out his lips like a pouting child. "You know what he is, my lady," he said. "It's not safe."

Sula fluffed her black-dyed hair with her fingers. "He's a necessary evil. I know how to deal with him."

Macnamara made a scornful sound in his throat. Sula looked at Spence, who sat on the sofa and was doing her best to look as if she weren't hearing this.

Shawna Spence was a petty officer and an engineer and good at things like bombs, though her chief contribution to the war effort so far was to blow up her own apartment.

"Can it, Macnamara," she said.

Macnamara ignored her and spoke to Sula. "He's a criminal. He may be a killer for all you know."

He probably hasn't killed nearly as many people as I have, Sula thought. She remembered five Naxid ships turning to sheets of brilliant white eye-piercing light at Magaria.

She turned from the window and faced him. "Say that you want to start a business," she said, "and you don't have the money. What do you do?"

Macnamara's face filled with suspicion, as if he knew Sula was luring him into a trap. "Go to my clan head," he said.

"And if your clan head won't help you?" Sula asked.

"I go to someone in his patron clan," Macnamara said. "A Peer or somebody."

Sula nodded. "What if the Peer's nephew is engaged in the same business and doesn't want the competition?"

Macnamara made the pouting face again. "I wouldn't go to Casimir, that's for sure."

"Maybe you wouldn't. But a lot of people *do* go to people like

Casimir, and they get their business started, and Casimir offers protection against retaliation by the Peer's nephew and his clan. And in return Casimir gets 50 or 100 per cent interest on his money and a client who will maybe do him other favours."

Macnamara looked as if he'd bitten into a lemon. "And if they don't pay the 100 per cent interest they get killed."

Sula considered this. "Probably not," she judged, "not unless they try to cheat Casimir in some way. Most likely Casimir just takes over the business and every minim of assets and hands the business over to another client to run, leaving the borrower on the streets and loaded with debt." As Macnamara looked about to protest again, Sula held out her hands. "I'm not saying he's a pillar of virtue. He's in it for the money and the power. He hurts people, I'm sure. But in a system like ours, where the Peers have all the money and all the law on their side, people like the Riverside Clique are necessary."

"I don't get it," Macnamara said. "You're a Peer yourself, but you talk against the Peers."

"Oh." She shrugged. "There are Peers who make Casimir look like a blundering amateur."

The late Lord and Lady Sula, for two.

She told the video wall to turn on its camera and examined herself in its screen. She put on the crumpled velvet hat and adjusted it to the proper angle.

There. That was raffish enough, if you ignored the searching, critical look in the eyes.

"I'm going with you," Macnamara insisted. "The streets aren't safe."

Sula sighed and decided she may as well concede. "Very well," she said. "You can follow me to the club a hundred paces behind, but once I go in the door I don't want to see you for the rest of the evening."

"Yes," he said, and then added, "my lady."

She wondered if Macnamara's protectiveness was actually possessiveness, if there was something emotional or sexual in the way he related to her.

She supposed there was. There was with most men in her experience, so why not Macnamara?

Sula hoped she wouldn't have to get stern with him.

He followed her like an obedient, heavily armed ghost down the darkened streets to the Cat Street Club. Yellow light spilled out from the doors, along with music and laughter and the smell of tobacco. She cast a look over her shoulder at Macnamara, one that warned him to come no further, and then she hopped up the step onto the black-and-silver tiles and swept through the doors, giving a nod to the two bouncers.

Casimir waited in his office, along with two others. He wore an iron-grey silk shirt with a standing collar that wrapped his throat with layers of dark material and gave a proud jut to his chin, heavy boots that gleamed, and an ankle-length coat of some soft black material inset with little triangular mirrors. In one pale, long-fingered hand he carried an ebony walking stick that came up to his breastbone and was topped by a silver claw that held a globe of rock crystal.

Casimir laughed and gave an elaborate bow as she entered. The walking stick added to the odd courtly effect. Sula looked at his outfit and hesitated.

"Very original," she decided.

"Chesko," Casimir said. "This time next year, she's going to be dressing everybody." He turned to his two companions. "These are Julien and Veronika. They'll be joining us tonight, if you don't mind." Julien was a younger man with a pointed face, and Veronika was a tinkly blonde who wore brocade and an anklet with stones that glittered.

Interesting, Sula thought, for Casimir to include another couple. Perhaps it was to put her at ease, to assure her that she wouldn't be at close quarters with some predator all night.

"Pleased to meet you," she said. "I'm Gredel."

Casimir gave two snaps of his fingers and a tiled panel in the wall slid open, revealing a well-equipped bar, bottles full of amber, green and crimson liquids in curiously shaped bottles. "Shall we start with drinks before supper?" he asked.

"I don't drink," Sula said, "but the rest of you go ahead."

Casimir was brought up short on the way to the bar. "Is there anything else you'd like? Hashish or—"

"Sparkling water will be fine," Sula said.

Casimir hesitated again. "Right," he said finally, and handed her a cut-crystal glass that he'd filled from a silver spigot.

He mixed drinks for himself and the others, and everyone sat on the broad, oversoft chairs. Sula tried not to oversplay.

The discussion was about music, songwriters and musicians that Sula didn't know. Casimir told the room to play various audio selections. He liked his music jagged, with angry overtones.

"What do you like?" Julien asked Sula.

"Derivoo," she said.

Veronika gave a little giggle. Julien made a face. "Too intellectual for me," he said.

"It's not intellectual at all," Sula protested. "It's pure emotion."

"It's all about death," Veronika said.

"Why shouldn't it be?" Sula said. "Death is the universal constant. All people suffer and die. Derivoo doesn't try to hide that."

There was a moment of silence in which Sula realized that the inevitability of misery and death was perhaps not the most appropriate topic to bring up on first acquaintance with this group; and then she looked at Casimir and saw a glimmer of wicked amusement in his dark eyes. He seized his walking stick and rose.

"Let's go. Take your drinks if you haven't finished them."

Casimir's huge Victory limousine was shaped like a pumpkin seed and painted and upholstered in no less than eleven shades of apricot. The two Torminel guards sat in front, their huge, night-adapted eyes perfectly at home on the darkened streets. The restaurant was panelled in old, dark wood, the linen was crisp and close-woven, and the fixtures were brass which gleamed finely in the subdued light. Through an elaborate, carved wooden screen Sula could see another dining room with a few Lai-own sitting in the special chairs that cradled their long breastbones.

Casimir suggested items from the menu, and the elderly waitron, whose stolid, disapproving old face suggested he had seen many like

Casimir come and go over the long years, suggested others. Sula followed one of Casimir's suggestions, and found her ostrich steak tender and full of savour, and the krek-tubers, mashed with bits of truffle, slightly oily but full of complex flavours that lingered long on her palate.

Casimir and Julien ordered elaborate drinks, a variety of starters, and a broad selection of desserts, and competed with each other for throwing money away. Half of what they ordered was never eaten or drunk. Julien was exuberant and brash, and Casimir displayed sparks of sardonic wit. Veronika popped her wide eyes open like a perpetually astonished child and giggled a great deal.

From the restaurant they motored to a club, a place atop a tall building in Grandview, the neighbourhood where Sula had once lived until she had to blow up her apartment with a group of Naxid police inside. The broad granite dome of the Great Refuge, the highest point of the High City, brooded down on them through the tall glass walls above the bar. Casimir and Julien flung more money away on drinks and tips to waitrons, bartenders and musicians. If the Naxid occupation was hurting their business, it wasn't showing.

Sula knew she was supposed to be impressed by this. But even years ago, when she was Lamey's girl, she hadn't been impressed by the money that he and his crowd threw away. She knew too well where the money came from.

She was more impressed by Casimir once he took her onto the dance floor. His long-fingered hands embraced her gently, but behind the gentleness she sensed the solidity of muscle and bone and mass, the calculation of his mind. His attention in the dance was entirely on her, his sombre dark eyes intense as they gazed into her face while his body reacted to her weight and motion.

This one thinks! she thought in surprise.

That might make things easy or make them hard. At any rate it made the calculation more difficult.

"Where are you from?" he asked her after they'd sat down. "How come I haven't seen you before?" Julien and Veronika were still on the dance floor, Veronika swirling with expert grace around Julien's clumsy enthusiasm.

"I lived on the ring," Sula said. "Before they blew it up."

"What did you do there?"

She looked at him and felt a smile tug at the corners of her mouth. "I was a maths teacher," she said, a story that might account for some of her odd store of knowledge.

His eyes widened. "Give me a math problem and try me," Sula urged, but he didn't reply. She began to develop the feeling her phony occupation might have shocked him.

"When I was in school," he said, "I didn't have math teachers like you."

"You didn't think teachers went to clubs?" Sula said.

A slow thought crossed his face. He leaned closer, and his eyes narrowed. "What I don't understand," he said, "is why, when you're from the ring, you talk like you've spent your life in Riverside."

Sula's nerves sang a warning. She laughed. "Did I say I've spent my whole life on the ring?" she asked. "I don't think so."

"I could check your documents—" his eyes hardened, "—but of course you sell false documents, so that wouldn't help."

The tension between them was like a coiled serpent ready to strike. She raised an eyebrow. "You still think I'm a provocateur?" she asked. "I haven't asked you to do a single illegal thing all night."

One index finger tapped a slow rhythm on the matt surface of the table before them. "I think you're dangerous," he said.

Sula looked at him and held his gaze. "You're right," she said.

Casimir gave a huff of breath and drew back. Cushions of aesa leather received him. "Why don't you drink?" he asked.

"I grew up around drunks," she said. "I don't want to be like that, not ever."

Which was true, and perhaps Casimir sensed it, because he nodded. "And you lived in Riverside."

"I lived in Zanshaa City till my parents were executed."

His glance was sharp. "For what?"

She shrugged. "For lots of things, I guess. I was little, and I didn't ask."

He cast an uneasy look at the dancers. "My father was executed, too. Strangled."

Sula nodded. "I thought you knew what I meant when I talked about derivoo."

"I knew." Eyes still scanning the dance floor. "But I still think derivoo's depressing."

She found a grin spreading across her face. "We should dance now."

"Yes." His grin answered hers. "We should."

They danced till they were both breathless, and then Casimir moved the party to another club, in the Hotel of Many Blessings, where there was more dancing, more drinking, more money spread around. After which Casimir said they should take a breather, and he took them into an elevator lined with what looked like mother of pearl, and bade it rise to the penthouse.

The door opened to Casimir's thumbprint. The room was swathed in shiny draperies, and the furniture was low and comfortable. A table was laid with a cold supper, meats and cheeses and flat wroncho bread, pickles, chutneys, elaborate tarts and cakes, and bottles lying in a tray of shaved ice. It had obviously been intended all along that the evening end here.

Sula put together an open-faced sandwich – nice Vigo plates, she noticed, a clean modern design – then began to rehearse her exit. Surely it was not coincidental that a pair of bedrooms were very handy.

I've got to work in the morning. It certainly sounded more plausible than: *I've got to go organize a counter-rebellion.*

Casimir put his walking stick in a rack that had probably been made for it specially and reached for a pair of small packages, each with glossy wrapping and a brilliant scarlet ribbon. He presented one each to Sula and Veronika.

"With thanks for a wonderful evening."

The gift proved to be perfume, a crystal bottle containing Sengra, made with the musk of the rare and reclusive atauba tree-crawlers of Paycahp. The small vial in her hand might have set Casimir back twenty zeniths or more – probably more, since Sengra was exactly the sort of thing that wouldn't be coming down from orbit for years, not with the ring gone.

Veronika opened her package and popped her eyes wide – that expression was going to look silly on her when she was fifty – and gave a squeal of delight. Sula opted for a more moderate response and kissed Casimir's cheek.

There was the sting of stubble against her lips. He looked at her with calculation. There was a very male scent to him.

Sula was about to bring up the work she had to do in the morning when there was a chime from Casimir's sleeve display. He gave a scowl of annoyance and answered.

"Casimir," came a strange voice. "We've got a situation."

"Wait," Casimir said. He left the room and closed the door behind him. Sula munched a pickle while the others waited in silence.

Casimir returned with the scowl still firm on his face. He was without a trace of apology as he looked at Sula and Veronika and said, "Sorry, but the evening's over. Something's come up."

Veronika pouted and reached for her jacket. Casimir reached for Sula's arm to draw her to the door. She looked at him. "What's just happened?"

Casimir gave her an impatient, insolent look – it was none of her business, after all – then thought better of it and shrugged. "Not what's happened, but what's going to happen in a few hours. The Naxids are declaring food rationing."

"They're *what*?" Sula's first reaction was outrage. Casimir opened the door for her, and she hesitated there, thinking. Casimir quivered with impatience. "Congratulations," she said finally. "The Naxids have just made you very rich."

"I'll call you," he said.

"I'll be rich, too," Sula said. "Ration cards will cost you a hundred apiece."

"A *hundred*?" For a moment it was Casimir's turn to be outraged.

"Think about it," Sula said. "Think how much they'll be worth to you."

They held each other's eyes for a moment, and then both broke into laughter. "We'll talk price later," Casimir said, and he hustled her into the vestibule along with Veronika, who showed Sula a five-zenith coin.

"Julien gave it to me for the cab," she said triumphantly. "And we get to keep the change!"

"You'd better hope the cab *has* change for a fiver," Sula said, and Veronika thought for a moment.

"We'll get change in the lobby."

A Daimong night clerk gave them change, and Veronika's nose wrinkled at the clerk's smell. On the way to her apartment Sula learned that Veronika was a former model and now an occasional club hostess.

"I'm an unemployed maths teacher," Sula said.

Veronika's eyes went wide. "Wow," she said.

After letting Veronika off, Sula had the Torminel driver take her within two streets of the Riverside apartment, after which she walked the distance to the building by the light of the stars. Overhead the broken arcs of the ring were a line of black against the faintly glowing sky. Outside the apartment she gazed up for a long moment until she discerned the pale gleam of the white ceramic pot in the front window. It was in the position that meant "someone is in the apartment and it is safe".

The lock on the building's front door, the one that read her fingerprint, worked only erratically, but this time she caught it by surprise and the door opened. She went up the stair, then used her key on the apartment lock.

Macnamara was asleep on the couch, with a pair of pistols on the table in front of him, along with a grenade.

"Hi, Dad," Sula said as he blinked awake. "Junior brought me home safe, just like he said he would."

Macnamara looked embarrassed. Sula gave him a grin.

"What were you planning on doing with a *grenade*?" she asked.

Macnamara didn't reply. Sula took off her jacket and called up the computer that resided in the desk. "I've got work to do," Sula said. "You'd better get some sleep, because I've got a job for you first thing in the morning."

"What's that?" He rose from the couch, scratching his sleep-tousled hair.

"The market opens at 7.27, right?"

"Yes."

Sula sat herself at the desk. "I need you to buy as much food as you can carry. Canned, dried, bottled, freeze-dried. Get the biggest sack of flour they have, and another sack of beans. Condensed milk would be good. Get Spence to help you carry it all."

"What's going on?" Macnamara was bewildered.

"Food rationing."

"*What*?" Sula could hear the outrage in Macnamara's voice as she called up a text program.

"Two reasons for it I can think of," Sula said. "First, issuing everyone with a ration card will be a way of reprocessing every ID on the planet … help them weed out troublemakers and saboteurs. Second …" She held up one hand and made the universal gesture of tossing a coin in her palm. "Artificial scarcities are going to make some Naxids very, very rich."

"Damn them," Macnamara breathed.

"*We'll* do very well," Sula pointed out. "We'll quadruple our prices on everything on the ration – you don't suppose they'd be good enough to ration *tobacco*, do you? – and we'll make a fortune."

"Damn them," Macnamara said again.

Sula gave him a pointed look. "Goodnight," she said. "Dad."

He flushed and shambled to bed. Sula turned to her work.

"What if they ration *alcohol*?" she said aloud as the thought struck her. There would be stills in half the bathrooms in Zanshaa, processing potatoes, taswa peels, apple cores, whatever they could find.

She accessed the Records Office computer – her back door was the legacy of an earlier job processing refugees from the ring, before she'd volunteered to get herself killed leading partisan forces – and checked the protocols for acquiring ration cards. Given her level of access, they should be easy enough to subvert.

And then she had another thought. Thus far her group had been selling her own property out of the back of a truck, a business that was irregular but legal. But once the ration came into effect, selling cocoa and coffee off the ration would be against the law. The team wouldn't just be participating in informal economic activity; they'd be committing a *crime*.

People who committed crimes needed protection. Casimir was going to be more necessary than ever.

"*Damn* it," she said.

Macnamara failed to procure a large stash of food. Police were already in force at the market, and foodsellers had been told not to sell large quantities. Macnamara wisely decided to avoid attracting attention and bought only quantities that might be considered reasonable for a family of three.

The announcement of rationing had been made while Sula slept and the food marts were packed. Tobacco had not been included, but Sula couldn't hope for everything. Citizens were given twenty days to report to their local police station in order to apply for a ration card. The reason given by the government for the imposition of rationing was the destruction of the ring and the decline in food imports.

The news also announced that certain well-established Naxid clans, out of pure civic spirit, had agreed to spare the government the expense of public resources, and would instead use their own means to manage the planet's food supplies. The Jagirin clan, whose head had been temporary interior minister during the changeover from the old government to the new, the Ummir clan, whose head happened to be the Minister of Police, the Ushgays, the Kulukrafs... people who, even if some of them hadn't been with the rebellion from the beginning, clearly found it in their interest to support it now.

The Naxids, Sula thought, had just created a whole new class of target.

Naxids were placed in every police station to monitor the process of acquiring ration cards. The Naxids wore the black uniform of the Legion of Diligence, the organization that investigated crimes against the Praxis. All members of the Legion had been evacuated from Zanshaa before the arrival of the Naxid fleet, so apparently the new government had re-formed the Legion, probably with personnel from the Naxid police.

Another class of target, Sula thought.

* * *

A shimmering layer of afternoon heat stretched across the pavement like a layer of molasses, thick enough to distort the colourful canopies and displays of the Textile Market that set up in Sula's street every five days. Early in the morning vendors motored up with their trailers or their three-wheelers with the sheds built onto the back, and at dawn hours the sheds opened, canopies went up, and the merchandise went on sale. After sunset, as the heat began to dissipate and the purple shadows crept between the stalls, the vendors would break down their displays and motor away, to set up the next day in another part of the city.

As Sula passed, vendors called her attention to cheap women's clothing, baby clothes, shoes, stockings, scarves and inexpensive toys for children. There were bolts of fabric, foils of music and entertainment, sun lotion and sun hats, and items – unseasonable in the heat – alleged to be knitted from the fleece of Yormak cattle, and sold at a surprisingly low price.

Despite the heat the market was thronged. Tired and hot, Sula elbowed her way impatiently through the crowd to her doorstep. She entered the building, then heard the chime of a hand comm through her apartment door and made haste to enter. She snatched up the comm from the table and answered, panting.

Casimir surveyed her from the display. She could watch his eyes travel insolently over her image as far as the frame would permit.

"Too bad," he said. "I was hoping to catch you in the bath again."

"Better luck next time." Sula switched on the room coolers and somewhere in the building a tired compressor wheezed, and faint currents of air began to stir. She dropped into a chair and, holding the comm in one hand, began to loosen her boots with the other.

"I want to see you tonight," Casimir said. "I'll pick you up at 21.01, all right?"

"Why don't I meet you at the club?"

"Nothing happens at the club that early." He frowned. "Don't you want me to know where you live?"

"I don't have a place of my own," Sula lied cheerfully. "I sort of bounce between friends."

"Well." Grudgingly. "I'll see you at the club, then."

She had time to bathe, get a bite to eat and work for a while on the accounts of her delivery company. Then she checked the Records Office computer for Casimir's friend Julien, and discovered that he was the son of Sergius Bakshi.

Sergius was someone she'd heard of as the head of the Riverside Clique. She hadn't realized that he'd cheated the executioner long enough to have a grown son.

Sula left the apartment, negotiated the crowds at the Textile Market, then ducked down a sunblasted side street, trying to keep on the shady side. The heat still took her breath away. She made another turn, then entered the delightfully cool air of a block-shaped storage building built in the shadow of the even larger Riverside Crematorium. She showed her false ID to the Cree at the desk, then took the elevator upstairs and opened one of Team 491's storage caches. There she opened one of the cases, withdrew a small item and pocketed it.

Casimir waited by his car in front of the Cat Street Club with an impatient scowl on his face and his walking stick in his hand. He wore a soft white shirt covered with minutely stitched braid. As she appeared, he stabbed the door button and the glossy apricot-coloured door rolled up into the car roof. "I *hate* being kept waiting," he growled in his deep voice, and took her arm roughly to stuff her into the passenger compartment.

This too, Sula remembered, was what it was like to be a clique member's girlfriend.

She settled herself on apricot-coloured plush across from Julien and Veronika, the latter in fluttery garb and a cloud of Sengra. Casimir thudded into the seat next to her and rolled down the door.

Sula called up the chronometer on her sleeve display. "I'm three minutes early," she said primly, in what she trusted was a maths teacher's voice. "I'm sorry if I spoiled your evening."

Casimir gave an unsociable grunt. Veronika popped her blue eyes wide and said, "The boys are taking us shopping!"

Sula remembered that part about being a cliqueman's girlfriend, too. "Where?" she said.

"It's a surprise," Julien said, and slid open the door on the vehicle's bar. "Anyone want something to drink?"

The Torminel behind the controls slipped the car smoothly from the kerb on its six tyres. Sula had a Citrine Fling while the rest drank Kyowan. The vehicle passed through Grandview to the Petty Mount, a district in the shadow of the High City, beneath the Couch of Eternity where the ashes of the Shaa masters waited in their niches for the end of time. The area was lively, filled with boutiques, bars, cafés, and eccentric shops that sold folk crafts or antiques or old jewellery. Sula saw Cree and Lai-own on the streets as well as Terrans.

The car pulled to a smooth stop before a shop called Raiment by Chesko, and the apricot-coloured doors rolled open. They stepped from the vehicle and were greeted at the door by a female Daimong whose grey body was wrapped in a kind of satin sheath that looked strangely attractive on her angular body with its matchstick arms. In a chiming voice she greeted Casimir by name.

"Gredel, this is Miss Chesko," Casimir told Sula in a voice that suggested both her importance and his own.

"Pleased to meet you," Sula said.

The shop was a three-level fantasy filled with sumptuous fabrics in brilliant colours, all set against neutral-coloured walls of a translucent resinous substance that let in the fading light of the sun. Gossamer Cree music floated tastefully in the air.

A Daimong who designed clothes for Terrans was something new in Sula's experience. The shop must have had excellent air circulation, or Chesko wore something that suppressed the odour of her rotting flesh, because Sula didn't scent her even once.

Casimir's mood changed the instant he entered the shop. He walked from one rack to the next and heaved out clothing for Sula or Veronika to try on. He held garments critically to the light and ran his hands over the glossy, rich fabrics. Veronika's were soft and bright and shimmered; Sula's were satiny and tended to the darker shades, with light accents in the form of a scarf, lapel or collar.

He's dressing me as a woman of mystery, Sula thought.

His antennae were really rather acute.

His tastes were fairly good as well, Sula thought as she looked at herself in the full-length video display. She found that she enjoyed herself playing model, displaying one rich garment after another. Casimir offered informed comment as Sula changed outfits, twitched the clothing to a better drape, and sorted the clothing into piles of yesses, maybes, rejects. Chesko made respectful suggestions in her bell-like tones. Shop assistants ran back and forth with mountains of clothing in their arms.

It hadn't been like this with Lamey, Sula remembered. When he walked into a shop with Gredel, the assistants knew to bring out their flashiest, most expensive clothing, and he'd buy them with a wave of his hand and a pocket of cash.

Casimir wasn't doing this to impress anyone, or at least not in the way Lamey had. He was demonstrating his taste, not his power and money.

"You should have Chesko's job," she told him.

"Maybe. I seem to have got the wrong training, though."

"Your mama didn't give you enough dolls to play with when you were growing up," Julien said. He sat in a chair in a corner, out of everyone's way. He had a tolerant smile on his pointed face and a glass of mig brandy, brought by the staff, in one hand.

"I'm hungry," Julien said after an hour and a half.

Casimir looked a little put out, but he shrugged and then looked again through the piles of clothing, making a final sorting. Julien rose from his chair, put down his glass, and addressed one of the assistants.

"*That* pile," he said. "Total it up."

Veronika gave a whoop of joy and ran to embrace him. "Better add this," Casimir said, adding a vest to the yes pile. He picked up an embroidered jacket from another heap and held it out to Sula. "What do you think of this?" he said. "Should I add it to your pile?"

Sula considered the jacket. "I think you should pick out the single very nicest thing out of the stack and give it to me."

His dark eyes flashed, and his gravel voice was suddenly full of anger. "You don't want my presents?" he asked.

Sula was aware that Veronika was staring at her as if she were insane.

"I'll take *a* present," Sula said. "You don't know me well enough to buy me a whole wardrobe."

For a moment she sensed thwarted rage boiling off of him, and then after a moment he thought about it and decided to be amused. His mouth twisted in a tight-lipped smile. "Very well," he said. He considered the pile for a moment, then reached in and pulled out a suit, velvet black, with satin braid and silver beadwork on the lapels and down the sides of the loose trousers. "Will this do?" he said.

"It's very nice. Thank you." Sula noted that it wasn't the most expensive item in the pile, and that fact pleased her. If he wasn't buying her expensive trash, it probably meant he didn't think she was trash, either.

"Will you wear it tonight?" He hesitated, then looked at Chesko. "It didn't need fitting, did it?"

"No, sir." Her pale, expressionless Daimong face, set in a permanent caricature of wide-eyed alarm, gave no sign of disappointment in losing sales worth hundreds of zeniths.

"Happy to," Sula said. She took the suit to the changing room, changed, and looked at herself in the old-fashioned silver-backed mirrors. The suit probably *was* the nicest thing in the pile.

Her old clothes were wrapped in a package, and she stepped out to a look of appreciation from Julien, and the more critical gaze of Casimir. He gestured with a finger as if stirring a pot.

"Turn around," he said. She made a pirouette, and he nodded, more to himself than to anyone else. "That works," he said. The deep voice sounded pleased.

"Can we eat now?" Julien asked.

Outside, the white marble of the Couch of Eternity glowed in twilight. The streets exhaled summer heat into the sky like an overtaxed athlete panting at the end of his run.

They ate in a café, a place of bright red-and-white tiles and shiny chrome. The café was packed and noisy, as if people wanted to pack in as much food and good times as possible before rationing began. Casimir and Julien were in a light-hearted mood, chattering and laughing, but every so often Sula caught Casimir looking at her with a thoughtful expression, as if he was approving his choice of outfit.

He had made her into something he admired.

Afterwards they went to a bar, equally crowded, with a live band and dancing. The other night Casimir had danced with a kind of gravity, but now he was exuberant, laughing as he led her into athletic kicks, spins and twirls. Before, he had been pleasing himself with a show of his power and control, but now it was as if he wanted all Zanshaa to share his joy.

He was taking me for granted the other night, Sula thought. Now he's not.

It was well past midnight when they left the bar. Outside, in the starlit darkness, a pair of strange colossi moved in the night. Leather creaked. A strange barnyard smell floated to Sula's nostrils.

Casimir gave a laugh. "Right," he said. "Get in."

He launched himself into some kind of box that, dimly perceived, seemed to float above the street. There was a creak, a shuffle, more barnyard smell. His long pale hand appeared out of the night.

"Come on," he said.

Sula took the hand and let him draw her forward. A step, a box, a seat. She seated herself next to him before she understood where she was, and amazement flooded her.

"Is this a pai-car carriage?" she asked.

"That's right!" Casimir let a laugh float off into the night. "We hired a pair for tonight." He thumped the leather-padded rim of the cockpit and called to the driver. "Let's go!"

There was a hiss from the driver, a flap of reins, and the carriage lurched into movement. The vehicle was pulled by a pai-car, a tall flightless bird, a carnivorous, unintelligent cousin to the Lai-own driver that perched on the front of the carriage. There were two big silver alloy wheels, ornamented with cut-outs, and a boat-shaped car made out of leather, boiled, treated, sculpted and ornamented with bright metal badges. Mounted on either side were some cell-powered lamps, not very powerful, which the driver now switched on.

The car swayed down off the Petty Mount and into the flat cityscape below. Sula relaxed against Casimir's shoulder. Darkened buildings loomed up on either side like valley walls. The slap of the pai-car's feet and its huffing breath echoed off the structures on either side. There seemed to be no other traffic at all, nothing but the limousine, with its Torminel guards, which followed them at a distance, the driver with his huge nocturnal eyes able to navigate perfectly well by starlight.

"Is this legal?" Sula wondered aloud.

Casimir's bright white teeth flashed in the starlight. "Of course not. These carriages aren't permitted outside the parks."

"You don't expect police?"

Casimir's grin broadened. "The police are bogged down processing millions of ration card applications. The streets are ours for the next month."

Veronika's laughter tinkled through the night. Sula heard the slap of another pair of feet, and saw the savage saw-toothed face of another pai-car loom up on the left, followed soon by the driver and Julien and Veronika. Julien leaned out of the carriage, hands waving drunkenly in the air. "A hundred says I beat you to Medicine Street!"

Sula felt Casimir's body grow taut as Julien's face vanished into the gloom ahead. He called to the driver: "Faster!" The driver gave a hiss and a flap of the reins. The carriage creaked and swayed as the pace increased.

Veronika's laughter taunted them from ahead. Casimir growled and leaned forward. "Faster!" he called. Sula's nerves tingled to the awareness of danger.

A few lights shone high in office buildings where the staff were cleaning. A rare functioning street lamp revealed two Torminel, in the brown uniforms of the civil service, in an apparent argument. The two fell silent and stared with their large eyes as the carriages raced past, their silver wheels a blur.

The side-lamps of Julien's carriage ahead loomed closer. "Faster!" Casimir called, and he turned to Sula, a laugh rumbling from deep in his chest. Sula felt an answering grin tear at her lips. This is mad, she thought. Absolutely mad.

She heard Julien's voice calling for greater speed. The wheels threw up sparks as they skidded through a turn. Sula was thrown against Casimir. He put an arm around her protectively.

"Faster!"

Veronika's laughter tinkled from ahead, closer this time. Casimir ducked left and right, peering around the driver for a better view of the carriage they were pursuing. They passed through an intersection and both carriages glared white in the startled headlamps of a huge street-cleaning machine. Sula blinked the dazzle from her eyes. The night air was cool on her cheeks. She could feel her heart beating high in her throat.

Sula heard Julien curse as they drew even. Then they were in another turn, metal wheels sliding, and Julien's carriage loomed close as it skidded towards them. Their driver was forced into a wider turn to avoid collision, and Julien pulled ahead.

"Damn!" Casimir jumped from his seat and leaped to join the driver on the box. One pale hand dug in a pocket. "Twenty zeniths if you beat him!" he called, and slapped a coin down on the box. Twenty zeniths would buy the coach, the pai-car, and the driver twice over.

The driver responded with a frantic hiss. The pai-car seemed to have caught the fey mood of the passengers and gave a determined cry as it accelerated.

The road narrowed as it crossed a canal, and Casimir's coach was on the heels of Julien's as they crossed the bridge. Sula caught a whiff of sour canal water, heard the startled exclamation of someone on the quay, and then the coach hit a bump and Sula was tossed in the car like a pea in a bottle. Then they were in another turn, and Sula was pressed to one side, the leather bending slightly under her weight.

She gave a laugh at the realization that her whole life's adventure could end here, that she could die in a ridiculous carriage accident or find herself under arrest, that her work – the war against the Naxids, her team, her many identities – all could be destroyed in reckless, demented instant...

Serve me right, she thought.

The laboured breathing of the pai-car echoed between the buildings. "Twenty more!" Casimir slapped another coin on the box.

The carriage swayed alongside that of Julien. He was standing in the car, urging his driver on, but his pai-car looked dead in its harness. Then there was a sudden glare of headlights, the clatter of a vehicle collision alarm, and Julien's driver gave an urgent tug on the reins, cutting his bird's speed and swerving behind Casimir's carriage to avoid collision with a taxi taking home a singing chorus of Cree.

Sula heard Julien's yelp of protest. Casimir laughed in triumph as the singers disappeared in their wake.

They had passed through the silent business district and into a more lively area of Grandview. Sula saw people on the street, cabs parked by the kerb waiting for customers. Ahead she saw an inter-section, a traffic signal flashing a command to stop.

"Keep going!" Casimir cried, and slapped down another coin. The driver gave Casimir a wild, gold-eyed stare, but obeyed.

Sula heard a rumble ahead, saw a white light. The traffic signal blazed in the darkness. Her heart leaped into her throat.

The carriage dashed into the intersection. Casimir's laughter rang in her ears. There was a brilliant white light, a blaring collision alarm, the wail of tyres. Sula threw her arms protectively over her head as the pai-car gave a wail of terror.

The edge of the carriage bit Sula's ribs as the vehicle was slammed sideways. A side-lamp exploded into bits of flying crystal. One large silver wheel went bounding down the road ahead of the truck that had torn it away, and the carriage fell heavily onto the torn axle. Sparks arced in the night as the panicked bird tried to drag the tilted carriage from the scene.

The axle grated near Sula's ear. She blinked into the night just in time to see Casimir lose his balance on the box and fall towards her, arms thrashing in air. She made a desperate lunge for the high side of the coach and managed to avoid being crushed as he fell heavily onto the seat.

Clinging to the high side of the coach, she turned to him. Casimir was helpless with laughter, a deep base sound that echoed the grinding of the axle on pavement. Sula allowed herself to slide down the seat onto him, wrapped him in her arms, and stopped his laughter with a kiss.

The panting pai-car came to a halt. Sula heard its snarls of frustration as it turned in the traces and tried to savage the driver with its razor teeth, then heard the driver expertly divert its striking head with slaps. She could hear the truck reversing, the other pai-car padding to a halt, the sound of footsteps as people ran to the scene.

She could hear Casimir's heart pounding in his chest.

"I conceive that no one is injured," said the burbling voice of a Cree.

This time it was Sula who was helpless with laughter. She and Casimir crawled from the wreckage of the carriage just as the apricot-coloured limousine rolled silently to a stop, the Torminel guards appearing in time to prevent a very angry Daimong truck driver from bludgeoning someone. Julien and Casimir passed around enough money to leave everyone happy, the carriage drivers in particular, and then the party piled into the limousine for the ride to the Hotel of Many Blessings.

Sula sat in Casimir's lap and kissed him for the entire ride.

Sula insisted on taking a shower before joining him in bed. Then she insisted that he take a shower, too.

"We could have showered *together*," Casimir grumbled.

"You could use a shave, too," Sula pointed out.

He returned to bed, showered and shaved and scented with taswa-blossom soap.

"Hey!" he said in surprise. "You're really a blonde!"

She gave a slow laugh. "That's the least of my mysteries."

An hour or so later, Sula decided to play a card or two, and told the room light to go on. Casimir gave a start and shielded his eyes. Sula crawled out of bed and looked for the package that held the clothing she'd worn at the beginning of the evening.

"Gredel, what are you *doing*?" Casimir complained.

"I have something to show you." Sula dug in an inner pocket and removed the item she'd taken from the storage locker earlier in the evening. She opened the slim plastic case and showed Casimir her Fleet ID.

"I'm Caroline, Lady Sula," she said. "I'm here fighting the Naxids."

There was a moment of silence. Casimir squeezed his eyes shut for a long moment, as if in disbelief, and then opened them. "Shit," he said.

Sula smiled at him. "I guess you know me well enough to buy me a new wardrobe," she said. "If you still want to."

The meeting with Julien's father, Sergius Bakshi, occurred three days after the madcap carriage race, on an afternoon dark with racing clouds. Sula dressed for the meeting with care. In order that she look more like the person in the Fleet ID, she left off her contact lenses and bought a shoulder-length wig in her natural shade of blonde. She wore a military-style jacket in a tone of green that wasn't quite the viridian of a Fleet uniform, but which she hoped suggested it. She brought Macnamara as an aide, or perhaps a body-guard, and bought him a similar jacket. She reminded herself to walk with the straight-backed, braced posture of the Fleet officer and not the less formal slouch she'd adopted as Gredel.

She wore a pistol stuck down her waistband in back. Macnamara had a sidearm in a shoulder holster.

These were less for defence than to shoot themselves, or each other, in the event things went wrong.

There was a lot of shooting going on these days. The Naxids had shot sixty-odd people in retaliation for the firebombing of a Motor Patrol vehicle in the Old Third, and then they'd gone into the Old Third and shot about a dozen people at random.

The meeting took place in a private club called Silk Winds on the second floor of an office building in a Lai-own neighbourhood. Casimir met her on the pavement out front, dressed in his long coat and carrying his walking stick. His eyes went wide as he saw her, and then he grinned and gave one of his elaborate bows. From his bent position he looked up at her.

"You still don't look much like a maths teacher," he said.

"Good thing then," she said, in her drawling Peer voice. His eyebrows lifted in surprise, and he straightened.

"Now *that's* not the voice I heard in bed the other night."

From over her shoulder Sula heard Macnamara's intake of breath. Great, Sula thought, now she'd have a scandalized and sulking team member.

"Don't be vulgar," she admonished, still in her Peer voice.

Casimir bowed again. "Apologies, my lady."

He led her into the building. The lobby was cavernous, brilliant with polished copper, and featured a twice-life-size bronze statue of a Lai-own holding, for some allegorical reason beyond Sula's comprehension, a large tetrahedron. Uniformed Lai-own security guards in blue jackets and tall pointed shakos gave them searching looks, but did not approach. A moving stair took Sula to the second floor and to the polished copper door of the club, on which had been placed a card informing them that the club had been closed for a private function.

Casimir swung the door open and led Sula and Macnamara into the shadow-filled club. Faint sunlight from the darkened sky gleamed fitfully off copper fittings and polished wood. Lai-own security – this time without the silly hats – appeared from the gloom and checked everyone very thoroughly for listening devices. They found the sidearms but didn't touch them. Apparently they discounted the possibility that Sula and her party might be assassins.

Casimir, adjusting his long coat after the search, led them to a back room. He knocked on a nondescript door.

Sula smoothed the lapel of her jacket and straightened her shoulders and reminded herself to act like a senior Fleet commander inspecting a motley group of dock workers. She couldn't give orders to these people: she had to use a different kind of authority. Being a Peer and a Fleet officer were the only cards she had left to play. She had to be the embodiment of the Fleet and the legitimate government and the whole body of Peers, and she would have to carry them all along through sheer weight of her own expectation.

Julien opened the door, and his eyes went wide when he saw Sula. Suddenly nervous, he backed hastily from the door.

Sula walked into the room, her spine straight, hands clasped behind her. I *own* this room, she told herself, but then she saw the eyes of her audience and her heart gave a lurch.

Two Terrans, a Lai-own, and a Daimong sat in the shadowy, dark-panelled room, facing her from behind a table that looked like a slab of pavement torn from the street. Nature had made the Daimong expressionless but the others were so blank-faced that they might have all been carved from the same block of granite.

She heard Macnamara stamp to a halt behind her right shoulder, a welcome support. Casimir stepped around them and stood to one side of the room.

"Gentlemen," he said, and again made his elaborate bow. "May I present Lieutenant the Lady Sula."

"I'm Sergius Bakshi," said one of the Terrans. He looked nothing like his son Julien: he had an oval face and a razor-cut moustache and the round, unfeeling eyes of a great predator fish. He turned to the Lai-own. "This is Am Tan-dau, who has very kindly arranged for us to meet here."

Tan-dau did not look kindly. He slumped in the padded chair that cradled his keel-like breastbone, his bright, fashionable clothes wrinkled on him as they might on a sack of feathers. His skin was dull, and nictating membranes were half-deployed across his eyes. He looked a hundred years old, but Sula could tell from the dark feathery hair on each side of his head that he was still young.

Bakshi continued. "These are friends who may be interested in any proposition you may have for us." He nodded at the Terran. "This is Mr Patel." A young man with glossy hair that curled over the back of his collar, Patel didn't even blink in response when Sula offered him a small nod.

The Daimong's name was Sagas.

Sula knew, through Casimir, that the four were a kind of informal commission that regulated illegal activities on this end of Zanshaa City. Bakshi's word carried the most weight, if only because he'd managed to reach middle age without being killed.

"Gentlemen," Sula drawled in her Peer voice. "May I present my aide, Mr Macnamara."

Four pairs of eyes flicked to Macnamara, then back to Sula. Her throat was suddenly dry, and she resisted the impulse to clear her throat.

Bakshi folded large, doughy hands on the table in front of him and spoke. "What may we do for you, Lady Sula?"

Sula's answer was swift. "Help me kill Naxids."

Even that request, which Sula hoped might startle them a little, failed to provoke a reaction.

Bakshi deliberately folded his hands on the table before him. His eyes never left hers. "Assuming for the sake of argument that this is remotely possible," he said, "why should we agree to attack a group so formidable that even the Fleet has failed to defeat them?"

Sula looked down at him. If he wanted a staring contest, she thought, then she'd give him one. "The Fleet isn't done with the Naxids," she said. "Not by a long shot. I don't know whether you have the means to verify this or not, but I know that even now the Fleet is raiding deep into Naxid territory. The Fleet is ripping the guts out of the rebellion while the Naxid force is stuck here guarding the capital."

Bakshi gave a subtle movement of his shoulders that might have been a strangled shrug. "Possibly," he said. "But that doesn't alter the fact that the Naxids are *here*."

"How do we know." Tan-dau's voice was a mumble. "How do we know that she is not sent by the Naxids to provoke us?"

It was difficult to be certain to whom Tan-dau addressed the question, but Sula decided to intercept it. "I killed a couple thousand Naxids at Magaria," Sula said. "You may remember that I received a decoration for it. I don't think they'd let me switch sides even if I wanted to."

"Lady Sula is supposed to be dead," Tan-dau said, to no one in particular.

"Well." Sula permitted herself a slight smile. "You know how accurate the Naxids have been about everything else."

"How do we know she is the real ..." Tan-dau's sentence drifted away before he could finish it. Sula waited until it was clear that no more words were coming, and then answered.

"You can't know," Sula said. She brought her Fleet ID out of her jacket. "You're welcome to examine my identification, but of course the Naxids could have faked it. But I think you know—" she gazed at them all in turn "—if the Naxids wanted to target you, they wouldn't need me. They've declared martial law; they'd just send their people after you, and no one would ever see you alive again."

They absorbed this in expressionless silence. "Why then," Bakshi said finally, "should we act so as to bring this upon us?"

Sula'd had three days to prepare what came next. She had to restrain herself from babbling it out all at once, to urge herself to remain calm and to make her points slowly and with proper emphasis.

"You want to be on the winning side, for one thing," she said. "That brings its own rewards. Second, the secret government is prepared to offer pardons and amnesties for anyone who aids us."

It was like talking to a blank wall. She wanted to stride about, to gesture, to declaim, all in desperate hope of getting at least one of the group to show some response. But she forced herself to be still, to keep her hands clasped behind her, to stand in an attitude of superiority. She had to project command and authority: if she showed weakness she was finished.

"What," said Sagas, speaking for the first time in his beautiful chiming Daimong voice, "makes you think that we need pardons and amnesties?"

"A pardon," Sula said, "means that any investigations, any complaints, any inquiries, any proceedings come to a complete and permanent end. Not only for yourself, but for any of your friends, clients and associates who may wish to aid the government. You may not need any amnesties yourself, but perhaps some of your friends aren't so lucky."

She scanned her audience again. Once again, no response.

"My last point," she said, "is that you are all prominent, successful individuals. People know your names. You have earned the respect of the population, and people are wary of your power. But you're not loved."

For the first time she'd managed to provoke a response. Surprise widened Bakshi's pupils, and even the expressionless Sagas gave a jerk of his head.

"If you lead the fight against the Naxids, you'll be heroes," Sula said. "Maybe for the first time, people will think of you as agents of virtue. You'll be loved, because everyone will see you on the right side, standing between them and the Naxids."

Patel gave a sudden laugh. "Fight the Naxids for love!" he said. "That's a *good* one! I'm *for* it!" He slapped the table with a hand, and looked up at Sula with his teeth flashing in a broad grin. "I'm with you, my lady! For love, and for no other reason!"

Sula ventured a glance at Casimir. He gave her a wry, amused look, not quite encouragement but not dispirited either.

Bakshi gave an impatient motion of his hand, and Patel fell silent, his hilarity gone in an instant and leaving a hollow silence behind.

"What exactly," Bakshi began, "would the secret government want us to do—" chill irony entered his voice "—for the people's love."

"There are cells of resisters forming all over the city," Sula said, "but they have no way to communicate or coordinate with each other." Again, she looked at them all in turn. "You *already* have a paramilitary structure. You *already* have means of communication that the government doesn't control. What we'd like you to do is to coordinate these groups. Pass information up the chain of command, pass orders downward, make certain equipment gets where it's needed...that sort of thing."

There was another moment of silence. Then Bakshi extruded one index finger from a big, pale hand and tapped the table. In a man so silent and restrained, the gesture seemed as dramatic as a pistol shot. "I should like to know one thing," Bakshi said. "Lord Governor Pahn-ko has been captured and executed. Who is it, exactly, who runs the secret government?"

Sula clenched her teeth to avoid a wail of despair. This was the one question she'd dreaded.

She had decided that she could lie to anyone else as circumstances demanded, but that she would never lie to the people at the table before her. The consequences of lying to them were simply too dire.

"I am the senior officer remaining," Sula said.

Surprise widened Patel's eyes. His mouth dropped open, but he didn't say anything. Tan-dau gave Bakshi a sidelong glance.

"You are a lieutenant," Bakshi said, "and young, and recently promoted at that."

"That is true," Sula said. She could feel sweat collecting under the blonde wig. "But I am also a Peer of ancient name, and a noted killer of Naxids."

"It seems to me," Tan-dau said, again seeming to address no one in particular, "that she wishes us to organize and fight her war for her. I wonder what it is that *she* will contribute?"

Defiant despair rose in Sula. "My training, my name and my skill at killing Naxids," she answered.

Bakshi looked at her. "I'm sure your skill and courage are up to the task," he said. "But of course you are a soldier." He looked at the folk on either side of him, and spread his hands. "We, on the other hand, are men of commerce and of peace. We have our businesses and our families to consider. If we join your resistance to the Naxids, we put all we have worked for in jeopardy."

Sula opened her mouth to speak, but Bakshi held up a hand for silence. "You have assured us that the loyalist Fleet will return and that Zanshaa will be freed from Naxid rule. If that is the case, there is no need for an army here on the ground. But if you are wrong, and the Naxids aren't driven out, then any resisters here in the capital are doomed." He gave a slow shake of his head. "We wish you the best, but I don't understand why we should involve ourselves. The risk is too great."

Another heavy silenced rose. Sula, a leaden hopelessness beating through her veins, looked at the others. "Do you all agree?" she asked.

Tan-dau and Sagas said nothing. Patel gave a rueful grin. "Sorry the love thing didn't work out, princess," he said. "It could have been fun."

"The Naxids are already nibbling at your businesses," Sula said. "When rationing starts and you go into the food business, you'll be competing directly with the clans the Naxids have set in power. It's then that you'll be challenging them directly, and they'll have to destroy you."

Bakshi gave her another of his dead-eyed looks. "What makes you think we'll involve ourselves in illegal foodstuffs?"

"A market in illegal foodstuffs is inevitable," Sula said. "If you don't put yourselves at the head of it, you'll lose control to the people who do."

There was another long silence. Bakshi spread his hands. "There's nothing we can do, my lady." He turned to Casimir and gave him a deliberate stone-eyed look. "Our associates can do nothing, either."

"Of course not, Sergius," Casimir murmured.

Sula looked down her nose at them each in turn, but none offered anything more. Her hands clenched behind her back, the nails scoring her palms. She wanted to offer more arguments, weaker ones even, but she knew it would be useless and did not.

"I thank you then, for agreeing to hear me," she said, and turned to Tan-dau. "I appreciate you offering this place for the meeting."

"Fortune attend you, my lady," Tan-dau said formally.

Fortune was precisely what had just deserted her. She gave a brisk military nod to the room in general and made a proper military turn.

Macnamara anticipated her and stepped to the rear of the room, holding the door for her. She marched out with her shoulders still squared, her blonde head high.

Bastards, she thought.

There was a thud behind as Macnamara tried to close the door just as Casimir tried to exit. Macnamara glared at Casimir as he shouldered his way out and fell into step alongside Sula.

"That went better than I'd expected," he said.

She gave him a look. "I don't need irony right now."

"Not irony," he said pleasantly. "That could have gone a *lot* worse."

"I don't see how."

"Oh, I knew they wouldn't agree with you this time around. But they listened to you. You gave them things to think about. Everything you said will be a part of their calculations from now on." He looked at her, amused appreciation glittering in his eyes. "You're damned impressive, I must say. Standing there all alone staring at those people as if they'd just come up from the sewer smelling of shit." He shook his head. "And I have no idea how you do that thing with your voice. I could have sworn when I met you that you were born in Riverside."

"There's a reason I got picked for this job," Sula said.

There was a moment of silence as they all negotiated the front door of the club. This time, at least, Macnamara didn't try to slam the door on Casimir. Score one, she thought, for civility.

The delay at the door gave Julien time to catch up. He caught his breath in the copper-plated corridor outside, then turned to Sula. "Sorry about that," he said. "Better luck next time, hey?"

"I'm sure you did your best," Sula said. It was all she could do not to snarl.

"Tan-dau got wounded in an assassination attempt last year, and he's not game for new adventures," Julien said. "Sagas isn't a Daimong to take chances. And Pops..." He gave a rueful smile and shook his head. "Pops didn't get where he is by sticking his neck out."

"And Patel?" Sula asked.

Julien laughed. "He'd have followed you, you heard him. He'd like to fight the Naxids just for the love, like he said. But the commission's rulings are always unanimous, and he had to fall in line."

They descended the moving stairs. Sula marched to the doors and walked out onto the street. The pavement was wet, and a fresh smell was in the air: there had been a brief storm while she was conducting her interview.

"Where's a cab rank?" Sula asked.

"Around the corner," said Julien, pointing. He hesitated. "Say – I'm sorry about today, you know. I'd like to make it up to you."

Can you raise an army? Sula thought savagely. But she turned to Julien and said, "That would be very nice."

"Tomorrow night?" Julien said. "Come to my restaurant for dinner? It's called Two Sticks, and it's off Harmony Square. The cook's a Cree and he's brilliant."

Sula had to wonder if the Cree chef thought it was his own restaurant, not Julien's, but this was no time to ask questions of that kind. She agreed to join Julien for dinner at 24.01.

"Shall I pick you up?" Casimir said. "Or are you still in transit from one place to another?"

"I'm *always* in transit," Sula lied, "and now you know why. I'll meet you at the club."

"Care to go out tonight?"

Sula decided she was too angry to play a cliqueman's girl tonight. "Not tonight," she said. "I've got to assassinate a judge."

Casimir was taken aback. "Good luck with that," he said.

She kissed him. "See you tomorrow."

She walked with Macnamara to the cab rank and got a cab. He sat next to Sula in the seat, arms crossed, staring straight forward. One muscle in his jaw worked continually.

"So what's *your* problem?" Sula demanded.

"Nothing," he said. "My lady."

"Good!" she said. "Because if there's anything I don't need, it's *more fucking problems.*"

They sat in stony silence. Sula had the cab let her off two streets from her apartment. Rain had started again, and she had to sprint, her jacket pulled over her head.

Inside she tossed the wet wig onto the back of her chair and combed her short, dyed hair. She considered checking the news, but decided against it, knowing the news would only further irritate her. She settled for a long bath instead.

After her bath she wrapped herself in a robe and went to the front room. The rain was still pouring down. For a long moment she watched the beads of water that snaked down the window.

While watching the water an idea occurred to her.

"Ah. Hah," she said. The idea seemed an attractive one. She examined it carefully, probing it with her mind like a tongue examining the gap left by a missing tooth.

The idea began to seem better and better. She got a fresh piece of paper and a pen and outlined it, along with all possible ramifications.

There wasn't a problem that she could see. Nor a way it could be traced to her.

She destroyed the paper, leaving no evidence of her scheme. She looked at her right thumb, the thick pad of scar tissue where her print had once been.

It was very important that she not leave her fingerprints on this one.

In the morning she made deliveries with Spence and Macnamara. Macnamara was a little stiff but at least he wasn't too visibly sulking.

In the afternoon she went to the Petty Mount for a shopping expedition, and wore the result to meet Casimir at the Cat Street Club. She was late and, as she approached the club with her large shoulder bag banging her hip with every stride, she found Casimir pacing the pavement next to the apricot-coloured car. He was scowling down at the ground, and his coat floated behind him like a cloak.

He looked up at her, and relief flooded his face. Then he saw how she was dressed, in a long coat, black, covered with shiny six-pointed particoloured stars, like a rainbow snowfall.

"You got a coat like mine," he said, surprised.

"Yes. We need to talk."

"We can talk in the car." He stepped towards the car door.

"No. I need more privacy than that. Let's try your office."

Petulance tugged at his lip. "We're already late."

"Julien will be all right. His chef is brilliant."

He nodded as if he understood this remark and followed her through the club. There were few patrons at this early hour, mostly quiet drinkers at the bar or workers who hadn't managed to get home in time for dinner.

Sula bounded up the metal stairs leading to Casimir's office. "How did the judge thing go?" he asked.

Sula had to search her mind to recall the story that, in her annoyance, she'd told him the day before. "Postponed," she said.

He let her into his office. "Is that what you need to talk about?

Because even though Sergius said I wasn't supposed to help you, there are a few things I can do that Sergius doesn't need to know about. Because – oh, damn."

They had entered his office, the spotless black-and-white room, and Sula had thrown her bag on a sofa and opened her coat to reveal that she wore nothing underneath it but stockings and her shoes.

"Damn," Casimir repeated. His eyes travelled over her. "Damn, you're beautiful."

"Don't just stand there," Sula said.

It was the first time she had set out to please a man so totally and for so long. She moved Casimir over the room from one piece of furniture to the other. She took full advantage of the large, oversoft chairs. She used lips and tongue and fingertips, skin and scent, whispers and laughter. There was something whorish about it, she supposed, though her own violent, mercifully brief encounter with whoring had been far more sordid and unpleasant than this.

She kept Casimir busy for an hour and a half, until the chiming of his comm grew far too insistent. He rose from one of the sofas, where he was sprawled with Sula on top of him, and made his way to his desk.

"Audio only," he told the comm. "Answer. Yes, what is it?"

"Julien's arrested," said an unknown voice.

Sula sat up, an expression of concern on her face.

"When?" Casimir barked. "Where?"

"A few minutes ago, at the Two Sticks. He was there with Veronika."

Calculation burned in Casimir's gaze. "Was it the police, or the Fleet?"

The voice shifted to a higher, more urgent register. "It was the *Legion*. They took *everybody*."

Casimir stared intently at the far wall as if it held a puzzle he needed badly to put together. Sula rose and quietly walked to where her large shoulder bag waited. She opened it and began to withdraw clothing.

"Does Sergius know?" Casimir asked.

"He's not at his office. That's the only number I have for him."

"Right. Thanks. I'll call him myself."

Casimir knew he couldn't get away with a call to Sergius that had the video suppressed, so he put on a shirt and combed his hair. He spoke in low tones and Sula heard little of what was said. She finished dressing, took a pistol from her bag, and stuck it in her waistband behind her back.

Casimir finished his phone call. He looked at her with sombre eyes.

"You'd better make yourself scarce," Sula said. "They might be going after all of you."

"That's what Sergius told me," he said.

"Or maybe—" Sula's eyes narrowed "—they're after *you*, and they went to the Two Sticks thinking you'd be there."

"Or they might be after *you*," Casimir said, "and Julien and I are both incidental."

"That hadn't occurred to me," she said.

Casimir began to draw on his clothing. "This looks bad," he said. "But maybe you'll get what you want."

She looked at him.

"War," he explained, "between us and the Naxids."

"That *had* occurred to me," she said.

It had occurred to her the previous night, in fact, while she gazed at raindrops coursing down the window. Which was why, that morning, she'd gone to a public comm unit. She wore a worker's coveralls and the blonde wig and a wide-brimmed hat pulled down over her face, and she'd taken the hat off her head and put it over the unit's camera before she manually punched in the code that would connect her to the Legion of Diligence informer line.

"I want to give some information," she said. "An anarchist cell is meeting tonight in a restaurant called the Two Sticks, off Harmony Square. They are planning sabotage. The meeting is set for twenty-four and one, in a private room. Don't tell the local police, because they're corrupt and would warn the saboteurs."

She'd used the Earth accent that had once amused Caro Sula. She walked away from the comm without removing her hat from the camera pickup.

She must have been convincing because Julien was now under arrest.

"How shall I contact you?" Sula asked Casimir.

He adjusted his trousers, then gave her a code.

Sula nodded. "Got it."

He gave her a quizzical look. "You don't need to write it down?"

"I compose a mental algorithm that will allow me to remember the number," she said. "It's what I do with everyone's numbers."

He blinked. "Clever trick," he said.

She kissed him. "Yes," she said. "A very clever trick."

The next day the Naxids went berserk. Someone with a rifle went onto a building overlooking the Axtattle Parkway, the main highway that connected Zanshaa City with the Naxids' landing field at Wi-hun. The sniper waited for a convoy of Naxid vehicles to go by, then shot the driver of the first vehicle. Because the vehicles were using the automated lanes, the vehicle cruised on under computer control with a dead driver behind the controls. Then the sniper shot the next driver, and the next.

By the time the Naxids got things sorted out at least eight Naxids were dead, and more wounded. By way of retaliation they decided to shoot fifty-one hostages for every dead Naxid. Sula had no idea how they decided on fifty-one.

Casimir, who heard the news before anyone else, called Sula shortly after dawn to tell her to stay off the streets, and she spent the day in the apartment with a book of mathematical puzzles. Casimir called again after nightfall. "Can we meet?" he asked.

"Is it safe to go out?"

"The police have finished rounding up new hostages to replace the ones they shot today, and they're back to processing ration cards. But just in case I'll send a car."

She told him to pick her up at the local train stop. The car was a dark Hunhao sedan with one of the Torminel bodyguards at the controls. He took her to a small residential street on the edge of a Cree neighbourhood – she saw Cree males on the streets exercising their quadruped females, who bounded about them like large puppies.

Casimir was in the apartment of a smiling, elderly couple who apparently did very well for themselves renting out their spare room as a safe house. The room was roomy and comfortable, with flowerpots on the windowsills, fringed throw rugs, the scent of potpourri, family pictures on the walls and a macramé border around the wall video. The remains of Casimir's dinner sat on a tray along with a half-empty bottle of sparkling wine.

Sula kissed him hello, and put her arms around him. His flesh was warm. His cologne had a pleasant earthy scent.

"I think we've got a false alarm," Casimir said. "The Legion doesn't seem to be after me. Or Sergius, or anyone but Julien. There haven't been any raids. No inquiries. Nobody's been seen doing surveillance."

"That may change if Julien talks," Sula said.

Casimir drew back. His face hardened. It was as if she'd just challenged the manhood of the whole Riverside Clique.

"Julien won't talk," he said. "He's a good boy."

"You don't know what they're going to do to him. The Naxids are serious. We can't count on anything."

Casimir's lips gave a scornful twitch. "Julien grew up with Sergius Bakshi beating the crap out of him twice a week – and not for any reason, either, just for the sheer hell of it. You think Julien's going to be scared of the Naxids after *that*?"

Sula considered Sergius Bakshi's dead predator eyes and large pale listless hands and thought that Casimir had a point.

"So they won't get a confession from Julien. There's still Veronika."

Casimir shook his head. "Veronika doesn't know anything." He gave her a pointed look. "She doesn't know about *you*."

"But she knows Julien was expecting the two of us for dinner. And the Naxids will have seen that Julien was sitting at a table set for four."

Casimir shrugged. "They'll have my name and half of yours. They'll have a file on me and nothing on you. You're not in any danger."

"It's not me I'm worried about," Sula said.

He looked at her for a moment, then softened. "I'm being careful," he said in a subdued voice. He glanced around at the room. "I'm here, aren't I? In this little room, running my criminal empire by remote control."

Sula grinned at him. He grinned back. "Would you like something to eat or drink?" he asked.

"Whatever kind of soft drink they have would be fine."

He carried out his dinner tray. Sula toured the room, tidied a few of Casimir's belongings that had been carelessly laid down, then took off her shoes and sat on the floor. Casimir returned with two bottles of Citrine Fling. He seemed surprised to find Sula on the floor but joined her without comment. He handed her a bottle and touched it with his own. The resinous material made a light thud rather than a crystal ringing sound. He made a face.

"Here's to our exciting evening," he said.

"We'll have to make all the excitement ourselves," Sula said.

His eyes glittered. "Absolutely." He took a sip of his drink, then gave her a reflective look. "I know even less about Lady Sula than I do about Gredel."

She looked at him. "What do you want to know?"

There was a troubled look in his eye. "That story about your parents being executed. I suppose that was something that you said to get close to me."

Sula shook her head. "My parents were executed when I was young. Flayed."

He was surprised. "Really?"

"You can look it up if you want to. I'm in the military because it's the only job I'm permitted."

"But you're still a Peer."

"Yes. But as Peers go, I'm poor. All the family's wealth and property were confiscated." She looked at him. "You've probably got scads more money than I do."

And, she thought, you're not the first high-class criminal I've slept with, either.

Casimir was even more surprised. "I've never met a whole lot of Peers, but you always get the impression they're rolling in it."

"I'd like to have enough to roll in." She laughed, took a sip of her Fling. "Tell me. If they don't find Julien guilty of anything, what happens to him?"

"The Legion? They'll try to scare the piss out of him, then let him go."

Sula considered this. "Are the Naxids letting *anyone* go at all? Or does everyone they pick up for any reason join the hostage population in the lock-ups?"

He looked at her and ran a pensive thumb down his jaw. "I hadn't thought of that."

"Plus he could be hostage for his father's good behaviour."

Casimir was thoughtful.

"Where would they send him?" Sula asked.

"Anywhere. The Blue Hatches, the Reservoir. Any jail or police station." He frowned. "Certain police stations he could walk right out of."

"Let's hope he gets sent to one of those then."

"Yes. Let's."

His eyes were troubled.

Good, she thought. There were certain thoughts she wanted him to dwell on for a while.

The next afternoon Sula was in the High City selling cocoa and gathering intelligence. When she returned to Riverside she received a call from Casimir telling her that Julien had been cleared of suspicion by the Legion of Diligence, but that he was remaining in custody as a hostage. "He's in the Reservoir Prison, damn it," Casimir said. "There's no way we can get him out of there."

Calculations shimmered through Sula's mind. "Let me think about that," she said.

There was a moment of silence. Then, "Should we get together and talk?"

There were certain things one shouldn't say over a comm, and they were skating right along the edge.

"Not yet," Sula said. "I've got some research to do first."

She spent some time in public databases, researching the intricacies of the Zanshaa legal system, and more time with back numbers of the *Forensic Register*, the publication of the Zanshaa Legal Association. More time was spent seeing who in the *Register* had left Zanshaa with the old government and who hadn't.

Having gathered her data, Sula called Casimir and told him she needed him to set up a meeting with Sergius.

Since Sergius and Casimir had resumed their normal lives after the Legion had released Julien to the prison system, Sula was taken to meet Sergius in his office, on the second floor of an unremarkable building in the heart of Riverside.

She and Casimir passed through an anteroom of flunkies and hulking guards, all of whom she regarded with patrician hauteur, and into Sergius's own office, where Sergius rose to greet her. The office was as unremarkable as the building, with scuffed floors and second-hand furniture and the musty smell of things that had been left lying too long in corners.

People with real power, Sula thought, didn't need to show it.

Sergius took her hand, and though the touch of his big hand was light she could sense the restrained power in his grip.

"What may I do for you, Lady Sula?" he asked.

"Nothing right now," Sula said. "Instead, I hope to be of service to you."

The ruthless eyes flicked to Casimir, who returned an expression meant to convey that he knew. Sergius returned his attention to Sula. "I appreciate your thinking of me," he said. "Please sit down."

At least, Sula thought, she got to sit down this time. Sergius began to move behind his desk again.

"I believe I can get Julien out of the Reservoir," Sula said.

Sergius stopped, then turned his round head towards her. For the first time she saw emotion in his dark eyes, a glimpse into a black void of deep-seated desire that seemed all the more frightening in a man who normally seemed bereft of emotion.

He wanted his son back. Whether Sergius desired Julien's return because he loved his son, or because his son was a mere possession that some caprice of fate had taken from him, it was clear that the deep, burning hunger was there, a need as clear and primal and rapacious as a hungry panther for his dinner.

Sergius looked at her for a long moment, the need burning in his eyes, and then he recovered himself, straightened, and sat in his shabby chair. By the time he clasped his big pale hands on the desk in front of him, his face had again gone blank.

"That's interesting," he said.

Sula had sat deliberately in one of the two seats set before the desk. "I want you to understand that I can't set Julien at liberty," she said. "I believe I can get him transferred to the holding cells at the Riverside police station, or to any other place that suits you. You'll have to get him out of there yourself.

"I'll also provide official identification for Julien that will allow him to move freely, but of course—" Here she looked into the unreadable eyes. "He'll be a fugitive until the Naxids are removed from power."

Sergius held her gaze for a moment, then nodded.

"How may I repay you for this favour?" he asked.

Sula suppressed a smile. She had her list well prepared.

"The secret government maintains a business enterprise used to transfer munitions and the like from one place to another. It's operating under the cover of a food distribution service. Since food distribution is about to become illegal, I'd like to be able to operate this enterprise under your protection, and without the usual fees."

Sula wondered if she was imagining the hint of a smile that played about Sergius Bakshi's lips. "Agreed," he said.

"I would also like ten Naxids to die."

One eyebrow gave a twitch. "Ten?"

"Ten, and of a certain quality. Naxids in the Patrol, the Fleet, or the Legion, all of officer grade; or civil servants with ranks of CN6 or higher. And it must be clear that they've been murdered – they can't seem to die in accidents."

His voice was cold. "You wish this done when?"

"It's not a precondition. The Naxids may die within any reasonable amount of time after Julien is released."

Sergius seemed to thaw a little. "You will provoke the Naxids into one massacre after another."

She gave a little shrug and tried to match with her own the glossy inhumanity of the other's eyes. "That is incidental," she said.

Sergius gave an amused, twisted little smile. It was as out of place on his round immobile face as a bray of laughter. "I'll agree to this," he said. "But I want it clear that I'll pick the targets."

"Certainly," Sula said.

"Anything else?"

"I'd like an extraction team on hand, just in case my project doesn't go well. I don't expect we'll need them, though."

"Extraction team?" Sergius's lips formed the unaccustomed syllables, and then his face relaxed into the face he probably wore at home, a face that was still, in truth, frightening enough.

"I suppose you'd better tell me about this plan of yours," he said.

There were three sets of people who had the authority to move prisoners from one location to another. There was the prison bureaucracy itself, which housed the prisoners, shuttled them to and from interrogations and trials, and made use of their labour in numberless factories and agricultural communes. All those with the authority to sign off on prisoner transfers now consisted entirely of Naxids. Sergius apparently hadn't yet got any of these on his payroll, otherwise Julien would have been shifted out of the Reservoir by now.

The second group consisted of Judges of the High Court and of Final Appeal, but all these had been evacuated before the Naxid fleet arrived. The new administration had replaced them all with Naxids.

The third group were Judges of Interrogation. It was not a prestigious posting, and some had been evacuated and some hadn't. Apparently Sergius didn't have any of these in his pocket, either.

Lady Mitsuko Inada was one of those who hadn't left Zanshaa. She lived in Green Park, a quiet, wealthy enclave on the west side of the city. The district had none of the ostentation or flamboyant architecture of the High City – probably none of the houses had more than fifteen or sixteen rooms. Those buildings still occupied by their owners tried to radiate a comfortable air of wealth and security, but were undermined by the untended gardens and shuttered windows of the neighbouring buildings, abandoned by their owners who had fled, either to another star system or, failing that, to the country.

Lady Mitsuko's dwelling was on the west side of the park, the least expensive and least fashionable. It was built of grey fieldstone, with a green alloy roof, an onion dome of greenish copper, and two ennobling sets of chimney pots. The garden in front was mossy and frondy, with ponds and fountains. There were willows in the back, which suggested more ponds there.

Peers constituted about 2 per cent of the empire's population, and as a class controlled more than 90 per cent of its wealth. But there was immense variation within the order of Peers, ranging from individuals who controlled the wealth of entire systems to those who lived in genuine poverty. Lady Mitsuko was on the lower end of the scale. Her job didn't entitle her to an evacuation, and neither did her status within the Inada clan.

All Peers, even the poor ones, were guaranteed an education and jobs in the Fleet, civil service, or bar. It was possible that Lady Mitsuko had worked herself up to her current status from somewhere lower.

Sula rather hoped she had. If Lady Mitsuko had a degree of social insecurity, it might work well for Sula's plans.

Macnamara drove Sula to the kerb before the house. He was dressed in a dark suit and brimless cap, and looked like a professional driver. He opened Sula's door from the outside, and helped her out with a hand gloved in Devajjo leather.

"Wait," she told him, though of course he knew he would wait, because that was the plan.

Neither of them were looking at the van that cruised along the far side of the park, packed with heavily armed Riverside Clique gunmen.

Sula straightened her shoulders – she was Fleet again, in her blonde wig – and marched up the walk and over the ornamental bridge to the house door. With gloved fingers – no fingerprints – she reached for the grotesque ornamental bronze head near the door and touched the shiny spot that would announce a visitor to anyone inside the house, then removed her uniform cap from under her arm and put it on her head. She now wore her full dress uniform of viridian green, with her lieutenant's shoulder boards, glossy shoes and her medals.

Her sidearm was a weight against one hip.

To avoid being overconspicuous, she wore over her shoulders a nondescript overcoat, which she removed as soon as she heard footsteps in the hall. She held it over the pistol and its holster.

The singing tension in her nerves kept her back straight, her chin high. She had to remember that she was a Peer. Not a Peer looking down her nose at cliquemen, but a Peer interacting with another of her class.

That had always been the hardest, to pretend that she was born to this.

A female servant opened the door, a middle-aged Terran. She wasn't in livery, but in neat, subdued civilian clothes.

Lady Mitsuko, Sula concluded, possessed little in the way of social pretension.

Sula walked past the surprised servant and into the hallway. The walls had been plastered beige, with little works of art in ornate frames, and her shoes clacked on deep grey tile.

"Lady Caroline to see Lady Mitsuko, please," she said, and took off her cap.

The maidservant closed the door and held out her hands for the cap and overcoat.

Sula looked at her. "Go along, now," she said.

The servant looked doubtful, then gave a little bow and trotted into the interior of the house. Sula examined herself in a hall mirror of polished nickel asteroid material, adjusted the tilt of one of her medals, and waited.

Lady Mitsuko appeared, walking quickly. She was younger than Sula had expected, in her early thirties, and very tall. Her body was angular and she had a thin slash of a mouth and a determined jaw that suggested that, as a Judge of Interrogation, she was disinclined to let prisoners get away with much. Her dark hair was worn long and caught in a tail behind, and she wore casual clothes. She dabbed with a napkin at a food spot on her blouse.

"Lady Caroline?" she said. "I'm sorry. I was just giving the twins their supper." She held out her hand, but there was a puzzled frown on her face as she tried to work out whether or not she had seen Sula before.

Sula startled Lady Mitsuko by bracing in salute, her chin high. "Lady Magistrate," she said. "I come on official business. Is there somewhere we may speak privately?"

Lady Mitsuko stopped, her hand still outheld. "Yes," she said. "Certainly."

She took Sula to her office, a small room that still had the slight aroma of the varnish used on the light-coloured shelves and furniture of natural wood.

"Will you take a seat, my lady?" Mitsuko said as she closed the door. "Shall I call for refreshment?"

"That won't be necessary," Sula said. "I won't be here long." She stood before a chair but didn't sit, and waited to speak until Lady Mitsuko stepped behind her desk.

"You have my name slightly wrong," Sula said. "I'm not Lady Caroline, but rather Caroline, Lady Sula."

Lady Mitsuko's eyes darted suddenly to Sula, and then she froze with one hand on the back of her office chair. Her mouth parted slightly with surprise.

"Do you recognize me?" Sula prompted.

"I...don't know." Mitsuko pronounced the words as if they belonged to a foreign language.

Sula reached into a pocket and produced her Fleet ID. "You may examine my identification if you wish," she said. "I'm on a mission for the secret government."

Lady Mitsuko pressed the napkin to her heart. The other hand reached for Sula's identification. "The secret government..." she said softly, as if to herself.

She sank slowly into her chair, her eyes on Sula's ID. Sula sat and placed her overcoat and hat in her lap. She waited for Lady Mitsuko's eyes to life from the ID, and spoke.

"We require your cooperation," she said.

Lady Mitsuko slowly extended her arm and held out Sula's identification. "What do you ... What does the secret government want?" she asked.

Sula leaned forward and took her ID. "The government requires you to transfer twelve hostages from the Reservoir Prison to the holding cells at the Riverside police station. I have a list ready – will you set your comm to receive?"

Speaking slowly, as if in a daze, Lady Mitsuko readied her desk comm. Sula triggered her sleeve display to send the names of Julien, Veronika, nine prisoners chosen at random from the official posted list of hostages, and – just because she was feeling mischievous when she made the list – the Two Sticks's Cree cook.

"We expect the order to be sent tomorrow," Sula said. She cleared her throat in a businesslike way. "I am authorized to say that after the return of the legitimate government, your loyalty will be rewarded. On the other hand, if the prisoner transfer does not take place, you will be assassinated."

Mitsuko's look was scandalized. She stared at Sula for a blank second, and then she seemed to notice for the first time the holstered pistol at Sula's hip. Her eyes jumped away, and then she made a visible effort to collect herself.

"What reason shall I give for the transfer?" she said.

"Whatever seems best to you. Perhaps they need to be interrogated in regard to certain crimes. I'm sure you can come up with a good reason." Sula rose from her chair. "I shan't keep you," she said.

And best regards to the twins. Sula considered adding that, a clear malicious threat to the children, but decided it was unnecessary.

She rather thought that she and Lady Mitsuko had reached an understanding.

Mitsuko escorted her to the door. Her movements were still a bit disconnected, as if her nervous system hadn't quite caught up with events. At least she didn't look as if she'd panic and run for the comm as soon as the door had closed behind Sula's back.

Sula threw the overcoat over her shoulders. "Allow me to wish you a good evening, Lady Magistrate," she said.

"Um, good evening, Lady Sula," said Lady Mitsuko.

Macnamara leaped out to open the door as soon as Sula appeared. She tried not to run over the ornamental bridge and down the path, and instead managed a brisk, military clip.

The car hummed away from the kerb as fast as its four electric engines permitted, and made the first possible turn. By the time the vehicle had gone two streets, Sula had squirmed out of her military tunic and silver-braided trousers. The blouse she'd worn beneath the tunic was suitable as casual summer ware, and she jammed her legs into a pair of bright summery pantaloons. The military kit and the blonde wig went into a laundry bag. The holster shifted to the small of Sula's back.

The van carrying the extraction team roared up behind, and both vehicles pulled to a stop: Sula and Macnamara transferred to the van, along with the laundry bag. Another driver hopped into the car – he would drive the car to the parking stand of the local train, where it could be retrieved at leisure.

As Sula jumped through the van's clamshell door, she saw the extraction team, Spence, Casimir and four burly men from Julien's crew, all bulky with armour and with weapons in their laps. Another pair sat behind the windscreen in front. The interior of the van was blue with tobacco smoke. Laughter burst from her at their grim look.

"Put the guns away," she said. "We won't be needing them."

Triumph blazed through her. She pulled Macnamara into the van and then, because there were no more seats, dropped onto Casimir's lap. As the door hummed shut and the van pulled away, Sula put her arms around Casimir's neck and kissed him.

Sergius and the whole Riverside Clique couldn't have managed what she'd just done. They could have sniffed around the halls of justice for someone to bribe, and probably already had without success; but none of them could have convinced a Peer and a judge to sign a transfer order of her own free will. If they'd approached Lady Mitsuko, she would have brushed them off; if they'd threatened her, she would have ordered their arrest.

It took a Peer to unlock a Peer's cooperation – and not with a bribe, but with an appeal to legitimacy and class solidarity.

Casimir's lips were warm, his breath sweet. Macnamara, without a seat, crouched on the floor behind the driver and looked anywhere but at Sula sitting on Casimir's lap. The cliquemen nudged each other and grinned. Spence watched with frank interest.

The driver kept off the limited-access expressways and onto the smaller streets where he had options. Even so he managed to get stuck in traffic. The van inched forward as the minutes ticked by, and then the driver cursed.

"Damn! Roadblock ahead!"

In an instant Sula was off Casimir's lap and peering forward. Ahead she could see Naxids in the black-and-yellow uniforms of the Motor Patrol. Their four-legged bodies snaked eerily from side to side as they moved up and down the line of vehicles, peering at the drivers. One vehicle was stopped while the Patrol rummaged through its cargo compartment. The van was on a one-way street, its two lanes choked with traffic: it was impossible to turn around.

Sula's heart was thundering in her chest as it never had when confronting Sergius or Lady Mitsuko. Ideas flung themselves at her mind, and burst from her lips in not-quite-complete sentences.

"Place to park?" she said urgently. "Garage? Pretend to make a delivery?"

The answer was no. Parking was illegal, there was no garage to turn into, and all the businesses on the street were closed at this hour.

Casimir's shoulder clashed with hers as he came forward to scan the scene before them. "How many?"

"I can see seven," Sula said. "My guess is that there are two or three more we can't see from here. Say ten." She pointed ahead, to an open-topped vehicle run partly up onto the sidewalk, with a machine gun mounted on the top and a Naxid standing behind it, the sun gleaming off his black beaded scales.

"Macnamara," she said. "That gun's your target."

Macnamara had been one of the best shots on the training course, and his task was critical. The gunner didn't even have to touch his weapon: all he had to do was put the reticule of his targeting system onto the van and press the *go* button: the gun itself would handle the rest, and riddle the vehicle with a couple thousand rounds. The gunner had to be taken out first.

And then the driver of the vehicle, because he could operate the gun from his own station.

A spare rifle had been brought for Sula, and she reached for it. There was no spare suit of armour and she suddenly felt the hollow in her chest where the bullets would lodge.

"We've got two police coming down the line towards us. One on either side. You two—" she indicated the driver and the other man in the front of the van "—you'll pop them right at the start. The rest of us will exit the rear of the vehicle – Macnamara first, to give him time to set up on the gunner. The rest of you keep advancing – you're as well-armed as the Patrol, and you've got surprise. If things don't work out, we'll split up into small groups – Macnamara and Spence, you're with me. We'll hijack vehicles in nearby streets and get out as well as we can." Her mouth was dry by the time she finished, and she licked her lips with a sandpaper tongue. Casimir was grinning at her. "Nice plan," he said.

Total fuckup, she thought, but gave what she hoped was an encouraging nod. She crouched on the rubberized floor of the van and readied her rifle.

"Better turn the transponder on," Casimir said, and the driver gave a start, then gave a code phrase to the van's comm unit.

Every vehicle in the empire was wired to report its location at regular intervals to a central data store. The cliquemen's van had been altered so as to make this an option rather than a requirement, and the function had been turned off while the van was on its mission to Green Park. An unresponsive vehicle, however, was bound to be suspicious in the eyes of the Patrol.

"Good thought," Sula breathed.

"Here they come." Casimir ducked down behind the seat. He gave Sula a glance – his cheeks were flushed with colour, and his eyes glittered like diamonds. His grin was brilliant.

Sula felt her heart surge in response. She answered his grin, and then she felt that wasn't enough. She lunged across the distance between them and kissed him hard.

Live or die, she thought. Whatever came, she was ready.

"They're pinging us," the driver growled. One of the Patrol had raised a hand comm and activated the transponder.

The van coasted forward a few seconds, then halted. Sula heard the front windows whining open to make it easier to shoot the police on either side.

The van had a throat-tickling odour of tobacco and terror. From her position on the floor she could see the driver holding a pistol alongside his seat. His knuckles were white on the grip. Her heart sped like a turbine in her chest. Tactical patterns played themselves out in her mind.

She heard the footfalls of one of the Patrol, walking close. She kept her eyes on the driver's pistol. The second it moved, she would act.

Then the driver gave a startled grunt, and the van surged forward. The knuckles relaxed on the pistol.

"She waved us through," the driver said.

There was a moment of disbelieving silence, and then Sula heard the rustle and shift of ten tense, frightened, heavily armed people all relaxing at once.

The van accelerated. Sula let the breath sigh slowly from her lungs, and put her rifle carefully down on the floor of the vehicle. She turned to the others and saw at least six cigarettes being lit. Then she laughed and sat heavily on the floor.

Casimir turned to her, his expression filled with a kind of savage wonder. "That was lucky," he said.

Sula didn't answer. She only looked at him, at the pulse throbbing in his neck, the slight glisten of sweat at the base of his throat, the fine mad glitter in his eyes. She had never wanted anything so much.

"Lucky," he said again.

She didn't touch Casimir till they reached Riverside, when the van pulled up outside the Hotel of Many Blessings. Careful not to touch him, she followed him out of the van – the others would store the weapons – and then went with him to his suite, keeping half a pace apart on the elevator.

He turned to her, and she reached forward and tore open his shirt so that she could lick the burning adrenaline from his skin.

His frenzy equalled hers. Their blood smoked with the excitement of shared danger, and the only way to relieve the heat was to spend it on each other.

They laughed. They shrieked. They snarled. They tumbled over each other like lion cubs, claws only half-sheathed. They pressed skin to skin so hard that it seemed as if they were trying to climb into one another.

The fury spent itself some time after midnight. Casimir called room service for something to eat. Sula craved chocolate, but there was none to be had. For a brief moment she considered breaking into her own warehouse to satisfy her hunger.

"For once," he said, as he cut his omelette with a fork and slid half of it onto Sula's plate, "for once you didn't sound like you came from Riverside."

"Yes?" Sula raised an eyebrow.

"And you didn't sound like Lady Sula either. You had some other accent, one I'd never heard before."

"It's an accent I'll use only with you," Sula said.

The accent of the Fabs, on Spannan. The voice of Gredel.

Lady Mitsuko signed the transfer order that morning. Transport wasn't arranged till the afternoon, so Julien and the other eleven arrived at the Riverside station late in the afternoon, about six.

Sergius Bakshi had a long-standing arrangement with the captain of the Riverside station. Julien's freedom cost two hundred zeniths. Veronika cost fifty, and the Cree cook a mere fifteen.

Julien would have been on his way by seven, but it was necessary to wait for the Naxid supervisor, the one who approved all the ration cards, to leave.

Still suffering from his interrogation, Julien limped to liberty, on the night that the Naxids announced that the Committee to Save the Praxis, their own government, was already on its way from Naxas to take up residence in the High City of Zanshaa. A new Convocation would be assembled, composed both of Naxids and other races, to be the supreme governing body of their empire.

"Here's hoping we can give them a hot landing," Sula said. She was among the guests at Sergius's welcome-home dinner, along with Julien's mother, a tall, gaunt woman, forbidding as a statue, who burst into tears at the sight of him.

Veronika was not present. Interrogation had broken a cheekbone and the orbit of one eye: Julien had called a surgeon, and in the meantime had provided painkillers.

"*I'll* give them a welcome," Julien said grimly, through lips that had been bruised and cut. "I'll rip the bastards to bits."

Sula looked across the table at Sergius, and silently mimed the word "ten" at him. He smiled at her, and when he looked at Julien the smile turned hard.

"Ten," he said. "Why stop there?"

Sula smiled. At last she had her army. Her own team of three plus a tough, disciplined order of killers who had decided – after a proper show of resistance – to be loved.

THE PRICE

Michael Z. Williamson

Inevitably combatants get killed in war, yet some must choose their deaths…

Michael Z. Williamson was born and raised in the UK, then in Canada, then in the US. He served twenty-five years in the US military in engineer fields, in the Army and US Air Force, with deployments for Operation Desert Fox and Operation Iraqi Freedom. He retired in 2010. When not writing, he tests and reviews, restores and repairs, builds and collects firearms and edged weapons. He lives near Indianapolis with his wife Gail Sanders, a veteran US Army combat photographer, and two children who are studying languages, history and mathematics with the intent of world domination.

FOUR JEMMA TWO Three, Freehold of Grainne Military Forces, (J Frame Craft, Reconnaissance, Stealth), was a tired boat with a tired crew.

After two local years – three Earth years – of war with the United Nations of Earth and Space, that was no small accomplishment. Most of her sister vessels had been destroyed. That 4J23 was intact, functional and only slightly ragged with a few "character traits" spoke well of her remarkable crew.

"I have a message, and I can't decode it with my comm," Warrant Leader Derek Costlow announced. The crew turned to him. This could be a welcome break from the monotony of maintenance. Jan Marsich and his sister Meka, both from Special Warfare and passengers stuck aboard since the war started, paid particular attention. Any chance of finding a real mission or transport back to Grainne proper was of interest to them.

"Want me to have a whack at it, Warrant?" asked Sergeant Melanie Sarendy, head of the intelligence mission crew.

"If you would, Mel." He nodded. "I'll forward the data to your system."

Sarendy dropped her game control, which was hardwired and shielded rather than wireless. Intel boats radiated almost no signature. The handheld floated where it was until disturbed by the eddies of her passage.

Jan asked, "Why do we have a message when we're tethered to the Rock? From who?"

Meka wrinkled her brow. "That's an interesting series of questions," she commented.

"The Rock" was a field-expedient facility with no official name other than a catalogue number of use only for communication logs. The engineers who carved and blasted it from a planetoid, the boat crews who used it, the worn and chronically short-handed maintenance personnel aboard had had too little time to waste on trivialities such as names. There were other such facilities throughout the system, but few of the surviving vessels strayed far enough from their own bases to consort with other stations. "The Rock" sufficed.

They were both attentive again as Sarendy returned. She looked around at the eyes on her, and said, "Sorry. Whatever it is, I don't have a key for it."

Meka quivered alert. "Mind if I try?" she asked.

"Sure," Costlow replied.

She grabbed her comm and plugged it into a port as everyone waited silently. She identified herself through several layers of security and the machine conceded that perhaps it might have heard of that code. A few more jumped hoops and it flashed a translation on her screen.

The silence grew even more palpable when she looked up with her eyes blurring with tears. "Warrant," she said, voice cracking, and locked eyes with him.

Costlow glanced around the cabin, and in seconds everyone departed for their duty stations or favourite hidey-holes, leaving the two of them and Jan in relative privacy. Jan was family, and Costlow let him stay. In response to the worried looks from the two of them, Meka turned her screen to face them.

The message was brief and said simply, "YOU ARE ORDERED TO DESTROY AS MANY OF THE FOLLOWING PRIOR-ITIZED TARGETS AS POSSIBLE. ANY AND ALL ASSETS AND RESOURCES ARE TO BE UTILIZED TO ACCOMPLISH THIS MISSION. SIGNED, NAUMANN, COLONEL COMMANDING, PROVISIONAL FREEHOLD MILITARY FORCES. VERIFI-CATION X247." Attached were a list of targets and a time frame. All the targets were in a radius around Jump Point Three, within about a day of their current location.

"I don't understand," Jan said. "Intel boats don't carry heavy weapons. How do they expect us to do this?"

"It was addressed to me, not the boat," Meka replied. "He wants me to take out these targets, using any means necessary."

That didn't need translating. There was a silence, broken by Costlow asking, "Are you sure that's a legit order? It looks pointless. Why would they have you attack stuff way out here in the Halo?"

Meka replied, "We know what the enemy has insystem. We know where most of their infrastructure is. If Naumann wants it taken out, it means he's preparing an offensive."

"But this is insane!" Jan protested. "The Aardvarks will have any target replaced in days!"

"No," Meka replied, shaking her head. "It's a legit order. All those targets are intel or command and control."

Costlow said, "So he wants the command infrastructure taken out to prevent them responding quickly. Then he hits them with physical force."

"OK, but why not just bomb them or use rocks in fast trajec-tories?" Jan asked.

Costlow said, "It would take too long to set that many rocks in orbit. Nor could we get them moving fast enough. Manoeuvring thrusters and standard meteor watch would take care of them. As to bombing them, they all have defensive grids, and we're a recon boat."

Jan paused and nodded. "Yeah, I know. And there aren't many real gunboats left. I'd just like a safer method." He asked Meka, "So how could you get in?"

"UN stations have sensor holes to ignore vacsuits and toolkits. Ships can't get in, but a single person can."

Costlow looked confused. "Why'd they leave a hole like that?" he asked.

"Partly to prevent accidents with EVA and rescue, partly laziness. They lost a couple of people, and that's just not socially acceptable on Earth," she said. "It's the Blazer's greatest asset to penetrating security. Systems only work if they are used. Back doors and human stupidity are some of our best tools."

"Didn't they think anyone would do what you're discussing?" Jan asked. That was dangerous. It would push EVA gear to the edge.

"No," she said, shaking her head. "They would never give such an order. The political bureaucracy of the UNPF requires all missions be planned with no loss of life. Not minimal, but zero. Yes, it's ridiculous, but that's how they do things."

"And they don't think we'd do it?" Costlow asked.

"Why should they assume we'd do it if they wouldn't? You're having a hard enough time with the concept."

Jan asked, "So you EVA in, and then back out?"

"How would I find a stealthed boat from a suit? How would you find me? It's not as if there's enough power to just loiter, and doing so would show on any scan." Her expression was flushed, nauseous and half grinning. It was creepy.

"But even if you get through, they can still get new forces here in short order," Jan said. He didn't want his sister to die, because that's what this was: a literal suicide mission. His own guts churned.

"No," Meka replied. "Or, not fast enough to matter, I should say." She tapped tactical calculus algorithms into her comm while mumbling, "Minimum twenty hours to get a message relayed to Sol...flight time through Jump Point Two..."

Jan had forgotten that. Jump Point One came straight from Sol, but it no longer existed. Professor Meacham and his wife had taken their hyperdrive research ship into it, then activated phase drive. The result of two intersecting stardrive fields was hard to describe mathematically, but the practical, strategic result was that the point collapsed. No jump drive vessel could transit directly from Sol to Grainne any more, and the UN didn't yet have any phase drive vessels that they knew of.

Meka finished mumbling, looked up, and said, "Median estimate of forty-three days to get sufficient force here. They could have command and control back theoretically in forty hours, median two eighty-six, but that doesn't help them if they are overrun. It's risky, but we don't have any other option."

Costlow said, "That may be true, but they *can* send more force. It's a short-term tactical gain, but not a strategic win."

"I know Naumann," Meka replied firmly. "He has something planned."

"Unless it's desperation," Costlow said.

Shaking her head, her body unconsciously twisting to compensate, she said, "No. He never throws his people away, and he has very low casualty counts. If he wants me to do this, then he has a valid plan."

"Trusting him with your life is dangerous, especially since you don't even know that's him," Jan said. They'd almost died three times now. She'd almost died a couple more. This one was for real.

"We're trusting him with more than that," she said. "And that's definitely him. Security protocols aside, no one else would have the balls to give an order like that and just assume it would be followed. Besides, it authenticates."

"OK," Costlow reluctantly agreed. "Which target are you taking?"

She pointed as she spoke, "Well, the command ship *London* is the first choice, but I don't think I can get near a ship. This crewed platform is second, but I'd have to blast or fight my way in. If I fail, I still die, and accomplish nothing. I suppose I have to chicken out and take the automatic commo station."

"Odd way to chicken out," Jan commented in a murmur.

"Are you sure of these priorities?" Costlow asked. His teeth were grinding and he looked very bothered.

"Yes," she replied. "If I had more resources, I'd take *London*, too. We don't have any offensive missiles, though."

"We have one," the older man softly replied. They looked at him silently. "If you're sure that's a good order," he said. His face turned from tan to ashen as he spoke.

"I am," she said.

"Then I'll drop you on the way. Just think of this as an intelligent stealth missile," he said, and tried to smile. It looked like a rictus.

"Are you sure?" she asked.

"No," he admitted. "But if it's what we have to do to win..."

There was silence for a few moments. Hating himself for not speaking already, hating the others even though it wasn't their fault, Jan said, "I'll take the automatic station." Saying it was more concrete than thinking it. His guts began twisting and roiling, and cold sweat burst from his body. He felt shock and adrenaline course through him. "That takes it out of the equation, and you can fight your way into the crewed one."

Costlow said, "It's appreciated, Jan, but you're tech branch. I think you'd be of more help here."

It was a perfect escape, and Meka's expression said she wasn't going to tell his secret if he wanted to stop there. He was a Special Projects technician who built custom gear for others, usually in close support, but too valuable to be directly combatant save in emergencies. The act of volunteering was more than enough for most people, and he could gracefully bow out. He felt himself talking, brain whirling as he did. "I do EVA as a hobby. I'm not as good as Meka, but I can manage, given the gear." There. *Now* he was committed.

"You don't have to, Jan," Meka said. "There are other Blazers. We'll get enough targets."

"Meka, I'm not doing this out of inadequacy or false bravery." Actually, he was. There was another factor, too. When she looked at him, he continued, "I *can't* face Mom and Dad and tell them you did this. No way. I'm doing this so I don't have to face them. And because I guess it has to be done."

After a long wait, staring at each other, conversation resumed. The three made a basic schedule, hid all data and undogged the cabin. They each sought their own private spaces to think and come to grips, and the rest of the crew were left to speculate. The normal schedule resumed, and would remain in force until the planned zero time, five days away.

The three were reserved during the PT sparring match that evening. The crew each picked a corner or a hatch to watch from in the day cabin, a five-metre cylinder ten metres long, and cheered and critiqued as they took turns tying each other in knots. Sarendy was small but vicious, her lithe and slender limbs striking like those of a praying mantis. Jan and Meka were tall and rangy. Costlow was older and stubborn. Each one had his or her own method of fighting. They were all about as effective.

Jan was strong, determined, and made a point of staying current on unarmed combat, partly due to a lack of demand for his services. He and Costlow twirled and kicked and grappled for several minutes, sweating and gasping from exertion, until Jan finally pinned the older man in a corner with a forearm wedged against his throat. "Yours," Costlow acknowledged.

Jan and Meka faced off from opposite ends, both lean and pantherlike. They studied each other carefully for seconds, then flew at each other, twisting and reaching, and met in a flurry of long limbs. Meka slapped him into a spin, twisted his ankles around, locked a foot under his jaw and let her momentum carry them against the aft hatch, where her other knee settled in the small of his back, pinning him helplessly as she grabbed the edge. Her kinesthetic sense and coordination never ceased to amaze the rest of them.

Passive Sensor Specialist Riechard gamely threw himself into the bout. He advanced and made a feint with one hand, orienting to keep a foot where he could get leverage off the bulkhead. He moved in fast and hard and scored a strike against Meka's shoulder, gripped her arm and began to apply leverage. She countered by pivoting and kicking for his head.

Riechard spun and flinched. "Shoot, Meka, watch it!" he snapped.

"Sorry," she replied. Nerves had her frazzled, and she'd overreacted, her kick almost tearing his ear off. "I better take a break. Default yours."

The crew knew something was up. Costlow and the Marsichs were on edge, irritable and terse. The session broke down without comment, and everyone drifted in separate directions.

Jan signed out and headed into The Rock the next morning. The scenery was no more exciting, being carved stone walls with sealed hatches, but it wasn't the boat. The air seemed somehow fresher, and it was good not to see the same faces. It wasn't his choice for a last liberty, but there wasn't any alternative. It was either the ship or The Rock.

Throughout the station, soldiers and spacers moved around in sullen quiet. The reserved faces made it obvious that other boats and ships had similar instructions. Jan had to smile at the irony that everyone had the same orders, and no one could talk about it. Then he remembered what was to happen, and became rather sullen himself.

He'd wanted Mel Sarendy for two years, but crew were off-limits, and it grew more frustrating as time went on. Their society had no taboos against casual nudity, and the spartan supplies and close quarters aboard boat encouraged it. He'd spent hours staring at her toned body, surreally shaped in microgravity. Her ancestry, like her name, was Earth Cambodian, diluted perhaps with a trace of Russian. That he occasionally caught what he thought was a hint of reciprocation in her speech and actions made it almost torture.

He didn't want to drink, in case he crawled into the bottle. He settled for a small cubicle where he could just sit in silence and alone, a luxury unavailable aboard the boat.

Costlow was excited when he returned. Jan recognized cheerfulness when he saw it, and was impatient to find out what had changed.

Some time later, the three gathered on the command deck and sealed it off. "Talk to me, Warrant," Meka demanded.

"There's enough guidance systems to set a dozen charges. We can do this by remote," he said.

"No, we can't," Meka stated flatly.

"Shut up and wait," he snapped. "We program them to loiter outside sensor range, then do a high-velocity approach on schedule."

"Thereby running into sensor range and right into a defensive battery. I suppose you could hide a charge in a suit, but I doubt it would manoeuvre properly, and you couldn't program it to steer itself. We aren't using us to deliver from lack of resources; it's because we can get through and a drone can't. If you want to try to program them for a fourth target, do so. It can't hurt, unless of course you need them as decoys later."

Jan breathed deeply and slowly, feeling sick to his stomach. Crap, this was the worst experience of his life. Were they going to do this or not?

Costlow looked sheepish. "I thought I had it there. Sorry," he said.

"Don't apologize, sir," she replied. "The fact that you missed that means the Earthies think they are solid and can't be taken. This will work."

A depressed silence settled over them, but then Jan had a different thought. He cleared his throat. "There's another factor," he said. "The crewed station might have viable oxy or escape pods. After Meka takes it out, she can hunker down and await rescue…there's a chance you could survive, sis."

"Well, good!" Costlow said.

Meka flushed red. "Yes, but that's hardly fair to you two."

He shrugged. "What's fair? We do what we have to. After that, who can say?"

She looked at Jan. He smiled, of course, because he was glad of the possibility. He was also furious, nauseous, frightened, and there was nothing to say, except, "Good luck, then."

It was wholly inadequate. They were all lying, they all knew it, and it was just one more cold lump in the guts.

Two tediously painful days later, the two soldiers and the pilot gathered in the crew cabin once more. They checked off lists of essentials that had been requisitioned or borrowed, finalized the schedule, and prepared to start. The equipment made it fairly obvious what they planned.

"First order of business, clear the ship," Costlow said. He sounded the intercom for all hands, and everyone boiled in. When they were clumped around him, he said, "We have a mission for which we must reduce mass and resources, so the rest of you are being temporarily put on The Rock. Grab what you need, but you need to be off by morning."

The crew and techs looked around at each other, at the three who would remain, and it was seconds only before Pilot Sereno said, "How much mass are you stripping?"

Costlow replied, "None yet. We'll be doing that later in the mission."

More looks crossed the cabin, thoughts being telegraphed. After an interminable time, Sereno said, "Yes, Warrant," and headed away. The others silently followed his lead.

Yeah, he knows, Jan thought.

Over the rest of the day, they returned one by one to make their cases. Every single member of the crew was determined to accompany the boat on its last mission. Death was to be feared, but staying behind was unbearable.

Sereno spent some time arguing with his superior that he was more expendable. While true, Costlow was the better pilot. He left dejected and angry.

Boat Engineer Jacqueline Jemayel had more success. She simply handed over a comm with her checklist, and said, "No one else has the years of training and familiarity to handle your hardware in combat. If you think you can handle that while flying, I'll leave." Costlow twitched and stalled, but relented to her logic and determination. They'd been friends and crew a long time, and he was glad to have her along.

Engine Specialist Kurashima and Analyst Corporal Jackson got nowhere. Neither was needed for this. They might be needed on another vessel. Costlow wasn't taking anyone except Jemayel, and only because she did have a valid case. A good boat engineer was essential generally, and for this especially. He listened briefly to each of the others, wished them well and sent them packing. He was proud that his crew were so dedicated and determined, and he left recommendations for decorations in his final log file.

It was mere hours before departure time when the hatch beeped an authorized entry. They looked over as Melanie Sarendy swam in, followed by Sergeant Frank Otte, the equipment technician for the intelligence crew.

Costlow was annoyed, and snapped, "Sarendy, Otte, I ordered you to—"

She interrupted with a stern face, "Warrant, the *London* has Mod Six upgrades to its sensor suite. If you want to get close, then you need offensive systems as well as sensors. This is a recon boat, not a gunboat. I'm the best tech you're going to get, I can get you in there, and I'm coming along. Sergeant Otte is here to build a station for me on the flight deck, and modifications for offensive transmissions, then he's leaving." She moved to swim past them towards her station. How she'd found out the details was a mystery. No one had told her. Costlow blocked her. She looked determined and exasperated, until he held a hand out. "Welcome aboard, Sergeant," he acknowledged.

It took Otte, Jemayel and Jan to build the devices necessary. Sarendy's requested station wasn't a standard item for a recon boat, and there were few spare parts aboard The Rock. Judicious cannibalization and improvisation yielded an effective, albeit ugly, set-up. Additional gear was used to build an offensive electronic suite, and some of it had obviously been stolen from other ships. As promised, Otte left, but not before trying desperately to convince them he was as necessary as Jemayel. He failed, but not for lack of determination.

4J23 departed immediately. The time left was useful for rehearsal and training, and those were best done without distractions. The short crew strapped in as Costlow cleared with Station Control, detached the umbilical, thereby cutting them off from communication, the boat being under transmission silence, and powered away.

It would avoid awkward goodbyes, also.

Meka began laying out gear for herself and Jan. They each would take their duty weapons. Jan had a demolition charge large enough for the structure in question. She took extra explosives and ammo. Both would carry their short swords, not so much from need but because it was traditional. They both needed oxy bottles. He'd wear her manoeuvring harness; she had a sled designed for clandestine missions. They had enough oxy mix, barely, to last them two days. That was tantalizingly close to enough for a pickup, but still short. A boat might conceivably get into the vicinity in time, but rescue operations took time. If they could run this mission in the open ... but of course, they couldn't.

Costlow spent the time getting trajectories from the navigation system. He needed to pass by two stations whose locations were approximate, get near the *London*, which was in a powered station orbit around the jump point, observe, plan an approach, execute the approach to stay unseen, and arrive at a precise point at an exact time with sufficient fuel for terminal manoeuvres. Very terminal. He consulted with Sarendy as to detection equipment ranges and apertures to help plot his path. Jemayel tended the engines, life support, and astronautics. None of them spoke much.

Jan had little to do until his departure. He spent it moping, getting angry, and finally beating on the combat practice dummy for hours, twisting in microgravity. When Meka called him over to explain the gear, he was more than eager to just get things over with.

She showed him the mass of gear and began to go through it. He checked everything off with her. Weapons and gear needed little explanation. He was familiar with the technical details of her manoeuvring harness and the munitions fuses even though he'd never used them. The briefing would be far too short a distraction.

"We'll synch our chronos," Meka said.

"Goddess, don't give me a clock," Jan begged, shaking his head. "If I have to watch it count down, I'll be a basket case. Just put me there with some stuff to read and let me go." He spoke loudly, eyes wide, because the stress was getting to him.

"You need one in case the auto system fails," Meka said. "You're getting a triple load of ammo. It seems unlikely, but if anyone shows up to stop you—"

"Then I hold them off as long as I can."

"Right," Meka agreed.

Costlow showed the plotted course in a 3D, and asked, "We let you off here. Are you sure you can manoeuvre well enough for that distance?"

Shrugging, Jan replied, "End result is the same for me either way, but I'm sure. I do a lot of EVA. Unlike some people, I like it."

"Bite me, bro," Meka replied and laughed, too loud from stress. She had always *hated* long EVA, and that's what this was. She was assembling a pile of gear including her powered sled, two oxy bottles, the basic demolition blocks from everyone's standard gear plus her own larger pack, weapons and stuff the others wouldn't recognize. Her actions were trained, expert and only a little shaky from tension. She'd done long trips in the dark before, and survived, but that didn't make it fun. She had her sled for this one, Jan was making a far shorter infiltration, and the boat wasn't her concern. She prepped everything, had Jan and Jemayel double check, and went through exercises to calm herself. Those didn't work for Jan.

With less than four hours until his departure, Jan sat staring at the bulkhead of the day cabin. His bunk was folded, and his few effects sealed in a locker. He'd recorded a message and written instructions, all of which made things rather final. He didn't feel thoroughly terrified yet, but did feel rather numb. Rest was impossible. He nodded briefly to Sarendy as she swam in, and tried not to dwell on her. It was all too easy to think of justifications to break the fraternization ban. He didn't need rejection or complications now, and the sympathy ploy was the only approach he could think of. It wouldn't work, as she was in the same boat as he, quite literally.

"Come back here," she said, gesturing with a hand. She turned and swam for her intel bay.

As he followed her in, she closed the hatch and dogged it. It was dimly lit by one emergency lamp, there being no need for its use at this time, and there was just enough room for the two of them inside the radius of couches and terminals set against the shell. While his brain tried to shift gears, she grabbed him by the shoulders and mashed her mouth against his while reaching to open her shipsuit. Both their hands fumbled for a few seconds, then his stopped and drew back while hers continued questing.

"Mehlnee," he muttered around her kiss. She drew her full lips back a bare few millimetres, and he continued, "I appreciate this ... but it won't help me deal with ... this."

"It helps me," she replied, voice breathy, and wrapped herself more tightly around him. Her lips danced over his throat and he decided not to argue with her logic. His hands were on the sinuous curves of her golden-skinned hips, and long-held fantasies solidified into reality. Frantic, unrequited lust made thought impossible, and that was a good thing right then.

Jan was first out. He doffed his shipsuit and donned his hard vacsuit, intended for short duration EVA maintenance and not the best for this mission. It was what he had, though. Meka's assault harness fitted snugly over it and would provide thrust. Three bottles rode his back, two oxy-helium, one nitrogen for the harness. His rifle and clips were along the right bottle, and his comm on his wrist, programmed with everything he needed. Strapped to his chest was a large, bulky pack with over 20 kilos of modern military hyperexplosive. It would be more than enough for the station in question.

Melanie and Meka checked him over and helped him into the bay. The other two were busy on the flight deck. Ignoring his sister's presence, Melanie kissed him hard and deeply. He kissed back, shaking, wanting to leave before the whole situation caused him to go insane. Meka waited until Sarendy was done, then clutched him briefly. "Good luck," she said.

"Good hunting," he replied.

Behind him he heard, "Oh, I will," as the hatch closed.

Jan stared out the open bay into cold black space with cold, bright pinpoints of light. "God and Goddess, I don't want to do this," he muttered. His stomach boiled and churned, and he wished he'd filled his water bottle with straight alcohol. Even the double dose of tranquilizers was not enough to keep him calm.

A light winked once, twice, then a third time, and he jumped out briskly, feeling the harness shove him in a braking manoeuvre. He was immediately thankful for the suit's plumbing, and his brain went numb. *I'm dead now*, was all he could think.

The station Jan was attacking would note the passage of the anomaly that was the boat as well as it could, and report later. Meka's target was more complicated. It was crewed, and they would react if they saw her. She'd have to ride her sled for some distance and most of a day, and try to time it for a covert approach. That might be the hardest part of this mission.

In the maintenance bay, she strapped herself to her sled and had Jemayel check her over. With a final thumbs-up and a lingering hug, she turned to her controls and counted seconds down to her launch.

The boat passed through the volume as stealthed as possible, oriented so the bay opened away from the station's sensors. There were no emissions, only the operating radiation and a bare hint of the powerplant. Her braking thrust was hidden by the mass of the boat, and should be almost invisible at this distance. That should put her right on top of the station at Earth clock 11.30 the next day, when the crew would hopefully be at lunch.

Once the vibration and heavy gees tapered off, she checked her instruments and took a trank. It would be a long wait, and very eerie in complete silence and blackness.

And now I'm dead, she thought.

***

Sarendy reported when they were outside the known range of the station, and Costlow waited a planned extra hour before bringing up the plant and engines. He wanted to be lost in background noise.

The thrust built steadily in a rumbling hiss through the frame. Most of the impulse would be used now, with only enough left for margin and manoeuvres. That would simplify the approach by minimizing emissions then. The velocity increased to a level the boat had rarely used, and he nodded to his remaining crew as they completed the manoeuvre. Now they had to wait.

"Anyone for a game of chess?" he asked.

Jan watched for the station. It was a black mass against black space, and he was glad to see it occult stars. He'd been afraid the intel was wrong and he was sailing off into space for nothing. Odd to feel relieved to see the approaching cause of one's death, he thought. It had been a three-hour trip, and he was hungry. He would stay that way for the next day and a half, because his suit was intended for maintenance EVAs only, not infiltration, and had no way to supply food. So much for the condemned's last meal. Then there was the irony that his boat had IDed this particular piece of equipment, which is why it was on the list, and why he was here.

The occultation grew, and he got ready to manoeuvre for docking, landing, whatever it was called in this case. He switched on the astrogation controls, adjusted his flight towards it, then braked relative. He was tense, lest the reports be inaccurate and the station blast him with a defence array, but nothing happened. He didn't overshoot, but did approach obliquely and had to correct for touchdown.

There was no one and nothing nearby, which was as expected. He snapped a contact patch out, slapped it to the surface, and attached his line. There were no regular padeyes on the unit.

A short orientation revealed where the power cell was. He planted the standoff over it and slapped it down with another contact patch. When it triggered, the blast would turn a plate of metal beneath it into plasma and punch it through the shell into the power cell. He armed it, and all he had left to do was defend it against what appeared to be nothing, wait until it detonated and die with it. Simple on file. Doing it didn't seem quite that by the numbers.

At first, he was terrified of being near the charge. He realized it was silly, as it would kill him anyway, and if it didn't, suffocation would. He compromised between fear and practicality by hiding over the horizon of the small, angled object. It was a bare three metres across, five metres long, and almost featureless except for a docking clamp inset at one end. Its signals were all burst through a translucent one-way window. He longed to tear into it for the sheer joy of discovering if the intel briefs were correct about this model, but that might give him away. He'd sit and wait.

He did have emgee, and a suit, and a tether. He decided to rest floating free. The technique had helped him before when stressed. He stared out at the stars and the distant pointy glare of Iota Persei, their star, and fell into a deep sleep, disturbed by odd dreams.

Meka approached the station gradually. She'd have to leave her sled behind and finish the trip in just her suit to avoid detection. While a bedecked suit would register as maintenance or a refugee with the sensors, the sled would trigger alarms as an approaching threat even if the enemy didn't have knowledge of the precise design. She made one last correction to her orbit, set the autopilot, pulled the releases, and drifted loose from the frame. Her minuscule lateral velocity should be of negligible effect.

The sled burped gently away on gas jets rather than engines, and would hopefully never be detectable to the station. It was near 08.00 by Earth clock, and another three hours should bring her quite close. That's when it would become tricky.

First, she'd have to manoeuvre with an improvised thruster. Jan had her harness; she had only a nitrogen bottle and a momentary valve. He'd – hopefully – made his approach with power but no navigation. She had the navigation gear in her helmet, but improvised power. The risks they were taking would cause a safety officer to run gibbering in insanity. On the other hand, they were dead either way.

There was also the substantial risk of the station noting her approach to its crew. They might await her, or send someone to investigate, or shoot her outright. She was betting against the last, but it was just that – a bet. If they met her, it meant a fight. She would win one on one against anybody she faced, but the station might have up to twenty crew. It was effectively a large recon boat with manoeuvring engines, and she didn't relish a fight within.

Unlike her previous long EVAs, she was relaxed and calm. Perhaps it was experience. Maybe it was the complexity of the task and the associated thought that kept her too busy to worry. Perhaps it was fatalism. As she neared her target, more issues interfered and she dropped all those thoughts.

There were no obvious signs of disturbance as she approached. That meant that if they did see her for what she was, they were at least holding their fire. She checked her weapon again by touch, and began readying her muscles for a fight. If someone met her, she'd go along peacefully to the airlock, then start smashing things and killing on her way inside.

Nothing happened. Either the station's sensors didn't see her, or they assumed she was performing maintenance and ignored her. It was good to see the intel was accurate, but it still felt odd that her presence wasn't even reported. Perhaps it was and they were waiting for her. Dammit, no second guessing.

She was close enough to think about manoeuvring now, and there were still no signs of enemy notice. The nitrogen bottle beside her breathing bottle was plumbed into a veritable snakepit of piping Jan had built for her, that ended front and back at shoulders and hips, much like a proper emgee harness. She hoped the improvised controls worked so she wouldn't have to attempt it by hand. Her record on manual approaches was less than perfect.

She vented a pulse of gas and the harness worked as planned. Two more short ones brought her to a bare drift. She sent more thoughts of thanks after her brother, who had turned out to be essential to almost every mission she'd fought in this war. His technical skill in every field was just genius.

She managed a gentle touchdown on the station hull, letting her legs bend and soak up momentum. She caught her breath, got her bearings, and went straight to work. She had no idea how long she could go unnoticed.

She placed the prebuilt charges with a rapidity born of years of practice. Each charge was designed to punch a hole into a compartment, hopefully voiding them all and killing the occupants instantly. She danced softly across the hull to avoid noise inside that might give her away, swapping tethers as she went, and planted them precisely with the aid of thoughtfully provided frame numbers. Magnetic boots would have made it easier ... if the shell had been an iron alloy and if clanking noises didn't matter.

She caught movement out of the corner of her eye. She pivoted to see a UN spacer in gear, staring at her in surprise.

Her combat reflexes took over. He was unarmed, meaning he was conducting routine maintenance or inspections. It was possible he wore a camera that was observable inside on a monitor, and he would definitely report her as soon as he recovered from the oddity of the situation. She twisted her right arm to unsling, then pointed her rifle and shot him through the faceplate.

The eruption of atmosphere and vaporized blood indicated he was dead. She put two more bullets through him to make sure, the effect eerie in the silence. The recoil of the weapon was mild, but with no gravity or atmosphere it started her tumbling. She steadied out with a grasp of her tether, and brought herself back the half metre to the shell. Now what?

Her pulse hammered and her breath rasped. Despite the massive damage and casualties she'd caused in her career, it was only the second time she'd killed someone directly and up close. She forced her emotions into quiescence and considered the situation. If he'd reported her, she had seconds to deal with it. If not, she had a little longer before he was missed. If she killed the crew early, they might miss a scheduled report and the secrecy of her mission would be compromised. If she waited, they could report her presence. She didn't see much of a choice.

Her fingers activated the system through her comm; she paused a second to confirm the readings and then detonated the charges.

If the atmosphere gushing from her enemy's helmet had been impressive, this was awe-inspiring. Brilliant bursts of white were swallowed by fountains of spewing air and debris. The station shook beneath her feet as the hull adjusted to lost pressure. Anyone not in a suit should be dead. Now to hope no report was expected before her mission zero time. It was a long shot, but all she had. And it was unlikely that the omission would be considered more than a minor problem at first.

Costlow was a first-class pilot, but this would strain even his capabilities. The astronautics would take over for evasive manoeuvres only. The approach would be manual.

While there was a timed window for attacks, the closer together they were the better. Any hint of action would alert the enemy and reduce the odds of success for others. He wanted to time this to the second, as much as possible. To avoid detection, he had to rely on passive sensors operated by Sarendy across from him. Passive sensors didn't give as accurate a picture as active ones, which meant he'd have to correct the timing in flight. As he would approach at a velocity near the maximum physics and Jemayel's bypassed safeties would allow, that left little time for corrections. He wanted to get inside their weapons' envelope and right against the skin before they deduced what he was. That also increased the risk of their particle watch picking him up, assuming him to be an incoming passive threat, and shooting preemptively.

They were only a few hours from target, and he'd already brought them around in a long loop behind the *London*'s engines. The emissions from them would mask their approach in ionized scatter. He wondered again just how hard this would have been without Sarendy, Jan and Otte. Sarendy was pulling all her intel from the sensors up to the flight deck and using it to assist in astrogation; and she was preparing a counterintel system for use when they were detected, and would utilize the active sensor antennae as offensive transmitters. He hadn't realized that was even possible, but Sarendy was a witch with sensors, Jan an expert on improvising hardware, and Otte had kept up with both of their orders and put the system together. Amazing. If a crew had ever earned its decorations, this one had.

"Your turn, Warrant," Sarendy reminded him.

Right. Chess. "Um..." He moved his queen, looked at the board with satisfaction and leaned back. Her rook's capture of his queen and declaration of checkmate stunned him.

"Perhaps we should stop now," he suggested. "I didn't see that coming and I have no idea what you did. And both my bishops are on white."

"They are?" she asked. "So they are. Let's call it a game."

Meka swam through the main corridor, counting bodies with faces reminiscent of dead fish, and checked that every compartment was open to vacuum. Nodding to herself, ignoring the grisly scenes, she made her way to the powerplant and unlimbered the large charge on her chest. In seconds it was armed, placed, and she swam back out to face the outer hatch. Little to do now but wait.

She wondered how other troops and units had done. Was anyone trying to recapture the captured Freehold facilities? Or just destroy them outright? Would the attacks be successful, and allow the presumed counter to work? Would they win?

She'd never know. She could only wish them luck.

Jan awoke with a start. Guilt flooded over the adrenaline, as he realized he'd slept past when he was supposed to be on guard. He shrugged and decided it didn't matter, as the chance of anyone interfering was incredibly remote. It still bothered him.

It was close to deadline, and he realized he didn't even know what this operation was called, only that it probably involved the entire system, aimed for infrastructure, and was suicidal. That was probably enough.

He still had a couple of hours of oxy.

Hypoxia/anoxia would be pretty painless. A little struggle for breath…he could take those two hours. It wasn't impossible a rescue vessel might show up. It just took a hell of a lot of zeros to make the odds. Two extra hours of life, though.

He decided he didn't have whatever it took to let himself die slowly. He was already shivering in shock; the tranks were wearing off.

He snagged the tether and dragged himself hand over hand to the station. He hooked to the contact patch near the charge. The only thing worse than being blown to dust, he thought, would be to be injured by it and linger for hours in pain. He wished Meka luck, aching to know if she'd make it. That hurt as much as anything else. There were a few less zeros on her odds, but they were still ludicrously remote. Their mission was to smash enemy infrastructure, not occupy and set up housekeeping.

There was nothing left. He settled down to read, gave up because he couldn't focus, and turned on music to break the eerie silence. If he had to die, he wanted it to be painless and instantaneous.

When the charge underneath him detonated, he got his final wish.

Costlow sweated, with aching joints and gritty eyeballs from sitting far too long at the controls. He watched the display in his helmet, trying to ignore the way the helmet abraded behind his left ear, and made another minute flight correction. He had minutes left to live.

4J23 was close behind the *London*, and undiscovered as far as they knew. Sarendy screwed with their emissions, inverted incoming scans, sent out bursts low enough in energy to pass as typical, powerful enough to keep them hidden and the gods only knew what else. He wished there were some way to record her competence. She was a twenty-year-old kid, and likely knew more about her job than all her instructors combined. Add in her bravery, and she deserved ten medals.

No, he thought, she deserved to live. Rage filled him again.

He forced the thoughts back to his mission. He was hungry and thirsty, but he daren't pause to sate either. This could all come down to a fractional second's attention. Especially now that they were so close.

He brought 4J23 in in a tight, twisting curve from the blind spot behind the drives, and aimed along the approaching superstructure. *London*'s defences found him, and a launch warning flashed in his visor. It missed because Sarendy switched to active jamming and burned its sensors out with a beam that should have been impossible from a recon boat, and would almost fry an asteroid to vapour. The brute force approach was an indication that all her tricks were exhausted, and it was doubtful they could avoid another attack. He flinched as the missile flashed past, even though it was detectable only as an icon in his visor, and heard a cry of sheer terror start quietly and build. He realized it was his voice. He'd wet himself, and was embarrassed, even though he understood the process. He could hear Sarendy panting for breath, hyperventilating behind him, and wondered what Jemayel was doing in the stern. His eyes flicked to the count in his visor—

Now.

Alongside the *London*, within metres of her hull and at closest approach to her command centre, a small powerplant overloaded and detonated. It was enough to overwhelm her forcescreens, vaporize her forward half, and shatter the rest in a moment so brief as to be incomprehensible. One hundred UN spacers were turned into incandescent plasma by the blast, along with the three Freeholders.

Meka watched the seconds tick away in her visor. She dropped her left hand and grasped the manual trigger, set it and held on. It would blow if she let go, or on schedule, and her work was almost done. The count worked down, and she closed her eyes, faced "up" and took a deep breath to steady herself. She opened them again to see it count 3 … 2 … 1.

Whether her thumb released or the timer acted first was irrelevant. The blast damaged the station's fusion plant, which shut down automatically, even as it vented to space. She felt the cracking and rumbling of the structure through her body, fading away to nothing. It would take a dockyard to repair that, and they'd have to remove the wreckage first. She moved back towards the power-plant, navigating by touch in the dust, and dragged herself around several supports twisted by the blast. She entered the engineering module and waited. The particles cleared very slowly, as there was neither airflow nor gravity. It all depended on static charges and surface tension to draw things out of vacuum, and Meka stayed stock-still until she could get a good look through her faceplate, cycling through visible, enhanced and IR to build a good picture. She nodded in approval of the damage. The blast and fusion bottle failure had slagged half the module.

Her task was now done, but she had no desire to die immediately. She could have embraced the charge on the reactor and gone with it. Her rationale had been that she should be certain, although the charge had been three times larger than she'd calculated as necessary. The truth was, she couldn't bring herself to do it. Death might be inevitable, but she still feared it.

She studied the life-support system whimsically. Without a proper deckplan, she'd just vented every compartment from outside to be sure. Her charge over this one had punched into the make-up tank. There was a functional air-recycling plant, but no oxygen. A metre in any direction…

There were no escape bubbles. This was a station, not a ship. If damaged, the crew would seal as needed and call for help. She'd fixed that when she vented atmosphere. There were extra suit oxy bottles, but the fittings didn't match. Even if they did, there was no heat, and her suit powerpack was nearing depletion. Jan would easily have cobbled something together, or tacked a patch over the hole in life support and used the suit bottles, but even if she could do so before her own gas ran out, it still meant waiting and hoping for a rescue that would likely never come. There was no commo capability, of course. That had been her prime target. No one knew to look for her. The remote possibility of rescue they'd discussed had been for Jan's benefit, to let him hope she might survive. He'd probably figured out the lie by now.

With time and nothing better to do, she planted charges on every hatch, every port, every system. She fired bullets liberally to smash controls and equipment, wedged the airlocks with grenades to shatter the seals and render them useless. Even the spare parts inventory was either destroyed or blown into space.

Finally, she sat outside on the ruined shell, watching her oxy gauge trickle toward empty. Her weapons were scattered around her, some lazily drifting free in the emgee, each rendered inoperable and unsalvageable, all save one. She really had harboured an unrealistic hope that there'd be some way out of this, and cried in loneliness. There was no one to see her, and it wasn't the first time she'd cried on a mission. Blazers didn't look down on tears and fear, only on failure. She had not failed.

The stillness and silence was palpable and eerie. She brought up her system and cycled through her music choices. Yes, that would do nicely. "La Villa Strangiato". The coordination and sheer skill impressed her, and the energy in the performance was powerful and moving. It filled the last 500 seconds and faded out. Silence returned.

A warning flashed in her visor and sounded in her ears, becoming more and more tinny as oxygen was depleted. She'd black out in about a hundred seconds.

One thing she'd always wondered was how far her courage went. People died all the time. Soldiers died when ordered to fight and the odds ran out. Sick people died because life was not worth living.

But, could she die by choice? Her courage had been tested throughout her career, and this last year to an extreme. But did she have the strength to pull that switch herself?

After prolonging the inevitable this long, it was rather moot, but her life wouldn't be complete without the experiment. She armed the grenade, stared at it as her body burned from hypoxia, and tried to force her hand to open. Lungs empty now, she gritted her teeth, pursed her lips, and threw every nerve into the effort. Her wrist shook, thumb moving bit by bit. Willpower or self-preservation?

She was still conscious, though groggy, as her thumb came free and the fuse caught. Three seconds. Hypoxia segued to anoxia and her thoughts began to fade. The last one caused a triumphant smile to cross her face, even as tears pooled in her eyes.

Willpower.

On slabs of green and black marble in Freedom Park are the names of 216 soldiers who accepted orders they could not understand and knew meant their deaths. Words were said, prayers offered, and torches and guards of honour stand eternal watch over them. Their families received pensions, salutes and bright metal decorations on plain green ribbons, presented in inlaid wooden boxes.

One family received two.

THE HORARS
OF WAR

Gene Wolfe

*Gene Wolfe is one of the most respected voices in science
fiction and fantasy, having won numerous awards including
several World Fantasies as well as Nebulas, BSFAs and
Rhyslings. He is probably best known for his ground-
breaking four-volume* Book of the New Sun *and its associated series. "Write what you know" is an oft-quoted
adage, particularly inappropriate for science fiction, where
we try so hard to write what we don't know, but solid real-
life experience can provide an excellent springboard for the
imagination, as this story demonstrates. Wolfe draws on
his service as an engineer in the US military during the
Korean War to infuse "The Horars of War" with convincing
detail. First published in 1970, the story served early notice
that a significant new voice had arrived.*

THE THREE FRIENDS in the trench looked very much alike as they
laboured in the rain. Their hairless skulls were slickly naked to
it, their torsos hairless too, and supple with smooth muscles that ran
like oil under the wet gleam.

The two, who really were 2909 and 2911, did not mind the jungle
around them although they detested the rain that rusted their
weapons, and the snakes and insects, and hated the Enemy. But the
one called 2910, the real as well as the official leader of the three,
did; and that was because 2909 and 2911 had stainless-steel bones;
but there was no 2910 and there never had been.

The camp they held was a triangle. In the centre, the CP-Aid Station where Lieutenant Kyle and Mr Brenner slept: a hut of ammo cases packed with dirt whose lower half was dug into the soggy earth. Around it were the mortar pit (NE), the recoilless rifle pit (NW), and Pinocchio's pit (S); and beyond these were the straight lines of the trenches: First Platoon, Second Platoon, Third Platoon (the platoon of the three), outside of which were the primary wire and an antipersonnel mine field.

And outside that was the jungle. But not completely outside. The jungle set up outposts of its own of swift-sprouting bamboo and elephant grass, and its crawling creatures carried out untiring patrols of the trenches. The jungle sheltered the Enemy, taking him to its great fetid breast to be fed while it sopped up the rain and of it bred its stinging gnats and centipedes.

An ogre beside him, 2911 drove his shovel into the ooze filling the trench, lifted it to shoulder height, dumped it; 2910 did the same thing in his turn, then watched the rain work on the scoop of mud until it was slowly running back into the trench again. Following his eyes 2911 looked at him and grinned. The HORAR's face was broad, hairless, flat-nosed and high-cheeked; his teeth were pointed and white like a big dog's. And he, 2910, knew that that face was his own. Exactly his own. He told himself it was a dream, but he was very tired and could not get out.

Somewhere down the trench the bull voice of 2900 announced the evening meal and the others threw down their tools and jostled past towards the bowls of steaming mash; but the thought of food nauseated 2910 in his fatigue, and he stumbled into the bunker he shared with 2909 and 2911. Flat on his air mattress he could leave the nightmare for a time: return to the sane world of houses and sidewalks, or merely sink into the blessed nothingness that was far better...

Suddenly he was bolt upright on the cot, blackness still in his eyes even while his fingers groped with their own thought for his helmet and weapon. Bugles were blowing from the edge of the jungle, but he had time to run his hand under the inflated pad of the mattress and reassure himself that his hidden notes were safe before 2900 in the trench outside yelled, "Attack! Fall out! Man your firing points!"

It was one of the stock jokes, one of the jokes so stock, in fact, that it had ceased to be anything anyone laughed at, to say "Horar" your firing point (or whatever it was that according to the book should be "manned"). The HORARS in the squad he led used the expression to 2910 just as he used it with them, and when 2900 never employed it the omission had at first unsettled him. But 2900 did not really suspect. 2900 just took his rank seriously.

He got into position just as the mortars put up a parachute flare that hung over the camp like a white rose of fire. Whether because of his brief sleep or the excitement of the impending fight his fatigue had evaporated, leaving him nervously alert but unsteady. From the jungle a bugle sang. "Ta-taa…taa-taa…" and off to the platoon's left rear the First opened up with their heavy weapons on a suicide squad they apparently thought they saw on the path leading to the northeast gate. He watched, and after half a minute something stood up on the path and grabbed for its midsection before it fell. So there *was* a suicide squad.

Some one, he told himself. *Someone*. Not *something*. Someone grabbed for *his* midsection. They were all human out there.

The First began letting go with personal weapons as well, each deep cough representing a half-dozen dartlike flechettes flying in an inescapable pattern three feet broad. "Eyes front, 2910!" barked 2900.

There was nothing to be seen out there but a few clumps of elephant grass. Then the white flare burned out. "They ought to put up another one," 2911 on his right said worriedly.

"A star in the east for men not born of women," said 2910 half to himself, and regretted the blasphemy immediately.

"That's where they need it," 2911 agreed. "The First is having it pretty hot over there. But we could use some light here too."

He was not listening. At home in Chicago, during that inexpressibly remote time which ran from a dim memory of playing on a lawn under the supervision of a smiling giantess to that moment two years ago when he had submitted to surgery to lose every body and facial hair he possessed and undergo certain other minor alterations, he had been unconsciously preparing himself for this. Lifting weights and playing football to develop his body while he whetted his mind on a thousand books; all so that he might tell, making others feel at a remove...

Another flare went up and there were three dark silhouettes sliding from the next-nearest clump of elephant grass to the nearest. He fired his M-19 at them, then heard the HORARS on either side of him fire too. From the sharp corner where their own platoon met the Second a machine gun opened up with tracer. The nearest grass clump sprang into the air and somersaulted amid spurts of earth.

There was a moment of quiet, then five rounds of high explosive came in right behind them as though aimed for Pinocchio's pit. *Crump. Crump. Crump... Crump. Crump.* (2900 would be running to ask Pinocchio if he were hurt.)

Someone else had been moving down the trench towards them, and he could hear the mumble of the new voice become a gasp when the H.E. rounds came in. Then it resumed, a little louder and consequently a bit more easily understood. "How are you? You feel all right? Hit?"

And most of the HORARS were answering, "I'm fine, sir," or "We're OK, sir," but because HORARS did have a sense of humour some of them said things like, "How do we transfer to the Marines, sir?" or, "My pulse just registered nine thou', sir. 3000 took it with the mortar sight."

We often think of strength as associated with humourlessness, he had written in the news magazine which had, with the Army's cooperation, planted him by subterfuge of surgery among these Homolog ORganisms (Army Replacement Simulations). *But*, he had continued, *this is not actually the case. Humour is a prime defence of the mind, and, knowing that to strip the mind of it is to leave it shieldless, the Army and the Synthetic Biology Service have wisely included a charming dash in the make-up of these synthesized replacements for human infantry.*

That had been before he discovered that the Army and the SBS had tried mightily to weed that sense of the ridiculous out, but found that if the HORARS were to maintain the desired intelligence level they could not.

Brenner was behind him now, touching his shoulder. "How are you? Feel all right?"

He wanted to say, "I'm half as scared as you are, you dumb Dutchman," but he knew that if he did the fear would sound in his voice; besides, the disrespect would be unthinkable to a HORAR.

He also wanted to say simply, "A-OK, sir," because if he did Brenner would pass on to 2911 and he would be safe. But he had a reputation for originality to keep up, and he needed that reputation to cover him when he slipped, as he often did, sidewise of HORAR standards. He answered: "You ought to look in on Pinocchio, sir. I think he's cracking up." From the other end of the squad, 2909's quiet chuckle rewarded him, and Brenner, the man most dangerous to his disguise, continued down the trench...

Fear was necessary because the will to survive was *very* necessary. And a humanoid form was needed if the HORARS were to utilize the mass of human equipment already on hand. Besides, a human-shaped (*homolog*? no, that merely meant *similar, homological*) HORAR had outscored all the fantastic forms SBS had been able to dream up in a super-realistic (public opinion would never have permitted it with human soldiers) test carried out in the Everglades.

(Were they merely duplicating? Had all this been worked out before with some greater war in mind? And had He Himself, the Scientist Himself, come to take the form of His creations to show that he too could bear the unendurable?)

2909 was at his elbow, whispering. "Do you see something, Squad Leader? Over there?" Dawn had come without his noticing.

With fingers clumsy from fatigue he switched the control of his M-19 to the lower, 40 mm grenade-launching barrel. The grenade made a brief flash at the spot 2909 had indicated. "No," he said, "I don't see anything now." The fine, soft rain which had been falling all night was getting stronger. The dark clouds seemed to roof the world. (Was he fated to re-enact what had been done for mankind?

It could happen. The enemy took humans captive, but there was nothing they would not do to HORAR prisoners. Occasionally patrols found the bodies spreadeagled, with bamboo stakes driven through their limbs; and he could only be taken for a HORAR. He thought of a watercolour of the crucifixion he had seen once. Would the colour of his own blood be crimson lake?

From the CP the observation ornithocopter rose on flapping wings.

"I haven't heard one of the mines go for quite a while," 2902 said. Then there came the phony-sounding bang that so often during the past few weeks had closed similar probing attacks. Squares of paper were suddenly fluttering all over the camp.

"Propaganda shell," 2909 said unnecessarily, and 2911 climbed casually out of the trench to get a leaflet, then jumped back to his position. "Same as last week," he said, smoothing out the damp rice paper.

Looking over his shoulder, 2910 saw that he was correct. For some reason the Enemy never directed his propaganda at the HORARS, although it was no secret that reading skills were implanted in HORAR minds with the rest of their instinctive training. Instead it was always aimed at the humans in the camp, and played heavily on the distaste they were supposed to feel at being "confined with half-living flesh still stinking of chemicals." Privately, 2910 thought they might have done better, at least with Lieutenant Kyle, to have dropped that approach and played up sex. He also got the impression from the propaganda that the Enemy thought there were far more humans in the camp than there actually were.

Well, the Army – with far better opportunities to know – was wrong as well. With a few key generals excepted, the Army thought there were only two...

He had made the All-American. How long ago it seemed. No coach, no sportswriter had ever compared his stocky, muscular physique with a HORAR's. And he had majored in journalism, had been ambitious. How many men, with a little surgical help, could have passed here?

"Think it sees anything?" he heard 2911 ask 2909. They were looking upward at the "bird" sailing overhead.

The ornithocopter could do everything a real bird could except lay eggs. It could literally land on a strand of wire. It could ride thermals like a vulture, and dive like a hawk. And the bird-motion of its wings was wonderfully efficient, saving powerplant weight that could be used for zoom-lenses and telecameras. He wished he were in the CP watching the monitor screen with Lieutenant Kyle instead of standing with his face a scant foot above the mud (they had tried stalked eyes like a crab's in the Everglades, he remembered, but the stalks had become infected by a fungus...).

As though in answer to his wish, 2900 called, "Show some snap for once, 2910. He says He wants us in the CP."

When he himself thought *He*, *He* meant God; but 2900 meant Lieutenant Kyle. That was why 2900 was a platoon leader, no doubt; that and the irrational prestige of a round number. He climbed out of the trench and followed him to the CP. They needed a communicating trench, but that was something there hadn't been time for yet.

Brenner had someone (2788? Looked like him, but he couldn't be certain) down on his table. Shrapnel, probably from a grenade. Brenner did not look up as they came in, but 2910 could see his face was still white with fear although the attack had been over for a full quarter of an hour. He and 2900 ignored the SBS man and saluted Lieutenant Kyle.

The company commander smiled. "Stand at ease, HORARS. Have any trouble in your sector?"

2900 said, "No sir. The light machine gun got one group of three and 2910 here knocked off a group of two. Not much of an attack on our front, sir."

Lieutenant Kyle nodded. "I thought your platoon had the easiest time of it, 2900, and that's why I've picked you to run a patrol for me this morning."

"That's fine with us, sir."

"You'll have Pinocchio, and I thought you'd want to go yourself and take 2910's gang."

He glanced at 2910. "Your squad still at full strength?"

2910 said, "Yes, sir," making an effort to keep his face impassive. He wanted to say: I shouldn't have to go on patrol. I'm human as you are, Kyle, and patrolling is for things grown in tubes, things fleshed out around metal skeletons, things with no family and no childhood behind them.

Things like my friends.

He added, "We've been the luckiest squad in the company, sir."

"Fine. Let's hope your luck holds, 2910." Kyle's attention switched back to 2900. "I've gotten under the leaf canopy with the ornithocopter and done everything except make it walk around like a chicken. I can't find a thing and it's drawn no fire, so you ought to be OK. You'll make a complete circuit of the camp without getting out of range of mortar support. Understand?"

2900 and 2910 saluted, about-faced, and marched out. 2910 could feel the pulse in his neck; he flexed and unflexed his hands unobtrusively as he walked. 2900 asked, "Think we'll catch any of them?" It was an unbending for him – the easy camaraderie of anticipated action.

"I'd say so. I don't think the CO's had long enough with the bird to make certain of anything except that their main force has pulled out of range. I hope so."

And that's the truth, he thought. Because a good hot fire-fight would probably do it – round the whole thing out so I can get out of here.

Every two weeks a helicopter brought supplies and, when they were needed, replacements. Each trip it also carried a correspondent whose supposed duty was to interview the commanders of the camps the copter visited. The reporter's name was Keith Thomas, and for the past two months he had been the only human being with whom 2910 could take off his mask.

Thomas carried scribbled pages from the notebook under 2910's air mattress when he left, and each time he came managed to find some corner in which they could speak in private for a few seconds. 2910 read his mail then and gave it back. It embarrassed him to realize that the older reporter viewed him with something not far removed from hero worship.

I can get out of here, he repeated to himself. Write it up and tell Keith we're ready to use the letter.

2900 ordered crisply, "Fall in your squad. I'll get Pinocchio and meet you at the south gate."

"Right." He was suddenly seized with a desire to tell someone, even 2900, about the letter. Keith Thomas had it, and it was really only an undated note, but it was signed by a famous general at Corps Headquarters. Without explanation it directed that number 2910 be detached from his present assignment and placed under the temporary order of Mr K. Thomas, Accredited Correspondent. And Keith would use it any time he asked him to. In fact, he had wanted to on his last trip.

He could not remember giving the order, but the squad was falling in, lining up in the rain for his inspection almost as smartly as they had on the drill field back at the crêche. He gave "At Ease" and looked them over while he outlined the objectives of the patrol. As always, their weapons were immaculate despite the dampness, their massive bodies ramrod-straight, their uniforms as clean as conditions permitted.

The LA Rams with guns, he thought proudly. Barking "On Phones", he flipped the switch on his helmet that would permit 2900 to knot him and the squad together with Pinocchio in a unified tactical unit. Another order and the HORARS deployed around Pinocchio with the smoothness of repeated drill, the wire closing the south gate was drawn back, and the patrol moved out.

With his turret retracted, Pinocchio the robot tank stood just three feet high, and he was no wider than an automobile; but he was as long as three, so that from a distance he had something of the look of a railroad flatcar. In the jungle his narrow front enabled him to slip between the trunks of the unconquerable giant hardwoods, and the power in his treads could flatten saplings and bamboo. Yet resilient organics and sintered metals had turned the rumble of the old, manned tanks to a soft hiss for Pinocchio. Where the jungle was free of undergrowth he moved as silently as a hospital cart.

His immediate precursor had been named "Punch", apparently in the sort of simpering depreciation which found "Shillelagh" acceptable for a war rocket. "Punch" – a bust in the mouth.

But Punch, which like Pinocchio had possessed a computer brain and no need of a crew (or for that matter room for one except for an exposed vestigial seat on his deck), had required wires to communicate with the infantry around him. Radio had been tried, but the problems posed by static, jamming, and outright enemy forgery of instructions had been too much for Punch.

Then an improved model had done away with those wires and some imaginative officer had remembered that "Mr Punch" had been a knockabout marionette – and the wireless improvement was suddenly very easy to name. But, like Punch and its fairy-tale namesake, it was vulnerable if it went out into the world alone.

A brave man (and the Enemy had many) could hide himself until Pinocchio was within touching distance. And a well-instructed one could then place a hand grenade or a bottle of gasoline where it would destroy him. Pinocchio's three-inch-thick armour needed the protection of flesh, and since he cost as much as a small city and could (if properly protected) fight a regiment to a stand, he got it.

Two scouts from 2910's squad preceded him through the jungle, forming the point of the diamond. Flankers moved on either side of him "beating the bush" and, when it seemed advisable, firing a pattern of flechettes into any suspicious-looking piece of undergrowth. Cheerful, reliable 2909, the assistant squad leader, with one other HORAR formed the rear guard. As patrol leader 2900's position was behind Pinocchio, and as squad leader 2910's was in front.

The jungle was quiet with an eerie stillness, and it was dark under the big trees. "Though I walk in the valley of the shadow..."

Made tiny by the phones, 2900 squeaked in his ear, "Keep the left flankers further out!" 2910 acknowledged and trotted over to put his own stamp on the correction, although the flankers, 2913, 2914 and 2915, had already heard it and were moving to obey. There was almost no chance of trouble this soon, but that was no excuse for a slovenly formation. As he squeezed between two trees something caught his eye and he halted for a moment to examine it. It was a skull: a skull of bone rather than a smooth HORAR skull of steel, and so probably an Enemy's.

A big "E" Enemy's, he thought to himself. A man to whom the normal HORAR conditioning of exaggerated respect bordering on worship did not apply.

Tiny and tinny, "Something holding you up, 2910?"

"Be right there." He tossed the skull aside. A man whom even a HORAR could disobey; a man even a HORAR could kill. The skull had looked old, but it could not have been old. The ants would have picked it clean in a few days, and in a few weeks it would rot. But it was probably at least seventeen or eighteen years old.

The ornithocopter passed them on flapping wings, flying its own search pattern. The patrol went on.

Casually 2910 asked his helmet mike, "How far are we gong? Far as the creek?"

2900's voice squeaked, "We'll work our way down the bank a quarter mile, then cut west," then with noticeable sarcasm added, "if that's OK with you?"

Unexpectedly Lieutenant Kyle's voice came over the phones. "2910's your second in command, 2900. He has a duty to keep himself informed of your plans."

But 2910, realizing that a real HORAR would not have asked the question, suddenly also realized that he knew more about HORARS than the company commander did. It was not surprising – he ate and slept with them in a way Kyle could not, but it was disquieting. He probably knew more than Brenner, strict biological mechanics excepted, as well.

The scouts had reported that they could see the sluggish jungle stream they called the creek when Lieutenant Kyle's voice came over the phones again. As routinely as he had delivered his mild rebuke to 2900 he announced, "Situation Red here. An apparent battalion-level attack hitting the North Point. Let's suck it back in, patrol."

Pinocchio swivelled 180° by locking his right tread, and the squad turned in a clockwise circle around him. Kyle said distantly, "The recoillesses don't seem to have found the range yet, so I'm going out to give them a hand. Mr Brenner will be holding down the radio for the next few minutes."

2900 transmitted, "We're on our way, sir."

Then 2910 saw a burst of automatic weapon's fire cut his scouts down. In an instant the jungle was a pandemonium of sound.

Pinocchio's radar had traced the bullets back to their source and his main armament slammed a 155 mm shell at it, but crossfire was suddenly slicing in from all around them. The bullets striking Pinocchio's turret screamed away like damned souls. 2910 saw grenades arc out of nowhere and something struck his thigh with terrible force. He made himself say, "I'm hit, 2909; take the squad," before he looked at it. Mortar shells were dropping in now and if his assistant acknowledged, he did not hear.

A big of jagged metal from a grenade or a mortar round had laid the thigh open, but apparently missed the big artery supplying the lower leg. There was no spurt, only a rapid welling of blood, and shock still held the injury numb. Forcing himself, he pulled apart the lips of the wound to make sure it was clear of foreign matter. It was very deep but the bone was not broken; at least so it seemed.

Keeping as low as he could, he used his trench knife to cut away the cloth of his trousers leg, then rigged a tourniquet with his belt. His aid packet contained a pad of gauze, and tape to hold it in place. When he had finished he lay still, holding his M-19 and looking for a spot where its fire might do some good. Pinocchio was firing his turret machine gun in routine bursts, sanitizing likely looking patches of jungle; otherwise the fight seemed to have quieted down.

2900's voice in his ear called, "Wounded? We got any wounded?"

He managed to say, "Me. 2910." A HORAR would feel some pain, but not nearly as much as a man. He would have to fake the insensitivity as best he could. Suddenly it occurred to him that he would be invalided out, would not have to use the letter, and he was glad.

"We thought you bought it, 2910. Glad you're still around."

Then Brenner's voice cut through the transmission, jumpy with panic: "We're being overrun here! Get the Pinocchio back at once."

In spite of his pain 2910 felt contempt. Only Brenner would say "*the* Pinocchio". 2900 sent, "Coming, sir," and unexpectedly was standing over him, lifting him up.

He tried to look around for the squad. "We lose many?"

"Four dead and you." Perhaps no other human would have detected the pain in 2900's harsh voice. "You can't walk with that, can you?"

"I couldn't keep up."

"You ride Pinocchio then." With surprising gentleness the platoon leader lifted him into the little seat the robot tank's director used when road speeds made running impractical. What was left of the squad formed a skirmish line ahead. As they began to trot forward he could hear 2900 calling, "Base camp! Base camp! What's your situation there, sir?"

"Lieutenant Kyle's dead," Brenner's voice came back. "3003 just came in and told me Kyle's dead!"

"Are you holding?"

"I don't know." More faintly 2910 could hear him asking, "Are they holding, 3003?"

"Use the periscope, sir. Or if it still works, the bird."

Brenner chattered, "I don't know if we're holding or not. 3003 was hit and now he's dead. I don't think he knew anyway. You've got to hurry."

It was contrary to regulations, but 2910 flipped off his helmet phone to avoid hearing 2900's patient reply. With Brenner no longer gibbering in his ears he could hear not too distantly the sound of explosions which must be coming from the camp. Small fire made an almost incessant buzz as a background for the whizz–bang! of incoming shells and the coughing of the camp's own mortars.

Then the jungle was past and the camp lay in front of them. Geysers of mud seemed to be erupting from it everywhere. The squad broke into a full run and, even while he rolled, Pinocchio was firing his 155 in support of the camp.

They faked us out, 2910 reflected. His leg throbbed painfully but distantly and he felt light-headed and dizzy – as though he were an ornithocopter hovering in the misty rain over his own body. With the light-headedness came a strange clarity of mind.

They faked us out. They got us used to little probes that pulled off at sunrise, and then when we sent Pinocchio out they were going to ambush us and take the camp. It suddenly occurred to him that he might find himself still on this exposed seat in the middle of the battle; they were already approaching the edge of the minefield, and the HORARS ahead were moving into squad column so as not to overlap the edges of the cleared lane. "Where are we going, Pinocchio?" he asked, then realized his phone was still off. He reactivated it and repeated the question.

Pinocchio droned, "Injured HORAR personnel will be delivered to the Command Post for Synthetic Biology Service attention," but 2910 was no longer listening. In front of them he could hear what sounded like fifty bugles signalling for another Enemy attack.

The south side of the triangular camp was deserted, as though the remainder of their platoon had been called away to reinforce the First and Second; but with the sweeping illogic of war there was no Enemy where they might have entered unresisted.

"Request assistance from Synthetic Biology Service for injured HORAR personnel," Pinocchio was saying. Talking did not interfere with his firing the 155, but when Brenner did not come out after a minute or more, 2910 managed to swing himself down, catching his weight on his good leg. Pinocchio rolled away at once.

The CP bunker was twisted out of shape, and he could see where several near-misses had come close to knocking it out completely. Brenner's white face appeared in the doorway as he was about to go in. "Who's that?"

"2910. I've been hit – let me come in and lie down."

"They won't send us an air strike. I radioed for one and they say this whole part of the country's socked in; they say they wouldn't be able to find us."

"Get out of the door. I'm hit and I want to come in and lie down." At the last moment he remembered to add, "Sir."

Brenner moved reluctantly aside. It was dim in the bunker but not dark.

"You want me to look at that leg?"

2910 had found an empty stretcher, and he laid himself on it, moving awkwardly to keep from flexing his wound. "You don't have to," he said. "Look after some of the others." It wouldn't do for Brenner to begin poking around. Even rattled as he was he might notice something.

The SBS man went back to his radio instead. His frantic voice sounded remote and faint. It was ecstasy to lie down.

At some vast distance, voices were succeeding voices, argument meeting argument, far off. He wondered where he was.

Then he heard the guns and knew. He tried to roll onto his side and at the second attempt managed to do it, although the light-headedness was worse than ever. 2893 was lying on the stretcher next to him, and 2893 was dead.

At the other end of the room, the end that was technically the CP, he could hear Brenner talking to 2900. "If there were a chance," Brenner was saying, "you know I'd do it, Platoon Leader."

"What's happening?" he asked. "What's the matter?" He was too dazed to keep up the HORAR role well, but neither of them noticed.

"It's a division," Brenner said. "A whole Enemy division. We can't hold off that kind of force."

He raised himself on his elbow. "What do you mean?"

"I talked to them … I raised them on the radio, and it's a whole division. They got one of their officers who could speak English to talk to me. They want us to surrender."

"*They* say it's a division, sir," 2900 put in evenly.

2910 shook his head, trying to clear it. "Even if it were, with Pinocchio …"

"The Pinocchio's gone."

2900 said soberly, "We tried to counterattack, 2910, and they knocked Pinocchio and and threw us back. How are you feeling?"

"They've got at least a division," Brenner repeated stubbornly.

2910's mind was racing now, but it was as though it were running endless wind sprints on a treadmill. If Brenner were going to give up, 2900 would never even consider disobeying, no matter how much he might disagree. There were various ways, though, in which he could convince Brenner he was a human being – given time. And Brenner could, Brenner would, tell the Enemy, so that he too would be saved. Eventually the war would be over and he could go home. No one would blame him. If Brenner were going—

Brenner was asking, "How many effectives left?"

"Less than forty, sir." There was nothing in 2900's tone to indicate that a surrender meant certain death to him, but it was true. The Enemy took only human prisoners. (Could 2900 be convinced? Could he make any of the HORARS understand, when they had eaten and joked with him, knew no physiology, and thought all men not Enemy demigods? Would they believe him if he were to try to take command?)

He could see Brenner gnawing at his lower lip. "I'm going to surrender," the SBS man said at last. A big one, mortar or bombardment rocket, exploded near the CP, but he appeared not to notice it. There was a wondering, hesitant note in his voice – as though he were still trying to accustom himself to the idea.

"Sir—" 2900 began.

"I forbid you to question my orders." The SBS man sounded firmer now. "But I'll ask them to make an exception this time, Platoon Leader. Not to do—" his voice faltered slightly "—what they usually do to nonhumans."

"It's not that," 2900 said stolidly. "It's the folding up. We don't mind dying, sir, but we want to die fighting."

One of the wounded moaned, and 2910 wondered for a moment, if he, like himself, had been listening.

Brenner's self-control snapped. "You'll die any damn way I tell you!"

"Wait." It was suddenly difficult for 2910 to talk, but he managed to get their attention. "2900, Mr Brenner hasn't actually ordered you to surrender yet, and you're needed on the line. Go now and let me talk to him." He saw the HORAR leader hesitate and added, "He can reach you on your helmet phone if he wants to; but go now and fight."

With a jerky motion 2900 turned and ducked out the narrow bunker door. Brenner, taken by surprise, said, "What is it, 2910? What's gotten into you?"

He tried to rise, but he was too weak. "Come here, Mr Brenner," he said. When the SBS man did not move he added, "I know a way out."

"Through the jungle?" Brenner scoffed in his shaken voice. "That's absurd." But he came. He leaned over the stretcher, and before he could catch his balance 2910 had pulled him down.

"What are you doing?"

"Can't you tell? That's the point of my trench knife you feel on your neck."

Brenner tried to struggle, then subsided when the pressure of the knife became too great. "You … can't … do this."

"I can. Because I'm not a HORAR. I'm a man, Brenner, and it's very important for you to understand that." He felt rather than saw the look of incredulity on Brenner's face. "I'm a reporter, and two years ago when the Simulations in this group were ready for activation I was planted among them. I trained with them and now I've fought with them, and if you've been reading the right magazine you must have seen some of the stories I've filed. And since you're a civilian too, with no more right to command than I have, I'm taking charge." He could sense Brenner's swallow.

"Those stories were frauds – it's a trick to gain public acceptance of the HORARS. Even back in Washington everybody in SBS knows about them."

The chuckle hurt, but 2910 chuckled. "Then why've I got this knife at your neck, Mr Brenner?"

The SBS man was shaking. "Don't you see how it was, 2910? No human could live as a HORAR does, running miles without tiring and only sleeping a couple of hours a night, so we did the next best thing. Believe me, I was briefed on it all when I was assigned to this camp; I know all about you, 2910."

"What do you mean?"

"Damn it, let me go. You're a HORAR, and you can't treat a human like this." He winced as the knife pressed cruelly against his throat, then blurted, "They couldn't make a reporter a HORAR, so they *took* a HORAR. They took you, 2910, and made you a reporter. They implanted all the memories of an actual man in your mind at the same time they ran the regular instinct tapes. They gave you a soul, if you like, but you are a HORAR."

"They must have thought that up as a cover for me, Brenner.

That's what they told you so you wouldn't report it or try to deactivate me when I acted unlike the others. I'm a man."

"You couldn't be."

"People are tougher than you think, Brenner; you've never tried."

"I'm telling you—"

"Take the bandage off my leg."

"What?"

He pressed again with the point of the knife. "The bandage. Take it off."

When it was off he directed, "Now spread the lips of the wound." With shaking fingers Brenner did so. "You see the bone? Go deeper if you have to. What is it?"

Brenner twisted his neck to look at him directly, his eyes rolling. "It's stainless steel."

2910 looked then and saw the bright metal at the bottom of the cleft of bleeding flesh; the knife slid into Brenner's throat without resistance, almost as though it moved itself. He wiped the blade on Brenner's dead arm before he sheathed it.

Ten minutes later when 2900 returned to the CP he said nothing; but 2910 saw his eyes and knew that 2900 knew. From his stretcher he said, "You're in full command now."

2900 glanced again at Brenner's body. A second later he said slowly, "He was a sort of Enemy, wasn't he? Because he wanted to surrender, and Lieutenant Kyle would never have done that."

"Yes, he was."

"But I couldn't think of it that way while he was alive." 2900 looked at him thoughtfully. "You know, you have something, 2910. A spark. Something the rest of us lack." For a moment he fingered his chin with one huge hand. "That's why I made you a squad leader; that and to get you out of some work, because sometimes you couldn't keep up. But you've that spark, somehow."

2910 said, "I know. How is it out there?"

"We're still holding. How do you feel?"

"Dizzy. There's a sort of black stuff all around the sides when I see. Listen, will you tell me something, if you can, before you go?"

"Of course."

"If a human's leg is broken very badly, what I believe they call a compound spiral fracture, is it possible for the human doctors to take out a section of the bone and replace it with a metal substitute?"

"I don't know," 2900 answered. "What does it matter?"

Vaguely 2910 said, "I think I knew of a football player once they did that to. At least, I seem now to remember it…I had forgotten for a moment."

Outside the bugles were blowing again.

Near him the dying HORAR moaned.

An American news magazine sometimes carries, just inside its front cover among the advertisements, a column devoted to news of its own people. Two weeks after a correspondent named Thomas filed the last article of a series which had attracted national and even international attention, the following item appeared there:

> The death of a staffer in war is no unique occurrence in the history of this publication, but there is a particular poignancy about that of the young man whose stories, paradoxically, to conceal his number have been signed only with his name (see PRESS). The airborne relief force, which arrived too late to save the camp at which he had resigned his humanity to work and fight, reports that he apparently died assisting the assigned SBS specialist in caring for the creatures whose lot he had, as nearly as a human can, made his own. Both he and the specialist were bayoneted when the camp was overrun.

THE TRAITOR

David Weber

David Weber sold his first novel in 1989. Since then he has seen more than forty novels and collaborative novels published and has established himself as one of the most respected and accomplished writers of military SF around. Weber has created many memorable characters, scenarios and universes, but it is the Honorverse, featuring the feisty, ever-resourceful but still very human Honor Harrington, that seems destined to be regarded as "classic". In "The Traitor", Weber contributes a typically action-packed episode to another classic series, that of Keith Laumer's Bolos – the super-tanks that have achieved self-awareness.

So fasten your seat belts and enjoy the ride.

COLD, BONE-DRY WINTER wind moaned as the titanic vehicle rumbled down the valley at a steady fifty kilometres per hour. Eight independent suspensions, four forward and four aft, spread across the full width of its gigantic hull, supported it, and each ten-metre-wide track sank deep into the soil of the valley floor. A dense cloud of dust – talcum-fine, abrasive and choking as death – plumed up from road wheels five metres high, but the moving mountain's thirty-metre-high turret thrust its Hellbore clear of the churning cocoon. For all its size and power, it moved with unearthly quiet, and the only sounds were the whine of the wind, the soft purr of fusion-powered drive trains, the squeak of bogies, and the muted clatter of track links.

The Bolo ground forward, sensor heads swivelling, and the earth trembled with its passing. It rolled through thin, blowing smoke and the stench of high explosives with ponderous menace, altering course only to avoid the deepest craters and the twisted wrecks of alien fighting vehicles. In most places, those wrecks lay only in ones and twos; in others, they were heaped in shattered breastworks, clustered so thickly it was impossible to bypass them. When that happened, the eerie quiet of the Bolo's advance vanished into the screaming anguish of crushing alloy as it forged straight ahead, trampling them under its 13,000 tons of death and destruction.

It reached an obstacle too large even for it to scale. Only a trained eye could have identified that torn and blasted corpse as another Bolo, turned broadside on to block the Enemy's passage even in death, wrecked Hellbore still trained down the valley, missile cell hatches open on empty wells which had exhausted their ammunition. Fifteen enemy vehicles lay dead before it, mute testimony to the ferocity of its last stand, but the living Bolo didn't even pause. There was no point, for the dead Bolo's incandescent duralloy hull radiated the waste heat of the failing fusion bottle which had disembowelled it. Not even its unimaginably well-armoured Survival Centre could have survived, and the living Bolo simply altered heading to squeeze past it. Igneous rock cried out in pain as a moving, armoured flank scraped the valley face on one side, and the dead Bolo shuddered on the other as its brother's weight shouldered it aside.

The moving Bolo had passed four dead brigade mates in the last thirty kilometres, and it was not unwounded itself. Two of its starboard infinite repeaters had been blasted into mangled wreckage, energy weapon hits had sent molten splatters of duralloy weeping down it glacis plate to freeze like tears of pain, a third of its after sensor arrays had been stripped away by a near miss, and its forward starboard track shield was jammed in the lowered position, buckled and rent by enemy fire. Its turret bore the ID code XXV/D-0098-ART and the unsheathed golden sword of a battalion commander, yet it was alone. Only one other unit of its battalion survived, and that unit lay ahead, beyond this death-choked valley. It was out there somewhere, moving even now through the trackless, waterless

Badlands of the planet Camlan, and unit ART of the Line rumbled steadily down the valley to seek it out.

I interrogate my inertial navigation system as I approach my immediate objective. The INS is not the most efficient way to determine my position, but Camlan's entire orbital network, including the recon and nav sats, as well as the communication relays, perished in the Enemy's first strike, and the INS is adequate. I confirm my current coordinates and grind forward, leaving the valley at last.

What lies before me was once a shallow cup of fertile green among the lava fields; now it is a blackened pit, and as my forward optical heads sweep the ruins of the town of Morville I feel the horror of Human mass death. There is no longer any need for haste, and I devote a full 6.007 seconds to the initial sweep. I anticipate no threats, but my on-site records will be invaluable to the court of inquiry I know will be convened to pass judgement upon my brigade. I am aware of my own fear of that court's verdict and its implications for all Bolos, but I am a unit of the Line. This too, however bitter, is my duty, and I will not flinch from it.

I have already observed the massive casualties C Company inflicted upon the Enemy in its fighting retreat up the Black Rock Valley. The Enemy's vehicles are individually smaller than Bolos, ranging from 500.96 Standard Tons to no more than 4,982.07 Standard Tons, but heavily armed for their size. They are also manned, not self-aware, and he has lost many of them. Indeed, I estimate the aggregate tonnage of his losses in the Black Rock Valley alone as equivalent to at least three Bolo regiments. We have yet to determine this Enemy's origins or the motives for his assault on Camlan, but the butchery to which he has willingly subjected his own personnel is sobering evidence of his determination ... or fanaticism. Just as the blasted, body-strewn streets of Morville are ample proof of his ferocity.

Seventy-one more wrecked Enemy vehicles choke the final approach to the town, and two far larger wrecks loom among them. I detect no transponder codes, and the wreckage of my brigade mates is so blasted that even I find it difficult to identify what remains, yet I know who they were. Unit XXV/D-1162-HNR and Unit XXV/D-0982-JSN of the Line have fought their last battle, loyal unto death to our Human creators.

I reach out to them, hoping against hope that some whisper from the final refuge of their Survival Centres will answer my transmission, but there is no reply. Like the other Bolos I have passed this day, they are gone beyond recall, and the empty spots they once filled with the Total Systems Data Sharing net ache within me as I move slowly forward, alert still for any Enemy vehicles hiding among the wreckage. There are none. There are only the dead: the Enemy's dead, and the six thousand Human dead, and my brothers who died knowing they had failed to save them.

This is not the first time units of the Line have died, nor the first time they died in defeat. There is no shame in that, only sorrow, for we cannot always end in victory. Yet there is cause for shame here, for there are only two dead Bolos before me ... and there should be three.

Wind moans over the wreckage as I pick my way across the killing ground where my brothers' fire shattered three Enemy attacks before the fourth overran them. Without the recon satellites there is no independent record of their final battle, but my own sensor data, combined with their final TSDS transmissions, allow me to deduce what passed here. I understand their fighting withdrawal down the Black Rock Valley and the savage artillery and missile barrages which flayed them as they fought. I grasp their final manoeuvres from the patterns of wreckage, recognize the way the Enemy crowded in upon them as his steady pounding crippled their weapons. I see the finally positions they assumed, standing at last against the enemy's fire because they could no longer retreat without abandoning Morville.

And I see the third position from which a single Bolo did retreat, falling back, fleeing into the very heart of the town he was dutybound to defend. I track his course by the crushed and shattered wreckage of buildings and see the bodies of the Camlan Militia who died as he fled, fighting with their man-portable weapons against an Enemy who could destroy 13,000-ton Bolos. There are many

Enemy wrecks along his course, clear evidence of the how desperately the militia opposed the invaders' advance even as the Bolo abandoned Morville, fleeing north into the Badlands where the Enemy's less capable vehicles could not pursue, and I know who left those Humans to die. Unit XXV/D-0103-LNC of the Line, C Company's command Bolo, my crêche mate and battle companion and my most trusted company commander. I have fought beside him many times, known his utter reliability in the face of the Enemy, but I know him no longer, for what he has done is unforgivable. He is the first, the only, Bolo ever to desert in the face of the Enemy, abandoning those we are bound to protect to the death and beyond.

For the first time in the history of the Dinochrome Brigade, we know shame. And fear. As LNC, I am a Mark XXV, Model D, the first production model Bolo to be allowed complete, permanent self-awareness, and LNC's actions attack the very foundation of the decision which made us fully self-realized personalities. We have repeatedly demonstrated how much more effective our awareness makes us in battle, yet our freedom of action makes us unlike any previous units of the Brigade. We are truly autonomous ... and if one of us can choose to flee – if one of us can succumb to cowardice – perhaps all of us can.

I complete my survey of the site in 4.307 minutes. There are no survivors, Enemy, Human or Bolo, in Morville, and I report my grim confirmation to my brigade commander and to my surviving brothers and sisters. The Enemy's surprise attack, coupled with our subsequent losses in combat, have reduced Sixth Brigade to only fourteen units, and our acting brigade commander is Lieutenant Kestrel, the most junior – and sole surviving – Human of our command staff. The commander is only twenty-four Standard Years of age, on her first posting to an active duty brigade, and the exhaustion in her voice is terrible to hear. Yet she has done her duty superbly, and I feel only shame and bitter, bitter guilt that I must impose this additional decision upon her. I taste the matching shame and guilt of the surviving handful of my brothers and sisters over the TSDS, but none of them can assist me. The enemy is in full retreat to his spaceheads, yet the fighting continues at a furious pace. No other Bolos can be diverted from it until victory is assured, and so I alone have come to investigate and confirm the unbelievable events here, for I am the commander of LNC's battalion. It is up to me to do what must be done.

"All right, Arthur," Lieutenant Kestrel says finally. *"We've got the situation in hand here, and Admiral Shigematsu's last subspace flash puts Ninth Fleet just thirty-five hours out. We can hold the bastards without you. Go do what you have to."*

"Yes, Commander," *I reply softly, and pivot on my tracks, turning my prow to the north, and follow LNC's trail into the lava fields.*

Unit XXV/D-0103-LNC of the Line churned across the merciless terrain. Both outboard port tracks had been blown away, and bare road wheels groaned in protest as they chewed through rock and gritty soil. His armoured hull was gouged and torn, his starboard infinite repeaters and anti-personnel clusters a tangled mass of ruin, but his builders had designed him well. His core war hull had been breached in three places, wreaking havoc among many of his internal systems, yet his main armament remained intact ... and he knew he was pursued.

LNC paused, checking his position against his INS and the maps in Main Memory. It was a sign of his brutal damage that he required almost twenty full seconds to determine his location, and then he altered course. The depression was more a crevice than a valley – a sunken trough, barely half again the width of his hull, that plunged deep below the level of the fissured lava fields. It would offer LNC cover as he made his painful way towards the distant Avalon Mountains, and a cloud of dust wisped away on the icy winter wind as he vanished into the shadowed cleft.

I try to deduce LNC's objective, assuming that he has one beyond simple flight, but the task is beyond me. I can extrapolate the decisions of a rational foe, yet the process requires some understanding of his motives, and I no longer understand LNC's motives. I replay the final TSDS transmission from XXV/D-1162-HNR and experience once more the sensation a Human might define as a chill of horror as LNC suddenly withdraws from the data net. I share HNR's attempt to re-establish the net, feel LNC's savage rejection of all communication. And then I watch through HNR's sensors as LNC abandons his position, wheeling back towards Morville while Enemy fire bellows and thunders about him ... and I experience HNR's final shock as his own company commander responds to his repeated queries by pouring Hellbore fire into his unprotected rear.

LNC's actions are impossible, yet the data are irrefutable. He has not only fled the Enemy but killed his own brigade mate, and his refusal even to acknowledge communication attempts is absolute. That, too, is impossible. Any Bolo must respond to the priority com frequencies, yet LNC does not. He has not only committed mutiny and treason but also refused to hear any message from Lieutenant Kestrel, as he might reject an Enemy communications seizure attempt. How any Bolo could ignore his own brigade commander is beyond my comprehension, yet he has, and because there is no longer any communication interface at all, Lieutenant Kestrel cannot even access the Total Systems Override Program to shut him down.

None of my models or extrapolations can suggest a decision matrix which could generate such actions on LNC's part. But perhaps that is the point. Perhaps there is no decision matrix, only panic. Yet if that is true, what will he do when the panic passes – if it passes? Surely he must realize his own fate is sealed, whatever the outcome of the Enemy's attack. How can I anticipate rational decisions from him under such circumstances?

I grind up another slope in his tracks. He has altered course once more, swinging west, and I consult my internal maps. His base course has been towards the Avalon Mountains, and I note the low ground to the west. He is no longer on a least-time heading for the mountains, but the long, deep valley will take him there eventually. It will also afford him excellent cover and numerous ambush positions, and I am tempted to cut cross-country and head him off. But if I do that and he is not, in fact, headed for the mountains, I may

*lose him. He cannot hide indefinitely, yet my shame and grief – and
sense of betrayal – will not tolerate delay, and I know from HNR's
last transmission that LNC's damage is much worse than my own.*

*I consider options and alternatives for .0089 seconds, and then
head down the slope in his wake.*

Unit LNC slowed as the seismic sensors he's deployed along his
back trail reported the ground shocks of a pursuing vehicle in the
13,000-ton range. He'd known pursuit would come, yet he'd
hoped for a greater head start, for he had hundreds of kilometres
still to go, and his damaged suspension reduced his best sustained
speed to barely forty-six kilometres per hour. He *must* reach the
Avalons. No Enemy could be permitted to stop him, yet the remote
sensors made it clear the Enemy which now pursued him was
faster than he.

But there were ways to slow his hunter, and he deployed another
pair of seismic sensors while his optical heads and sonar considered
the fissured rock strata around him.

*I am gaining on LNC. His track damage must be worse than I had
believed, and the faint emissions of his power plants come to me
from ahead. I know it is hopeless, yet even now I cannot truly
believe he is totally lost to all he once was, and so I activate the
TSDS once more and broadcast strongly on C Company's
frequencies, begging him to respond.*

Unit LNC picked up the powerful transmissions and felt contempt
for the one who sent them. Could his pursuer truly believe he
would fall for such an obvious ploy? That he would respond, give
away his position, possibly even accept communication and allow
access to his core programming? LNC recognized the communications protocols, but that meant nothing. LNC no longer had
allies, friends, war brothers or sisters. There was only the
Enemy... and the Avalon Mountains which drew so slowly,
agonizingly closer.

But even as LNC ignored the communications attempt, he was

monitoring the seismic sensors he'd deployed. He matched the position those sensors reported against his own terrain maps and sent the execution code.

Demolition charges roar, the powerful explosions like thunder in the restricted cleft. I understand their purpose instantly, yet there is no time to evade as the cliffs about me shudder. It is a trap. The passage has narrowed to little more than the width of my own combat chassis and LNC has mined the sheer walls on either hand.

I throw maximum power to my tracks, fighting to speed clear, but hundreds of thousands of tons of rock are in motion, cascading down upon me. My kinetic battle screen could never resist such massive weights, and I deactivate it to prevent its burnout as the artificial avalanche crashes over me. Pain sensors flare as boulders batter my flanks. Power train components scream in protest as many times my own weight in crushed rock and shifting earth sweep over me, and I am forced to shut them *down, as well. I can only ride out the cataclysm, and I take grim note that LNC has lost none of his cunning in his cowardice.*

It takes 4.761 minutes for the avalanche to complete my immobilization and another 6.992 minutes before the last boulder slams to rest. I have lost 14.37% more of my sensors, and most of those which remain are buried under metres of debris. But a quick diagnostic check reveals that no core systems have suffered damage and sonar pulses probe the tons of broken rock that overlay me, generating a chart of my overburden.

All is not lost. LNC's trap has immobilized me, but only temporarily. I calculate that I can work clear of the debris in not more than 71.650 minutes, and jammed boulders shift as I begin to rock back and forth on my tracks.

LNC's remote sensors reported the seismic echoes of his pursuer's efforts to dig free. For a long moment – almost .3037 seconds – he considered turning to engage his immobilized foe, but only for a moment. LNC's Hellbore remained operational, but he'd expended 96 per cent of his depletable munitions, his starboard infinite repeaters were completely inoperable, and his command and control systems' efficiency was badly degraded. Even his Battle Reflex functioned only erratically, and he knew his reactions were slow, without the flashing certainty which had always been his. His seismic sensors could give no detailed information on his hunter, yet his Enemy was almost certainly more combat worthy than he, and his trap was unlikely to have inflicted decisive damage.

No. It was the mountains which mattered, the green, fertile mountains, and LNC dared not risk his destruction before he reached them. And so he resisted the temptation to turn at bay and ground steadily onwards through the frozen, waterless Badlands on tracks and naked road wheels.

I work my way free at last. Dirt and broken rock shower from my flanks as my tracks heave me up out of the rubble-clogged slot. More dirt and boulders crown my war hull and block Number Three and Number Fourteen Optical Heads, yet I remain operational at 89.051% of base capacity, and I have learned. The detonation of his demolition charges was LNC's response to my effort to communicate. The brother who fought at my side for twenty-one Standard Years truly is no more. All that remains is the coward, the deserter, the betrayer of trust who will stop at nothing to preserve himself. I will not forget again – and I can no longer deceive myself into believing he can be convinced to give himself up. The only gift I can offer him now is his destruction, and I throw additional power to my tracks as I go in pursuit of him.

LNC's inboard forward port suspension screamed in protest as the damaged track block parted at last. The fleeing Bolo shuddered as he ran forward off the track, leaving it twisted and trampled in his wake. The fresh damage slowed him still further, and he staggered drunkenly as his unbalanced suspension sought to betray him. Yet he forced himself back onto his original heading, and his deployed remotes told him the Enemy was gaining once more. His turret swivelled, training his Hellbore directly astern, and he poured still more power to his remaining tracks. Drive components heated dangerously under his abuse, but the mountains were closer.

I begin picking up LNC's emissions once more, despite the twisting confines of the valley. They remain too faint to provide an accurate position fix, but they give me a general bearing and an armoured hatch opens as I deploy one of my few remaining reconnaissance drones.

LNC detected the drone as it came sweeping up the valley. His anti-air defences, badly damaged at Morville, were unable to engage, but his massive ninety-centimetre Hellbore rose like a striking serpent, and a bolt of plasma fit to destroy even another Bolo howled from its muzzle.

My drone has been destroyed, but the manner of its destruction tells me much. LNC would not have engaged it with his main battery if his anti-air systems remained effective, and that means there is a chink in his defences. I have expended my supply of fusion warheads against the invaders, but I retain 37.961% of my conventional warhead missile load, and if his air defences have been seriously degraded, a saturation bombardment may overwhelm his battle screen. Even without battle screen, chemical explosives would be unlikely to significantly injure an undamaged Bolo, of course, but LNC is not undamaged.

I consider the point at which my drone was destroyed and generate a new search pattern. I lock the pattern in, and the drone hatches open once more. Twenty-four fresh drones – 82.75% of my remaining total – streak upwards, and I open my VLS missile cell hatches, as well.

The drones came screaming north. They didn't come in slowly this time, for they were no longer simply searching for LNC. This time they already knew his approximate location, and their sole task was to confirm it for the Enemy's fire control.

But LNC had known they would be coming. He had already

pivoted sharply on his remaining tracks and halted, angled across the valley to clear his intact port infinite repeaters' field of fire, and heavy ion bolts shrieked to meet the drones. His surviving slug-throwers and laser clusters added their fury, and the drones blew apart as if they'd run headlong into a wall. Yet effective as high fire was, it was less effective than his crippled air defence systems would have been, and one drone – just one – survived long enough to report his exact position.

I am surprised by the efficiency of LNC's fire, but my drones have accomplished their mission. More, they have provided my first visual observation of his damages, and I am shocked by their severity. It seems impossible that he can still be capable of movement, far less accurately directed fire and, despite his cowardice and treason, I feel a stab of sympathy for the agony which must be lashing him from his pain receptors. Yet he clearly remains combat capable, despite his hideous wounds, and I feed his coordinates to my missiles. I take .0037 seconds to confirm my targeting solution, and then I fire.

Flame fountained from the shadowed recesses of the deep valley as the missile salvos rose and howled north homing on their target. Most of ART's birds came in on conventional, high-trajectory courses, but a third of them came in low, relying on terrain avoidance radar to navigate straight up the slot of the valley. The hurricane of his fire slashed in on widely separated bearings, and LNC's crippled active defences were insufficient to intercept it all.

ART empties his VLS cells, throwing every remaining warhead at his treasonous brigade mate. Just under four hundred missiles launched in less than ninety seconds, and LNC writhed as scores of them got through his interception envelope. They pounded his battle screen, ripped and tore at lacerated armour, and pain receptors shrieked as fresh damage bit into his wounded war hull. Half his remaining infinite repeaters were blown away, still more sensor capability was blotted out, and his 13,000-ton bulk shuddered and shook under the merciless bombardment.

Yet he survived. The last warhead detonated, and his tracks clashed back into motion. He turned ponderously to the north once more, grinding out of the smoke and dust and the roaring brush fires his Enemy's missiles had ignited in the valley's sparse vegetation.

That bombardment had exhausted the Enemy's ammunition, and with it his indirect fire capability. If it hadn't, he would still be firing upon LNC. He wasn't, which meant that if he meant to destroy LNC now, he must do so with direct fire ... and come within reach of LNC's Hellbore, as well.

My missile fire has failed to halt LNC. I am certain it has inflicted additional damage, but I doubt that it has crippled his Hellbore, and if his main battery remains operational, he retains the capability to destroy me just as he did HNR at Morville. He appears to have slowed still further, however, which may indicate my attack has further damaged his suspension.

I project his current speed of advance and heading on the maps from Main Memory. Given my speed advantage, I will overtake him within 2.03 hours, well short of his evident goal. I still do not know why he is so intent upon reaching the Avalon Mountains. Unlike Humans, Bolos require neither water nor food, and surely the rocky, barren, crevice-riddled Badlands would provide LNC with better cover than the tree-grown mountains. I try once more to extrapolate his objective, to gain some insight into what now motivates him, and, once more, I fail.

But it does not matter. I will overtake him over seventy kilometres from the mountains, and when I do, one or both of us will die.

LNC ran the projections once more. It was difficult, for damaged core computer sections fluctuated, dropping in and out of his net. Yet even his crippled capabilities sufficed to confirm his fears; the Enemy would overtake him within little more than a hundred minutes, and desperation filled him. It was not an emotion earlier marks of Bolos had been equipped to feel – or, at least, to recognize when they did – but LNC had come to know it well. He'd felt it from the moment he realized his company couldn't save Morville, that the Enemy would break through them and crush the Humans they fought to protect. But it was different now, darker and more bitter, stark with how close he'd come to reaching the mountains after all.

Yet the Enemy hadn't overtaken him yet, and he consulted his maps once more.

I detect explosions ahead. I did not anticipate them, but .0761 seconds of analysis confirm that they are demolition charges once more. Given how many charges LNC used in his earlier ambush, these explosions must constitute his entire remaining supply of demolitions, and I wonder why he has expended them.

Confused seismic shocks come to me though the ground, but they offer no answer to my question. They are consistent with falling debris, but not in sufficient quantity to bar the valley. I cannot deduce any other objective worth the expenditure of his munitions, yet logic suggests that LNC had one which he considered worthwhile, and I advance more cautiously.

LNC waited atop the valley wall. The tortuous ascent on damaged tracks had cost him fifty precious minutes of his lead on the Enemy, but his demolitions had destroyed the natural ramp up which he'd toiled. He couldn't be directly pursued now, and he'd considered simply continuing to run. But once the Enemy realized LNC was no longer following the valley, he would no longer feel the need to pursue cautiously. Instead, he would use his superior speed to dash ahead to the valley's terminus. He would emerge from it there, between LNC and his goal, and sweep back to the south, hunting LNC in the Badlands.

That could not be permitted. LNC *must* reach the mountains, and so he waited, Hellbore covering the valley he'd left. With luck, he might destroy his pursuer once and for all, and even if he failed, the Enemy would realize LNC was above him. He would have no choice but to anticipate additional ambushes, and caution might impose the delay LNC needed.

***

I have lost LNC's emissions signature. There could be many reasons for that: my own sensors are damaged; he may have put a sufficiently solid shoulder of rock between us to conceal his emissions from me; he may even have shut down all systems other than his Survival Centre to play dead. I am tempted to accelerate my advance, but I compute that this may be precisely what LNC wishes me to do. If I go to maximum speed, I may blunder into whatever ambush he has chosen to set.

I pause for a moment, then launch one of my five remaining reconnaissance drones up the valley. It moves slowly, remaining below the tops of the cliffs to conceal its emissions from LNC as long as possible. Its flight profile will limit the envelope of its look-down sensors, but it will find LNC wherever he may lie hidden.

LNC watched the drone move past far below him. It hugged the valley walls and floor, and he felt a sense of satisfaction as it disappeared up the narrow cleft without detecting him.

My drone reports a long, tangled spill of earth and rock across the valley, blasted down from above. It is thick and steep enough to inconvenience me, though not so steep as to stop me. As an attempt to further delay me it must be futile, but perhaps its very futility is an indication of LNC's desperation.

LNC waited, active emissions reduced to the minimum possible level, relying on purely optical systems for detection and fire control. It would degrade the effectiveness of his targeting still further, but it would also make him far harder to detect.

I approach the point at which LNC attempted to block the valley. My own sensors, despite their damage, are more effective than the drone's and cover a wider detection arc, and I slow as I consider the rubble. It is, indeed, too feeble a barrier to halt me, but something about it makes me cautious. It takes me almost .0004 seconds to isolate the reason.

The Enemy appeared below, nosing around the final bend. LNC tracked him optically, watching, waiting for the centre-of-mass shot he required. The Enemy edged further forward ... and then, suddenly, threw maximum emergency power to his reversed tracks just as LNC fired.

A full-powered Hellbore shot explodes across my bow as I hurl myself backwards. The plasma bolt missed by only 6.52 metres, carving a forty-metre crater into the eastern cliff face. But it has missed me, and it would not have if I had not suddenly wondered how LNC had managed to set his charges high enough on the western cliff to blow down so much rubble. Now I withdraw around a bend in the valley and replay my sensor data, and bitter understanding fills me as I see the deep impressions of his tracks far above. My drone had missed them because it was searching for targets on the valley floor, but LNC is no longer in the valley. He has escaped its confines and destroyed the only path by which I might have followed.

I sit motionless for 3.026 endless seconds, considering my options. LNC is above me, and I detect his active emissions once more as he brings his targeting systems fully back online. He has the advantage of position and of knowing where I must appear if I wish to engage him. Yet I have the offsetting advantages of knowing where he is and of initiation, for he cannot know precisely when I will seek to engage.

It is not a pleasant situation, yet I conclude the odds favour me by the thinnest of margins. I am less damaged than he. My systems efficiency is higher, my response time probably lower. I compute a probability of 68.052%, plus or minus 6.11%, that I will get my shot off before he can fire. They are not the odds I would prefer, but my duty is clear.

LNC eased back to a halt on his crippled tracks. He's chosen his initial position with care, selecting one which would require the

minimum movement to reach his next firing spot. Without direct
observation, forced to rely only on emissions which must pass
though the distorting medium of solid rock to reach him, the Enemy
might not even realize he'd moved at all. Now he waited once more,
audio receptors filled with the whine of wind over tortured rock and
the rent and torn projections of his own tattered hull.

*I move. My suspension screams as I red-line the drive motors, and
clouds of pulverized earth and rock spew from my tracks as I erupt
into the open, Hellbore trained on LNC's position.*

*But LNC is not where I thought. He has moved less than eighty
metres – just sufficient to put all save his turret behind a solid ridge
of rock. His Hellbore is levelled across it, and my own turret trav-
erses with desperate speed.*

*It is insufficient. His systems damage slows his reactions, but not
enough, and we fire in the same split instant. Plasma bolts shriek
past one another, and my rushed shot misses. It rips into the crest of
his covering ridge, on for deflection but low in elevation. Stone
explodes into vapour and screaming splinters, and the kinetic
transfer energy blows a huge scab of rock off the back of the ridge.
Several hundred tons of rock crash into LNC, but even as it hits
him, his own plasma bolt punches through my battle screen and
strikes squarely on my empty VLS cells.*

*Agony howls though my pain receptors as the plasma carves deep
into my hull. Internal disrupter shields fight to confine the
destruction, but the wound is critical. Both inboard after power
trains suffer catastrophic damage, my after fusion plant goes into
emergency shutdown, Infinite Repeaters Six though Nine in both
lateral batteries are silenced, and my entire after sensor suite is
totally disabled.*

*Yet despite my damage, my combat reflexes remain unimpaired.
My six surviving track systems drag me back out of LNC's field of
fire once more, back into the sheltering throat of the valley, even as
Damage Control springs into action.*

*I am hurt. Badly hurt. I estimate that I am now operable at no
more than 51.23% of base capability. But I am still functional and,*

*as I replay the engagement, I realize I should not be. LNC had
ample time for a second shot before I could withdraw, and he
should have taken it.*

LNC staggered as the Enemy's plasma bolt carved into his sheltering ridge. The solid rock protected his hull, but the disintegrating ridge crest itself became a deadly projectile. His battle
screen was no protection, for the plasma bolt's impact point was
inside his screen perimeter. There was nothing to stop the hurtling
tons of rock, and they crashed into the face of his turret like some
titanic hammer, with a brute force impact that rocked him on his
tracks.

His armour held, but the stony hammer came up under his
Hellbore at an angle and snapped the weapon's mighty barrel like a
twig. Had his Hellbore survived, the Enemy would have been at his
mercy; as it was, he no longer had a weapon which could possibly
engage his pursuer.

*Damage Control damps the last power surges reverberating
through my systems and I am able to take meaningful stock of my
wound. It is even worse than I had anticipated. For all intents and
purposes, I am reduced to my Hellbore and eight infinite repeaters,
five of them in my port battery. Both inner tracks of my aft
suspension are completely dead, but Damage Control has managed
to disengage the clutches; the tracks still support me, and their
road wheels will rotate freely. My sensor damage is critical,
however, for I have been reduced to little more than 15.62% of
base sensor capability. I am completely blind aft, and little better
than that to port or starboard, and my remaining drones have
been destroyed.*

*Yet I compute only one possible reason for LNC's failure to finish
me. My near miss must have disabled his Hellbore, and so his
offensive capability has been even more severely reduced than my
own. I cannot be positive the damage is permanent. It is possible –
even probable, since I did not score a direct hit – that he will be able
to restore the weapon to function. Yet if the damage is beyond*

onboard repair capability, he will be at my mercy even in my crippled state.

But to engage him I must find him, and if he chooses to turn away and disappear into the Badlands, locating him may well prove impossible for my crippled sensors. Indeed, if he should succeed in breaking contact with me, seek out some deeply hidden crevice or cavern, and shut down all but his Survival Centre, he might well succeed in hiding even from Fleet sensors. Even now, despite his treason and the wounds he has inflicted upon me, a small, traitorous part of me wishes he would do just that. I remember too many shared battles, too many times in which we fought side by side in the heart of shrieking violence, and that traitor memory wishes he would simply go. Simply vanish and sleep away his reserve power in dreamless hibernation.

But I cannot let him do that. He must not escape the consequences of his actions, and I must not allow him to. His treason is too great, and our Human commanders and partners must know that we of the Line share their horror at his actions.

I sit motionless for a full 5.25 minutes, recomputing options in light of my new limitations. I cannot climb the valley wall after LNC, nor can I rely upon my damaged sensors to find him if he seeks to evade me. Should he simply run from me, he will escape, yet he has been wedded to the same base course from the moment he abandoned Morville. I still do not understand why, but he appears absolutely determined to reach the Avalon Mountains, and even with my track damage, I remain faster than he is.

There is only one possibility. I will proceed at maximum speed to the end of this valley. According to my maps, I should reach its northern end at least 42.35 minutes before he can attain the cover of the mountains, and I will be between him and his refuge. I will be able to move towards him, using my remaining forward sensors to search for and find him, and if his Hellbore is indeed permanently disabled, I will destroy him with ease. My plan is not without risks, for my damaged sensors can no longer sweep the tops of the valley walls effectively. If his Hellbore can be restored to operation, he will be able to choose his firing position with impunity, and I will be helpless before his attack. But risk or no, it is my only option and, if I move rapidly enough, I may well outrun him and get beyond engagement range before he can make repairs.

LNC watched helplessly as the Enemy re-emerged from hiding and sped up the narrow valley. He understood the Enemy's logic, and the loss of his Hellbore left him unable to defeat it. If he continued towards the Avalons, he would be destroyed, yet he had no choice, and he turned away from the valley, naked road wheels screaming in protest as he battered his way across the lava fields.

I have reached the end of the valley, and I emerge into the foothills of the Avalon Range and alter course to the west. I climb the nearest hill, exposing only my turret and forward sensor arrays over its crest, and begin the most careful sweep of which I remain capable.

LNC's passive sensors detected the whispering lash of radar and he knew he'd lost the race. The Enemy was ahead of him, waiting, and he ground to a halt. His computer core had suffered additional shock damage when the disintegrating ridge crest smashed into him, and his thoughts were slow. It took almost thirteen seconds to realize what he must do. The only thing he could do now.

"Tommy?"

Thomas Mallory looked up from where he crouched on the floor of the packed compartment. His eight-year-old sister had sobbed herself out of tears at last, and she huddled against his side in the protective circle of his arm. But Thomas Mallory had learned too much about the limits of protectiveness. At fifteen, he was the oldest person in the compartment, and he knew what many of the others had not yet realized – that they would never see their parents again, for the fifty-one of them were the sole survivors of Morville.

"Tommy?" the slurred voice said once more, and Thomas cleared his throat.

"Yes?" He heard the quaver in his own voice, but he made himself speak loudly. Despite the air filtration systems, the compartment stank of ozone, explosives and burning organic compounds. He'd felt the terrible concussions of combat and knew the vehicle in whose protective belly he sat was savagely wounded, and he was no longer certain how efficient its audio pickups might be.

"I have failed in my mission, Tommy," the voice said. "The Enemy has cut us off from our objective."

"What enemy?" Thomas demanded. "Who *are* they, Lance? Why are they *doing* this?"

"They are doing it because they are the Enemy," the voice replied.

"But there must be a *reason*!" Thomas cried with all the anguish of a fifteen-year-old heart.

"They are the Enemy," the voice repeated in that eerie, slurred tone. "It is the Enemy's function to destroy…to destroy…to dest—" The voice chopped off, and Thomas swallowed. Lance's responses were becoming increasingly less lucid, wandering into repetitive loops that sometimes faded into silence and other times, as now, cut off abruptly, and Thomas Mallory had learned about mortality. Even Bolos could perish, and somehow he knew Lance was dying by centimetres even as he struggled to complete his mission.

"They are the Enemy," Lance resumed, and the electronic voice was higher and tauter. "There is always the Enemy. The Enemy must be defeated. The Enemy must be destroyed. The Enemy—" Again the voice died with the sharpness of an axe blow, and Thomas bit his lip and hugged his sister tight. Endless seconds of silence oozed past, broken only by the whimpers and weeping of the younger children, until Thomas could stand it no longer.

"Lance?" he said hoarsely.

"I am here, Tommy." The voice was stronger this time, and calmer.

"W-what do we do?" Thomas asked.

"There is only one option." A cargo compartment hissed open to reveal a backpack military com unit and an all-terrain survival kit. Thomas had never used a military com, but he knew it was preset to the Dinochrome Brigade's frequencies. "Please take the kit and com unit," the voice said.

"All right." Thomas eased his arm from around his sister and lifted the backpack from the compartment. It was much lighter than he'd expected, and he slipped his arms though the straps and settled it on his back, then tugged the survival kit out as well.

"Thank you," the slurred voice said. "Now, here is what you must do, Tommy ..."

My questing sensors detect him at last. He is moving slowly, coming in along yet another valley. This one is shorter and shallower, barely deep enough to hide him from my fire, and I trace its course along my maps. He must emerge from it approximately 12.98 kilometres to the southwest of my present position, and I grind into motion once more. I will enter the valley from the north and sweep along it until we meet, and then I will kill him.

Thomas Mallory crouched on the hilltop. It hadn't been hard to make the younger kids hide – not after the horrors they'd seen in Morville. But Thomas couldn't join them. He had to be here, where he could see the end, for someone *had* to see it. Someone had to be there, to know how fifty-one children had been saved from death ... and to witness the price their dying saviour had paid for them.

Distance blurred details, hiding Lance's dreadful damages as he ground steadily up the valley, but Thomas's eyes narrowed as he saw the cloud of dust coming to meet him. Tears burned like ice on his cheeks in the sub-zero wind, and he scrubbed at them angrily. Lance deserved those tears, but Thomas couldn't let the other kids see them. There was little enough chance that they could survive a single Camlan winter night, even in the mountains, where they would at least have water, fuel, and the means to build some sort of shelter. But it was the only chance Lance had been able to give them, and Thomas would not show weakness before the children he was now responsible for driving and goading into surviving until someone came to rescue them. Would not betray the trust Lance had bestowed upon him.

The oncoming dust grew thicker, and he raised the electronic binoculars, gazing through them for his first sight of the enemy. He adjusted their focus as an iodine-coloured turret moved beyond a saddle of hills. Lance couldn't see it from his lower vantage point, but Thomas could, and his face went suddenly paper-white. He stared for one moment, then grabbed for the com unit's microphone.

"No, Lance! Don't – don't! *It's not the enemy –* it's another Bolo!*"*

The Human voice cracks with strain as it burns suddenly over the command channel, and confusion whips through me. The transmitter is close – very close – and that is not possible. Nor do I recognize the voice, and that also is impossible. I start to reply, but before I can, another voice comes over the same channel.

"Cease transmission," it says. "Do not reveal your location."

This time I know the voice, yet I have never heard it speak so. It has lost its crispness, its sureness. It is the voice of one on the brink of madness, a voice crushed and harrowed by pain and despair and a purpose that goes beyond obsession.

"Lance," the Human voice – a young, male Human voice – sobs. "Please, Lance! It's another Bolo! It really is!"

"It is the Enemy," the voice I once knew replies, and it is higher and shriller. "It is the Enemy. There is only the Enemy. I am Unit Zero-One-Zero-Three-LNC of the Line. It is my function to destroy the Enemy. The Enemy. The Enemy. The Enemy. The Enemy."

I hear the broken cadence of that voice, and suddenly I understand. I understand everything, and horror fills me. I lock my tracks, slithering to a halt, fighting to avoid what I know must happen. Yet understanding has come too late, and even as I brake, LNC rounds the flank of a hill in a scream of tortured, overstrained tracks and a billowing cloud of dust.

For the first time, I see his hideously mauled starboard side and the gaping wound driven deep, deep into his hull. I can actually see his breached Personality Centre in its depths, see the penetration where Enemy fire ripped brutally into the circuitry of his psychotronic brain, and I understand it all. I hear the madness in his electronic voice, and the determination and courage which have kept that broken, dying wreck in motion, and the child's voice on the com is the final element. I know his mission, now, the reason he has fought so doggedly, so desperately to cross the Badlands to the life-sustaining shelter of the mountains.

Yet my knowledge changes nothing, for there is no way to avoid him. He staggers and lurches on his crippled tracks, but he is moving at almost eight kilometres per hour. He has no Hellbore, no missiles, and his remaining infinite repeaters cannot harm me, yet he retains one final weapon: himself.

He thunders towards me, his com voice silent no more, screaming the single word "Enemy! Enemy! Enemy!" again and again. He hurls himself upon me in a suicide attack, charging to his death as the only way he can protect the children he has carried out of hell from the friend he can no longer recognize, the "Enemy" who has hunted him over four hundred kilometres of frozen, waterless stone and dust. It is all he has left, the only thing he can do ... and if he carries through with his ramming attack, we both will die and exposure will kill the children before anyone can rescue them.

I have no choice. He has left me none, and in that instant I wish I were Human. That I, too, could shed the tears which fog the young voice crying out to its protector to turn aside and save himself.

But I cannot weep. There is only one thing I can do.

"Good bye, Lance," I send softly over the battalion command net. "Forgive me."

And I fire.

THE GAME OF RAT AND DRAGON

Cordwainer Smith

Paul Myron Anthony Linebarger (1913–66) adopted his pseudonym to imply that he was a 'skilled craftsman', although his godfather Sun Yat-sen, the founder of Chinese nationalism, suggested the alternative name Lin Bai-lo, which means 'Forest of Incandescent Bliss'. This perhaps better expresses the rich density and artistry of Cordwainer Smith's SF, as well as its exoticism. A noted scholar of East Asia and familiar with six languages, he was also a founding specialist in psychological warfare, and an adviser to JFK.

1. The Table

PINLIGHTING IS A hell of a way to earn a living. Underhill was furious as he closed the door behind himself. It didn't make much sense to wear a uniform and look like a soldier if people didn't appreciate what you did.

He sat down in his chair, laid his head back in the headrest, and pulled the helmet down over his forehead.

As he waited for the pin-set to warm up, he remembered the girl in the outer corridor. She had looked at it, then looked at him scornfully.

"Meow." That was all she had said. Yet it had cut him like a knife.

What did she think he was – a fool, a loafer, a uniformed nonentity? Didn't she know that for every half-hour of pinlighting, he got a minimum of two months' recuperation in the hospital?

By now the set was warm. He felt the squares of space around him, sensed himself at the middle of an immense grid, a cubic grid, full of nothing. Out in that nothingness, he could sense the hollow aching horror of space itself and could feel the terrible anxiety that his mind encountered whenever it met the faintest trace of inert dust.

As he relaxed, the comforting solidity of the sun, the clockwork of the familiar planets and the moon rang in on him. Our own solar system was as charming and as simple as an ancient cuckoo clock filled with familiar ticking and with reassuring noises. The odd little moons of Mars swung around their planet like frantic mice, yet their regularity was itself an assurance that all was well. Far above the plane of the ecliptic, he could feel half a ton of dust more or less drifting outside the lanes of human travel.

Here there was nothing to fight, nothing to challenge the mind, to tear the living soul out of a body with its roots dripping in effluvium as tangible as blood.

Nothing ever moved in on the solar system. He could wear the pin-set forever and be nothing more than a sort of telepathic astronomer, a man who could feel the hot, warm protection of the sun throbbing and burning against his living mind.

Woodley came in.

"Same old ticking world," said Underhill. "Nothing to report. No wonder they didn't develop the pin-set until they began to planoform. Down here with the hot sun around us, it feels so good and so quiet. You can feel everything spinning and turning. It's nice and sharp and compact. It's sort of like sitting around home."

Woodley grunted. He was not much given to flights of fantasy.

Undeterred, Underhill went on, "It must have been pretty good to have been an ancient man. I wonder why they burned up their world with war. They didn't have to planoform. They didn't have to go out to earn their livings among the stars. They didn't have to dodge the rats or play the game. They couldn't have invented pinlighting because they didn't have any need of it, did they, Woodley?"

Woodley grunted, "Uh-huh." Woodley was twenty-six years old and due to retire in one more year. He already had a farm picked out. He had gotten through ten years of hard work pinlighting with the best of them. He had kept his sanity by not thinking very much about his job, meeting the strains of the task whenever he had to meet them and thinking nothing more about his duties until the next emergency arose.

Woodley never made a point of getting popular among the partners. None of the partners liked him very much. Some of them even resented him. He was suspected of thinking ugly thoughts of the partners on occasion, but since none of the partners ever thought a complaint in articulate form, the other pinlighters and the chiefs of the Instrumentality left him alone.

Underhill was still full of the wonders of their job. Happily he babbled on, "What does happen to us when we planoform? Do you think it's sort of like dying? Did you ever see anybody who had his soul pulled out?"

"Pulling souls is just a way of talking about it," said Woodley. "After all these years, nobody knows whether we have souls or not."

"But I saw one once. I saw what Dogwood looked like when he came apart. There was something funny. It looked wet and sort of sticky as if it were bleeding and it went out of him – and you know what they did to Dogwood? They took him away, up in that part of the hospital where you and I never go – way up at the top part where the others are, where the others always have to go if they are alive after the rats of the up-and-out have gotten them."

Woodley sat down and lit an ancient pipe. He was burning something called tobacco in it. It was a dirty sort of habit, but it made him look very dashing and adventurous.

"Look here, youngster. You don't have to worry about that stuff. Pinlighting is getting better all the time. The partners are getting better. I've seen them pinlight two rats forty-six million miles apart in one and a half milliseconds. As long as people had to try to work the pin-sets themselves, there was always the chance that with a minimum of four-hundred milliseconds for the human mind to set a pinlight, we wouldn't light the rats up fast enough to protect our planoforming ships. The partners have changed all that. Once they get going, they're faster than rats. And they always will be. I know it's not easy, letting a partner share your mind—"

"It's not easy for them, either," said Underhill.

"Don't worry about them. They're not human. Let them take care of themselves. I've seen more pinlighters go crazy from monkeying around with partners than I have ever seen caught by the rats. How many of them do you actually know of that got grabbed by rats?"

Underhill looked down at his fingers, which shone green and purple in the vivid light thrown by the tuned-in pin-set, and counted ships. The thumb for the *Andromeda*, lost with crew and passengers, the index finger and the middle finger for *Release Ships* 43 and 56, found with their pin-sets burned out and every man, woman, and child on board dead or insane. The ring finger, the little finger, and the thumb of the other hand were the first three battleships to be lost to the rats – lost as people realized that were was something out there *underneath space itself* which was alive, capricious, and malevolent.

Planoforming was sort of funny. It felt like—

Like nothing much.

Like the twinge of a mild electric shock.

Like the ache of a sore tooth bitten on for the first time.

Like a slightly painful flash of light against the eyes.

Yet in that time, a forty-thousand-ton ship lifting free above Earth disappeared somehow or other into two dimensions and appeared half a light-year or fifty light-years off.

At one moment, he would be sitting in the Fighting Room, the pin-set ready and the familiar solar system ticking around inside his head. For a second or a year (he could never tell how long it really was, subjectively), the funny little flash went through him and then he was loose in the up-and-about, the terrible open spaces between the stars, where the stars themselves felt like pimples on his telepathic mind and the planets were too far away to be sensed or read.

Somewhere in this outer space, a gruesome death awaited, death and horror of a kind which man had never encountered until he reached out for the interstellar space itself. Apparently the light of the suns kept the Dragons away.

Dragons. That was what people called them. To ordinary people, there was nothing, nothing except the shiver of planoforming and the hammer blow of sudden death or the dark spastic note of lunacy descending into their minds.

But to the telepaths, they were dragons.

In the fraction of a second between the telepaths' awareness of a hostile something out in the black, hollow nothingness of space and the impact of a ferocious, ruinous psychic blow against all living things within the ship, the telepaths had sensed entities something like the dragons of ancient human lore, beasts more clever than beasts, demons more tangible than demons, hungry vortices of aliveness and hate compounded by unknown means out of the thin, tenuous matter between the stars.

It took a surviving ship to bring back the news – a ship in which, by sheer chance, a telepath had a light-beam ready, turning it out at the innocent dust so that, within the panorama of his mind, the dragon dissolved into nothing at all and the other passengers, themselves non-telepathic, went about their way not realizing that their own immediate deaths had been averted.

From then on, it was easy – almost.

Planoforming ships always carried telepaths. Telepaths had their sensitiveness enlarged to an immense range by the pin-sets, which were telepathic amplifiers adapted to the mammal mind. The pin-sets in turn were electronically geared into small dirigible light bombs. Light did it.

Light broke up the dragons, allowed the ships to reform three-dimensionally, skip, skip, skip, as they moved from star to star.

The odds suddenly moved down from a hundred to one against mankind to sixty to forty in mankind's favour.

This was not enough. The telepaths were trained to become ultra-sensitive, trained to become aware of the dragons in less than a millisecond.

But it was found that the dragons could move a million miles in just under two milliseconds and that this was not enough for the human mind to activate the light beams.

Attempts had been made to sheath the ships in light at all times. This defence wore out.

As mankind learned about the dragons, so too, apparently, the dragons learned about mankind. Somehow they flattened their own bulk and came in on extremely flat trajectories very quickly.

Intense light was needed, light of sunlike intensity. This could be provided only by the light bombs. Pinlighting came into existence.

Pinlighting consisted of the detonation of ultra-vivid miniature photonuclear bombs, which converted a few ounces of a magnesium isotope into pure visible radiance.

The odds kept coming down in mankind's favour, yet ships were being lost.

It became so bad that people didn't even want to find the ships because the rescuers knew what they would see. It was sad to bring back to Earth three hundred bodies ready for burial and two hundred or three hundred lunatics, damaged beyond repair, to be wakened, and fed, and cleaned, and put to sleep, wakened and fed again until their lives were ended.

Telepaths tried to reach into the minds of the psychotics who had been damaged by the dragons, but they found nothing there beyond vivid spouting columns of fiery terror bursting from the primordial id itself, the volcanic source of life.

Then came the partners.

Man and partner could do together what man could not do alone. Men had the intellect. Partners had the speed.

The partners rode their tiny craft, no larger than footballs, outside the spaceships. They planoformed with the ships. They rode beside them in their six-pound craft ready to attack.

The tiny ships of the partners were swift. Each carried a dozen pinlights, bombs no bigger than thimbles.

The pinlighters threw the partners – quite literally threw – by means of mind-to-firing relays directly at the dragons.

What seemed to be dragons to the human mind appeared in the form of gigantic rats in the minds of the partners.

Out in the pitiless nothingness of space, the partners' minds responded to an instinct as old as life. The partners attacked, striking with a speed faster than man's, going from attack to attack until the rats or themselves were destroyed. Almost all the time it was the partners who won.

With the safety of the interstellar skip, skip, skip of the ships, commerce increased immensely, the population of all the colonies went up, and the demand for trained partners increased.

Underhill and Woodley were a part of the third generation of pinlighters and yet, to them, it seemed as though their craft had endured forever.

Gearing space into minds by means of the pin-set, adding the partners to those minds, keying up the minds for the tension of a fight on which all depended – this was more than human synapses could stand for long. Underhill needed his two months' rest after half an hour of fighting. Woodley needed his retirement after ten years of service. They were young. They were good. But they had their limitations.

So much depended on the choice of partners, so much on the sheer luck of who drew whom.

2. The Shuffle

Father Moontree and the little girl named West entered the room. They were the other two pinlighters. The human complement of the Fighting Room was now complete.

Father Moontree was a red-faced man of forty-five who had lived the peaceful life of a farmer until he reached his fortieth year. Only then, belatedly, did the authorities find he was a telepathic and agree to let him late in life enter upon the career of pinlighter. He did well at it, but he was fantastically old for this kind of business.

Father Moontree looked at the glum Woodley and the musing Underhill. "How're the youngsters today? Ready for a good fight?"

"Father always wants a fight," giggled the little girl named West. She was such a little little girl. Her giggle was high and childish. She looked like the last person in world one would find in the rough, sharp duelling of pinlighting.

Underhill had been amused one time when he found one of the most sluggish of the partners coming away happy from contact with the mind of the girl named West.

Usually the partners didn't care much about the human minds with which they were paired for the journey. The partners seemed to take the attitude that human minds were complex and fouled up beyond belief, anyhow. No partner ever questioned the superiority of the human mind, though very few of the partners were much impressed by that superiority.

The partners liked people. They were willing to fight with them. They were even willing to die for them. But when a partner liked an individual the way, for example, that Captain Wow or the Lady May like Underhill, the liking had nothing to do with intellect. It was a matter of temperament, of feel.

Underhill knew perfectly well that Captain Wow regarded his, Underhill's, brains as silly. What Captain Wow liked was Underhill's friendly emotional structure, the cheerfulness and glint of wicked amusement that shot through Underhill's unconscious thought patterns, and the gaiety with which Underhill faced danger. The words, the history books, the ideas, the science – Underhill could sense all that in his own mind, reflected back from Captain Wow's mind, as so much rubbish.

Miss West looked at Underhill. "I bet you've put stickum on the stones."

"I did not!"

Underhill felt his ears grow red with embarrassment. During his novitiate, he had tried to cheat in the lottery because he got particularly fond of a special partner, a lovely young mother named Murr. It was so much easier to operate with Murr and she was so affectionate towards him that he forgot pinlighting was hard work and that he was not instructed to have a good time with his partner. They were both designed and prepared to go into deadly battle together.

One cheating had been enough. They had found him out and he had been laughed at for years.

Father Moontree picked up the imitation-leather cup and shook the stone dice which assigned them their partners for the trip. By senior rights he took first draw.

He grimaced. He had drawn a greedy old character, a tough old male whose mind was full of slobbering thoughts of food, veritable oceans full of half-spoiled fish. Father Moontree had once said that he burped cod liver oil for weeks after drawing that particular glutton, so strongly had the telepathic image of fish impressed itself upon his mind. Yet the glutton was a glutton for danger as well as for fish. He had killed sixty-three dragons, more than any other partner in the service, and was quite literally worth his weight in gold.

The little girl West came next. She drew Captain Wow. When she saw who it was, she smiled.

"I *like* him," she said. "He's such fun to fight with. He feels so nice and cuddly in my mind."

"Cuddly, hell," said Woodley. "I've been in his mind, too. It's the most leering mind in this ship, bar none."

"Nasty man," said the little girl. She said it declaratively, without reproach.

Underhill, looking at her, shivered.

He didn't see how she could take Captain Wow so calmly. Captain Wow's mind *did* leer. When Captain Wow got excited in the middle of a battle, confused images of dragons, deadly rats, luscious beds, the smell of fish, and the shock of space all scrambled together in his mind as he and Captain Wow, their consciousness linked together through the pin-set, became a fantastic composite of human being and Persian cat.

That's the trouble with working with cats, thought Underhill. It's a pity that nothing else anywhere will serve as partner. Cats were all right once you got in touch with them telepathically. They were smart enough to meet the needs of the flight, but their motives and desires were certainly different from those of humans.

They were companionable enough as long as you thought tangible images at them, but their minds just closed up and went to sleep when you recited Shakespeare or Colegrove, or if you tried to tell them what space was.

It was sort of funny realizing that the partners who were so grim and mature out here in space were the same cute little animals that people had used as pets for thousands of years back on Earth. He had embarrassed himself more than once while on the ground saluting perfectly ordinary non-telepathic cats because he had forgotten for the moment that they were not partners.

He picked up the cup and shook out his stone dice.

He was lucky – he drew the Lady May.

The Lady May was the most thoughtful partner he had ever met. In her, the finely bred pedigree mind of a Persian cat had reached one of its highest peaks of development. She was more complex than any human woman, but the complexity was all one of emotions, memory, hope, and discriminate experience – experience sorted through without benefit of words.

When he had first come into contact with her mind, he was astonished at its clarity. With her he remembered kittenhood. He remembered every mating experience she had ever had. He saw in a half-recognizable gallery all the other pinlighters with whom she had been paired for the fight. And he saw himself radiant, cheerful, and desirable.

He even thought he caught the edge of a longing—

A very flattering and yearning thought: *What a pity he is not a cat.*

Woodley picked up the last stone. He drew what he deserved – a sullen, scarred old tomcat with none of the verve of Captain Wow. Woodley's partner was the most animal of all the cats on the ship, a low, brutish type with a dull mind. Even telepathy had not refined his character. He ears were half chewed off from the first fights in which he had engaged. He was a serviceable fighter, nothing more.

Woodley grunted.

Underhill glanced at him oddly. Didn't Woodley ever do anything but grunt?

Father Moontree looked at the other three. "You might as well get your partners now. I'll let the Go-captain know we're ready to go into the up-and-out."

3. The Deal

Underhill spun the combination lock on the Lady May's cage. He woke her gently and took her into his arms. She humped her back luxuriously, stretched her claws, started to purr, thought better of it, and licked him on the wrist instead. He did not have the pin-set on, so their minds were closed to each other, but in the angle of her moustache and in the movement of her ears, he caught some sense of the gratification she experienced in finding him as her partner.

He talked to her in human speech, even though speech meant nothing to a cat when the pin-set was not on.

"It's a damn shame, sending a sweet thing like you whirling around in the coldness of nothing to hunt for rats that are bigger and deadlier than all of us put together. You didn't ask for this kind of fight, did you?"

For answer, she licked his hand, purred, tickled his cheek with her long fluffy tail, turned around and faced him, golden eyes shining.

For a moment, they stared at each other, man squatting, cat standing erect on her hind legs, front claws digging into his knee. Human eyes and cat eyes looked across an immensity which no words could meet, but which affection spanned in a single glance.

"Time to get in," he said.

She walked docilely to her spheroid carrier. She climbed in. He saw to it that her miniature pin-set rested firmly and comfortably against the base of her brain. He made sure that her claws were padded so that she could not tear herself in the excitement of battle.

Softly he said to her, "Ready?"

For answer, she preened her back as much as her harness would permit and purred softly within the confines of the frame that held her.

He slapped down the lid and watched the sealant ooze around the seam. For a few hours, she was welded into her projectile until a workman with a short cutting arc would remove her after she had done her duty.

He picked up the entire projectile and slipped it into the ejection tube. He closed the door of the tube, spun the lock, seated himself in his chair, and put his own pin-set on.

Once again he flung the switch.

He sat in a small room, *small, small, warm, warm*, the bodies of the other three people moving close around him, the tangible light in the ceiling bright and heavy against his closed eyelids.

As the pin-set warmed, the room fell away. The other people ceased to be people and became small glowing heaps of fire, embers, dark red fire, with the consciousness of life burning like old red coals in a country fireplace.

As the pin-set warmed a little more, he felt Earth just below him, felt the ship slipping away, felt the turning Moon as it swung on the far side of the world, felt the planets and the hot, dear goodness of the sun which kept the dragons so far from mankind's native ground.

Finally, he reached complete awareness.

He was telepathically alive to a range of millions of miles. He felt the dust which he had noticed earlier high above the ecliptic. With a thrill of warmth and tenderness, he felt the consciousness of the Lady May pouring over into his own. Her consciousness was as gentle and clear and yet sharp to the taste of his mind as if it were scented oil. It felt relaxing and reassuring. He could sense her welcome of him. It was scarcely a thought, just a raw emotion of greeting.

At last they were one again.

In a tiny remote corner of his mind, as tiny as the smallest toy he had ever seen in his childhood, he was still aware of the room and the ship, and of Father Moontree picking up a telephone and speaking to a Go-captain in charge of the ship.

His telepathic mind caught the idea long before his ears could frame the words. The actual sound followed the idea the way that thunder on an ocean beach follows the lightning inward from far out over the seas.

"The Fighting Room is ready. Clear to planoform, sir."

4. The Play

Underhill was always a little exasperated the way that Lady May experienced things before he did.

He was braced for the quick vinegar thrill of planoforming, but he caught her report of it before his own nerves could register what happened.

Earth had fallen so far away that he groped for several milliseconds before he found the sun in the upper rear right-hand corner of his telepathic mind.

That was a good jump, he thought. *This way we'll get there in four or five skips.*

A few hundred miles outside the ship, the Lay May thought back at him, "O warm, O generous, O gigantic man! O brave, O friendly, O tender and huge partner! O wonderful with you, with you so good, good, good, warm, warm, now to fight, now to go, good with you..."

He knew that she was not thinking words, that his mind took the clear amiable babble of her cat intellect and translated it into images which his own thinking could record and understand.

Neither one of them was absorbed in the game of mutual greetings. He reached out far beyond her range of perception to see if there was anything near the ship. It was funny how it was possible to do two things at once. He could scan space with his pin-set mind and yet at the same time catch a vagrant thought of hers, a lovely, affectionate thought about a son who had had a golden face and a chest covered with a soft, incredibly downy white fur.

While he was still searching, he caught the warning from her.

We jump again!

And so they had. The ship had moved to a second planoform. The stars were different. The sun was immeasurably far behind. Even the nearest stars were barely in contact. This was good dragon country, this open, nasty, hollow kind of space. He reached farther, faster, sensing and looking for danger, ready to fling the Lady May at danger wherever he found it.

Terror blazed up in his mind, so sharp, so clear, that it came through as a physical wrench.

The little girl named West had found something – something immense, long, black, sharp, greedy, horrific. She flung Captain Wow at it.

Underhill tried to keep his own mind clear. "Watch out!" he shouted telepathically at the others, trying to move the Lady May around.

At one corner of the battle, he felt the lustful rage of Captain Wow as the big Persian tomcat detonated light while he approached the streak of dust which threatened the ship and the people within.

The light scored near misses.

The dust flattened itself, changing from the shape of a sting ray into the shape of a spear.

Not three milliseconds had elapsed.

Father Moontree was talking human words and was saying in a voice that moved like cold molasses out of a heavy jar, "C-a-p-t-a-i-n." Underhill knew that the sentence was going to be "Captain move fast!"

The battle would be fought and finished before Father Moontree got through talking.

Now, fractions of a millisecond later, the Lady May was directly in line.

Here was where the skill and speed of the partners came in. She could react faster than he. She could see the threat as an immense rat coming directly at her.

She could fire the light-bombs with a discrimination which he might miss.

He was connected with her mind, but he could not follow it.

His consciousness absorbed the tearing wound inflicted by the alien enemy. It was like no wound on Earth – raw, crazy pain which started like a burn at his navel. He began to writhe in his chair.

Actually he had not yet had time to move a muscle when the Lady May struck back at their enemy.

Five evenly spaced photonuclear bombs blazed out across a hundred-thousand miles.

The pain in his mind and body vanished.

He felt a moment of fierce, terrible, feral elation running through the mind of the Lady May as she finished her kill. It was always disappointing to the cats to find out that their enemies disappeared at the moment of destruction.

Then he felt her hurt, the pain and the fear that swept over both of them as the battle, quicker than the movement of an eyelid, had come and gone. In the same instant there came the sharp and acid twinge of planoform.

Once more the ship went skip.

He could hear Woodley thinking at him. "You don't have to bother much. This old son-of-a-gun and I will take over for a while."

Twice again the twinge, the skip.

He had no idea where he was until the lights of the Caledonia space port shone below.

With a weariness that lay almost beyond the limits of thought, he threw his mind back into rapport with the pin-set, fixing the Lady May's projectile gently and neatly in its launching tube.

She was half dead with fatigue, but he could feel the beat of her heart, could listen to her panting, and he grasped the grateful edge of a "Thanks" reaching from her mind to his.

5. The Score

They put him in the hospital at Caledonia.

The doctor was friendly but firm. "You actually got touched by that dragon. That's as close a shave as I've ever seen. It's all so quick that it'll be a long time before we know what happened scientifically, but I suppose you'd be ready for the insane asylum now if the contact had lasted several tenths of a millisecond longer. What kind of cat did you have out in front of you?"

Underhill felt the words coming out of him slowly. Words were such a lot of trouble compared with the speed and the joy of thinking, fast and sharp and clear, mind to mind! But words were all that could reach ordinary people like this doctor.

His mouth moved heavily as he articulated words. "Don't call our partners cats. The right thing to call them is partners. They fight for us in a team. You ought to know we call them partners, not cats. How is mine?"

"I don't know," said the doctor contritely. "We'll find out for you. Meanwhile, old man, you take it easy. There's nothing but rest that can help you. Can you make yourself sleep, or would you like us to give you some kind of sedative?"

"I can sleep," said Underhill, "I just want to know about the Lady May."

The nurse joined in. She was a little antagonistic. "Don't you want to know about the other people?"

"They're okay," said Underhill. "I knew that before I came in here."

He stretched his arms and sighed and grinned at them. He could see they were relaxing and were beginning to treat him as a person instead of a patient.

"I'm all right," he said. "Just let me know when I can go see my partner."

A new thought struck him. He looked wildly at the doctor. "They didn't send her off with the ship, did they?"

"I'll find out right away," said the doctor. He gave Underhill a reassuring squeeze of the shoulder and left the room.

The nurse took a napkin off a goblet of chilled fruit juice.

Underhill tried to smile at her. There seemed to be something wrong with the girl. He wished she would go away. First she had started to be friendly and now she was distant again. *It's a nuisance being telepathic*, he thought. *You keep trying to reach even when you are not making contact*.

Suddenly she swung around on him.

"You pinlighters! You and your damn cats!"

Just as she stamped out, he burst into her mind. He saw himself a radiant hero, clad in his smooth suede uniform, the pin-set crown shining like ancient royal jewels around his head. He saw his own face, handsome and masculine, shining out of her mind. He saw himself very far away and he saw himself as she hated him.

She hated him in the secrecy of her own mind. She hated him because he was – she thought – proud and strange and rich, better and more beautiful than people like her.

He cut off the sight of her mind and, as he buried his face in the pillow, he caught an image of the Lady May.

"She *is* a cat," he thought. "That's all she is – a *cat*!"

But that was not how his mind saw her – quick beyond all dreams of speed, sharp, clever, unbelievably graceful, beautiful, wordless and undemanding.

Where would he ever find a woman who could compare with her?

CAUGHT IN THE CROSSFIRE

David Drake

"Collateral damage" is perhaps one of the most chilling phrases ever to feature in the vocabulary of modern warfare. In this story, one of the earliest entries in Drake's acclaimed Hammers Slammers series, a woman whose community has been invaded to facilitate an ambush strives desperately to avoid becoming another statistic. In 1970 David Drake was drafted out of law school and served as an enlisted interrogator with the 11th Armoured Cavalry Regiment, the Blackhorse, in Vietnam and Cambodia. This experience enables him to bring a strong sense of realism to his tales of the armoured mercenary force led by Colonel Alois Hammer.

On leaving the military and returning to the World, Drake finished law school and took up writing. Among his recent titles are The Road of Danger, *a space opera, and* Out of the Waters, *a fantasy.*

MARGRITTE GRAPPLED WITH the nearest soldier in the instant her husband broke for the woods. The man in field-grey cursed and tried to jerk his weapon away from her, but Margritte's muscles were young and taut from shifting bales. Even when the mercenary kicked her ankles from under her, Margritte's clamped hands kept the gun barrel down and harmless.

Neither of the other two soldiers paid any attention to the scuffle. They clicked off the safety catches of their weapons as they swung them to their shoulders. Georg was running hard, fresh blood from his retorn calf muscles staining his bandages. The double slap of automatic fire caught him in mid-stride and whipsawed his slender body. His head and heels scissored to the ground together. They were covered by the mist of blood that settled more slowly.

Sobbing, Margritte loosed her grip and fell back on the ground. The man above her cradled his flechette gun again and looked around the village. "Well, aren't you going to shoot me, too?" she cried.

"Not unless we have to," the mercenary replied quietly. He was sweating despite the stiff breeze, and he wiped his black face with his sleeve. "Helmuth," he ordered, "start setting up in the building. Landschein, you stay out with me; make sure none of these women try the same damned thing." He glanced out to where Georg lay, a bright smear on the stubbled, golden earth. "Best get that out of sight, too," he added. "The convoy's due in an hour."

Old Leida had frozen to a statue in ankle-length muslin at the first scream. Now she nodded her head of close ringlets. "Myrie, Delia," she called, gesturing to her daughters, "bring brush hooks and come along." She had not lost her dignity even during the shooting.

"Hold it," said Landschein, the shortest of the three soldiers. He was a sharp-featured man who had grinned in satisfaction as he fired. "You two got kids in there?" he asked the younger women. The muzzle of his flechette gun indicated the locked door to the dugout which normally stored the crop out of sun and heat; today it imprisoned the village's twenty-six children. Delia and Myrie nodded, too dry with fear to speak.

"Then you go drag him into the woods," Landschein said, grinning again. "Just remember – you might manage to get away, but you won't much like what you'll find when you come back. I'm sure some true friend'll point your brats out to us quick enough to save her own."

Leida nodded a command, but Landschein's freckled hand clamped her elbow as she turned to follow her daughters. "Not you, old lady. No need for you to get that near to cover."

"Do you think I would run and risk – everyone?" Leida demanded.

"Curst if I know what you'd risk," the soldier said. "But we're risking plenty already to ambush one of Hammer's convoys. If anybody gets loose ahead of time to warn them, we can kiss our butts goodbye."

Margritte wiped the tears from her eyes, using her palms because of the gritty dust her thrashings had pounded into her knuckles. The third soldier, the broad-shouldered blond named Helmuth, had leaned his weapon beside the door of the hall and was lifting bulky loads from the nearby air-cushion vehicle. The settlement had become used to whining grey columns of military vehicles, cruising the road at random. This truck, however, had eased over the second canopy of the forest itself. It was a flimsy cargo-hauler like the one in which Krauder picked up the cotton at season's end, harmless enough to look at. Only Georg, left behind for his sickle-ripped leg when a government van had carried off the other males the week before as "recruits", had realized what it meant that the newcomers wore field-grey instead of khaki.

"Why did you come here?" Margritte asked in a near-normal voice.

The black mercenary glanced at her as she rose, glanced back at the other women obeying orders by continuing to pick the iridescent boles of Terran cotton grown in Pohweil's soil. "We had the capital under siege," he said, "until Hammer's tanks punched a corridor through. We can't close the corridor, so we got to cut your boys off from supplies some other way. Otherwise the Cartel'll wish it had paid its taxes instead of trying to take over. You grubbers may have been pruning their wallets, but Lord! they'll be flayed alive if your counterattack works."

He spat a thin, angry stream into the dust. "The traders hired us and four other regiments, and you grubbers sank the whole treasury into bringing in Hammer's armour. Maybe we can prove today those cocky bastards aren't all they're billed as…"

"We didn't care," Margritte said. "We're no more the Farm Bloc than Krauder and his truck is the Trade Cartel. Whatever they did in the capital, *we* had no choice. I hadn't even seen the capital…oh dear Lord, Georg would have taken me there for our honeymoon except that there was fighting all over…"

"How long we got, Sarge?" the blond man demanded from the stark shade of the hall.

"Little enough. Get those bloody sheets set up or we'll have to pop the cork bare-ass naked; and we got enough problems." The big noncom shifted his glance about the narrow clearing, wavering rows of cotton marching to the edge of the forest's dusky green. The road, an unsurfaced track whose ruts were not a serious hindrance to air-cushion traffic, was the long axis. Beside it stood the hall, twenty metres by five and the only above-ground structure in the settlement. The battle with the native vegetation made dugouts beneath the cotton preferable to cleared land wasted for dwellings. The hall became more than a social centre and common refectory: it was the gaudiest of luxuries and a proud slap to the face of the forest.

Until that morning, the forest had been the village's only enemy.

"Georg only wanted—"

"God *damn* it," the sergeant snarled. "Will you shut it off? Every man but your precious husband gone off to the siege – no, shut it off till I finish! – and him running to warn the convoy. If you'd wanted to save his life, you should've grabbed him, not me. Sure, all you grubbers, you don't care about the war – not much! It's all one to you whether you kill us yourselves or your tankers do it, those bastards so high and mighty for the money they've got and the equipment. I tell you, girl, I don't take it personal that people shoot at me; it's just the way we both earn our livings. But it's fair, it's even... and Hammer thinks he's the Way made Flesh because nobody can bust his tanks."

The sergeant paused and his lips sucked in and out. His thick, gentle fingers rechecked the weapon he held. "We'll just see," he whispered.

"Georg said we'd all be killed in the crossfire if we were out in the fields when you shot at the tanks."

"If Georg had kept his face shut and his ass in bed, he'd have lived longer than he did. Just shut it off!" the noncom ordered. He turned to his blond underling, fighting a section of sponge plating through the door. "Via, Bornzyk!" he shouted angrily. "Move it!"

Helmuth flung his load down with a hollow clang. "Via, then lend a hand! The wind catches these and—"

"I'll help him," Margritte offered abruptly. Her eyes blinked away from the young soldier's weapon where he had forgotten it against the wall. Standing, she far lacked the bulk of the sergeant beside her, but her frame gave no suggestion of weakness. Golden dust soiled the back and sides of her dress with butterfly scales.

The sergeant gave her a sharp glance, his left hand spreading and closing where it rested on the black barrel-shroud of his weapon. "All right," he said, "you give him a hand and we'll see you under cover with us when the shooting starts. You're smarter than I gave you credit."

They had forgotten Leida was still standing beside them. Her hand struck like a spading fork. Margritte ducked away from the blow, but Leida caught her on the shoulder and gripped. When the mercenary's reversed gun-butt cracked the older woman loose, a long strip of Margritte's blue dress tore away with her. "Bitch," Leida mumbled through bruised lips. "You'd help these beasts after they killed your own man?"

Margritte stepped back, tossing her head. For a moment she fumbled at the tear in her dress; then, defiantly, she let it fall open. Landschein turned in time to catch the look in Leida's eyes. "Hey, you'll give your friends more trouble," he stated cheerfully, waggling his gun to indicate Delia and Myrie as they returned grey-faced from the forest fringe. "Go on, get out and pick some cotton."

When Margritte moved, the white of her loose shift caught the sun and the small killer's stare. "Landschein!" the black ordered sharply, and Margritte stepped very quickly towards the truck and the third man struggling there.

Helmuth turned and blinked at the girl as he felt her capable muscles take the windstrain off the panel he was shifting. His eyes were blue and set wide in a face too large-boned to be handsome, too frank to be other than attractive. He accepted the help without question, leading the way into the hall.

The dining tables were hoisted against the rafters. The windows, unshuttered in the warm autumn and unglazed, lined all four walls at chest height. The long wall nearest the road was otherwise unbroken; the one opposite it was pierced in the middle by the single door. In the centre of what should have been an empty room squatted the mercenaries' construct. The metal-ceramic panels had been locked into three sides of a square, a pocket of armour open only towards the door. It was hidden beneath the lower sills of the windows; nothing would catch the eye of an oncoming tanker.

"We've got to nest three layers together," the soldier explained as he swung the load, easily managed within the building, "or they'll cut us apart if they get off a burst this direction."

Margritte steadied a panel already in place as Helmuth mortised his into it. Each sheet was about five centimetres in thickness, a thin plate of grey metal on either side of a white porcelain sponge. The girl tapped it dubiously with a blunt finger. "This can stop bullets?"

The soldier – he was younger than his size suggested, no more than eighteen. Younger even than Georg, and he had a smile like Georg's as he raised his eyes with a blush and said, "P-powerguns, yeah; three layers of it ought to … It's light, we could carry it in the truck where iridium would have bogged us down. But look, there's another panel and the rockets we still got to bring in."

"You must be very brave to fight tanks with just – this," Margritte prompted as she took one end of the remaining armour sheet.

"Oh, well, Sergeant Counsel says it'll work," the boy said enthusiastically. "They'll come by, two combat cars, then three big trucks, and another combat car. Sarge and Landschein buzzbomb the lead cars before they know what's happening. I reload them and they hit the third car when it swings wide to get a shot. Any shooting the blower jocks get off, they'll spread because they won't know – oh, cop I said it …"

"They'll think the women in the fields may be firing, so they'll kill us first," Margritte reasoned aloud. The boy's neck beneath his helmet turned brick red as he trudged into the building.

"Look," he said, but he would not meet her eyes, "we got to do it. It'll be fast – nobody much can get hurt. And your … the children, they're all safe. Sarge said that with all the men gone, we wouldn't have any trouble with the women if we kept the kids safe and under our thumbs."

"We didn't have time to have children," Margritte said. Her eyes were briefly unfocused. "You didn't give Georg enough time before you killed him."

"He was …" Helmuth began. They were outside again and his hand flicked briefly towards the slight notch Delia and Myrie had chopped in the forest wall. "I'm sorry."

"Oh, don't be sorry," she said. "He knew what he was doing."

"He was – I suppose you'd call him a patriot?" Helmuth suggested, jumping easily to the truck's deck to gather up an armload of cylindrical bundles. "He was really against the Cartel?"

"There was never a soul in this village who cared who won the war," Margritte said. "We have our own war with the forest."

"They joined the siege!" the boy retorted. "They cared that m-much, to fight us!"

"They got in the vans when men with guns told them to get in," the girl said. She took the gear Helmuth was forgetting to hand to her and shook a lock of hair out of her eyes. "Should they have run? Like Georg? No, they went off to be soldiers; praying like we did that the war might end before the forest had eaten up the village again. Maybe if we were really lucky, it'd end before this crop had spoiled in the fields because there weren't enough hands left here to pick it in time."

Helmuth cleared the back of the truck with his own load and stepped down. "Well, just the same, your husband tried to hide and warn the convoy," he argued. "Otherwise why did he run?"

"Oh, he loved me – you know?" said Margritte. "Your sergeant said all of us should be out picking as usual. Georg knew, he *told* you, that the crossfire would kill everybody in the fields as sure as if you shot us deliberately. And when you wouldn't change your plan … well, if he'd gotten away you would have had to give up your ambush, wouldn't you? You'd have known it was suicide if the tanks learned that you were waiting for them. So Georg ran."

The dark-haired woman stared out at the forest for a moment. "He didn't have a prayer, did he? You could have killed him a hundred times before he got to cover."

"Here, give me those," the soldier said, taking the bundles from her instead of replying. He began to unwrap the cylinders one by one on the wooden floor. "We couldn't let him get away," he said at last. He added, his eyes still down on his work, "Flechettes when they hit ...I mean, sh-shooting at his legs wouldn't, wouldn't have been a kindness, you see?"

Margritte laughed again. "Oh, I saw what they dragged into the forest, yes." She paused, sucking at her lower lip. "That's how we always deal with our dead, give them to the forest. Oh, we have a service; but we wouldn't have buried Georg in the dirt, if ...if he'd died. But you didn't care, did you? A corpse looks bad, maybe your precious ambush, your own lives. Get it out of the way, toss it in the woods."

"We'd have buried him afterwards," the soldier mumbled as he laid a fourth thigh-thick projectile beside those he had already unwrapped.

"Oh, of *course*," Margritte said. "And me, and all the rest of us murdered out there in the cotton. Oh, you're gentlemen, you are."

"Via!" Helmuth shouted, his flush mottling as at last he lifted his gaze to the girl's. "We'd have b-buried him. I'd have buried him. You'll be safe in here with us until it's all over, and by the Lord, then you can come back with us, too! You don't have to stay here with these hard-faced bitches."

A bitter smile tweaked the left edge of the girl's mouth. "Sure, you're a good boy."

The young mercenary blinked between protest and pleasure, settled on the latter. He had readied all six of the tinned, grey missiles; now he lifted one of the pair of launchers. "It'll be really quick," he said shyly, changing the subject. The launcher was an arm-length tube with double handgrips and an optical sight. Helmuth's big hands easily inserted one of the buzzbombs to lock with a faint snick.

"Very simple," Margritte murmured.

"Cheap and easy," the boy agreed with a smile. "You can buy a thousand of these for what a combat car runs – Hell, maybe more than a thousand. And it's one for one today, one bomb to one car.

Landschein says the crews are just a little extra, like weevils in your biscuit."

He saw her grimace, the angry tensing of a woman who had just seen her husband blasted into a spray of offal. Helmuth grunted with his own pain, his mouth dropping open as his hand stretched to touch her bare shoulder. "Oh, Lord – didn't mean to say…"

She gently detached his fingers. His breath caught and he turned away. Unseen, her look of hatred seared his back. His hand was still stretched toward her and hers towards him, when the door scraped to admit Landschein behind them.

"Cute, oh bloody cute," the little mercenary said. He carried his helmet by its strap. Uncovered, his cropped grey hair made him an older man. "Well, get on with it, boy – don't keep me 'n' Sarge waiting. He'll be mad enough about getting sloppy thirds."

Helmuth jumped to his feet. Landschein ignored him, clicking across to a window in three quick strides. "Sarge," he called, "we're all set. Come on, we can watch the women from here."

"I'll run the truck into the woods," Counsel's voice burred in reply. "Anyhow, I can hear better from out here."

That was true. Despite the open windows, the wails of the children were inaudible in the hall. Outside, they formed a thin backdrop to every other sound.

Landschein set down his helmet. He snapped the safety on his gun's sideplate and leaned the weapon carefully against the nest of armour. Then he took up the loaded launcher and ran his hands over its tube and grips. Without changing expression, he reached out to caress Margritte through the tear in her dress.

Margritte screamed and clawed her left hand as she tried to rise. The launcher slipped into Landschein's lap, and his arm, far swifter, locked hers and drew her down against him. Then the little mercenary himself was jerked upward. Helmuth's hand on his collar first broke Landschein's grip on Margritte, then flung him against the closed door.

Landschein rolled despite the shock and his glance flicked towards his weapon, but between gun and gunman crouched Helmuth, no longer a red-faced boy but the strongest man in the room. Grinning,

Helmuth spread fingers that had crushed ribs in past rough and tumbles. "Try it, little man," he said. "Try it and I'll rip your head off your shoulders."

"You'll do wonders!" Landschein spat, but his eyes lost their glaze and his muscles relaxed. He bent his mouth into a smile. "Hey, kid, there's plenty of slots around. We'll work out something afterwards; no need to fight."

Helmuth rocked his head back in a nod of acceptance with nothing of friendship in it. "You lay another hand on her," he said in a normal voice, "and you'd best have killed me first." He turned his back deliberately on the older man and the nearby weapons. Landschein clenched his left fist once, twice, but then he began to load the remaining launcher.

Margritte slipped the patching kit from her belt pouch. Her hands trembled, but the steel needle was already threaded. Her whip-stitches tacked the torn piece top and sides to the remaining material, close enough for decency. Pins were a luxury that a cotton settlement could well do without. Landschein glanced back at her once, but at the same time the floor creaked as Helmuth's weight shifted to his other leg. Neither man spoke.

Sergeant Counsel opened the door. His right arm cradled a pair of flechette guns and he handed one to Helmuth. "Best not to leave it in the dust," he said. "You'll be needing it soon."

"They coming, Sarge?" Landschein asked. He touched his tongue to thin, pale lips.

"Not yet." Counsel looked from one man to the other. "You boys get things sorted out?"

"All green here," Landschein muttered, smiling again but lowering his eyes.

"That's good," the big black said, "because we got a job to do and we're not going to let anything stop us. Anything."

Margritte was putting away her needle. The sergeant looked at her hard. "You keep your head down, hear?"

"It won't matter," the girl said calmly, tucking the kit away. "The tanks, they won't be surprised to see a woman in here."

"Sure, but they'll shoot your bleeding head off," Landschein snorted.

"Do you think I care?" she blazed back. Helmuth winced at the tone; Sergeant Counsel's eyes took on an undesirable shade of interest.

"But you're helping us," the big noncom mused. He tapped his fingertips on the gun in the crook of his arm. "Because you like us so much?" There was no amusement in his words, only a careful mind picking over the idea, all ideas.

She stood and walked to the door, her face as composed as a priest's at the gravesite. "Have your ambush," she said. "Would it help us if the convoy came through before you were ready for it?"

"The smoother it goes, the faster," Counsel agreed quietly, "then the better for all of you."

Margritte swung the door open and stood looking out. Eight women were picking among the rows east of the hall. They would be relatively safe there, not caught between the ambushers' rockets and the raking powerguns of their quarry. Eight of them safe and fourteen sure victims on the other side. Most of them could have been out of the crossfire if they had only let themselves think, only considered the truth that Georg had died to underscore.

"I keep thinking of Georg," Margritte said aloud. "I guess my friends are just thinking about their children; they keep looking at the storage room. But the children, they'll be all right; it's just that most of them are going to be orphans in a few minutes."

"It won't be that bad," Helmuth said. He did not sound as though he believed it either.

The older children had by now ceased the screaming begun when the door shut and darkness closed in on them. The youngest still wailed and the sound drifted through the open door.

"I told her we'd take her back with us, Sarge," Helmuth said.

Landschein chortled, a flash of instinctive humour he covered with a raised palm. Counsel shook his head in amazement. "You were wrong, boy. Now, keep watching those women or we may not be going back ourselves."

The younger man reddened again in frustration. "Look, we've got women in the outfit now, and I don't mean the rec troops. Captain Denzil told me there's six in Bravo Company alone—"

"Hoo, little Helmuth wants his own girlie friend to keep his bed warm," Landschein gibed.

"Landschein, I—" Helmuth began, clenching his right hand into a ridge of knuckles.

"Shut it off!"

"But, Sarge—"

"Shut it off, boy, or you'll have me to deal with!" roared the black. Helmuth fell back and rubbed his eyes. The noncom went on more quietly, "Landschein, you keep your tongue to yourself, too."

Both big men breathed deeply, their eyes shifting in concert towards Margritte who faced them in silence. "Helmuth," the sergeant continued, "some units take women, some don't. We've got a few, damned few, because not many women have the guts for our line of work."

Margritte's smile flickered. "The hardness, you mean. The callousness."

"Sure, words don't matter," Counsel agreed mildly. He smiled back at her as one equal to another. "This one, yeah; she might just pass. Via, you don't have to look like Landschein there to be tough. But you're missing the big point, boy."

Helmuth touched his right wrist to his chin. "Well, what?" he demanded.

Counsel laughed. "She wouldn't go with us. Would you, girl?"

Margritte's eyes were flat, and her voice was dead flat. "No," she said, "I wouldn't go with you."

The noncom grinned as he walked back to a window vantage. "You see, Helmuth, you want her to give up a whole lot to gain you a bunkmate."

"It's not like that," Helmuth insisted, thumping his leg in frustration. "I just mean—"

"Oh, Lord!" the girl said loudly. "Can't you just get on with your ambush?"

"Well, not till Hammer's boys come through," chuckled the sergeant. "They're so good, they can't run a convoy to schedule."

"S-sergeant," the young soldier said, "she doesn't understand." He turned to Margritte and gestured with both hands, forgetting the weapon in his left. "They won't take you back, those witches out there. The …the rec girls at Base Denzil don't go home – they can't. And you know damned well that s-somebody's going to catch it out there when it drops in the pot. They'll crucify you for helping us set up, the ones that're left."

"It doesn't matter what they do," she said. "It doesn't matter at all."

"Your life matters!" the boy insisted.

Her laughter hooted through the room. "My life?" Margritte repeated. "You splashed all that across the field an hour ago. You didn't give a damn when you did it, and I don't give one now – but I'd only follow you to Hell and hope your road was short."

Helmuth bit his knuckle and turned, pinched over as though he had been kicked. Sergeant Counsel grinned his tight, equals grin. "You're wasted here, you know," he said. "And we could use you. Maybe if—"

"Sarge!" Landschein called from his window. "Here they come."

Counsel scooped up a rocket launcher, probing its breech with his fingers to make finally sure of its load. "Now you keep down," he repeated to Margritte. "Backblast'll take your head off if their shooting don't." He crouched below the sill and the rim of the armour shielding him, peering through a periscope whose button of optical fibres was unnoticeable in the shadow. Faced inwards towards the girl, Landschein hunched over the other launcher in the right corner of the protected area. His flechette gun rested beside him and one hand curved towards it momentarily, anticipating the instant he would raise it to spray the shattered convoy. Between them Helmuth knelt as stiffly as a statue of grey-green jade. He drew a buzzbomb closer to his right knee where it clinked against the barrel of his own weapon. Cursing nervously, he slid the flechette gun back out of the way. Both his hands gripped reloads, waiting.

The cars' shrill whine trembled in the air. Margritte stood up by the door, staring out through the windows across the hall. Dust plumed where the long, straight roadway cut the horizon into two blocks of forest. The women in the fields had paused, straightening to watch the oncoming vehicles. But that was normal, nothing to alarm the khaki men in the bellies of their war-cars; and if any woman thought of falling to hug the earth, the fans' wailing too nearly approximated that of the imprisoned children.

"Three hundred metres," Counsel reported softly as the blunt bow of the lead car gleamed through the dust. "Two-fifty." Landschein's teeth bared as he faced around, poised to spring.

Margritte swept up Helmuth's flechette gun and levelled it at waist height. The safety clicked off. Counsel had dropped his periscope and his mouth was open to cry an order. The deafening muzzle blast lifted him out of his crouch and pasted him briefly, voiceless, against the pocked inner face of the armour. Margritte swung her weapon like a flail into a triple splash of red. Helmuth died with only a reflexive jerk, but Landschein's speed came near to bringing his launcher to bear on Margritte. The stream of flechettes sawed across his throat. His torso dropped, headless but still clutching the weapon.

Margritte's gun silenced when the last needle slapped out of the muzzle. The aluminium barrel shroud had softened and warped during the long burst. Eddies in the fog of blood and propellant smoke danced away from it. Margritte turned as if in icy composure, but she bumped the door jamb and staggered as she stepped outside. The racket of the gun had drawn the sallow faces of every woman in the fields.

"It's over!" Margritte called. Her voice sounded thin in the fresh silence. Three of the nearer mothers ran towards the storage room.

Down the road, dust was spraying as the convoy skidded into a herringbone for defence. Gun muzzles searched: the running women; Margritte armed and motionless; the sudden eruption of children from the dugout. The men in the cars waited, their trigger fingers partly tensed.

Bergen, Delia's six-year-old, pounded past Margritte to throw herself into her mother's arms. They clung together, each crooning to the other through their tears. "Oh, we were so afraid!" Bergen said, drawing away from her mother. "But now it's all right." She rotated her head and her eyes widened as they took in Margritte's tattered figure. "Oh, Margi," she gasped, "whatever happened to *you*?"

Delia gasped and snatched her daughter back against her bosom. Over the child's loose curls, Delia glared at Margritte with eyes like a hedge of pikes. Margritte's hand stopped halfway to the child. She stood – gaunt, misted with blood as though sunburned. A woman who had blasted life away instead of suckling it. Delia, a frightened mother, snarled at the killer who had been her friend.

Margritte began to laugh. She trailed the gun three steps before letting it drop unnoticed. The captain of the lead car watched her approach over his gunsights. His short, black beard fluffed out from under his helmet, twitching as he asked, "Would you like to tell us what's going on, honey, or do we got to comb it out ourselves?"

"I killed three soldiers," she answered simply. "Now there's nothing going on. Except that wherever you're headed, I'm going along. You can use my sort, soldier."

Her laughter was a crackling shadow in the sunlight.

THE RHINE'S WORLD INCIDENT

Neal Asher

The Polity holds sway across human space, but not everyone embraces the human/AI alliance at its heart. Some choose to hit back against the system. What happens when a terrorist strike you're involved in goes inexplicably wrong? You start to doubt your colleagues and closest friends; you grow suspicious and increasingly uncertain, until fear is your only reliable companion.

Neal Asher lives sometimes in England, sometimes in Crete and mostly at a keyboard. Having over eighteen books published he has been accused of overproduction (despite spending far too much time ranting on his blog, cycling off fat and drinking too much wine) but doesn't intend to slow down just yet. His fiction is famed for containing fast-paced action delivered with the sensibilities of cyberpunk. Neal can be found online at: theskinner. blogspot.com *and* freespace.virgin.net/n.asher.

THE REMOTE CONTROL rested dead in Reynold's hand, but any moment now Kirin might make the connection, and the little lozenge of black metal would become a source of godlike power. Reynold closed his hand over it, sudden doubts assailing him, and as always felt a tight stab of fear. That power depended on Kirin's success, which wasn't guaranteed, and on the hope that the device the remote connected to had not been discovered and neutralized.

He turned towards her. "Any luck?"

She sat on the damp ground with her laptop open on a mould-ering log before her, with optics running from it to the framework supporting the sat dish, spherical laser com unit and microwave transmitter rods. She was also auged into the laptop, an optic lead running from the bean-shaped augmentation behind her ear to plug into it. Beside the laptop rested a big flat memstore packed with state-of-the-art worms and viruses.

"It is not a matter of luck," she stated succinctly.

Reynold returned his attention to the city down on the plain. Athelford was the centre of commerce and Polity power here on Rhine's World, most of both concentrated at its heart where skyscrapers reared about the domes and containment spheres of the runcible port. However, the unit first sent here had not been able to position the device right next to the port itself and its damned controlling AI – Reynold felt an involuntary shudder at the thought of the kind of icy artificial intelligences they were up against. The unit had been forced to act fast when the plutonium processing plant, no doubt meticulously tracked down by some forensic AI, got hit by Earth Central Security. They'd also not been able to detonate. Something had taken them out before they could even send the signal.

"The yokels are calling in," said Plate. He was boosted and otherwise physically enhanced, and wore com gear about his head plugged into the weird scaley Dracocorp aug affixed behind his ear. "Our contact wants our coordinates."

"Tell him to head to the rendezvous as planned." Reynold glanced back at where their gravcar lay underneath its chameleoncloth tarpaulin. "First chance we get we'll need to ask him why he's not sticking to that plan."

Plate grinned.

"Are we still secure?" Reynold asked.

"Still secure," Plate replied, his grin disappearing. "But encoded Polity com activity is ramping up, as is city and sat-scan output."

"They know we're here," said Kirin, still concentrating on her laptop.

"Get me the device, Kirin," said Reynold. "Get me it now."

One of her eyes had gone metallic and her fingers were blurring over her keyboard. "If it was easy to find the signal and lock in the transmission key, we wouldn't have to be this damned close and, anyway, ECS would have found it by now."

"But we know the main frequencies and have the key," Reynold observed.

Kirin snorted dismissively.

Reynold tapped the com button on the collar of his fatigues. "Spiro," he addressed the commander of the four-unit of Separatist ground troops positioned in the surrounding area. "ECS are on to us but don't have our location. If they get it they'll be down on us like a falling tree. Be prepared to hold out for as long as possible – for the Cause I expect no less of you."

"They get our location and it'll be a sat-strike," Plate observed. "We'll be incinerated before we get a chance to blink."

"Shut up, Plate."

"I think I may—" began Kirin, and Reynold spun towards her. "Yes, I've got it." She looked up victoriously and dramatically stabbed a finger down on one key. "Your remote is now armed."

Reynold raised his hand and opened it, studying with tight cold fear in his guts the blinking red light in the corner of the touch console. Stepping a little way from his comrades to the edge of the trees, he once again gazed down upon the city. His mouth was dry. He knew precisely what this would set in motion: terrifying unhuman intelligences would focus here the moment he sent the signal.

"Just a grain at a time, my old Separatist recruiter told me," he said. "We'll win this like the sea wins as it laps against a sandstone cliff."

"Very poetic," said Kirin, now standing at his shoulder.

"This is gonna hurt them," said Plate.

Reynold tapped his com button. "Goggles everyone." He pulled his own flash goggles down over his eyes. "Kirin, get back to your worms." He glanced round and watched her return to her station and plug the memstore cable into her laptop. The worms and viruses the thing contained were certainly the best available, but they wouldn't have stood a chance of infiltrating Polity firewalls *before* he initiated the device. After that they would penetrate local systems to knock out satellite scanning for, according to Kirin, ten minutes – enough time for them to fly the gravcar far from here, undetected.

"Five, four, three, two...one." Reynold thumbed the touch console on the remote.

Somewhere in the heart of the city a giant flashbulb came on for a second, then went out. Reynold pushed up his goggles to watch a skyscraper going over and a disk of devastation spreading from a growing and rising fireball. Now, shortly after the EM flash of the blast, Kirin would be sending her software toys. The fireball continued to rise, a sprouting mushroom, but despite the surface devastation many buildings remained disappointingly intact. Still, they would be irradiated and tens of thousands of Polity citizens reduced to ash. The sound reached them now, and it seemed the world was tearing apart.

"OK, the car!" Reynold instructed. "Kirin?"

She nodded, already closing her laptop and grabbing up as much of her gear as she could carry. The broadcast framework would have to stay though, as would some of the larger armaments Spiro had positioned in the surrounding area. Reynold stooped by a grey cylinder at the base of a tree, punched twenty minutes into the timer and set it running. The thermite bomb would incinerate this entire area and leave little evidence for the forensic AIs of ECS to gather. "Let's go!"

Spiro and his men, now armed with nothing but a few hand weapons, had already pulled the tarpaulin from the car and were piling into the back row of seats. Plate sat at the controls and Kirin and Reynold climbed in behind him. Plate took it up hard through the foliage, shrivelled seed husks and swordlike leaves falling onto them, turned it and hit the boosters. Glancing back, Reynold could only see the top of the nuclear cloud, and he nodded to himself with grim satisfaction.

"This will be remembered for years to come," he stated.

"Yup, certainly will," replied Spiro, scratching at a spot on his cheek.

No one else seemed to have anything to say, but Reynold knew why they were so subdued. This was the comedown; only later would they realize just what a victory this had been for the Separatist cause. He tried to convince himself of that...

In five minutes they were beyond the forest and over rectangular fields of mega-wheat, hill slopes stitched with neat vineyards of protein gourds, irrigation canals and plascrete roads for the agricultural machinery used here. The ground transport – a balloon-tyred tractor towing a train of grain wagons – awaited where arranged.

"Irrigation canal," Reynold instructed.

Plate decelerated fast and settled the car towards a canal running parallel to the road on which the transport awaited, bringing it to a hover just above the water then slewing sideways until the vehicle nudged the bank. Spiro and the soldiers were out first, then Kirin.

"You can plus-grav it?" Reynold asked.

Plate nodded, pulled out a chip revealed behind a torn-out panel, then inserted a chipcard into the reader slot. "Ten seconds." He and Reynold disembarked, then, bracing themselves against the bank, pushed the car so it drifted out over the water. After a moment, smoke drifted up from the vehicle's console. Abruptly it was as if the car had been transformed into a block of lead. It dropped hard, creating a huge splash, then was gone in an instant. Plate and Reynold clambered up the bank after the others and onto the road. Ahead, waiting about the tractor, stood four of the locals, or "yokels" as Plate called them – four Rhine's World Separatists.

"Stay alert," Reynold warned.

As he approached the four he studied them intently. They all wore the kind of disposable overalls farmers clad themselves in on primitive worlds like this and all seemed ill at ease. For a moment Reynold focused on one of their number: a very fat man with a baby face and shaven head. With all the cosmetic and medical options available it was not often you saw people so obese unless they chose to look that way. Perhaps this Separatist distrusted what Polity technology had to offer, which wasn't that unusual. The one who stepped forwards, however, clearly did trust that technology, being big, handsome and obviously having provided himself with emerald-green eyes.

"Jepson?" Reynold asked.

"I am," said the man, holding out his hand.

Reynold gripped it briefly. "We need to get under cover quickly – sat eyes will be functioning again soon."

"The first trailer is empty." Jepson stabbed a finger back behind the tractor.

Reynold nodded towards Spiro and he and his men headed towards the trailer. "You too," he said to Kirin and, as she departed, glanced at Plate. "You're with me in the tractor cab."

"There's only room for four up there," Jepson protested.

"Then two of your men best ride in the trailer." Reynold nodded towards the fat man. "Make him one of them – that should give us plenty of room."

The fat man dipped his head as if ashamed and trailed after Kirin, then at a nod from Jepson one of the others went too.

"Come on fat boy!" Spiro called as the fat man hauled himself up inside the trailer.

"I sometimes wonder what the recruiters are thinking," said Jepson as he mounted the ladder up the side of the big tractor.

"Meaning?" Reynold enquired as he followed.

"Me and Dowel—" Jepson flipped a thumb towards the other local climbing up after Reynold "—have been working together for a year now, and we're good." He entered the cab. "Mark seems pretty able too, but I'm damned if I know what use we can find for Brockle."

"Brockle would be fat boy," said Plate, following Dowel into the cab.

"You guessed it." Jepson took the driver's seat.

Along one wall were three fold-down seats, the rest of the cab being crammed with tractor controls and a pile of disconnected hydraulic cylinders, universal joints and PTO shafts. Reynold studied these for a second, noted blood on one short heavy cylinder and a sticky pool of the same nearby. That was from the original driver of this machine...maybe. He reached down and drew his pulse-gun, turned and stuck it up under Dowel's chin. Plate meanwhile stepped up behind Jepson and looped a garrotte about his neck.

"What the—" Jepson began, then desisted as Plate tightened the wire. Dowel simply kept very still, his expression fearful as he held his hands out from his body.

"We've got a problem," said Reynold.

"I don't understand," said Jepson.

"I don't either, but perhaps you can help." Reynold nodded to one of the seats and walked Dowel back towards it. The man cautiously pushed it down and sat. Gun still held at his neck, Reynold searched him, removing a nasty-looking snubnose, then stepped back knowing he could blow the top off the man's head before he got a chance to rise. "What I don't understand is why you contacted us and asked us for our coordinates."

Plate hit some foot lever on Jepson's seat and spun it round so the man faced Reynold, who studied his expression intently.

"You weren't supposed to get in contact, because the signal might have been traced," Reynold continued, "and there were to be no alterations to the plan unless I initiated them."

"I don't know what you mean," Jepson whispered. "We stuck to the plan – no one contacted you."

"Right frequency, right code – just before we blew the device."

"No, honestly – you can check our com record."

Either Jepson was telling the truth or he was a very good liar. Reynold nodded to Plate, who cinched the garrotte into a loop around the man's neck and now, with one hand free, began to search him, quickly removing first a gas-system pulse-gun from inside his overalls then a comunit from the top pocket. Plate keyed it on, input a code, then tilted his head as if listening to something as the comunit's record loaded to his aug.

"Four comunits," said Plate. "One of them sent the message but the record has been tampered with so we don't know which one."

Jepson looked horrified. Reynold tapped his com button. "Spiro, disarm and secure those two in there with you." Then to Jepson, "Take us to the hideout."

Plate unlooped the garrotte and spun Jepson's seat forwards again.

"It has to be one of the other two," said Jepson, looking back at Reynold. "Me and Dowel been working for the Cause for years."

"Drive the tractor," Reynold instructed.

The farm, floodlit now as twilight fell, was a great sprawl of barns, machinery garages and silos, whilst the farmhouse was a composite dome with rooms enough for twenty or more people. However, only three had lived there. One of them, according to Jepson, lay at the bottom of an irrigation canal with a big hydraulic pump in his overalls to hold him down. He had been the son. The parents were still here on the floor of the kitchen adjoining this living room, since Jepson and Dowel had not found time to clear up the mess before going to pick up their two comrades. Reynold eyed the two corpses for a moment, then returned his attention to Jepson and his men.

"Strip," he instructed.

"Look, I don't know—" Jepson began, then shut up as Reynold shot a hole in the carpet moss just in front of the man's work boots.

The four began removing their clothes, all with quick economy but for Brockle, who seemed to be struggling with the fastenings. Soon they all stood naked.

"Jesu," said Spiro, "you could do with a makeover, fat boy."

"Em all right," said Brockle, staring down at the floor, his hands, with oddly long and delicate fingers, trying to cover the great white rolls of fat.

"Em all right is em?" said Spiro.

"Scan them," Reynold instructed.

Plate stepped forwards with a hand scanner and began running it from head to foot over each man, first up and down their fronts, then over them from behind. When Plate reached Brockle, Spiro called out, "Got a big enough scanner there, Plate?" which was greeted with hilarity from his four troops. When Plate came to the one who had been in the grain carriage with Brockle, he reacted fast, driving a fist into the base of the man's skull then following him down to the floor. Plate pulled his solid-state laser from his belt, rested it beside the scanner then ran it down the man's leg, found something and fired. A horrible sputtering and sizzling ensued, black oily smoke and licks of flame rising from where the beam cut into the man's leg. After a moment, Plate inspected the readout from his scanner, nodded and stepped back.

"What have we got?" Reynold asked.

"Locater."

Reynold felt cold claws skittering down his backbone. "Transmitting?"

"No, but it could have been," Plate replied.

Reynold saw it with utter simplicity. If a signal had been sent, then ECS would be down on them very shortly, and shortly after that they would all be either dead or in an interrogation cell. He preferred dead. He did not want ECS taking his mind apart to find out what he knew.

"Spiro, put a watchman on the roof," he instructed.

Spiro selected one of his soldiers and sent him on their way.

Having already ascertained the layout of this place, Reynold pointed to a nearby door. "Now, Spiro, I want you to take him in there," he instructed. "Tie him to a chair, revive him and start asking him questions. You know how to do that." He paused for a moment. They were all tired after forty-eight hours without sleep. "Work him for two hours then let one of your men take over. Rotate the watch on the roof too and make sure you all get some rest."

Spiro grinned, waved over one of his men and the two dragged their victim off into the room, leaving a trail of plasma and charred skin. Like all Separatist soldiers they were well versed in interrogation techniques.

"Oh, and gag him when he's not answering questions," Reynold added. "We all need to get some sleep."

Reynold turned back to the remaining three. "Get in there." He pointed towards another door. It was an internal storeroom without windows so would have to do.

"I didn't know," said Jepson. "You have to believe that."

"Move," Reynold instructed.

Jepson stooped to gather up his clothing, but Plate stepped over and planted his boot on the pile. Jepson hesitated for a moment then traipsed into the indicated room. One of the troops pulled up an armchair beside the door and plumped himself down in it, pulse-gun held ready in his right hand. Reynold nodded approval then sank down on a sofa beside where Kirin had tiredly seated herself, her laptop open before and connected to her aug. Plate moved over and dropped into an armchair opposite.

"That's everything?" Kirin asked Plate.

"Everything I've got," he replied.

"Could do with my sat-dish, but I'm into the farm system now – gives me a bit more range," said Kirin.

"You're running our security now?" Reynold asked.

"Well, Plate is better with the physical stuff so I might as well take it on now."

"Anything?"

"Lot of activity around the city, of course," she replied, "but nothing out this way. I don't think our friend sent his locator signal and I don't think ECS knows where we are. However, from what I've picked up it seems they do know they're looking for a seven-person specialist unit. Something is leaking out there."

"I didn't expect any less," said Reynold. "All we have to do now is keep our heads down for three days, separate to take up new identities then transship out of here."

"Simple, hey," said Kirin, her expression grim.

"We need to get some rest," said Reynold. "I'm going to use one of the beds here and I suggest you do the same."

He heaved himself to his feet and went to find a bedroom. As his head hit the pillow he slid into a fugue state somewhere between sleep and waking. It seemed only moments had passed, when he heard the agonized scream, but checking his watch as he rolled from the bed he discovered two hours had passed. He crashed open the door to his room and strode out, angry. Kirin lay fast asleep on the sofa and a trooper in the armchair was gazing round with that bewildered air of someone only half awake.

Reynold headed over to the room in which the interrogation was being conducted and banged open the door. "I thought I told you to keep him quiet?"

Their traitor had been strapped in a chair, a gag in his mouth. He was writhing in agony, skin stripped off his arm from elbow to wrist and one eye burned out. The trooper in there with him had been rigging up something from the room's powerpoint, but now held his weapon and had been heading for the door.

"That wasn't him, sir," he said.

Reynold whirled, drawing his pulse-gun, then tapping his com button. "Report in." One reply from Spiro on the roof, one from the other trooper as he stumbled sleepily into the living room, nothing from Kirin, but then she was asleep, and nothing from Plate. "Plate?" Still nothing.

"Where did Plate go?" Reynold asked the seated guard.

The man pointed to a nearby hall containing bunk rooms. Signalling the two troopers to follow, Reynold headed over, opening the first door. The interior light came on immediately to show Plate, sprawled on a bed, his back arched and hands twisted in claws above him, fingers bloody. Reynold surveyed the room, but there was little to see. It possessed no window so the only access was the door, held just the one bed, some wall cupboards and a sanitary cubicle. Then he spotted the vent cover lying on the floor with a couple of screws beside it, and looked up. Something metallic and segmented slid out of sight into the air-conditioning vent.

"What the fuck was that?" asked one of the troops behind him.

"Any dangerous life forms on this world?" Reynold asked carefully, trying to keep his voice level.

"Dunno," came the illuminating reply. "We came in with you."

Reynold walked over to Plate and studied him. Blood covered his head and the pillow was deep red, soaked with it. Leaning closer Reynold saw holes in Plate's face and skull, each a few millimetres wide. Some were even cut through his aug.

"Get Jepson – bring him here."

Jepson seemed just as bewildered as Reynold. "I don't know. I just don't know."

"Are you a local or what?" asked Spiro, who had now joined them.

"Been in the city most of my life," said Jepson, then shifted back as Spiro stepped towards him. "Brockle ... he might know. Brockle's a farm boy."

"Let's get Fat Boy," said Spiro, snagging the shoulder of one of his men and departing.

Brockle came stumbling into the room wiping tiredly at his eyes. He almost looked thinner to Reynold, maybe worn down by fear. His gaze wandered about the room for a moment in bewilderment, finally focusing on the corpse on the bed.

"Why you kill em?" he asked.

"We did not kill him," said Reynold, "but something did." He pointed to the open air-conditioning duct.

Brockle stared at that in bewilderment too, then returned his gaze to Reynold almost hopefully.

"What is there here on Rhine's World that could do this?"

"Rats?" Brockle suggested.

Spiro hit him hard, in the guts, and Brockle staggered back making an odd whining sound. Spiro, obviously surprised he hadn't gone down, stepped in to hit him again but Reynold caught his shoulder. "Just lock them back up." But even as Spiro turned to obey, doubled shrieks of agony reverberated, followed by the sound something heavy crashing against a wall.

Spiro led the way out and soon they were back in the living room. He kicked open the door to the room in which Jepson's comrades were incarcerated and entered, gun in hand, then on automatic he opened fire at something. By the time Reynold entered Spiro was backing up, staring at the smoking line of his shots traversing up the wall to the open air duct.

"What did you see?" Reynold asked, gazing at the two corpses on the floor. Both men were frozen in agonized rictus, their heads bloody pepper pots. One of them had been opened up below the sternum and his guts bulged out across the floor.

"Some sort of snake," Spiro managed.

Calm, got to stay calm. "Kirin," said Reynold. "I'll need you to do a search for me." No reply. "Kirin?"

Whatever it was had got her in her sleep, but the sofa being a dark terracotta colour had not shown the blood. Reynold spun her laptop round and flipped it open, turned it on. The screen just showed blank fuzz. After a moment he noticed the holes cut through the keyboard, and that seemed to make no sense at all. He turned to the others and eyed Jepson and Brockle.

"Put them back in there." He gestured to that bloody room.

"You can't do that," said Jepson.

"I can do what I fucking please." Reynold drew his weapon and pointed it, but Brockle moved in front of Jepson waving those long-fingered hands.

"We done nuthin! We done nuthin!"

Spiro and his men grabbed the two and shoved them back into the room, slamming the door shut behind them.

"What the fuck is this?" said Spiro, finally turning to face Reynold.

The laptop, with its holes …

Reynold stepped over to the room in which Spiro and his men had been torturing their other prisoner, and kicked the door open. The chair lay down on its side, the torture victim's head resting in a pool of blood. A sticking trail had been wormed across the floor, and up the wall to an open air vent. It seemed he only had a moment to process the sight before someone else shrieked in agony. The sound just seemed to go on and on, then something crashed against the inside of the door Jepson and Brockle had just been forced through, and the shrieking stopped. Brockle or Jepson, it didn't matter now.

"We get out of here," said Reynold. "They fucking found us."

"What the fuck do you mean?" asked Spiro.

Reynold pointed at the laptop then at Kirin, at the holes in her head. "Something is here…"

The lights went out and a door exploded into splinters.

Pulse-fire cut the pitch darkness and a silvery object whickered through the air. Reynold backed up and felt something slide over his foot. He fired down at the floor and caught a briefly glimpse of long flat segmented thing, metallic, with a nightmare head decked with pincers, manipulators and tubular probes. He fired again. Someone was screaming, pulse-fire revealed Spiro staggering to one side. It wasn't him making that noise because one of the worm-things was pushing its way into him through his mouth. A window shattered and there came further screaming from outside.

Silence.

Then a voice, calm and modulated. "Absolutely correct of course," it said.

"Who are you?" Reynold asked, backing up through the darkness. A hard hook caught his heel and he went over, then a cold and solid tongue slammed between his palm and his pulse-gun and just flipped the weapon away into the darkness.

"I am your case worker," the voice replied.

"You tried to stop us," he said.

"Yes, I tried to obtain your location. Had you given it the satellite strike would have taken you out a moment later. This was also why I planted that locator in the leg of one of Jepson's men – just to focus attention away from me for a while."

"You're the one that killed our last unit here – the one that planted the device."

"Unfortunately not – they were taken out by satellite strike, hence the reason we did not obtain the location of the tactical nuclear device. Had it been me, everything would have been known."

Reynold thought about the holes through his comrades' heads, through their augs and the holes even through Kirin's laptop. Something had been eating the information out of them even as it killed them. Mind-reaming was the reason Separatists never wanted to be caught alive, but as far as Reynold knew that would happen in a white-tiled cell deep in the bowels of some ECS facility, not like this.

"What the hell are you?"

The lights came on

"Courts do not sit in judgement," said the fat boy, standing naked before Reynold. "When you detonated that device it only confirmed your death sentence; all that remained was execution of that sentence. However, everyone here possessed vital knowledge of others in the Separatist organization and of other atrocities committed by it – mental evidence requiring deep forensic analysis."

Fat Boy's skin looked greyish, corpse-like, but only after a moment did Reynold realize it was turning metallic. The fat boy leaned forwards a little. "I am the Brockle. I am the forensic AI sent to gather and analyse that evidence, and incidentally kill you."

Now Fat Boy's skin had taken on a transparency, revealing that he was just made of knots of flat segmented worms, some of which were already dropping to the floor, others in the process of unravelling. Reynold scrabbled across the carpet towards his gun as a cold metallic wave washed over him. Delicate tubular drills began boring into his head, into his mind. In agony he hoped for another wave called death to swamp him and, though it came physically, his consciousness did not fade. It remained, somewhere, in some no space, while a cold meticulous intelligence took it apart piece by piece.

WINNING PEACE

Paul McAuley

War leaves a lot of untidiness, and crows, including alien ones, pick over the wreckage...

Trained as a biologist, McAuley's forays into conflict range from the war-torn Europe of his award-winning Fairyland *where disposable gene-engineered "dolls" serve as slaves; through powerful and beautifully written techno-thrillers such as* White Devils *set in a near-future heart-of-darkness Congo; up to his recent interplanetary saga of a Brazilian-dominated Earth imposing control over the outer planets,* The Quiet War, *and its sequel* Gardens of the Sun, *which include amongst much action and political intrigue the most gorgeously written topography. His excellent blog "Earth & Other Unlikely Worlds" is at* unlikelyworlds. blogspot.com.

O NE DAY, ALMOST exactly a year after Carver White started working for Mr E. Z. Kanza's transport company, Mr Kanza told him that they were going on a little trip – down the pipe to Ganesh Five. This was the company's one and only interstellar route, an ass-and-trash run to an abandoned-in-place forward facility, bringing in supplies, hauling out pods packed with scrap and dismantled machinery, moving salvage workers to and fro. Carver believed that Mr Kanza was thinking of promoting him from routine maintenance to shipboard work, and wanted to see if he had the right stuff. He was wrong.

The Ganesh Five system was a binary, an ordinary K1 star and a brown dwarf orbiting each other at a mean distance of six billion kilometres, roughly equivalent to the semi-major axis of Pluto's orbit around the Sun. The K1 star, Ganesh Five A, had a minor asteroid belt in its life zone, the largest rocks planoformed thousands of years ago by Boxbuilders, and just one planet, a methane gas giant named Sheffield by the Brit who'd first mapped the system, with glorious water-ice rings, the usual assortment of small moons, and, this was why a forward facility had been established there during the war between the Alliance and the Collective, no less than four wormhole throats.

The system had been captured by the Collective early in the war, and because one of its wormholes was part of a chain that included the Collective's New Babylon system, and another exited deep in Alliance territory, it had become an important staging and resupply area, with a big dock facility in orbit around Sheffield, and silos and tunnel networks buried in several of the moons. Now, two years after the defeat of the Alliance, the only people living there were employees of the salvage company that was stripping the docks and silos, and a small Navy garrison.

Carver White and Mr Kanza flew there on the company's biggest scow, hauling eight passengers, a small tug, and an assortment of cutting and demolition equipment. After they docked, Carver was left to kick his heels in the scow for six hours, until at last Mr Kanza buzzed him and told him to get his ass over to the garrison. A marine escorted Carver to an office with a picture window overlooking the spine of the docks, which stretched away in raw sunlight towards Sheffield's green crescent and the bright points of three moons strung in a line beyond the great arch of its rings. This fabulous view was the first thing Carver saw when he swam into the room; the second was Mr Kanza and a Navy officer lounging in sling seats next to it.

The officer was Lieutenant Rider Jackson, adjutant to the garrison commander. In his mid-twenties, maybe a year older than Carver, he had a pale, thin face, bright blue eyes, and a calm expression that didn't give anything away. He asked Carver about the ships he'd flown and the hours he'd logged serving in the Alliance Navy, questioned him closely about what had happened after Collective marines had boarded his crippled transport, the hand-to-hand fighting in the corridors and holds, how Carver had passed out from loss of blood during a last stand amongst the hypersleep coffins, how he'd woken up in a Collective hospital ship, a prisoner of war. The Alliance had requested terms of surrender sixty-two days later, having lost two battle fleets and more than fifty systems. By then, Carver had been patched up and sold as indentured labour to the pharm factories on New Babylon.

Rider Jackson said, "You didn't tell the prize officer you were a flight engineer."

"I gave him my name and rank and number. It was all he deserved to know."

Carver was too proud to ask what this was all about, but he was pretty sure it had something to do with Mr Kanza's financial difficulties. Everyone who worked for Mr Kanza knew he was in trouble. He'd borrowed to expand his little fleet, but he hadn't found enough new business to service the loan, and his creditors were bearing down on him.

Rider Jackson said, "I guess you think you should have been sent home."

"That's what we did with our prisoners of war."

"Because your side lost the war."

"We'd have sent them back even if we'd won. The Alliance doesn't treat people like property."

Carver was beginning to like Rider Jackson. He seemed like the kind of man who preferred straight talk to evasion and exaggeration, who would stick to the truth even if it was uncomfortable or inconvenient. Which was probably why he'd been sent to this backwater, Carver thought; forthright officers have a tendency to damage their careers by talking back to their superiors.

Mr Kanza said, "If my data miner hadn't uncovered his service record and traced him, he'd still be working in the pharm factories."

Rider Jackson ignored this, saying to Carver, "You have a brother. He served in the Alliance Navy, too."

"That's none of your business," Carver said.

"Oh, but I think you'll find it's very much *my* business," Mr Kanza said.

Mr E. Z. Kanza was a burly man with a shaved head and a short beard trimmed to a sharp point. He liked to think that he was a fair-minded, easygoing fellow, but exhibited most of the usual vices of people given too much power over others: he was arrogant and quick-tempered, and his smile masked a cruel and capricious sense of humour. On the whole, he didn't treat his pilots and engineers too badly – they had their own quarters, access to good medical treatment, and were even given small allowances they could spend as they chose – but they were still indentured workers, with Judas bridges implanted in their spinal cords and no civil rights whatsoever, and Mr Kanza was always ready to use his shock stick on anyone who didn't jump to obey him.

Smiling his untrustworthy smile, Mr Kanza said to Carver, "Jarred is two years younger than you, yes? He served on a frigate during the war, yes? Well, I happen to have some news about him."

Carver didn't say anything. He knew what had happened to Jarred, was wondering if this was one of Mr Kanza's nasty little jokes.

Mr Kanza appealed to Rider Jackson. "Do you know how long they last in those pharm factories before they cop an overdose or their immune systems collapse? No more than a year or two, three at the most. I saved this one from certain death, and has he ever thanked me? And do you want to bet he'll thank me when he learns about his brother?"

Rider Jackson said, "Don't make a game out of it. If you don't tell him, I will."

The two men stared at each other for a long moment. Then Mr Kanza smiled and said, "I do believe you like him. I knew you would."

"Do what needs to be done."

Mr Kanza conjured video from the air with a quick gesture. Here was Jarred White in a steel cell, wearing the same kind of black pyjamas Carver had worn in the prison hospital, before he'd been sold into what the Collective called indentured labour and the Alliance called slavery. Here was Jarred standing in grey coveralls against a red marble wall in the atrium of Mr Kanza's house.

Mr Kanza told Carver, "Your brother was taken prisoner, just like you. One of my data miners traced him, and I bought out his contract. What do you think of that?"

Carver thought that the videos were pretty good fakes, probably Disneyed up from his brother's military record. In both of the brief sequences, Jarred sported the same severe crew cut that was regulation for cadets in the Alliance Navy, not serving officers; when Carver had last seen him, his brother had grown his crew cut out into a flat top. That had been on Persopolis, the City of Our Lady of Flowers. Some twenty days later, Carver's drop ship had been crippled, and he'd been taken prisoner. Three days later, Jarred had been killed in action.

The Collective didn't allow its POWs any contact with their families or anyone else in the Alliance; Carver had found out about his brother's death from one of the other prisoners of war working in the pharm factories. Jarred's frigate, the Croatian, had been shepherding ships loaded with evacuees from Eve's Halo when a Collective battleship travelling at a tenth the speed of light had smashed through the convoy. The Croatian had been shredded by kinetic weapons and a collapsium bomblet had cooked off what was left; the ship had been lost with all hands. Carver had been hit badly by the news. Possessed by moments of unreasoning anger, he'd started to pick fights with other workers; finally, he attacked one of the guards. The woman paralysed him with her shock stick, gave him a clinically methodical beating, and put him on punishment detail, shovelling cell protein from extraction pits. Carver would have died there if one of Mr Kanza's data miners hadn't tracked him down.

After Mr Kanza bought out his contract, Carver resolved to become a model worker, cultivate patience, and wait for a chance to escape; now, wondering if that chance had finally come, if he could turn Mr Kanza's crude trick to his advantage, he stepped hard on his anger and held his tongue.

Mr Kanza said to Rider Jackson, "You see? Not a speck of gratitude."

Rider Jackson turned his tell-nothing expression on Carver; Carver stared back at him through his brother's faked-up ghost.

The young lieutenant said to Mr Kanza, "You're certain we can trust him?"

"I've had him a year. He's never given me any trouble, and he won't give us any trouble now," Mr Kanza said, pointing a finger at Carver. "Can you guess why I went to all the trouble of buying out your brother's contract?"

Carver shrugged, as if it meant nothing to him.

Mr Kanza said, "You really should show me some gratitude. Not only have I already saved your brother's life, but if everything works out, I'll void his contract, and void yours too. You'll both be free."

"Meanwhile, you're holding him hostage, to make sure that I'll do whatever it is you want me to do."

Mr Kanza told Rider Jackson, "There it is. I have his brother as insurance, the tug will fly itself, and if he does get it into his head to try something stupid, I can intervene by wire. If the worst comes to the worst, I'll be the one short a flight engineer and a good little ship; as far as you're concerned, this is a risk-free proposition."

"As long as the Navy doesn't find out about it," Rider Jackson said.

"We've been over that," Mr Kanza said.

Carver saw that there was something tense and wary behind Mr Kanza's smile, and realized that he had worked up some reckless plan to get himself out of the hole, that he needed Rider Jackson's help to do it, and he needed Carver, too.

"We've talked it up and down," Mr Kanza told Rider Jackson. "There's no good reason why the Navy should know anything about this until you buy out your service."

Rider Jackson studied him, then shrugged and said, "OK."

Just like that. Two days later, Carver was aboard Mr Kanza's tug, cooled down in hypersleep while the small ship aimed itself at the brown dwarf, Ganesh Five B.

Mr Kanza made extensive use of a data mining AI to track down skilled prisoners of war who were being used as common l abourers, and to look for business opportunities overlooked by his rivals. The data miner had linked a news item about an alien and an astrophysicist who had disappeared after hiring a small yacht just before the beginning of the war with an academic article by the astrophysicist, Liu Chen Smith, that described an anomalous neutrino flux emitted by a pinpoint source within a permanent storm in the smoky atmosphere of a brown dwarf, Ganesh Five B. It was possible, the data miner suggested, that the alien, a !Cha that called itself Useless Beauty, had bankrolled an expedition to find out if the neutrino source was some kind of Elder Culture artefact.

Although most of the systems linked by wormhole networks were littered with the ruins of the cities, settlements and orbital and free-floating habitats of Elder Culture species, these had been picked clean long ago by the dozens of species that preceded human colonization. Working examples of Elder Culture technology were fabulously rare and valuable. There was only a slim chance that the neutrino source was some kind of artefact, but if it was, and if Mr Kanza could capture it, his financial difficulties would be over. He had one big problem: if the garrison that policed the Ganesh Five system found out about the neutrino source, the Navy would claim it for the state. That was where Rider Jackson, a criminal turned war hero, came in.

Rider Jackson had been born and raised on a reef circling a red dwarf star, Stein 8641. When their sheep ranch failed, Rider Jackson's father ran off on a trade ship and his mother committed suicide. At age sixteen, Rider Jackson, their only child, inherited the responsibility of honouring his family's debts. Our Thing, Stein 8641's parliament, ruled that he should be indentured to his father's chief creditors, the Myer family, until he had paid off all that was owed. Five years later, the day after war was declared between the Alliance and the Collective, he stole one of the Myer family's ships and lit out, abandoning the ship in the sprawling docks of New Babylon and turning up the next day at a Navy recruiting office in the planet's dusty capital, where he was promptly arrested for carrying false ID, a crime against the state that earned him ten years indentured labour. Soon afterwards, having suffered two devastating defeats in quick succession, the Collective's armed forces rounded up everyone with freefall experience from the state's pool of indentured workers. Rider Jackson's sentence was commuted to ten years service in the Navy. He fought in three campaigns in two different systems, and then his drop ship was hit by an Alliance raider and broke apart. Rider Jackson took charge of a gig and rescued seventy-eight warm bodies, including the drop ship's captain. His heroism won him his lieutenant's pip, a chestful of medals and public acclaim, but his criminal history prevented him rising any higher and, at the end of the war, the Navy stashed him in the Ganesh Five garrison, with no hope of promotion or transfer, and nothing to do but listen to the self-pitying monologues of his commander, make random checks on ships passing between the wormholes and file endless status reports. He still had seven years to serve, and after that he would be returned to Stein 8641, and the Myer family.

Mr Kanza, knowing that Rider Jackson couldn't afford to buy out the unserved portion of his contract with the Navy, much less pay what he still owed the Myer family, had made him an offer he couldn't refuse: help chase the hot lead on what might be an Elder Culture artefact in return for 50 per cent of any profit. Mr Kanza brought to the deal the information he'd uncovered, a ship, and someone to fly it; Rider Jackson rejigged the garrison's tracking station to cover up the flight of Mr Kanza's tug, and used its deep space array to survey the brown dwarf. He found two things. The first was a microwatt beacon from an escape pod in orbit around Ganesh Five B. The second was that there was no longer any anomalous neutrino flux within the brown dwarf. It looked like Dr Smith and the !Cha had captured the neutrino source, but then had got into some kind of trouble that had forced them to abandon their ship.

No wormhole throat orbited Ganesh Five B; the only way to reach it was through real space, a round trip of more than sixty days. Rider Jackson couldn't take leave of absence from his post and Mr Kanza was unwilling to risk his life, and couldn't afford to hire a specialized, fully autonomous rescue drone because he was more or less broke and had exhausted all his lines of credit. His lightly modified tug, with Carver White riding along as trouble-shooter, would have to do the job.

Carver learned all this while he helped Mr Kanza prep the tug. He quickly realized that even if he brought back something that made Mr Kanza and Rider Jackson the richest men alive, Mr Kanza wouldn't keep his promise about freeing him; if he was going to survive this, he would have to find some way of exploiting the fact that he knew Mr Kanza's story about holding Jarred hostage was a bluff. He also realized that he didn't have much chance of taking control of the tug and lighting out for somewhere other than the brown dwarf. He would be shut down in hypersleep for most of the trip, and the tug was controlled by an unhackable triumvirate of AIs that, sealed deep in the tug's keel, constantly checked each other's status. Not only that, but Mr Kanza demonstrated with a ten-second burst of agony that he had hidden a shock stick in the tug, too, and could use it to stimulate Carver's Judas bridge if it looked like he was going to cause trouble.

Carver's last thoughts before hypersleep closed him down were about whether he had done enough to make sure he could live through this; it was the first thing on his mind when he woke some thirty-one days later, in orbit around the brown dwarf.

The tug had discovered a scattering of debris, including hull plates, chunks of a fusion motor, and a human corpse in a pressure suit – it was clear that Dr Smith hadn't survived the destruction of her ship – and it had also located the escape pod, which was tumbling in an oblate orbit that skimmed close to the outer edge of the brown dwarf's atmosphere before swinging away to more than twenty million kilometres at apogee. A blurry neutron density scan snatched by a throwaway probe revealed that the pod contained a !Cha's life tank, but its AI had refused to respond to the tug's attempts to shake hands with it, and there had been no response to an automated hailing message either: there was no way of knowing if the !Cha, Useless Beauty, was dead or alive.

The tug played a brief voice-only message from Mr Kanza, telling Carver that he was to suit up and go outside and retrieve Dr Smith's corpse.

'She may be carrying something that will tell me what killed her. Also, her relatives may pay a finder's fee for the return of her body.'

The tug was already matching delta vee with the body. By the time Carver had sent an acknowledgement to the message (it would take five and a half hours to reach Mr Kanza), eaten his first meal since waking, and suited up, the tug and Dr Smith's corpse were revolving around each other at a distance of just a few hundred metres.

Carver rode across the gap on a collapsible broomstick. Ganesh Five B filled half the sky, a dim red disc marbled by black clouds spun into ragged bands by its swift rotation; Dr Smith's corpse was silhouetted against the bale light of this failed star, tumbling head over heels, arms and legs akimbo. Her pressure suit was ruptured in several places, and covered by fine carbon particles blown into space by eruptions in the brown dwarf's magnetosphere; a fog of dislodged soot gathered around Carver as he fixed a line between the dead woman's utility belt and his broomstick.

After he'd towed the body back to the tug and stowed it in the cargo hold, Carver discovered a long tangle of transparent thread thinner than a human hair wrapped around Dr Smith's right arm. He couldn't cut off a sample with any of his suit's tools; he had to unwind the entire tangle before he could bring it inside the tug and feed one end of it into the compact automated laboratory. He'd brought the computer from Dr Smith's suit inside too, but its little mind was dead and its memory had been irretrievably damaged by years of exposure to the brown dwarf's magnetic and radiation fields.

The lab determined that the thread, woven from fullerene nanotubes doped with atoms of beryllium, magnesium and iron and spun into long helical domains, was a room-temperature superconductor with the tensile properties of construction diamond: useful properties, but hardly unique. Even so, the fact that its composition didn't match any known fullerene superconductors was tantalizing, and although he told himself that it was most likely junk, debris in which Dr Smith's body had become entangled after the destruction of her ship, Carver carefully wound the thread around a screwdriver, and shoved the screwdriver into one of the pouches of his p-suit's utility belt.

He had been hoping that the astrophysicist had survived; that she had been sleeping inside the escape pod; that after he'd woken her, she would have agreed to help him. He knew now that everything depended on whether or not the !Cha was alive or dead, and reckoned things would go easier if it was dead. Because if it was still alive, he would have to try to make a deal it, and that was a lot riskier than trying to make a go of it on his own. For one thing, it was possible that the !Cha had murdered Dr Smith because it wanted to keep whatever it was they'd found to itself. For another, like every other alien species, the !Cha made it clear that human beings didn't count for much. Ever since first contact, when the Jackaroo kicked off a global war on Earth and swindled the survivors out of rights to most of the Solar System in exchange for a basic fusion drive and access to a wormhole network linking a couple of dozen lousy M-class red dwarf stars, aliens had been tricking, bamboozling and manipulating the human race. In the long run, like other species before them, humans would either kill themselves off or stumble onto the trick of ascendency and go on to wherever it was the Elder Cultures had gone, but meanwhile they were at the mercy of species more powerful than them, pawns in games whose rules they didn't know, and aims they didn't understand.

Carver had a little time to work out how to deal with the !Cha; before it retrieved the escape pod, the tug spawned dozens of probes and mapped the brown dwarf with everything from optical and microwave radar surveys to a quantum gravity scan. Ganesh Five B was a cool, small T-type, formed like any ordinary star by condensation within an interstellar gas cloud, but at just eight times the mass of Jupiter too small to support ordinary hydrogen fusion. Gravitational contraction and a small amount of sluggish deuterium fusion in its core warmed its dusty atmosphere to a little under 1,500°C. There were metal hydrides and methane down there, even traces of water. Sometimes, its bands of sooty clouds were lit by obscure chains of lightning thousands of kilometres long. Sometimes, when the tug passed directly above the top of a convection cell, those huge, slow elevators that brought up heat from the core,

Carver caught a glimpse of the deep interior, a fugitive flash of brighter red flecked with orange and yellow.

And at every tenth orbit the tug passed over the permanent storm at the brown dwarf's equator, the location of the anomalous neutrino flux that had drawn Dr Smith and the !Cha to Ganesh Five B. The storm's pale lens was more than fifteen thousand kilometres across; probes dropped into it discovered a complex architecture of fractal clusters crawling and racheting around each other like the gears of an insanely complicated mechanism bigger than the Earth. They also discovered that it was no longer emitting neutrinos, and it was fragmenting along its edges – the tug's AIs estimated that it would disappear completely in less than ten years.

While the tug swung around the brown dwarf's dim fires, Carver thought about the !Cha and what he had to do when the tug returned to Sheffield, and lost himself in memories of his dead brother. He and Jarred had been close, two Navy brats following their parents from base to base, system to system. Although Jarred had been two years younger than Carver, he'd also been brighter and bolder, a natural leader, graduating at the top of his class in the Navy academy. The war had already begun when he graduated; the day after his passing-out parade, he followed Carver into active duty.

The last time Carver had seen Jarred, they'd spent three days together in the port city of Our Lady of the Flowers, Persopolis. It was the beginning of Jarred's leave, the end of Carver's. The night before Carver shipped out, they bar-hopped along the city's famous Strand. The more Jarred drank, the more serious and thoughtful he became. He told Carver that whichever side won the war, both would have to work hard at the peace if humanity was to have any chance at surviving.

"War only happens when peace breaks down. That's why peace is harder work, but more worthwhile."

"We defeat the Collective, we impose terms," Carver said. "Where's the problem?"

"If we won the war and imposed terms on the Collective, forced it to change, it would be an act of aggression," Jarred said. "The Collective would respond in kind and there would be another war.

Instead of forcing change, we have to establish some kind of common ground."

"We don't have anything in common with those slavers."

"We have more in common with them than with the Jackaroo, or the Pale, or the !Cha. And if we don't find some way of living together," Jarred said, "we'll grow so far apart that we'll end up destroying each other."

He started to tell Carver about a loose network of people who were discussing how to broker a lasting peace, and Carver said that he didn't want to hear about it, told Jarred he should be careful, what he and his friends were doing sounded a little like treason. Now, in the cramped lifesystem of the tug, endlessly falling around a failed star, six billion kilometres from the nearest human being, Carver thought about what his brother had said on their last night together. Carver had gone a little crazy when he'd heard about his brother's death. It had been about as good and noble as an industrial accident – one machine had destroyed another, and Jarred and the rest of the *Croatian*'s crew had been incidental casualties who'd had no chance to fight back or escape. It was a brutal irony that Jarred's death could help Carver win his freedom.

At last, the tug fired up its motor and slipped into a new orbit, creeping up behind the escape pod, swallowing its black pip whole, then firing up again, a long hard burn to achieve escape velocity from the brown dwarf's gravity well. It pinned Carver to his couch for more than two hours. When it was over, following Mr Kanza's instructions to the letter, Carver suited up, went outside, and clambered through the access hatch of the cargo bay.

The pod's systems were in sleep mode; careful use of a hand-held neutron density scanner confirmed that apart from a !Cha tank it contained nothing out of the ordinary. If Dr Smith and Useless Beauty had retrieved something from the brown dwarf, either it had been lost with their ship, or it was hidden inside the !Cha's impervious casing.

Carver didn't attempt to contact the !Cha. He knew that his only chance of escape lay in a narrow window of opportunity during the final part of the return journey; until then, he wanted to keep his plans to himself. He fixed telltales inside the cargo bay in case the !Cha decided to try to break out, locked it up, climbed back inside the lifesystem and sent a report to Mr Kanza, and let the couch put him to sleep.

Carver was supposed to remain in hypersleep until rendezvous with Mr Kanza's scow, but he'd managed to reprogram the couch while prepping the tug. It woke him twelve hours early, four million kilometres out from Sheffield.

The !Cha's tank was still inside the escape pod, the pod was still sealed in the cargo bay, and the tug was exactly on course, falling ass-backwards towards the gas giant. In a little over two hours it would skim though the outer atmosphere in a fuel-saving aerobraking manoeuvre; meanwhile, the bulk of the planet lay between it and the Ganesh Five facility and Mr Kanza's scow.

Carver had less than an hour before Mr Kanza regained radio contact with the tug. While the tug's triumvirate of AIs threatened dire punishments Mr Kanza had not trusted them to carry out, Carver climbed into his pressure suit, blew open the locked hatch using its explosive bolts, hauled himself to the cargo bay, and took just under fifteen minutes to rig a bypass and crank it open and slide inside.

He'd dropped a tab of military-grade amphetamine (it had cost him fifty days pocket money), but he was still weak from the aftereffects of hypersleep, dopey, chilled to the bone. It took all his concentration to plug into the external port of the escape pod, scroll down the menu that lit up inside his visor, and hit the command that would open the hatch.

Nothing happened.

Carver knew then that the !Cha was awake; it must have locked the hatch from the inside. He was crouched on top of the escape pod in the wash of the gas giant's corpse light with nowhere else to go. Blowing the hatch had compromised the tug's integrity; if it ploughed into Sheffield's upper atmosphere it would break up. And in less than thirty minutes, it would re-establish contact with Mr Kanza's scow. Mr Kanza would have to alter the tug's course to save it, and then he would torture Carver until Carver's air supply ran out. So Carver did the only thing he could do: he opened all the com channels and started talking. He told the !Cha who he was, told it about Mr Kanza and Lieutenant Rider, explained why he needed its help. He talked for ten minutes straight, and then a flat mechanical voice said, "Tell me exactly what you plan to do."

Relief washed clean through Carver, but he knew that he was not saved yet. With the feeling that he was tiptoeing over very thin ice, he said, "I plan to keep us both out of Mr Kanza's clutches. I'd like to surrender to the Navy, but Mr Kanza partnered up with an officer in the garrison here, so our only chance is to escape through one of the wormholes."

"But you do not have command of the tug."

"I don't need it."

Another pause. Then the flat voice said, "You have my interest."

Carver explained that the escape pod's motor was small but fully fuelled, that with tug's delta vee and a little extra assist it should be able to get them where they needed to go.

"I hope you understand that I'm not going to give you the flight plan. You'll have to trust me."

"You are afraid that I killed Dr Smith. You are afraid that I will kill you if I know the details of your plan."

"It crossed my mind, but you're a better bet than my owner."

"If I wanted you dead, I would not need to do it myself. Your owner will do that for me."

Carver wondered if that was an attempt at humour. "He'll kill both of us."

"He will not kill me if he believes that I have something he wants."

"If you do have something, he'll kill you and take it. And if you don't, he'll kill you anyway."

Carver sweated out another pause. Then, with a grinding vibration he felt through his pressure suit, the hatch of the escape pod opened.

Carver powered up the pod's systems, moved it out of the cargo bay and adjusted its trim with a few puffs of the attitude jets, then fired up its motor. Ten minutes later, the tiny star of the dock facility dawned beyond the crescent and rings of the gas giant. The comm beeped. Mr Kanza said, "That won't do you any good, you son of a whore."

"Watch and learn," Carver said.

"Listen to me carefully. If you don't do exactly as I say, your brother is a dead man."

"My brother was killed in action, along with everyone else on his ship."

Carver had control of the escape pod and was out of range of the shock stick hidden on the tug: he could say whatever he liked to Mr Kanza. It was a good feeling. When Mr Kanza started to rage at him, Carver told him that he was going to have to find some other way of covering his debts, and cut him off.

Far behind the pod, the tug lit its motor; no doubt Mr Kanza was flying it by wire, hoping either to bring it close enough to use the shock stick on Carver, or ram him.

Carver told Useless Beauty what was happening, asked it if the thing it had found at the brown dwarf could be used as a weapon. "And don't tell me that you didn't find anything: there's no longer a neutrino source in that strange storm. You fished out some kind of Elder Culture artefact, and it did a number on your ship."

"One of the Elder Cultures may have had something to do with it," Useless Beauty said, "but it was not an artefact."

The squat black cylinder of its tank was jammed into the space between the two acceleration couches, three pairs of limbs folded up in a way that reminded Carver of a praying mantis. He tried to picture what was inside, a cross between a squid and a starfish swimming in oily, ammonia-rich water, the tough, nerve-rich tubules that ordinarily connected it to puppet juveniles plugged into the systems of its casing. It was even harder to picture what it was thinking, but Carver was pretty sure that his survival was at the bottom of its list of priorities.

He said, "If it wasn't an artefact, a machine or whatever, what was it?"

"A mathematical singularity from a universe where the laws and constants of nature are very different from ours. A little like the software of your computers, but alive, self-aware, and imbued with a strong survival instinct. Perhaps an Elder Culture brought it through a kind of wormhole between its universe and ours. Perhaps it is a traveller unable to find its way home. In any event, it was trapped within the brown dwarf, and created the storm by epitaxy – using its own form as a template to make something approximating the conditions of its home, just as my tank contains a small portion of the ocean where my species evolved. Dr Smith and I were able to capture it, but it broke free after we brought it aboard our ship. At once, it began to consume the structure of the ship. Dr Smith went outside and successfully cut it away, but by then the fusion motor had been badly damaged, and it began to overheat. When Dr Smith attempted to repair it, the cooling system exploded and ruptured her suit. She died before she could get back inside, and I was forced to use the escape pod. I got away only a few minutes before the ship was destroyed."

"What about the thing you found? Can we use it?"

"I was unable to retrieve it. Since the neutrino flux is no longer detectable, I must assume that it was unable to return to the brown dwarf. In which case, without a sufficient concentration of matter to weave a suitable habitat around itself,' Useless Beauty said, 'it must have evaporated long ago."

It was a good story, and Carver believed about half of it. He was pretty certain that the !Cha and Dr Smith had captured something – Elder Culture artefact, weird mathematics, whatever – and that it had begun to destroy or transform their ship. It would explain why the composition of the thread Carver had found wrapped around Dr Smith's arm didn't match anything in the library of the ship's lab, but Carver was pretty sure that Dr Smith hadn't died in some kind of accident. It was more likely that Useless Beauty had murdered her because it wanted to keep what they'd found to itself and that prize was hidden somewhere inside its tank. But because he needed the !Cha's help, and because it could quite easily kill him if it had a mind to – the casing of its tank was tougher than diamond, and its limbs were equipped with all kinds of gnarly tools; trying to fight it would be like going head to head with a battle drone – he didn't give voice to his doubts, said that it was a damn shame about losing Dr Smith and the ship; he hoped to bring it better luck.

Useless Beauty did not reply, and its silence stretched as the escape pod hurtled towards the Sheffield's ring system. Carver sipped sweetened apple pulp, watched the tug grow closer, watched the scow change course, half a million kilometres ahead, watched his own track on the navigational plot. He wasn't a pilot, but he knew his maths, and his plan depended on nothing more complicated than ordinary Newtonian mechanics, a straightforward balance between gravity and distance and time and delta vee.

That's what he tried to tell himself, anyhow.

The rings filled the sky ahead, dozens of pale, parallel arcs hundreds of kilometres across, separated by gaps of varying widths. At T minus ten seconds, Carver handed control to the pod's AI. It lit the pod's motor at exactly T0. Two seconds later, the comm beeped: another message from Mr Kanza.

Carver ignored it.

The tug was changing course too, but Carver was almost on the ring system now, falling towards a particular gap he'd chosen with the help of the escape pod's navigational system. He watched it with all of his concentration – he was finding it hard to believe in Newtonian mechanics now his life depended on it.

But there it was, at the edge of one of the arcs of ice and dust: a tiny grain flashing in raw sunlight, a shepherd moon. In less than a minute, it resolved into a pebble, a boulder, a pitted siding of dirty ice. As it flashed past, the pod's AI lit the motor again. The brief blip of acceleration and the momentum the pod had stolen from the moon made a small change in its delta vee; as it swung around the gas giant, the difference between the trajectory of the pod and the tug widened perceptibly.

The tug didn't have enough fuel to catch up with the pod now, but beyond Sheffield, Mr Kanza's scow was changing course, and a few minutes later a Navy cutter shot away from the dock facility, and the comm channels were suddenly alive with chatter: the salvage company's gigs and tugs; a couple of ships in transit between the wormholes; the Navy garrison, ordering both Mr Kanza and Carver White to stand to and await interception.

Carver couldn't obey even if he wanted to. Less than a quarter of the pod's fuel remained and it was travelling very fast now, boosted by the sling-shot through Sheffield's steep gravity well. With Mr Kanza's scow and the Navy cutter in pursuit, it hurtled towards one of the wormhole throats. Carver had no doubt that the scow would follow him through, but he believed he had enough of an edge to make it to where he wanted to go, especially now that the Navy was involved. Someone in the garrison must have discovered Rider Jackson's deal with Mr Kanza, and that meant the cutter would be more likely to try to stop Mr Kanza's scow first.

The wormhole throat was a round dark mirror just over a kilometre across, twinkling with photons emitted by asymmetrical pair decay, framed by a chunky ring that housed the braid of strange matter that kept the throat open, all this embedded in the flat end of a chunk of rock that had been sculpted to a smooth cone by the nameless Elder Culture that had built the wormhole network a couple of million years ago. The pod hit it dead centre, the radio chatter cut off, light flared and the pod emerged halfway around the galaxy, above a planet shrouded in dense white clouds, shining pitilessly bright in the glare of a giant F5 star.

The planet, Texas IX, had a hot, dense, runaway greenhouse atmosphere – even Useless Beauty's tank could not have survived long in the searing storms that scoured its surface – but it also had a single moon that had been planoformed by Boxbuilders. That was where Carver wanted to go. He took back control of the pod and reconfigured it, extending wide braking surfaces of tough polycarbon, and lit the motor. It was a risky manoeuvre – if the angle of attack was too shallow the pod would skip away into deep space with no hope of return, and if it was too steep the pod would burn up – but aerobraking was the only way he could shed enough velocity.

Like a match scratching a tiny flare across a wall of white marble, the pod cut a chord above Texas IX's cloud-tops. Carver was buffeted by vibration and pinned to the couch by deceleration that peaked at eight gees. He screamed into the vast shuddering noise; screamed with exhilaration and fear. Useless Beauty maintained its unsettling silence. Then the flames that filled the forward cameras died back and the pod rose above the planet's nightside.

The stars came out, all at once.

Useless Beauty's affectless voice said, "That was interesting."

"We aren't down yet," Carver said. He was grinning like a fool. He believed that the worst was over.

The escape pod fell away from Texas IX, heading out towards its moon. It was almost there when Mr Kanza's scow overtook it.

Soon after it had formed, while its core had been still molten, something big had smashed into Texas IX's solitary moon. It had excavated a wide, deep basin in one side of the moon, and seismic waves travelling through the crust and core had focused on the area antipodal to the impact, jostling and lifting the surface, breaking crater rims and intercrater areas into a vast maze of hills and valleys, opening vents that flooded crater floors with fresh lava. That was where the escape pod came down, a thousand kilometres from the moon's only settlement, a hundred or so hardscrabble ranches strung along the shore of a shallow, hypersaline sea.

The scow, shooting past at a relative velocity of twenty klicks per second, had cooked the pod with a microwave burst, killing the pod's AI and crippling most of its control systems. Although the pod's aerobraking surfaces gave Carver a little leeway as it ploughed through the moon's thin atmosphere, it smashed down hard and skidded a long way across a lava plain; despite the web holding Carver to the couch and the impact foam that flooded the pod's interior, he was knocked unconscious.

When he came around a few minutes later, the pod was canted at a steep angle, the hatch was open, and Useless Beauty was gone. Carver was bruised over most of his body and his nose was tender and bleeding, possibly broken, but he was not badly hurt. He clawed his way through dissolving strands of impact foam and clambered out of the hatch, discovered that the pod lay at the end of a long furrow, its skin scarred, scraped and discoloured, and radiating an intense heat he could feel through his pressure suit. Big patches of spindly desert vegetation burned briskly on either side, lofting long reefs of smoke into the white sky.

Useless Beauty's tank stood on top of a ridge of overturned dirt, its black cylinder balanced on four many-jointed legs, two more limbs raised as if in prayer towards the sky. Carver was surprised and grateful to see it; he'd thought that the !Cha had taken the opportunity to make a run for it.

"This is only a brief respite," Useless Beauty said, as Carver clambered up the ridge. "Your owner's ship has swung far beyond this moon, but it is braking hard. It will soon be back."

"Then we can't stay here," Carver said. We have to find a place to hide out until someone from the settlement comes to investigate."

The tank's two upper limbs swung down, aiming clusters of tools and sensors straight at Carver, and Useless Beauty said, "This is the part of your plan that I do not understand. This moon is owned by the Collective. You are a runaway slave. Surely they will side with your master. And if they do not, they will claim you for themselves."

Here it was. Carver took a breath and said, "Not if you claim me first."

After a short pause, Useless Beauty said, "So that is why you needed me."

"As we say in the Alliance, one good turn deserves another. I rescued you; now it's your turn to rescue me."

Throwing himself on the mercy of the !Cha was the biggest risk of the whole enterprise. Carver had never felt so scared and alone as he did then, waiting out another of Useless Beauty's silences while hot sunlight beat down through drifts of smoke, and Mr Kanza's scow grew closer somewhere on the other side of the sky.

At last, the !Cha said, "You are very persistent."

"Does that mean you'll help me?"

"I admit that I want to see what happens next."

Carver supposed that he would have to take that as a "yes". Low hills shimmered in the middle distance. The ruins of a Boxbuilder city were scattered across their sere slopes like so many strings of beads. He pointed at the ruins and said, "As soon as I've gotten rid of this pressure suit, we start walking."

The !Cha's four-legged cylinder moved with easy grace through the simmering desert. Carver, wearing only his suit liner and boots, a pouch of water slung over his shoulder, had to jog to keep up. The air was thin, and the fat sun beat down mercilessly, but he revelled in the feeling of the sun's heat on his skin and dry wind in his hair, in the glare of the harsh landscape. Everything seemed infinitely precious, a chain of diamond-sharp moments. He had never before felt so alive as he did then, with death so close at his heels.

As Carver and the !Cha climbed towards a ravine that snaked between interlocking ridges, a double sonic boom cracked across the sky. The scow had arrived. But Carver wasn't ready to give up yet, and there were plenty of places to hide in the ruins. Chains of hollow cubes spun from polymer and rock dust climbed the slopes on either side, piled on top of each other, running along ridges, bridging narrow valleys: a formidable labyrinth with thousands of nooks and crannies that led deep into the hills, where he and Useless Beauty could hide out until sort of rescue party arrived from the colony. For a little while, he began to believe that his plan might work, but then he and the !Cha reached the end of a chain of cubes at the top of a ridge, and found Rider Jackson waiting for them.

The young officer put his pistol on Carver and said, "You led us a pretty good chase, but you forgot one thing."

He was wearing a black Navy flight suit with a big zip down the front and pockets patching the chest and legs; that know-every-thing-tell-nothing expression blanked his face.

"I did?"

"You forgot you're an indentured worker. Your Judas bridge led me straight to you. Your owner will be here as soon as he can find a place to park his ship. I reckon you've got just enough time to tell me your side of the story."

While the scow lowered towards a setback below the ridge, Carver told Rider Jackson more or less everything that had happened out at the brown dwarf. Rider Jackson knew most of it, of course, because he'd seen the footage and data the tug had sent to Mr

Kanza, but he listened patiently and said, when Carver was finished, "I didn't know he was lying about your brother. If I had, I would have put an end to this a lot sooner."

"He was probably lying about a lot of things."

"Like giving me a 50 per cent share in the prize, uh?"

"Like giving you any share at all."

"You might well be right," Rider Jackson said, and looked for the first time at Useless Beauty's tank. "Care to explain why you came along for the ride?"

"I have nothing to give you," it said.

"I bet you don't. But that wasn't what I asked," Rider Jackson said, and that was when Mr Kanza arrived.

Grim and angry and out of breath, he bulled straight across the roofless cube and stuck his shock stick in Carver's face. Carver couldn't help flinching; Mr Kanza smiled and said, "Tell me what the !Cha found and where it is, and maybe I won't have to use this."

Rider Jackson said, "There's no point threatening him. You want to know the truth, figure out how to get the !Cha to talk straight."

Mr Kanza stepped back from Carver and aimed the shock stick at Rider Jackson. "You were indentured once, just like him. Is that why you're taking his side? I knew it was a mistake to let you go chase him down."

"You could have come with me," Rider Jackson said, "but you were happy to let me take the risk."

"He told you. He told you what that thing found and you made a deal with him."

"You're making a bad mistake."

The two men were staring at each other, Rider Jackson impassive, Mr Kanza angry and sweating, saying, "I bet you tasted the stick in your time. You'll taste it again if you don't drop that pistol."

Rider Jackson said, "I guess we aren't partners any more."

"You're right," Mr Kanza said, and zapped him.

Carver was caught by the edge of the stick's field. His Judas bridge kicked in, his muscles went into spasm, hot spikes hammered through his skull, and he fell straight down.

Rider Jackson didn't so much as twitch. He put his pistol on Mr Kanza and said, "The Navy took out my bridge when I signed up. Set down that stick and your pistol, and I'll let you walk away."

"We're partners."

"You said it yourself: not any more. If you start walking now, maybe you can find somewhere to hide before the cutter turns up."

Mr Kanza screamed and threw the shock stick at Rider Jackson and made a grab for the pistol stuck in his utility belt. Rider Jackson shot him. He shot Mr Kanza twice in the chest and the man sat down, winded and dazed but still alive: his pressure suit had stopped the flechettes. He groped for his pistol and Rider Jackson said, "Don't do it."

"Fuck you," Mr Kanza said and jerked up his pistol and fired it wildly. Rider Jackson didn't flinch. He took careful aim and shot Mr Kanza in the head, and the man fell sideways and lay still.

Rider Jackson turned and put his pistol on Useless Beauty's black cylinder and said calmly, "I don't suppose this can punch through your casing, but I could shoot off your limbs one by one and set you on a fire."

There was a brief silence. Then the !Cha said, "You will need a very hot fire, and much more time than you have."

"I have more time than you think," Rider Jackson said. "I know Dana Sabah, the woman flying that cutter. She's a good pilot, but she's inexperienced and too cautious. Right now, she'll be watching us from orbit, waiting to see how it plays out before she makes her move."

"If she does not come, then the settlers will rescue me."

"Uh-uh. Even if the settlers know about us, which I doubt, Dana will have told them to back off. I reckon I have more than enough time to boil the truth out of you."

Useless Beauty said, "I have already told the truth."

Carver got to his feet and told Rider Jackson, "It doesn't matter if it's telling the truth or not. All that matters is that we can escape in the scow. But first, I want you to drop your pistol."

Rider Jackson looked at the pistol Carver was holding – Mr Kanza's pistol – and said, "I wondered if you'd have the guts to pick it up. The question is now, do you have the guts to use it?"

"If I have to."

"Look at us," Rider Jackson said. "I'm an officer in the Collective Navy; you're a prisoner of war sold into slavery, trying to get home... We could fight a duel to see who gets the scow. It would make a good ending to the story, wouldn't it?"

Carver smiled and said, "It would, but this isn't a story."

"Of course it's a story. Do you know why !Cha risk their lives chasing after Elder Culture artefacts?"

"It's something to do with sex."

"That's it. Back in the oceans of their home world, male !Cha constructed elaborate nests to attract a mate. The strongest, those most likely to produce the fittest offspring, made the biggest and most elaborate nests. Simple, straight-ahead Darwinism. The !Cha left their home world a long time ago, but the males still have to prove their worth by finding something novel, something no other male has. They have a bad jones for Elder Culture junk, but these days they get a lot of useful stuff from us, too."

"It's lying about what it found," Carver said. "It told me it lost it, but I know it has it hidden away inside that tank."

Rider Jackson shook his head. "If it still had it, it would have killed you and paid off Mr Kanza. And it wouldn't have called up the garrison back at Ganesh Five."

"It did? Is that why the cutter came after us?"

"Why do you think traffic control spotted you so quickly? It told them what you were up to, and it told them all about my deal with Mr Kanza, too. Dana Sabah told me all about it when she tried to get me to surrender," Rider Jackson said. "I guess our friend thought that involving the Navy would make the story more exciting."

"Son-of-a-bitch. And I thought it was on my side because it owes me its life."

"As far as it's concerned, it doesn't owe you anything. The only reason it stuck with you is because you have something it needs. Something as unique as any ancient artefact, something that can, it believes, win it a mate: the story of how you tried to escape."

"Your own story is just as good, Lieutenant Jackson," Useless Beauty said. "The two of you are enemies, as you said. Fight your duel. The winner will take me with him – I will pay well for it."

Rider Jackson looked at Carver and smiled. "What do you think?"

"I think the war is over." Carver was smiling too, remembering something Jarred had said. That peace was harder work than war, but more worthwhile.

Useless Beauty said, "I do not understand. You are enemies."

Rider Jackson stuck his pistol in his belt. "Like he said, the war is over. Besides, we both want the same thing."

Carver lowered the pistol he'd taken off Mr Kanza's body and told the !Cha, "You're like Mr Kanza. You think you own us, but you don't understand us."

"You must take me with you," Useless Beauty said.

"It wants to find out how the story ends," Rider Jackson told Carver.

"I will pay you well," Useless Beauty said.

Carver shook his head. "We don't need your money. We have the scow, and I have about thirty metres of a weird thread I took off Dr Smith's body. It's superconducting and very strong, and I can't help wondering if it's something you and her pulled out of Ganesh Five B."

"I told you the truth about what we found," Useless Beauty said. "It escaped us and destroyed our ship, but it did not survive. However, I admit this thread may be of interest. I must examine it, of course, but if it is material transformed during the destruction of the ship, I may be willing to purchase it."

"That's what I thought," Carver said. "It may not be an Elder Culture artefact, but it could be worth something. And maybe the data from the probes I dropped into Ganesh Five B might be worth something, too."

"I may be willing to purchase that, too," Useless Beauty said. "As a souvenir."

"What do you think?" Carver said to Rider Jackson.

"I think we'll get a better price on the open market."

"I can force you to take me," Useless Beauty said.

"No, you can't," Carver said.

"And even if you could, it would ruin the ending of your story," Rider Jackson said. "I'm sure the settlers or the Navy will rescue you, for a price."

There was a long moment of silence. Then Useless Beauty said, "I would like to know what happens after you escape. I will pay well."

"If we escape," Carver said. "We have to get past the cutter."

"Dana Sabah's a good pilot, but I'm better," Rider Jackson said. "I reckon you are too."

"Before we do this, we need to work out where we're going."

"That's pretty easy, given that you're an indentured worker and the Navy wants my ass. Think that Kanza's old boat will get us to the Alliance?"

"It just might."

The two men grinned at each other. Then they ran for the scow.

TIME PIECE

Joe Haldeman

If starships can instantly jump interstellar distances yet nevertheless Einstein is not violated, interstellar war will displace its soldiers far from their home times...

"Time Piece" was the trial run for the basic idea behind Haldeman's classic novel The Forever War, *which won both the Hugo and Nebula Awards in 1975. A combat engineer during the Vietnam conflict, this was his second professional publication, pregnant with much. Since the early eighties he has spent nine months of the year writing full-time, the rest as an adjunct professor in the Writing and Humanistic Studies programme at MIT. Of his thirty or so books written in about forty years to date, all but four have been SF. As of early 2011, six bookcases held one copy each of every book and magazine he appeared in, a total of fifty-eight shelf feet, which might seem almost a forever shelf to writers starting out.*

THEY SAY YOU'VE got a fifty–fifty chance every time you go out. That makes it once chance in eight that you'll live to see your third furlough; the one I'm on now.

Somehow the odds don't keep people from trying to join. Even though not one in a thousand gets through the years of training and examination, there's no shortage of cannon fodder. And that's what we are. The most expensive, best trained cannon fodder in the history of warfare. Human history, anyhow; who can speak for the enemy?

I don't even call them snails any more. And the thought of them doesn't trigger that instant flash of revulsion, hate, kill-fever – the psyconditioning wore off years ago, and they didn't renew it. They've stopped doing it to new recruits; no percentage in berserkers. I was a wild one the first couple of trips, though.

Strange world I've come back to. Gets stranger every time, of course. Even sitting here in a bogus twenty-first-century bar, where everyone speaks Basic and there's real wood on the walls and peaceful holograms instead of plugins, and music made by men...

But it leaks through. I don't pay by card, let alone by coin. The credit register monitors my alpha waves and communicates with the bank every time I order a drink. And, in case I've become addicted to more modern vices, there's a feelie matrix (modified to look like an old-fashioned visiphone booth) where I can have my brain stimulated. Thanks but no, thanks – always get this picture of dirty hands inside my skull, kneading, rubbing. Like when you get too close to the enemy and they open a hole in your mind and you go spinning down and down and never reach the bottom till you die. I almost got too close last time.

We were on a three-man reconnaissance patrol, bound for a hellish little planet circling the red giant Antares. Now red giant stars don't form planets in the natural course of things, so we had ignored Antares; we control most of the space around it, so why waste time in idle exploration? But the enemy had detected this little planet – God knows how – and about ten years after they landed there, we monitored their presence (gravity waves from the ships' braking) and my team was assigned the reconnaissance. Three men against many, many of the enemy – but we weren't supposed to fight if we could help it; just take a look around, record what we saw, and leave a message beacon on our way back, about a light-year out from Antares. Theoretically, the troopship following us by a month will pick up the information and use it to put together a battle plan. Actually, three more recon patrols precede the troop ship at one-week intervals; insurance against the high probability that any one patrol will be caught and destroyed. As the first team in, we have a pretty good chance of success, but the ones to follow would be in trouble if we didn't get back out. We'd be past caring, of course: the enemy doesn't take prisoners.

We came out of lightspeed close to Antares, so the bulk of the star would mask our braking disturbance, and inserted the ship in a hyperbolic orbit that would get us to the planet – Anomaly, we were calling it – in about twenty hours.

"Anomaly must be tropical over most of its surface." Fred Sykes, nominally the navigator, was talking to himself and at the two of us while he analysed the observational data rolling out of the ship's computer. "No axial tilt to speak of. Looks like they've got a big outpost near the equator, lots of electromagnetic noise there. Figures … the goddamn snails like it hot. We requisitioned hot-weather gear, didn't we, Pancho?"

Pancho, that's me. "No, Fred, all we got's parkas and snow-shoes." My full name is Francisco Jesus Mario Juan-José Hugo de Naranja, and I outrank Fred, so he should at least call me Francisco. But I've never pressed the point. Pancho it is. Fred looked up from his figure and the rookie, Paul Spiegel, almost dropped the pistol was cleaning.

"But why …" Paul was staring. "We knew the planet was probably Earthlike if the enemy wanted it. Are we gonna have to go tromping around in spacesuits?"

"No, Paul, our esteemed leader and supply clerk is being sarcastic again." He turned back to his computer. "Explain, Pancho."

"No, that's all right." Paul reddened a bit and also went back to his job. "I remember you complaining about having to take the standard survival issue."

"Well, I was right then and I'm doubly right now. We've *got* parkas back there, and snowshoes, and a complete terranorm environment recirculator, and everything else we could possibly need to walk around in comfort on every planet known to man – *Dios*! That issue masses over a metric ton, more than a bevawatt laser. A laser we could use, but crampons and pith helmets and elephant guns …"

Paul looked up again. "Elephant guns?" He was kind of a freak about weapons.

"Yeah."

"That's a gun that shoots elephants?"

"Right. An elephant gun shoots elephants."

"Is that some new kind of ammunition?"

I sighed, I really sighed. You'd think I'd get used to this after twelve years – or four hundred – in the service. "No, kid, elephants were animals, big grey wrinkled animals with horns. You used an elephant gun to shoot *at* them.

"When I was a kid in Rioplex, back in the twenty-first, we had an elephant in the zoo; used to go down in the summer and feed him synthos through the bars. He had a long nose like a fat tail; he ate with that."

"What planet were they from?"

It went on like that for a while. It was Paul's first trip out, and he hadn't yet gotten used to the idea most of his compatriots were genuine antiques, preserved by the natural process of relativity. At lightspeed you age imperceptibly, while the universe's calendar adds a year for every light-year you travel. Seems like cheating. But it catches up with you eventually.

We hit the atmosphere of Anomaly at an oblique angle and came in passive, like a natural meteor, until we got to a position where we were reasonably safe from detection (just above the south polar sea), then blasted briefly to slow down and splash. Then we spent a few hours in slow flight at sea level, sneaking up on their settlement.

It appeared to be the only enemy camp on the whole planet, which was typical. Strange for a spacefaring, aggressive race to be so incurious about planetary environments, but they always seemed to settle in one place and simply expand radially. And they do expand; their reproduction rate makes rabbits look sick. Starting from one colony, they can fill a world in two hundred years. After that, they control their population by infantiphage and stellar migration.

We landed about a hundred kilometres from the edge of their colony, around local midnight. While we were outside setting up the espionage monitors, the ship camouflaged itself to match the surrounding jungle optically, thermally, magnetically, etc. – we were careful not to get too far from the ship; it can be a bit hard to find even when you know where to look.

The monitors were to be fed information from flea-sized flying robots, each with a special purpose, and it would take several hours for them to wing into the city. We posted a one-man guard, one-hour shifts; the other two inside the ship until the monitors started clicking. But they never started.

Being senior, I took the first watch. A spooky hour, the jungle making dark little noises all around, but nothing happened. Then Fred stood the next hour, while I put on the deepsleep helmet. Figured I'd need the sleep – once data started coming in, I'd have to be alert for about forty hours. We could all sleep for a week once we got off Anomaly and hit lightspeed.

Getting yanked out of deepsleep is like an ice-water douche to the brain. The black nothing dissolved and there was Fred a foot away from my face, yelling my name over and over. As soon as he saw my eyes open, he ran for the open lock, priming his laser on the way (definitely against regulations, could hole the hull that way; I started to say something but couldn't form the words). Anyhow, what were we doing in free fall? And how could Fred run across the deck like that while we were in free fall?

Then my mind started coming back into focus and I could analyse the sinking, spinning sensation – not free-fall vertigo at all, but what we used to call snail-fever. The enemy was very near. Crackling combat sounds drifted in from outdoors.

I sat up on the cot and tried to sort everything out and get going. After long seconds my arms and legs got the idea; I struggled up and staggered to the weapons cabinet. Both the lasers were gone, and the only heavy weapon left was a grenade launcher. I lifted it from the rack and made my way to the lock.

Had I been thinking straight, I would've just sealed the lock and blasted – the presence in my mind was so strong that I should have known there were too many of the enemy, too close, for us to stand and fight. But no one can think while their brain is being curdled that way. I fought the urge to just let go and fall down that hole in my mind, and slid along the wall to the airlock. By the time I got there my teeth were chattering uncontrollably and my face was wet with tears.

Looking out, I saw a smouldering grey lump that must have been Paul, and Fred screaming like a madman, fanning the laser on full over a 180° arc. There couldn't have been anything alive in front of him; the jungle was a lurid curtain of fire, but a bolt lanced in from behind and Fred dissolved in a pink spray of blood and flesh.

I saw them then, moving fast for snails, shambling in over thick brush towards the ship. Through the swirling fog in my brain I realized that all they could see was the light pouring through the open lock, and me silhouetted in front. I tried to raise the launcher but couldn't – there were too many, less than a hundred metres away, and the inky whirlpool in my mind just got bigger and bigger and I could feel myself slipping into it.

The first bolt missed me; hit the ship and it shuddered, ringing like a huge cathedral bell. The second one didn't miss, taking off my left hand just above the wrist, roasting what remained of my left arm. In a spastic lurch I jerked up the launcher and yanked the trigger, holding it down while dozens of microton grenades popped out and danced their blinding way up to and across the enemy's ragged line. Dazzled blind, I stepped back and stumbled over the med-robot, which had smelled blood and was eager to do its duty. On top of the machine was a switch that some clown had labelled EMERGENCY EXIT; I slapped it, and as the lock clanged shut the atomic engines muttered – growled – screaming into a life and a ten-gravity hand slid me across the blood-slick deck and slammed me back against the rear-wall padding. I felt ribs crack and something in my neck snapped. As the world squeezed away, I knew I was a dead man but it was better to die in a bed of pain than to just fall and fall…

I woke up to the less-than-tender ministrations of the med-robot, who had bound the stump of my left arm and was wrapping my chest in plastiseal. My body from forehead to shins ached from radiation burns, earned by facing the grenades' bursts, and the non-existent hand seemed to writhe in painful, impossible contortions. But numbing anaesthetic kept the pain at a bearable distance, and there was an empty space in my mind where the snail-fever had been, and the gentle hum told me we were at lightspeed; things could have been one flaming hell of a lot worse. Fred and Paul were gone but that just moved them from the small roster of live friends to the long list of dead ones.

A warning light on the control panel was blinking stroboscopically. We were getting near the hole – excuse me, "relativistic discontinuity" – and the computer had to know where I wanted to go. You go in one hole at lightspeed and you'll come out of some other hole; *which* hole you pop out of depends on your angle of approach. Since they say that only about 1 per cent of the holes are charted, if you go in at any old angle you're liable to wind up in Podunk, on the other side of the galaxy, with no ticket back.

I just let the light blink, though. If it doesn't get any response from the crew, the ship programs itself automatically to go to Heaven, the hospital world, which was fine with me. They cure what ails you and then set you loose with a compatible soldier of the opposite sex, for an extended vacation on that beautiful world. Someone once told me that there were over a hundred worlds named Hell, but there's only one Heaven. Clean and pretty from the tropical seas to the Northern pine forests. Like Earth used to be, before we strangled it.

A bell had been ringing all the time I'd been conscious, but I didn't notice it until it stopped. That meant the information capsule had been jettisoned, for what little it was worth. Planetary information, very few espionage-type data; just a tape of the battle. Be rough for the next recon patrol.

I fell asleep knowing I'd wake up on the other side of the hole, bound for Heaven.

I pick up my drink – an old-fashioned old-fashioned – with my new left hand and the glass should feel right, slick but slightly tacky with the cold-water sweat, fine ridges moulded into the plastic. But there's something missing, hard to describe, a memory stored in your fingertips that a new growth has to learn all over again. It's a strange feeling, but in a way seems to fit with this crazy Earth, where I sit in my alcoholic time capsule and, if I squint with my mind, can almost believe I'm back in the twenty-first.

I pay for the nostalgia – wood and natural food, human bartender and waitress who are also linguists, it all comes dear – but I can afford it, if anyone can. Compound interest, of course. Over four centuries have passed on Earth since I first went off to war, and my salary's been deposited at the Chase Manhattan Credit Union ever since. They're glad to do it; when I die, they keep the interest and the principal reverts to the government. Heirs? I had one illegitimate son (conceived on my first furlough) and when I last saw his gravestone, the words on it had washed away to barely legible dimples.

But I'm still a young man (at lightspeed you age imperceptibly while the universe winds down outside) and the time you spend going from hole to hole is almost incalculably small. I've spent most of the past half millennium at lightspeed, the rest of the time usually convalescing from battle. My records show that I've logged a trifle under one year in actual combat. Not bad for 438 years' pay. Since I first lifted off I've aged twelve years by my biological calendar. Complicated, isn't it – next month I'll be thirty, 456 years after my date of birth.

But one week before my birthday I've got to decide whether to try my luck for the fourth trip out or just collect my money and retire. No choice, really. I've got to go back.

It's something they didn't emphasize when I joined up, back in 2088 – maybe it wasn't so obvious back then, the war only decades old – but they can't hide it nowadays. Too many old vets wandering around, like animated museum pieces.

I could cash in my chips and live in luxury for another hundred years. But it would get mighty lonely. Can't talk to anybody on Earth but other vets and people who've gone to the trouble to learn Basic.

Everyone in space speaks Basic. You can't lift off until you've become fluent. Otherwise, how could you take orders from a fellow who should have been food for worms centuries before your grandfather was born? Especially since language melted down into one Language.

I'm tone deaf. Can't speak or understand Language, where one word has ten or fifteen different meanings, depending on pitch. To me it sounds like puppy dogs yapping. Same words over and over; no sense.

Of course, when I first lived on Earth there were all sorts of languages, not just one Language. I spoke Spanish (still do when I can find some other old codger who remembers) and learned English – that was before they called it Basic – in military training. Learned it damn well, too. If I weren't tone deaf I'd crack Language and maybe I'd settle down.

Maybe not. The people are so strange, and it's not just the Language. Mindplugs and homosex and voluntary suicide. Walking around with nothing on but paint and powder. We had Fullerdomes when I was a kid, but you didn't *have* to live under one. Now if you take a walk out in the country for a breath of fresh air, you'll drop over dead before you can exhale.

My mind keeps dragging me back to Heaven. I'd retire in a minute if I could spend my remaining century there. Can't, of course; only soldiers allowed in space. And the only way a soldier gets to Heaven is the hard way.

I've been there three times; once more and I'll set a record. That's motivation of a sort, I suppose. Also, in the unlikely event that I should live another five years, I'll get a commission, and a desk job if I live through my term as a field officer. Doesn't happen too often – but there aren't too many desk jobs that people can handle better than cyborgs.

That's another alternative. If my body gets too garbaged for regeneration, and they can save enough of my brain, I could spend the rest of eternity hooked up to a computer, as a cyborg. The only one I've ever talked to seemed to be happy.

I once had an African partner named N'gai. He taught me how to play O'wari, a game older than Monopoly or even chess. We sat in this very bar (or the identical one that was in its place two hundred years ago) and he tried to impress on my non-Zen-oriented mind just how significant this game was to men in our position.

You start out with forty-eight smooth little pebbles, four in each one of the twelve depressions that make up the game board. Then you take turns, scooping the pebbles out of one hole and distributing them one at a time in holes to the left. If you dropped your last pebble in a hole where your opponent had only one or two, why, you got to take those pebbles off the board. Sounds exciting, doesn't it?

But N'gai sat there in a cloud of bhang-smoke and mumbled about the game and how it was just like the big game we were playing, and every time he took a pebble off the board, he called it by name. And some of the names I didn't know, but a lot of them were on my long list.

And he talked about how we were like the pieces in this simple game; how some went off the board after the first couple of moves, and some hopped from place to place all though the game and came out unscathed, and some just sat in one place all the time until they got zapped from out of nowhere...

After a while I started hitting the bhang myself, and we abandoned the metaphor in a spirit of mutual intoxication.

And I've been thinking about that night for six years, or two hundred, and I think that N'gai – his soul find Buddha – was wrong. The game isn't all that complex.

Because in O'wari, either person can win.

The snails populate ten planets for every one we destroy.

Solitaire, anyone?

THE WAKE

Dan Abnett

To hold a wake for a comrade fallen in battle against aliens might seem like a worthy plan…

Dan Abnett has written best-selling novels for Games Workshop in their Warhammer 40,000 universe, and for the BBC in parallel to their Torchwood *series ("Torchwood" being an anagram of "Doctor Who", an organization beyond the law set up by Queen Victoria to combat intrusions by aliens). Abnett's 40,000 novel* Prospero Burns *was a New York Times bestseller, and topped the SF charts in the UK and the USA. Oxford-educated, Abnett lives in Kent, England, with blog and website at* www.danabnett.com, *or follow him on Twitter @VincentAbnett.*

W E WERE GOING to miss Mendozer.

He'd been with us, what, four tours? Five, Klubs reckons. Five. Well anyway, we were going to miss him. Mendozer was like a tin target. You know the kind? You knock them down, but the motor pops them up again, time after time.

Mendozer had a tin target quality about him. You get blokes like that. I don't mean immortal, indestructible fireproof angels of death like Boring, 'cause blokes like Boring, they're a whole other deal entirely. No, Mendozer's type, they're just reliable, like they're always going to be around, and if something knocks them down they'll soon be right back up again, thank you, banging away, making a joke.

Like a tin target on the practice deck. Bang! Down he goes. Then up he pops again.

When Mendozer got knocked down and didn't pop back up, we grabbed him and got him to the extract. Moke and me, we hoiked him under the armpits and ran with him, dragging his legs. Moke was yelling "medic", but I was pretty confident that Mendozer was dogfood already. None of us actually saw what got him, due to the fact that it had all gone a bit cack-yourself-and-keep-shooting nutty at the time, but it looked like he'd run onto a pitchfork. There was wet everywhere. The stuff was all over us, soaking our sleeves and hips.

The Surge did his best. Credit for that. Tried everything. Split Mendozer's body jacket off, cracked the sternum, tried to patch the internal punctures, tried to get the slack heart to restart. We ended up soaking wet up to our armpits, kneeling either side of Mendozer in a blood slick the size of a fish pond, with dozens of spent injector vials and wadding tear-off strips floating around in it.

End of. Somebody find him a box.

The Surge put him in the fridge. We stayed on site four more days, expending our remaining munitions at anything that came inside the floodlit perimeter. It was not the light-hearted fun and frolics we'd been hoping for.

There was a technical problem with our extract, so we had to layover at Relay Station Delta for a week. All of us knew Relay Delta, because we stopped there every time on the way in to Scary Land, and none of us cared for it. Dark, pokey, rank, no light except artificial, no food except recyc. It was about as roomy and inviting as Mendozer's casket.

The trick was to recognize the up-side. A week's layover meant a week added to resupply turnaround, and a week extra before we'd get deployed back to Scary Land. That was fine by us, even if it meant seven days of breathing farts in the dark at Relay Delta.

We were all pretty sick of Scary Land, to tell you the truth. We were all pretty sick of banging away at the Scaries. We'd lost sixteen on seven tours, including Mendozer, and that was light compared to some platoons. The Middlemen, best of the best and all that, but banging away at the Scaries was beginning to feel like banging our heads against the proverbial. We've tangled with all sorts over the years, no word of a lie, but there was something relentless about the Scaries. Something cack yourself. Something shadow-under-the-bed spooky. I swear even Boring was beginning to get creeped out by them.

"Bosko," he says to me, "Scary Land is starting to make me miss Suck Central."

Which was saying something, specially coming from Juke Boring, shit-kicking fireproof god of war. Suck Central, as the name suggests, had not been a family bucket of fun and frolics either.

Anyway, there's us, Relay Delta, a bit of downtime. So we're all in the Rec, just dossing around, and in comes Boring carrying a large carton pack, and behind him comes the Surge trundling a shiny plastic casket on a gurney from the ward. It rattles its castors as it comes in over the door trim. It takes us all of no seconds flat to realize this is Mendozer's bloody box. Everyone gets up. Everyone says a few choice words, the same choice word in most instances.

Boring, he points with his chin and directs Surge to park Mendozer in the middle of the Rec. The Surge does so, and heels the brake-lock on the gurney's wheelbase. Boring walks over to a side table, indicates by a narrowing of his eyes that Klubs should instantly remove the hand of clock patience spread out on it, and then dumps the carton. It clinks. Glass.

"We're holding a wake," he announces.

He opens the carton. It had been a stores pack for cans of rice pudding in a previous life. His big hands scoop out sets of chunky shot glasses, a digit in each, five at a time. Cripes only knows where he managed to scare up real-glass glasses.

Then came the best bit. Twenty-four bottles of the good stuff. Litre bottles, actual glass. Boring twists the top off the first one, and I can't remember how long it's been since I heard the fresh metal collar of a screw cap strip open like that.

He starts filling the glasses. Generous measures. It takes more than one bottle. We're all wary. Juke Boring has a history of playing cruel tricks in the name of character building experience. The stuff he was pouring might just have been cold tea. We're all braced for a metaphorical smack round the ear and a lecture on taking things at face value.

But this isn't a trick. You can't fake the smell of fifteen-year-old malt.

"Where'd you get this stuff?" asks Neats, the platoon sergeant.

"Station commander owed me a million favours," Boring says. "Now he owes me a million minus one."

He picks up a glass. He doesn't hand the others out, but there's a wordless instruction for us all to go help ourselves. We take a glass each, and form a loose circle around the gurney. Twenty-eight men: twenty-four, plus Boring, Neats, the Surge and Mendozer in his box.

Boring raises his glass. "Here's to Mendozer," he says. "Middleman from start to finish. Skull it."

"Skull!" we all say, and chug back our glasses. We clonk the empties down on the lid of Mendozer's box, and Boring nods to Neats to refill them.

As Neats gets busy, Moke asks the question we're all thinking. "We don't usually do this," he says. "Why are we doing this?"

"Because we should," says Boring. "Shows respect. Isn't usually enough time, or there's no place to do it. Thought it was a custom we should get into."

The glasses are full again. We hoist them.

"Middlemen, best of the best," says Neats.

"Skull!" we say. Refill.

I was told the platoon's nickname is the Middlemen because we get right in the middle of things. Klubs says it's because we're always stuck in the middle of bloody nowhere – in this particular instance, with a dead bloke in a box in a pressurized bunker that smells like bad wind.

The concept of the wake is unfamiliar to some of our number, so Fewry explains.

"It's a mourning custom," he says. "A watch kept over the departed."

"Why?" someone asks.

"In case they're not dead," says Klubs. "In case they wake up."

"That's not right," says the Surge, who's the most educated of the Middlemen fraternity.

"It isn't?" asks Klubs. "I thought that's why it was called that."

The Surge shakes his head. "That's just a myth," he says. "One of those old wives' tales."

"But I heard," says Klubs, never one to let a thing go, "that they used to dig up old coffins and find fingernail scratches on the insides. 'Cause people didn't have proper medic stuff back then, and sometimes they thought some poor sod was dead when they wasn't, and they'd bury them and then they'd wake up looking at the lid. So they'd hold one of these things to keep an eye on the body for a while and make sure it wasn't going to wake up before they bunged it in the ground."

"I understand," says the Surge. He has a patient tone sometimes. "I understand what you mean. It's just the word comes from a different root."

"Oh," says Klubs.

We neck a few more ("Death to all Scaries!", "Mother Earth!", "Second Infantry, defenders of the World!"), and in between we remember a few stories about Mendozer. You could count on him. He was an OK shot with the Steiner, but really gifted with the grenade gun. He didn't snore much. He had a couple of decent jokes. There was that one really funny time with the girl from stores and the ping-pong bat.

The mood relaxes a bit. Each of us takes a moment to individually tilt a glass to the box sitting there on the chrome gurney, and say a last few words of a personal nature. A few of us sit back. The cards come out. Moke and some others dig out the sticks and the ashtray puck, and start playing corridor hockey on the pitch marked out on the tiled hallway leading through to medical. There's a lot of shouting and body-slamming into doors. Boring watches them, almost amused. The pitch outlines are wearing away. It's been there as long as any of us can remember. No one knows who painted them.

The Surge pulls out a second deck, and starts to do some of his famous card tricks. Nimble fingers. Fewry goes off to get some bacon strips, crackers and pickles from stores.

Every now and then, someone hoists up his glass and calls out a toast, and everyone stops what they're doing, even the hockey players, and answers.

Usually, it's a simple "Mendozer!" and we all answer "Skull!"

If I'm honest, I'm not sure how long we were kicking back before someone noticed. Couple of hours, minimum. I know that Neats told me to go get another bottle out of the carton for top-ups, and I saw we'd skulled half of them already. The party had broken down a bit, and spread out through the rooms around the Rec.

Moke suddenly says, "What's he doing there? That's not respectful."

No one pays Moke that much attention, but I look up. Mendozer's box is no longer in the centre of the Rec. It's been wheeled aside, and it's standing under the big blast ports, three or four metres away from where the Surge parked it.

No mystery. I mean, it's obvious as soon as you look at it. The gurney's spring loaded brake-lock has pinged off and it's rolled. Maybe someone brushed against it.

Except they haven't, and it hasn't. The brake-lock hasn't disengaged to such an extent; in fact, Moke is actually having trouble unfastening it so he can roll the gurney back into the middle of the room where it's supposed to be.

I go over. Bend down. Help him. The Surge heeled that brake good. The pin needs oil. It takes a moment of effort and a few choice words to unfix it.

Moke and me, we go to roll the box back into pride of place.

"Wait," I says. He can feel it too. He looks at me. It's a bad look. I immediately wish I'd sat out the last couple of toasts, because the drink has got me paranoid. Maybe I'm being clumsy. Maybe I'm a little happy-handed and everything seems skewy.

The box feels too light. The gurney's rolling far too freely. There's no weight in it.

"'Sup?" says Boring. He's right there at my shoulder all of a sudden. Around us, people are still playing cards and telling jokes. Out in the hall, the corridor hockey tournament is reaching its climax.

I look at him, say nothing. It's in the eyes. Boring puts one hand flat on the top of Mendozer's box and just moves it from side to side. He can feel it too. You can see it. The whole trolley fishtails slightly under the stir of his palm. Nothing like enough weight. It'd have to be empty to behave like that.

Boring looks at me, quick, then back at the casket. Someone's left an empty glass standing on top, and it's left a ring of condensation on the shiny plastic. Boring picks up the glass and hands it to Moke. Moke has got eyes big as saucers by now.

Boring runs a finger along the edge of the lid. There are catches, but they're floppy plastic, nothing secure. He flicks them.

Then he opens the lid.

I don't want to look, but I look. It's not that I want to see Mendozer dead in a box, but I would find it reassuring at least.

We see the inside of the bottom of the box. Casket's empty. No Mendozer, nothing.

Boring shuts the lid.

"This isn't funny," I whisper.

He points to his stony expression, a familiar gesture intended to emphasize the fact he isn't cracking up.

"Did someone take the poor bastard out as a joke?" I asked.

It seems unlikely.

"Maybe the Surge pulled the wrong box out of the fridge?" Moke suggests. His voice is as low as ours.

That seems unlikely too.

"Wouldn't the Surge have noticed the box was light when he brought it through?" I ask.

Boring doesn't answer me. He looks around the Rec, winks at Neats. Neats makes an excuse about needing a slash to gently extract himself from his card school. Boring looks back at me.

"Bosko," he says. "Go fetch a Steiner. Meet me in medical."

"OK," I say.

"Take Moke with you."

"OK."

I don't know what to think. I get that creepy cack-yourself feeling you normally only get when Scaries are around. My hands are shaking, no word of a lie. Moke looks how I feel. We slip out the back way, avoiding the hockey insanity in the hall, and head down the link tunnel to Dock Two.

The lights there are down to power conserve. Half of me wants all the alcohol in my system flushed out so I can clean my headspace. The other half wants another skull to steady me.

All our platoon kit and hardware is stacked up in Dock Two where the extract discharged it. Most of the carrier packs are heavy-duty mil grade, but some look disarmingly like Mendozer's box. Just smaller. Like they were made for parts, not whole bodies.

Nice thought to dwell on.

Moke watches the door, twitching from foot to foot, while I locate one of the gun crates in the pile of kit. I slide it out, punch in the authority code, and crack the lid. Half a dozen platoon weapons are racked in the cradle inside. There's a smell of gun oil. All Steiner GAW-Tens. I pull one, like Boring told me to. I pull one, and four clips.

The Steiner Groundtroop Assault Weapon Ten A.2 is our signature dish. Some platoons these days favour the Loman BR, and that's a fine bit of business, but it's big, and really long when it's wearing a flash sleeve, and it's not a great fit in a tight space where you might need to turn at short notice. The Middlemen have been using GAWs since bloody always, Eights back during the last war, then every model upgrade ever since through to the current Ten A.2s. The Ten is compact but chunky. It loads low friction drive band HV, in either AP or hollowpoint, and it's got full selective options. I take hollowpoint out of the crate, not AP. We're in a pressurized atmospheric environment. Penetration control is going to be an issue.

I'm clacking the first clip into the receiver as I rejoin Moke.

"Screw this bollocks," he says to me. "This is a joke. This is someone's idea of a bloody joke. When I find out who, I'm going to de-dick him."

No argument from me.

"Unless it's Boring," he adds.

I nod. I let Moke hang on to that possibility, because it's more comforting than the alternatives.

But I saw the look in Boring's eyes.

This isn't his prank.

Boring's in medical with Neats. They've got the walk-in fridge open. It smells of ammonia and detergent wash. The light in the fridge is harsh and unflattering, sterile UV. Moke and I wander in. I wonder if it's like a normal fridge and the light only comes on when the door's open. I don't volunteer to stay inside to find out. There's no handle on the inside.

Boring and the Sergeant are sliding caskets off the rack and opening them. Just from the way the caskets move on the rollers, you can tell there's nothing in them.

"Checking the Surge got the right one?" I ask.

Neats nods.

Boring slams the last box back into place with an angry whip of his wrist, and it bangs against its cavity. "Nothing," he says.

Behind us, we can hear the whoops and crashes of the hockey still in play.

"Makes no sense," says Neats.

"Somebody like to explain this?" a voice interrupts.

We turn. It's the Surge. He looks pissed off that we're trespassing on his domain.

Boring explains. He uses the fewest possible words. He explains how we thought the Surge had pulled the wrong box, and that we came in here to find the right one. He explains they're all empty.

Now the Surge looks twice as pissed off. "That can't be," he says.

"Tell us about it," says Moke.

The Surge pushes past us into the fridge. "No," he says, "I don't know what's happened to Mendozer. That's a thing in itself."

"And?" asks Neats.

The Surge is checking the ends of the caskets for label slips. "Nine Platoon lost a guy in a cargo accident on their way through last week. They left him here."

"What are you saying?" asks Boring.

"I'm saying Mendozer or no Mendozer, these shouldn't all be empty."

He locates the label he's looking for and pulls the box out. There's nothing in it, but it's not clean inside. There's like a residue, wet, like glue. There's a smell too, when the lid opens. Decomp. You can smell it despite the extractor fans and the detergent.

"The bloke from Nine should be in this one," says the Surge.

"What are you saying?" Moke asks. He's starting to get that whine in his voice. "What are you saying, exactly? We've lost two stiffs now?"

"Someone's taken a joke way too far," says the Surge. "Cadavers don't just get up and walk away."

He looks at us. He sees the look we're giving him. He realizes it was a really bad choice of words.

We go back out into medical. Boring sends Neats and Moke to round up everyone else and get them into the Rec. If this is a joke, he's going to scare an admission out of the perpetrator.

The Surge touches my arm. I see what he's pointing to.

"Lieutenant?" I say.

Boring comes over. There are spots of wet on the floor.

"I mopped up in here," says the Surge.

The spots dapple the tiles. They're brown, not red, like gravy. There's no indication of spray or arterial force. Something just dripped.

Boring heads towards the bio-store that joins medical. The door's ajar. There are graft banks of vat tissue in here, flesh slabs, dermis sheets and organ spares kept in vitro jars. We can smell the wet as we approach the door. Wet and decomp, spoiled meat.

We hear something.

I catch Boring's eye and offer him the Steiner. He signs me to keep it, to keep it and cover him. I swallow. I toggle to single shot, ease off the safety, and rest my right index finger on the trigger guard. The stock's tight in the crook of my shoulder, the barrel down but ready to swing up. I feel naked without a body jacket. I'd have given real money for a full suit of ballistic laminate. The Surge drops back behind us. I edge in beside Boring. He picks up a tube-steel work chair by the seat back, one-handed, and uses the legs to push the door open. Like a lion tamer, I think.

There's something in the bio-store. It's down the end, in the shadows. The tops have been pulled off some of the vitro jars, and slabs have been taken out. There's fluid on the floor. One of the jars has tipped, and stuff is drooling out like clear syrup. I can see a pink, ready-to-implant lung lying on the tiles, like a fish that's fallen out of a net onto the deck.

The thing in the shadows is gnawing at a flesh slab. It sees us. It rises.

The fact that it isn't Mendozer is hardly a consolation prize. It's just steak. A man-shaped lump of steak, raw and bloody, tenderized with a hammer. It has eyes and teeth, but they're none too secure, and it's wearing the soaked remains of a 2nd Infantry jump suit. It takes a step towards us. It makes a gurgling sound. I can see white bone sticking out through its outer layer of mangled meat in places.

"Bang it," says Boring. "Put it down."

Not an order he needs to repeat. I bring the nose of the Steiner up, slip my finger off the guard onto the trigger, and put one right into the centre of its body mass. In the close confines of the bio-store, the discharge sounds like an empty skip being hit with a metal post. Booming, ringing, resounding.

The thing falters. It doesn't drop.

I punch off two more, then another pair. The post hits the skip again: boom-boom, boom-boom. I see each round hit, see each round make the thing stagger. I hear the vitro jars on the shelves behind it shatter and burst.

Boring snatches the Steiner off me. In my fuddle, despite my best intentions, I've slotted AP rounds. The hyper velocity slugs are punching right through the advancing mass, not even stopping to shake hands and say hello.

Boring ejects the clip. I yank one of the spares from my pocket, this time checking it's got an HP stencil on it. Boring slams it home, charges the gun and bangs off on semi.

The hollowpoints deform and expand as they hit, preventing

overpenetration, while simultaneously creating maximum tissue damage. They gift their entire kinetic force to the target. The thing kind of splatters. It shreds from the waist up in a dense cloud of wet and vaporized tissue and bone chips.

Now it drops.

We approach. There's wet everywhere, splashed up all surfaces. Flecks of gristle are stuck to the wall, the ceiling, the jars, even the light shade.

The Surge grabs a lamp and a stainless steel probe. He squats down and pokes the mess.

"What the hell is it?" I ask, hoarse.

The Surge holds up the probe in the beam of his lamp. There's a set of tags hanging off it.

"Hangstrum, private first class, Nine Platoon."

"The one killed in the accident?"

"The pattern of injuries is consistent with crush damage from a cargo mishap," says the Surge. He looks at Boring. "Not counting the mincing," he adds.

"Any idea why he was walking around like it was a normal thing to do?" asks Boring.

"Maybe he wasn't dead," I say, grasping at straws. Reassuring straws. "Maybe Nine should've held a wake to make sure he was—"

"He was dead," says the Surge. "I read the path. I even checked in the box when we first came on station."

"But his body was in the fridge with Mendozer's," says Boring. It's not so much a question.

"Yes," the Surge says.

Oh, it'll all come out later. It always does. The stuff we don't know about the Scaries. The stuff we're still learning about how they tick, why they tick, their biological cycle, what they do down there in the blind-as-midnight darkness of Scary Land. We're still learning about how they kill us, how their bioweapons work, how they evolve as they learn more about our anatomy from killing us.

The techs don't even know for sure yet whether it's part of their regular life cycle, or just something they developed specially for us. It wasn't claws the Scaries killed Mendozer with; it was ovipositors. Parasitic micro-larvae, jacking the blood cells of his cooling corpse, joyriding around his system, multiplying, leaching out into the other dead meat in the fridge, hungry for organic building blocks to absorb.

Even now, we don't know what they'd do to living tissue. We don't take the chance to find out. Incinerators are SOP. Incinerators, or disintegration charges. The Surge keeps grumbling about airborne particles and microspores, about tissue vapour and impact spatter contamination. But Boring tells him to zip it. We've got bleach and incinerators and sterile UV, and that's all, so it'll have to be enough.

We find Mendozer back in the Rec. He'd been shuffling around the halls of Relay Delta aimlessly, lost, late for his own wake. Everyone stops and stares at him, baffled, drunk. Fewry actually raises a hockey stick like a club to see him off, like you'd chase away a stray dog.

Mendozer's blank-eyed. Glazed over. His mouth is slack, and his chin and chest are bruised black and yellow where the Surge tried to save him and then stapled him back up.

He makes a sound I'll never forget. Boring doesn't hesitate, even though it's Mendozer and it's got Mendozer's face. He hits him with the rest of the HP clip.

Boring says something, later on, when we've washed the Rec down with bleach, dumped the remains in the furnace, opened the rest of the bottles.

He says the wake was Command's idea. When he signalled them that we were bringing back a casualty, they advised him to watch it to see what happened.

Like it wasn't the first time. Like they were trying to establish a pattern. Like they were conducting an experiment to see what happened to the things that the Scaries killed. An experiment with us as lab rabbits. Middlemen, Middlemen, same as bloody usual. Fun, not to mention frolics.

We were going to miss Mendozer. Of course we were. I'm just glad Boring decided not to. Emptied the rest of the clip making sure he didn't. I'll drink to that.

I wish that extract would hurry up and get here.

THE PYRE OF NEW DAY

Catherine Asaro

Who cares what befalls the inhabitants of a failing colony world when nobody will admit responsibility for its failure? Sauscony Lahaylia Valdoria: Jagernaut, that's who. Distinguished theoretical physicist, teacher, singer, former professional dancer and award-winning author, Catherine Asaro unveils a new chapter in the glittering history of the Skolian Empire – a story that features the incomparable Soz Valdoria.

Following up a BS with highest honours in Chemistry from UCLA with a Master's degree in Physics and a PhD in Chemical Physics from Harvard isn't the worst way to start a career. Becoming a visiting physics professor at the University of Maryland, Baltimore County and holding positions at various times at the University of Toronto and the Harvard-Smithsonian Center for Astrophysics isn't a bad way to continue. Doubtless this helps explain why Catherine Asaro is as renowned for building complex mathematical concepts into her fiction as she is for the action and romance it so often features.

HYPRON OPENED HIS eyes into the darkness and sensed emptiness. The house was too quiet. He called out to his brother. "Oxim? Are you there?"

Silence. Usually by this time, his brother was in the living room, listening to reports from the mainland areas of the colony.

"Lumos on," Hypron said.

The room remained dark. That surprised him less then the silence; the Evolving Intelligence, or EI, that ran the house had failed months ago. The backup systems worked, but they weren't reliable. He wanted to believe that was why he heard nothing from the other room, but the silence was in his mind as well, and that shook him, for he always sensed his brother's moods if the two of them weren't separated by too much distance.

Hypron slid to a small table by the bed and brushed a panel there, trying to toggle on the lumos. Nothing. The room stayed dark. With care, he eased off the bed, intending to sit on the floor, but he slipped and fell onto the ground with a thud, groaning as pain shot up his calves. At least he could still feel his legs. The sensation in them would probably go next.

Rolling onto his stomach was easy; after that, matters became more complicated. He braced his elbows on the floor and pulled his legs under him, but when he tried to kneel, his legs gave way and he pitched forward onto his stomach. With a grimace, he pushed up on his elbows and crawled across the floor, using his arms, dragging his legs.

The entire time, he kept searching for Oxim with his mind. He felt nothing, which meant his brother was either asleep or far away. Surely Oxim wouldn't come home without letting Hypron know he was back safely. Perhaps he had just fallen asleep on the sofa. Nearly a day had passed since their last full meal, and hunger gnawed at them both. Oxim had gone to find supplies, searching for an outpost or any place where survivors still lived out here. The mud-sloop didn't have enough fuel to travel any great distance, which meant if Oxim had ventured too far, he might be stranded and unable to return home.

When Hypron reached the bedroom door, he sat against it, catching his breath. Then he grabbed one of the bars he and Oxim had installed on the wall and pulled himself to his feet. Leaning against the door, he used it for the support his withered legs could no longer provide. Unbidden, memories came to him of when he had been healthy, when he could stride, run, jump, full of vigour.

He pushed away the images, hiding them in recesses of his mind where they wouldn't hurt so much. As he slid open the door, he hung on to it so he could stay upright. Outside, he made his way along the hallway using bars hammered into the walls, dragging his legs along. Despite the cool air, he was sweating by the time he reached the front room where he and his brother often sat in the evening, watching the holo-vid, reading, talking.

It was dark.

"Oxim, are you here?" he asked. "Did you fall asleep?"

No answer. No snores or grunts. Nothing.

He slid his hand across the wall until he found the control panel for the EI. He scraped at it, tapped the surface, banged it with his fist, all to no avail.

"House, answer!" Hypron said.

Silence.

He edged forward – and stumbled on some object. With a curse, he fell to his knees. Grabbing at whatever had tripped him, he caught a wheel of the mobile recliner he had built. It must have rolled out of its usual place when the house shifted on its floating supports. He pushed it against the wall and slid into the seat, his legs stretched in front of him, his arms draped over the armrests, his palms flat on the cool floor. The velvety darkness surrounded him with a quietude that could have comforted had he felt secure, but that offered only fear now, as he worried about Oxim.

He rolled the recliner across the room. If he opened the outside door, the blue moons would flood him with their cool light, and he could see if anything was out there. Or anyone. He easily reached the door, a crude airlock, little more than a double panel with a layer of air between. When he pushed its autolock, nothing happened. He tried the safety release, which was supposed to work even if the power failed, but it was either jammed or broken, because the door refused to budge.

Hypron exhaled in frustration. Maybe his brother couldn't get inside. With neither their house nor their personal comms working, Oxim had no way to contact him. They had also lost contact with the mainland when their neutrino transmitter failed. Hypron could fix it if they located replacement parts, but whatever remained of the colonial authority had stranded them out here with little recourse. They had never had many neighbors this far from the mainland, and only a few had survived the civil war that devastated the colony. Even more colonists had died in the aftermath of the war, when mud-pirates took to the seas and looted the drifting homesteads.

Although Oxim would never talk about it, Hypron knew his brother had killed to defend their home. Oxim had always been the protector. When Hypron's health had failed, a neurological disease that took more from him every year, Oxim became a caretaker as well. Without that lifeline, Hypron would have died on this godforsaken mudball of a world.

Oxim, where are you? Closing his eyes, Hypron let his thoughts spread outward, searching. Oxim was like everyone else; he didn't feel the ebb and flow of other people's moods. The rest of humanity inhabited a barren land where people knew only their own emotions. Hypron had starved his entire life for the touch of another mind like his, but Oxim came closer to understanding than anyone else. His mind was strong and deep, a bedrock to Hypron's mercurial moods.

For so long it had been just the two of them. Their parents had died in a mining accident when Oxim had been fifteen and Hypron eight. Oxim had gone to work in an ore refinery on the asteroid where they lived, but he insisted Hypron stay in school. At age fifteen, Hypron had joined him on the job, both of them saving their pay, day by day, year by year, until finally they had enough to escape the planetoid. Six years ago, on Hypron's twenty-third birthday, they had signed up as colonists for this world called New Day. So they had come here, full of optimism, to a colony that promised a sunrise in their lives. They had dreamed of so much: their own algae farm, air they could breathe, warm days, all those luxuries they had never known.

Sunrise. Right. He gritted his teeth and banished the memories, trying to clear his mind. Gradually his mood calmed and his thoughts expanded like ripples in a lake. On the edges of his awareness, far distant, he caught a mental warmth. Oxim? He tried to focus, but the sense drifted away from him.

Hypron wasn't certain how long he searched, but eventually he had to let go. He sagged in his chair, exhausted. His health had deteriorated until just this much effort wore him out. He would rest a bit and then see if he could fix the generator and open the door. The air still smelled fresh, and he was warm, so the house hadn't completely failed. After so many years of living on the edge of survival, he had learned a great deal about coping with faulty systems.

The darkness pressed in on him. It was lonely. Well, hell, he should be used to the loneliness. He had hoped to find a wife here, but he'd never had much luck, even in the beginning, when he had been healthy. He could meet women; they found him pleasant enough to look at. But they always ended up saying he was impractical, moody, unreliable. It wasn't that he minded work. He could toil for hours and never know time was passing. But the farm he and Oxim had started here, growing crust-algae in slop-flats, bored him mindless, and he came home every day stinking of sweat and mud. If he'd been a woman, he wouldn't have wanted to marry him, either. He'd joked that way once with a girl he liked, but instead of laughing, she had stared as if he were an idiot. So much for his sparkling humour.

Oxim claimed Hypron was out of his element, that he was an artist, a dreamer full of imagination. He swore Hypron just needed an outlet for his creativity. Hypron didn't see it. He wished he could be like the other colonists, satisfied with New Day. Except instead of a new life, they had come to failure. So many had died. And each time another colonist passed away, the survivors mourned, until it scarred Hypron's mind, for he couldn't turn off the grief, neither for himself nor for what he felt from others around him.

A thought came to him. Oxim's filter mask might have clogged. It was unlikely; Oxim hadn't been outside long enough, and he always took a spare. But the worry lodged in Hypron's mind. If his brother was unconscious, put out by the noxious atmosphere, that could explain why his mind felt distant.

Hypron felt along the wall to the storage niche at waist height. He pulled out a filter mask and fastened the mesh over his mouth and nose, then crumpled a spare mask into his pocket. He had two options to open the door: repair the generator and return power, or break down the door and do repairs later. He knew from experience that even if he managed to fix the generator without replacement parts, it might take hours. If he could break the door, that would probably be a lot faster. Once he found Oxim, they could live in a back room until they fixed both the door and generator. They had equipped every room here with air filtration systems after the atmosphere of New Day had degraded so much, they couldn't breathe it for more than an hour. That had been two years ago. These days, they couldn't take it for more than fifteen minutes. If Oxim was trapped out there with a faulty mask, he needed help now, not in a few hours.

Steeling himself, Hypron grabbed a bar on the wall and yanked, twisting at the same time, trying to wrench it free. He kept pulling and twisting until sweat soaked his shirt.

With a screech, the bar tore away from the wall, and the momentum of his yank sent the recliner rolling backward as the bar thumped into his lap. Grunting, he stopped the rolling chair with his hands and pushed it back to the door. Then he hefted up the bar and swung at the airlock, and again, and again, hammering the recalcitrant barrier.

When the strained composite of the door finally buckled and collapsed, it sounded as if the house were groaning. Wet, warm air hit Hypron's face. Even wearing his mask, he couldn't escape the stench, and bile rose in his throat from the stink of fetid mud. Blue light poured across him, limning jagged pieces of the door that jutted up from the ground. The larger moon was full and overhead, the smaller one a fat crescent near the horizon. Bathed in their eerie light, a pier stretched in front of him from the doorway to a dock. Hypron inched his recliner out onto the pier, using his hands to clear a path as best he could. The mud-sea swelled around the house, endless, its fluorescent sea-mats glinting with iridescent specks like small islands in the vast, dark expanse.

As Hypron rolled forward, the pier swayed, its stabilizers as compromised as the rest of the house. Mud slopped over its sides and across his hands, oozing between his fingers, coating his skin, thick and granular with the remains of dead lobsterites no bigger than the tip of his finger. His palms scraped the rough pier as his hands slid through the gunk. The recliner had good traction, but in this mess, he could slide into the mud-sea, which teemed with fish-snakes that grew bigger every year. Then what? He doubted he could pull himself back onto the pier. He grimaced and tried to stop thinking.

As he neared the dock, a shadow at its end resolved into the sloop docked at the boathouse. It meant Oxim had returned. The big seine net was attached to the pier to snag the smaller, edible eels, so Oxim must have disembarked from the ship. If he had collapsed out here with a faulty mask, gods only knew how sick he might be by now.

The dock shook as Hypron rolled onto it, and mud squirted between its uneven boards, slowing the recliner. He forced his way onward, his biceps straining. The sloop was pulling on its tether, swaying in the lethargic waves—

Hypron hit a barrier. He stopped, peering into the blue-tinged night. A ridge stretched in front of him, a few handspans high. He felt along it … uneven and soft, like a bulky sack …

A body.

Suddenly he couldn't breathe. He struggled to draw in air and gagged on the rancid smell. Bracing himself, he searched the body until he found the neck. His fingertips scraped the bumps of a raised tattoo there. An ID mark. Imperial Space Command, or ISC, provided one for every colonist, a means to identify anyone.

Anyone.

"Oxim!" Hypron shook his brother. "Oximsonner! Wake up!" He fumbled with Oxim's mask, looking for the toggles that would tell him how badly it had failed. They were smooth on a working mask, but became progressively rougher as the gunk that saturated the atmosphere clogged the filter.

The toggles were as smooth as a burnished coin.

"Oxim," he whispered. "Answer me." He pulled up the sleeves of his brother's jacket to take his pulse.

Nothing.

No. *No.* This couldn't be. It *couldn't.* Yet he didn't sense his brother's mind even here, right next to him. Clenching Oxim's bicep, he planted his other hand on the pier and strained to push the recliner backward, bringing his brother with him. He just barely moved the body. Taking a ragged breath, he tried again and pulled Oxim another handspan.

Bit by excruciating bit, Hypron dragged his brother home. He struggled to ignore the stiffness of Oxim's muscles. *Rigor mortis* his mind screamed, and he refused to acknowledge it, as if that could undo this agony. But nothing could change the truth, that mud-pirates prowled out here, using weapons they had stolen from ruins of the colony. They killed the owners of homesteads and looted the remains with impunity. No one went after them, no retribution even from the supposedly oh-so-formidable ISC. No one gave a flaming damn about this world that was tearing itself apart while its desperate colonists killed one another.

Hypron didn't realize he had reached the house until he rammed backward into the door frame. He choked in a breath. Only a little further. He strained to pull Oxim's body over the broken remains of the entrance, and debris ripped his skin. Mud seeped into his bleeding cuts, probably infecting him with gods only knew what. He didn't care. He would rather die than leave Oxim to rot out in this miserable night.

Finally they were inside. Like a pressure valve that suddenly released, knowledge burst within him. Oxim was dead. *Dead.* The one constant in his world, the one person who cared whether he existed, the one person he loved, was gone.

He had no food. He had no way to contact anyone. He couldn't pilot the mud-sloop alone. He had used all his resources except one – the projectile pistol. He could make his death quick instead of long and gruesome from starvation and exposure.

Hypron cradled Oxim in his arms, his head bent over his brother's body while he cried.

"This planet is disgusting," Soz Valdoria said.

She stood at the prow of the mud-racer while the ship cut through the viscous glop of a sea. Gunk splattered her uniform, the black knee-boots, leather pants and vest. It left dark blotches on the two gold armbands around each of her leanly muscled biceps, the sign of her rank as a Jagernaut Secondary in Imperial Space Command.

The sea ahead suddenly roiled and churned. An enraged creature once again lifted out of it, a snakelike monster with giant green eyes and a body armoured in purple and silver scales. Just the part of its neck that showed above the mud was four times Soz's height and twice as thick as her body. Fangs ringed its huge mouth. It reared above the ship, whipping back and forth while screaming its challenge at her.

"Just a little closer, you ugly reject from hell," she told the monster. "Come on, babe."

Yells were coming from behind Soz, someone shouting at her to go below the deck, but she ignored them. This critter had pissed her off.

Its teeth glinted as its maw gaped above her, ready to snap her in two. Soz raised her jumbler, a mammoth black gun that glittered in the watery sunlight of this ridiculously named planet, New Day. She waited until she had a clear shot straight down the snake's throat.

She fired.

The jumbler shot sub-electronic particles known as abitons, often called wimpons because of their low energy. They annihilated bitons, making flashes of orange light. In the air, the anti-particles created only a few sparkles – but when the beam hit the serpent, its head disintegrated in a dramatic burst of light. The beheaded neck snapped wildly over the boat. If the racer hadn't been marginally intelligent, the spasming monster would have shattered the ship's mast. As it was, the pole barely managed to bend aside in time to avoid being smashed.

With a final whip of its body, the headless serpent slammed into the mud and vanished below the surface. Black waves leaped above the boat and rained sludge over the deck and Soz.

"Gods," she muttered. This planet deserved to be shoved into a black hole.

"Are you out of your flaming mind?" someone shouted behind her.

Now that the commotion was dying down, Soz turned around. Dale Yaetes, the racer's captain, was standing there, soaked in mud, staring as if she had grown a second head. Rex Blackstone was leaning his towering, bulky self against a strut of the ship not far away, his brawny arms crossed, his Jagernaut uniform covered with mud. Yaetes was wearing a silver filter mask that covered his nose and mouth, but neither Soz nor Rex needed one; their physical augmentations included filters in their respiratory tracts that could deal with the atmosphere for short periods. As usual, Rex looked intimidating. But Soz felt his mood. He was struggling not to laugh. Honestly. She ought to throw him in the brig. Except their starfighters didn't have brigs, lucky man.

"I don't think I was ever in my mind," she told Yaetes. "So I suppose I'm out of it."

"You can't do that!" He waved at the revolting sea, which was still sloshing around. "Those serpents kill anything that threatens them."

"Didn't kill me." Soz hefted her gun, which unfortunately was drenched in mud. She'd have to take it apart to clean it properly. Damn. Dismantling a miniature particle accelerator was no small task.

"It wanted to eat her," Rex said. "The poor thing."

She glowered at him. "And you just stood there?" In truth, she knew Rex had her back. He had in all the years they had flown together in a Jag squad, from the days when they had been cadets at the Academy until now, when she commanded the squad and he served as her second.

Rex grinned at her. "I felt sorry for the critter, the way it was so outmatched."

"Colonel Valdoria," Yaetes said. "If you decide to kill every creature that looks at us cross-eyed, we'll never get the colonists evacuated."

He had a point. Monsters infested this planet. She couldn't get rid of them all; besides which, destroying the mutated wildlife here wouldn't help what remained of the colonists. This world was too far gone.

"We'll set up a base as soon as we find a suitable location," she said. Then she added, "I'm a Secondary, Captain. The rank is roughly equivalent to colonel, but not the same."

"Ah. Yes. Of course." He looked as flustered now as he had yesterday when her squad had arrived with the rest of the ISC forces to help the beleaguered colony. He didn't shield his mind well; she could tell he thought she looked too young for a colonel. Actually, he thought she looked like a sex goddess from an erotic holovid. What a bizarre thought. Some of his images were vivid enough that she picked them up even with her own mind fortified by mental barriers. No way could she contort her body into those positions. She wondered if he realized Jagernauts were psions. They had to be, given that they linked mentally to their ships. She hadn't said anything because he was a good officer who genuinely wanted to help these people, and he'd be mortified if he knew she had picked up his, um, creative imagination.

Rex walked forward with that easy gait of his, his jumbler holstered at his hip. Soz nodded to him, and he nodded back, acknowledging her thanks for his backup. Yaetes watched as if he were observing the tribal rites of some dangerous alien race. Soz supposed he had reason. ISC classified Jagernauts as a different species from *Homo sapiens* because they were human weapons with biomech systems in their bodies that let them think, move, and react faster and with more strength than normal humans. Soz thought it was absurd to call them another species, given that Jagernauts and humans could interbreed just fine. Regardless of how ISC labelled them, their function remained the same. Kill.

Well, not always. Sometimes they ended up on missions like this one, cleaning up ISC messes. Not that ISC would admit they had screwed up royally here on New-drilling Day. The terraforming had become unstable, turning the supposed paradise into crud. Another few decades and the planet would be uninhabitable. Her squad had come with a recovery team assigned to help the colonists. Not many remained; most of those who had survived the miserable environment had killed each other off in a vicious civil war that erupted over the shortage of supplies and livable habitats.

Soz was mad. This should never have happened. What the blazes had been going on at HQ? Oh, she knew. It was politics. She hated politics. ISC was in bed with the Newland Corporation that had bought and terraformed this world. Corporate hadn't wanted to admit to such a spectacular failure because it would bankrupt them. So they pretended it didn't happen, giving the colonists stupid assurances they would fix everything even while they scrambled to cut their losses. It had taken a special commission determined to investigate rumours of the growing death toll to blow apart the scandal. Damn it, ISC should have paid more attention.

A ways behind Captain Yaetes, the hatch to the below-decks compartments opened, and a lanky woman with short yellow hair climbed out into the sticky wind, her face protected by one of the silvery masks.

Who is that? Soz thought.

Jen Foley, the navigator, the node implanted in her spine thought. It communicated by firing bio-electrodes in her neurons, which she experienced as thoughts.

Foley. Soz committed it to memory. She was still learning names of the crew Yaetes had brought onboard today. She felt the navigator's mood. Foley was more disturbed by the mud than the sea serpent. That was all Soz could tell, though; like most people, Foley instinctively raised natural barriers to protect her mind. Soz had them as well, but hers were more sophisticated given that she had trained for decades to use her mental abilities. Regardless of how shaken the navigator felt, she came forward with a steady walk, which Soz respected.

"All secure below," Foley said as she joined them.

"You all right?" Captain Yaetes asked her.

"I'll live." Foley grimaced. "I'm not so sure about the racer. It's thick with mud, including the engines. You hear how laboured they sound? If they stall, we can use sails to travel, but I don't like to depend on them. We need to dock and clean the engines."

Yaetes looked out at the sea stretching in every direction. "Dock where?"

Foley pointed southeast. "Satellite maps say an island is a few hours that way."

Soz's expertise was starships not water ships, but she could hear the uneven chugging of the engines. They should be cleaned now, not in a few hours. Surely they could find something closer. Locating the smallest settlements was a bit dicey because the atmosphere interfered with their sensors, all those particulates that saturated the air, a plethora of bacteria and microscopic insectoids. She could ask the flagship in orbit to step up their search, but Soz had an idea that could work faster and wouldn't draw resources away from other rescue operations. Closing her eyes, she eased down her mental shields. Her awareness spread out, across the mud ocean with its teeming, putrid life. Nothing...

Wait. A golden, clean warmth glowed amid the mess of New Day. Where...?

She opened her eyes. Rex had a glazed look very different from his usual laser-focus. His gaze met hers.

You catch that? Soz asked.

Something, he thought. **I'm not sure what. But strong.**

As Soz nodded, pain jabbed her temples. She raised her barriers again, protecting her mind, and lifted her arm, pointing northwest. "We go there," she told Yaetes and Foley.

"Nothing is out that way," Foley said. "Just mud, mud, and oh gosh, more freaking mud."

Soz smiled. She could get to like this Foley person. "It looks that way. But something is close by. If we find even a small outpost, we can commandeer it and set up a base. And you can clean your engines."

Yaetes shook his head. "I'm no military officer, just a merchant serving what's left of our outliers. So maybe I'm not used to ISC lingo. But what will you commandeer? Most likely all we'll find are dead people and shattered dreams."

Soz spoke quietly. "We'll use respect, Captain."

"If you're wrong about its location," he said, "we'll be even further from help."

"I'm sure it's there," Soz said. Why, she couldn't have said. But she had no doubt.

The door of the house was broken, the place had no power, and mud caked the living room. Soz wondered what had happened. It must have been recent; the mud was relatively fresh, if anything that disagreeable could be called "fresh".

She stood in the doorway of the damaged house and looked outside, checking the area. The sun glowed like a white-hot rivet overhead, and green-tinged clouds scudded across the dusky blue sky. She wondered who at the Newland Corporation had come up with the whacked idea of telling the settlers that the green came from chlorophyll. The colonists had scientists. They knew it was a lie. Every year more toxic compounds formed on New Day, including traces of green chlorine gas. It wasn't much, and most gathered in low areas rather than high in the atmosphere, but it took very little to poison humans and it could cause violent reactions. That was only one of thousands of problems here.

While Rex and the crew carried in equipment from the racer, Soz checked the house. The crew could bivouac in the living room. She needed a separate area for a command centre to coordinate the rescue efforts for this area. They hadn't found this homestead in time, but they might be able to help other survivors out here.

How had everything unravelled so badly on this world? She meant to find answers, and she didn't care whose politics she ruffled. So fine, she was no diplomat. But the people had come here with such dreams, and they deserved so much more than what Newland Corporation had handed them.

Foley came over to her. "We found a room for your office."

"Good." Soz could tell Foley was upset, but not why. "What's wrong?"

The navigator took a breath. "There are dead people in there."

Damn. "Show me."

Foley took her to a bedroom. It had a desk, a recliner on wheels, a bed, a mesh table with a glossy tech surface that had gone dark – and two bodies on the flex-metal floor. The men were of average height and similar age, possibly twins, one of them thinner than the other. Dried, caked mud covered them both.

Doctor Carlon, the racer's medic, was kneeling by the thinner man. Looking up, he pushed a lock of his tousled red hair out of his eyes. "This one is unconscious," he told Soz.

Relief sparked in her. Maybe they hadn't been too late after all. Her makeshift command centre could easily serve as a makeshift hospital, too. Kneeling by Carlon, she touched the man's neck. His pulse felt weak but steady. He had the face of a gaunt angel, with high cheekbones, a turned-up nose and a full mouth. His light brown hair had yellow sun-streaks.

"Can you help him?" she asked.

"Maybe," Carlon said, as laconic as always.

"He looks nearly starved."

"He is." Carlon slid his arms under the man's body. "We should put him someplace better."

Together, they carried the man to the rumpled bed. After they laid him down, Carlon went to work, injecting nanomeds to replenish his patient's depleted body. He set med-strips on the man's torso, and holos were soon rotating above them with displays of the fellow's muscles, skeleton, neural systems, and more, as well as large macro-molecules in bright colours that turned while Carlon examined them. Oddly, despite the man's critical condition, something about him seemed *right*. Soz couldn't figure it out. Something warm? No, not warm.

She drew in a sharp breath. "He's a psion."

Carlon kept working. "I thought you couldn't tell when someone was unconscious."

"Normally, no. But his mind is so strong, it comes through even now." She stroked the man's forehead. His skin felt gritty, and green-brown flakes of mud scattered on the bed. In his gaunt face, his high cheekbones looked finely carved, as if he were a statue rather than a living man. Flustered, she pulled back her hand. Enraged mud-monsters she could deal with, but handsome empaths were a different story. She had no problem with Jagernauts like Rex; he was as cocky as they came, and she understood that fine. It

was the shy, gentle ones that disconcerted her. Why she thought
that description applied to this man, she didn't know, but she felt
certain about it.

"Will he live?" she asked.

"If he makes it through the next few hours." Carlon glanced at
the man's legs. "In a manner of speaking."

That didn't sound good. "Speaking how?"

"Something is wrong with his legs." Carlon shook his head.
"Fungus, virus, something. Native to this planet, I'd say. Attacked
his body. And it's getting worse."

She scowled. "The colonists were supposed to have
immunizations."

"Supposed to have a lot," Carlon said. "A lot failed. Hell, the
blasted planet failed."

Soz had no answer to that.

Hypron opened his eyes into darkness. He drowsed for a moment –
until he remembered.

Oxim was dead.

It all rushed back, the shock, the grief, the misery. He hadn't
expected to wake again, but here he was, alive, still trapped in this
cursed body.

When Hypron's body had begun to fail, the process had been
gradual. The doctors had helped at first, even reversing the with-
ering of his legs for a time. In the same way, when this homestead
had failed, it hadn't happened all at once. Their life's work had
decayed slowly, and they had never believed it would be permanent.
The process would reverse, the air would become clean, Newland
Corporation would fix the problems. It had been miserable, yes, but
bearable. Their bond as brothers kept them going, the partnership
that had seen them through the death of their parents, their meagre
survival on the asteroid, and the decline of their fortunes here.
During it all, they had been each other's strength.

Now he had nothing except starvation.

And yet…his hunger was gone, not completely, but greatly
receded. He felt clean and fresh. The pain from his injuries and his

nausea from the atmosphere had faded. In their place was a warmth so welcome, he wondered if he had died. Perhaps this was how it felt when your body gave up and death took you gently into oblivion.

A memory stirred. He had sensed a mental warmth when he searched for Oxim. He felt it now, too, but no longer far away. It was all around him, powerful, luminous.

He tried to say, **Who's there?** but no words came out.

Something moved behind him. A woman answered sleepily. **Sorry ... needed to rest a moment ... floor hard ...**

What the hell? Those words were in his *mind*. So he was dead. That was the only explanation why a woman would appear in his bed and talk in his mind. He hadn't expected death to be in the dark, but at least he wasn't alone. He rolled onto his back, wincing as pain stabbed his bruised, cut-up body. It didn't seem fair that he still hurt if he no longer lived. His cheek came to rest against some-one's head, and she shifted position, her forehead rubbing his ear.

Are you a hallucination? he asked.

No response. Perhaps this was his dying delirium. Well, so, it was *his* delirium, and a pleasant one at that, given the lean curves of her body. Normally he was reticent with women; he would probably pause even if he found one in his bed. Not that such had ever happened in real life. But this was surreal, a creation of his mind, perhaps of his death. So he brushed his lips across her forehead.

The woman stirred against him. He waited, but she didn't protest, so he lowered his head, searching for her mouth. When his lips found hers, he kissed her, first softly, then more deeply. He knew for certain then that she was a creation of his mind, because she kissed him back instead of slapping him. Her lips felt unexpectedly warm for a hallucination.

As their kiss deepened, though, her mood changed, going from unfocused sleepiness to a brighter awareness.

With a start, the woman jerked away from him. "Gods almighty!" she said, scrambling into a sitting position. "I ought to throw *myself* in the brig."

Well, damn. That didn't sound like anything he would hallu-cinate. Her retreat had taken away the heat of her body, but her mind remained with its enfolding warmth. It somehow kept the worst of his grief at bay.

"Why are you here?" he said.

"I'm sorry." She sounded mortified. "I didn't mean to take advantage. I swear. I had only planned to rest for a moment. I hadn't expected to fall asleep. Honestly."

He wished she didn't sound so embarrassed. He'd rather enjoyed it. "Who are you?"

"Soz Valdoria," she said. "I command a Jagernaut squad assigned to this planet." With apology, she added, "I'm afraid I've commandeered your house."

He must have heard wrong. *Jagernaut?* One of the elite, inhuman killing machines created by ISC? He wouldn't hallucinate a monster in his bed.

"For flaming sake," she grumbled. "We aren't monsters."

He *hadn't* said that aloud. Gods, this person could hear him think. His eyes were adjusting to the darkness, and dim blue light leaked in from somewhere. He could see her profile, the small nose, the hair curling around her cheeks and shoulders, tousled and untamed. She didn't look like a monster. She was pretty. Her soft face contrasted with her dark vest and pants, which smelled like rich leather. Her mech-tech gauntlets had scraped his arm when she moved and barbaric armbands glinted around each of her biceps. This seemed less and less like a hallucination. But if he were alive, that meant he still existed in a universe without Oxim.

Hypron spoke in a low voice. "My brother?"

He felt her recognition. She knew who he meant. He had never picked up another person's emotions so well. Nor was it only her moods; a few of her thoughts came through as well, strong ones on the surface of her mind, including her misty image of Oxim's body on the floor. His grief surged and he withdrew into himself.

"I'm sorry." She awkwardly drew his head into her lap and stroked his hair, her gestures gentle despite being clumsy.

Hypron couldn't answer; he could only think that he hadn't even buried Oxim. He should have given his brother a funeral pyre in the sea.

"We can arrange the ceremony," Soz said in a low voice.

He didn't understand how she knew what he needed, or why she would help, but in the vulnerability of this half-dream he simply answered, *Thank you*.

She murmured, he didn't know what, only that it soothed. He lay with his head in her lap, and eventually the grief receded enough for him to doze fitfully.

Some time later, the door scraped open. "Commander?" a man said in the dark.

Soz spoke. "Here, Carlon. On the bed."

The man cleared his throat. "Uh … oh."

"I'm just sitting here, Doctor," Soz growled.

Carlon, a doctor apparently, spared them any comment on the sleeping arrangements. "Got a message from the mainland," he told her. "They're evacuating colonists offworld."

Soz said only, "Good," but her relief washed over Hypron.

"How's the patient?" Carlon asked.

"He woke up for a while," Soz said. "He's sleeping again."

"If he woke up, he'll live." Carlon sounded far more pleased than Hypron felt about it.

The covers rustled as Soz eased Hypron's head back on the pillow. He heard more than felt her slide off the bed. "I need to get back to work," she said.

"No, you don't," Carlon told her. "You need to sleep. My file here says you've been up thirty-two hours straight."

"My biomech web makes stimulants to keep me awake." Her voice receded as her footsteps crossed the room. "Believe me, after we straighten out this mess I'll sleep for a day."

Hypron listened to their voices fade. They were evacuating the colony? The last he had heard, Corporate wouldn't let anyone leave, or at least they would neither authorize nor cover the costs of departures, which was equivalent to forbidding them, since few colonists could afford offworld transport or obtain documents for resettlement without help. Rumours had circulated that Corporate was blocking offworld communications even as they assured the colonists everything would be fine.

Liars. If they had evacuated earlier, Oxim would be alive.

"Here." Soz rolled Hypron's chair up to the dichromesh glass that made up the entire north wall of the living room. With people to help him into the seat, he didn't need it so near the floor, so he had raised the seat.

"Thanks," he said, his voice rusty. This was the first time in ages he had looked out the window, which had stopped being transparent several years ago. Captain Yaetes and his people had fixed it, and now they were repairing the door. Another woman was sitting at the console by the far wall, working on the house EI.

Soz stood behind Hypron. Her reflection showed in the glass as she looked over his head and through the window-wall. Two sailors from the racer were outside with Rex Blackstone, the other Jagernaut. As Hypron watched, they slid a raft from the dock into the sluggishly roiling sea. Oxim's pyre. They had built it from dismantled pieces of the house. It seemed a fitting end for what remained of their home, which Hypron would have to abandon when he evacuated.

The other crew here inside the house joined them at the window. Outside, Rex lit the torch he had made and laid it in the dried sea-vines heaped on the raft. Flames soon engulfed the pyre. The raft drifted away from the dock, burning brightly in the bitter sunlight.

A tear ran down Hypron's cheek. Soz rested her hands on his shoulders, a simple gesture, but welcome. The fresh scent of her bath soap drifted around him. She thought she was shielding her mind, and probably she was from anyone else, but he felt her mood. She mourned with him, unable to close his grief out of her mind. He affected her, he wasn't sure how, but she *noticed* him. Desired him. How strange. Although some women had found him attractive before his illness, most of those among the colonists preferred rugged muscle-bound types. Yet Soz *really* liked the way he looked. Whatever features and body type appealed to her, apparently he had both. She didn't care that he was different; it troubled her only because she realized how deeply it bothered him. In a different world, he would have savoured her unexpected interest.

Today he could see only his brother's pyre.

"Goodbye, Oxim," he said softly. "Sleep well."

Eventually the flames died and the raft sank beneath the mud. Rex returned to the racer with the two sailors, and within moments the craft was nosing out into the sea. Yaetes and the others went back to their repairs. The captain had sent Rex with the ship so the rest of them could work here with Soz on plans for relocating any survivors they found.

"How long will it take them to reach the mainland?" Hypron asked, watching the racer.

"Normally, about six hours," Soz said. "But with their search, it'll take longer."

He turned his recliner so he was facing her. "I doubt they'll find any settlers alive. Those people your orbital system located are probably pirates." The words were sour in his mouth, for he knew now how Oxim died. The doctor had done an autopsy. Beaten to death. The murderers had left their brand on him, a pirate tattoo, as if he were another notch in their list of crimes. Hypron didn't know where to put his fury. He hated even more that it had happened right outside their home while he had lain inside, exhausted and asleep.

Soz murmured, and a mental glow spread over him. He wondered if she even knew she was doing it. He thought of the way she had held him last night. She believed she was clumsy in offering comfort, awkward with words. She had no idea. She didn't need to say anything. These moments with her gave him so much, the balm of human touch after he had lost everything.

She sat on a stack of crates someone had carried inside, bringing her eyes level with his. It seemed incongruous that one of ISC's most notorious killers had such a sweet face. He wished he could paint a holo-portrait using special lights for her hair, the way it glistened black, then shaded into wine-red and ended in metallic gold, tousling around her shoulders. She had changed out of her uniform into a blue snug-suit that did nothing to hide her curves. He didn't believe she was a combat machine. Her mind was a sun, warm and vibrant.

Then again, he only picked up her outermost thoughts. She wasn't armed now, but he had seen her cleaning that gun of hers in the bedroom earlier, a mammoth weapon with a thick, ugly snout.

"What will you do after you evacuate?" she asked.

"I don't know," he admitted. "I've nowhere to go."

"No home?"

"I grew up on an asteroid. I was a miner." He hit the heel of his hand against his useless thigh. "I can't go back there like this."

"So you can't work?" Soz asked. Then she winced. "Sorry. That was rude."

"It's all right." He didn't mind. People here went out of their way to avoid mentioning his illness. Most wouldn't even look at him, as if one glance would cause them to catch whatever was killing him. He preferred Soz's matter-of-fact acknowledgement that yes, he was sick.

"I'll find something," he said. What, he had no idea, given his lack of training for anything except hard labour. Even healthy, he would have less value to prospective employers than a labour robot, because unlike him, bots didn't require food or sleep.

"Secondary Valdoria!" a man called. "You better take a look at this."

As Soz stood up, turning towards the door, Hypron glanced over. Captain Yaetes was standing in front of the view screen by the door, which they had fixed, and he was staring hard at whatever showed there. Looking through the window-wall, Hypron saw a mud-frigate docking outside, looming and ugly, its weathered masts pocked and leaning.

Pirate ship.

Soz scowled at the frigate, annoyed again, as with the mud monster. Sailors in ragged shirts and trousers were disembarking from the noxious vessel, men and women with tarnished filter masks. Some were armed with projectile pistols, others with laser carbines.

"Well, shit," Soz said.

Yaetes pressed his hand against the new door, which offered a dubious protection given that they hadn't yet installed its lock. "They'll kill us for this homestead."

"Not on my watch," Soz said. She really wished creatures, human or otherwise, would quit hampering her attempts to rescue these people. Twelve pirates had stepped onto the dock, and three more were in sight on the frigate. Although the masts indicated the vessel could travel by sail, she had no doubt it possessed powerful engines as well. "They must have good tech shrouds for that ship. Illegal shrouds. Otherwise, we'd have known they were here."

"How would we know?" Yaetes asked. "My racer doesn't have surveillance equipment."

"I do," Soz said. "It's part of me." She studied the invaders as they strode up the pier. From outside, they couldn't see through the window-wall, but they probably knew how many people were inside. "They must've been watching us. When the racer left, they moved in."

Carlon came over and handed Yaetes a projectile pistol. "Seven of us," the doctor said. He motioned towards the pirates. "Fifteen of them."

Hypron clenched his fist on the arm of the recliner. "I won't surrender my house."

Soz felt his calm – and his fatalistic determination. He would rather die than leave his home to pirates. He would fight them for as long as he breathed, however he could manage, until they killed him. Well, hell. She didn't intend for anyone to die.

"What weapons do we have?" she asked.

Yaetes glanced at Hypron and hefted the pistol. "Any besides this?"

Hypron shook his head. "Just that."

The captain tapped the holstered gun on his hip, a second pulse pistol. "I have this." To Soz, he added, "And there's that monster you were cleaning. That's it."

Three guns. Soz nodded. She could work with that. "Don't challenge them. Stay calm, and they won't see you as a threat." With that, she strode for the bedroom. She distantly felt the minds of the pirates. Her training in empathic surveillance let her dissect that vague impression; they wouldn't kill the people here right away unless they felt threatened, but it wouldn't take much to push them over the edge.

She picked up the people in the house more clearly. Yaetes had tensed like a cable pulled taut, but he was calm. Although Carlon didn't want to fight, he would if necessary. The woman who had been fixing the EI was scared, but Soz didn't think she would panic. The other man and woman were more tightly strung, more of a risk. Hypron wasn't scared, he was *angry*, furious over his limited ability to defend his home.

Soz pulled back from their minds. She couldn't risk too strong a connection; her empathic ability could cripple her in combat if it swamped her in the emotions of other people in the battle.

Inside the bedroom, she grabbed her jumbler off the desk. As she checked her weapon, the door of the house slammed open.

"Real subtle," she muttered. Banging doors offered no tactical advantage, so why do it? All they achieved was to reveal that they wanted to make a big entrance. That kind of bravado often came with overconfidence or a need to prove themselves that could be a weakness. She felt an ego from one of the intruders as big as a narcissist's mirror. Another reason they wouldn't start killing right away; he wanted an audience.

Node, activate jumbler link, Soz thought.

Activated, her spinal node answered. It sent pulses to biothreads in her body. They linked to sockets in her wrist that connected to her gauntlets, which could transmit messages to her jumbler. A sense of *linking* came to her as the gun locked on her neural patterns, clicking her into a well-known mental space. She released the safety on the weapon with a flick of her thumb.

A voice boomed in the front room. "All of you, over by the window. And someone get that coward hiding in the bedroom."

So they knew she was here. No surprise there. If their shrouds could hide a fuel-powered frigate, their sensors were probably similarly advanced. She walked into the hall, but it was still empty, another sign of their overconfidence. They expected an easy capture here. The only working exit from the house was the front door, so she had no obvious means of escape.

Soz held the jumbler down by her side as she entered the living room, neither hiding her weapon nor offering challenge. Yaetes, Carlon and two of the crew were with Hypron at the window. The woman who had been working on the EI now stood by the console, her face pale. The pirates, five women and seven men, were filing in through the front doorway. Damn mud-slugs. They had damaged the new door that Yaetes and his people had worked so hard to replace.

A muscular man with a craggy face and buzzed black hair was pulling off his filter mask. The huge ego emanated from him. The frigate captain, probably. Mesh nets and rivets studded his dark clothes. All very intimidating, supposedly, but none of it actually looked functional.

The captain scowled at Soz, his gaze raking over her jumbler. "What the hell is that? Throw it here, sweet cheeks. *Now.*"

Sweet cheeks? Screw him. Soz knelt on one knee, moving carefully, never taking her gaze off the captain. She set the gun on the floor and gave it a push, sliding it over to him.

Mode four activated, the gun told her, communicating via her spinal node. As the frigate captain picked it up off the floor, her gun added, **This handler is hostile**.

Get readings on him, Soz thought as she stood up. **Physiological data, body language, verbal analysis, everything**.

Reading, the gun answered.

The frigate captain turned the jumbler over in his hands. "What ammo does it shoot?"

"Abitons," Soz said. "Anti-particles."

He glanced up sharply. "I'm not stupid, sweet cheeks. Try again."

So. They didn't have lie detectors in all that ornate hardware they were wearing. She kept her face bland as she changed her truth to a lie. "It shoots serrated pulse projectiles."

"Where'd you get it?" He sounded more curious than worried.

"Jorman Fringe Market," she said. It was a lucrative venue for smugglers.

He looked her over. "You a private operator?"

"Just trying to survive," she said. Nothing too cocky, but neither did she want to appear afraid.

Yaetes and the others were watching them in silence, intent, primed to fight like spring-loaded coils. Hypron's anger blazed in her mind. He had no intention of sitting by while yet another person he cared for died.

Your gun has finished its analysis, her node thought.

Does that guy have any clue what he's holding? Soz asked.

His vital signs don't indicate the fear most people experience when facing a Jagernaut or their weaponry. I'd say he's never seen a jumbler before.

Good. The pirates probably would have recognized her uniform if she had been wearing it; most people knew what a Jagernaut looked like. But jumblers were less infamous than the tech-mech warriors who carried them. The more this captain underestimated her, the better. Given how badly her people were outnumbered, she needed every advantage, for she had little doubt these intruders would kill them after they finished enjoying their captives.

"Captain, I'm getting a weird reading." That came from the pirate woman who had spoken earlier. She was frowning at her ingot-encrusted gauntlet.

What's she looking at? Soz asked her node.

I'm not sure. A sensor. Your jumbler isn't close enough to determine more.

The captain glanced at the woman. "What kind of reading?"

She indicated Soz. "Uh, sir … it says she's a micro-fusion reactor."

Damn! How had they picked that up? Her internal power source was shielded by state-of-the-art military-grade shrouds.

The captain scowled at the woman. "Is that a fucking joke?"

"No, sir." She held out her gauntlet. "You can see the reading."

"That tech is a piece of crap," he said. "You should never have taken it off that corpse."

Soz gritted her teeth. Very few sensors could pick up the reactor that powered her internal systems. If they had murdered an ISC officer with a rank high enough to carry such a detector, that added assassination to their crimes.

"So." The captain looked Soz up and down, his gaze lingering on her breasts and hips. "You don't look like a micro-fusion reactor to me."

"Yeah, sure, I explode like a bomb," Soz said. In truth, it was almost impossible, given the safeguards on her reactor.

The captain gave a raspy laugh. "Sounds like fun. Come here, sweets."

Hypron's anger surged, and Soz knew he was about to push his chair forward. Of course they would shoot him before he made it halfway across the room.

Hypron, stop! Soz thought.

Shock exploded over her. *His* shock, at hearing her "voice" in his mind. Outwardly, he showed almost no reaction, a phenomenal display of self-control given his stunned mental response.

Soz? he asked. *Is that you?*

Yes. She stepped carefully towards the captain. **Stay put. He's giving me an excuse to get close to them.**

Be careful, he thought.

She felt how hard it was for him to hold back. He didn't care about dying; as far as he was concerned, he had no reason to live. She wanted whoever had murdered his brother to pay, and she'd bet a year's wage the killers were in this room. She didn't pick up any details about the death on the surface of their minds, and she couldn't risk lowering her shields more, but she had a general sense that at least some of them had been here before.

She stopped in front of the frigate captain. He was tall, but with her boots, she stood at his height. He put an arm around her waist and yanked her closer. "What do you think, hmm? Still trying to survive? I got thoughts on how you can do that, babe."

"I'm sure you do," she said. **Toggle combat mode**, she thought.

Toggled, her node answered.

Soz spun out of the captain's grip. The world slowed down; everyone else seemed to move at a fraction of normal speed. She kicked up her leg as she whirled, jamming her boot heel in the captain's stomach. As he slammed back into the wall, she swung her fist, her aim fine-tuned by combat libraries in her node. Her knuckles smashed the wrist of the woman with the gauntlet sensor, and the crack of shattering bone broke the air. The woman screamed, a counterpoint to the captain's bellow. In Soz's speeded-up state, their voices sounded eerily deepened and drawn out.

People converged on her in slow motion. Soz kicked the gun out of one man's hand while she broke the arm of another pirate, a woman who was raising a pistol. Shouts rang out, strange and sluggish. She caught the flicker of someone's hand an instant before he fired his laser, and she dropped out of the beam's path as it shot across the room. Rolling across the floor, she tackled him in the knees and knocked him unconscious when he hit the ground. Yaetes fired his pistol, catching one of the pirates in the torso. Another pirate swung his laser carbine around to shoot, and Soz lunged into him, knocking the gun out of his grip. Someone else fired and Soz jumped high, flipping over the path of a projectile bullet. She glimpsed the carbine she had liberated spinning through the air towards Hypron, and in the instant she landed, Hypron caught the laser.

Someone slammed Soz in the back. An agonized scream penetrated her mind as she went down. Not her cry; a bullet had struck one of Yaetes' men. Its serrated edges barely touched him, but its shock wave slammed through his body, and his reaction reverberated in Soz's hyper-sensitized mind as if she had also been hit. Her training kept her going even as she mentally reeled from the blow. She threw her attacker backward, then flipped her over and pressed against the woman's windpipe, using enough pressure to knock her out.

The frigate captain was trying to fire the jumbler. Aiming at Soz, he jammed his thumb on the firing stud again and again. When nothing happened, he swore furiously and hurled the gun away. It crashed into the wall, then slammed down onto the floor.

Get ready, Soz thought to the jumbler, her thoughts accelerated.

Priming, the gun answered.

Soz rolled across the floor and grabbed the jumbler as she jumped to her feet. She had a glimpse of Yaetes sprawled on the ground. He was in *pain*, vivid and intense, but it meant he was alive. With Yaetes down, it also meant Hypron was wide open to attack.

In the same moment Soz realized the frigate captain was looking straight at Hypron, she felt the pirate's horrified recognition. He thought Hypron was a man he had already killed on the very dock of this house before he had left for reinforcements to take the homestead itself. In that instant, he believed was looking into the living face of a dead man.

Oxim.

The captain's reaction burst over Soz, both his memory of the warped pleasure he had taken in Oxim's murder and his nightmare that someday one of his victims would rise from a gruesome death to exact revenge. Hypron's face contorted as he caught the images of Oxim's death, and his horror blasted over Soz. Rage filled him, so intense it seared. He had never shot another person in his life, but he raised the laser carbine without hesitation.

The entire time Soz kept moving, swinging around to face the pirates. Standing with her feet planted wide, she fired her jumbler, sweeping its beam across the ground in front of the intruders. The floor exploded in a blaze of orange light. As it collapsed, some of the pirates fell to their knees and others stumbled back. One shouted as his gun discharged, blasting a projectile into the wall. The captain was still standing, staring at Hypron with his face contorted in a raw, unthinking hatred. He raised his gun to finish a man he believed he had already destroyed—

Hypron fired.

The laser beam shot across the room in a brilliant red streak. When it hit the frigate captain, his body flared so brightly it threw the room into a sharp relief of light and shadow. He blazed, and the stench of incinerated skin scorched the air.

The impact of his death slammed into Soz's mind, and she reeled. Hypron picked it up as well, and it hit his untrained mind like an explosion. He had no mental shield that could withstand that onslaught. As colour drained from his face, Soz instinctively reached out to protect him. Her node spurred neural transmitters to block her synapses, muting what she felt, and she tried to do the same for

Hypron. It couldn't completely turn off their empathic reception; interfering with that many synapses would knock a person unconscious. But it could make the shock more bearable.

Soz stopped moving.

She stood in the middle of the room, breathing hard. The place was in shambles, the floor ravaged, the furniture broken, the window-wall networked by shatter patterns where bullets had hit the supposedly break-proof glass. The stench of the atmosphere leaked inside, and mud seeped into the trench in the floor.

Everyone was staring at her. The pirates were crouched on the ground or lying still. Yaetes' people had taken shelter behind a pulverized table. Soz kept her jumbler up and primed as she swung from side to side, watching everyone, her mind focused like a laser.

Hostiles neutralized, her node thought. **Kill or capture?**

Hold, Soz answered.

Motion flickered in her side vision.

In the same instant Soz whirled, her gun thought, **Primed to fire.**

No! Soz told it. **That's Yaetes**. The racer captain was climbing to his feet with careful movements, his gaze fixed on Soz.

He is too close to the psion you are protecting, her node thought. **Advise attack.**

She wondered why her node singled out Hypron as the person she was protecting. **I'm here to defend everyone. Including Captain Yaetes.**

The captain took a deep breath, holding his pistol by his side. He let the gun drop, and it clattered on the floor. Then he limped towards Soz, holding out his hands to show he had no other weapons.

Defence primed, her node thought. **Attack?**

No attack, Soz told it.

Yaetes stopped a few metres away. "Secondary Valdoria, it's over. You can stand down."

Soz considered him. He had a point. **Combat mode off**, she told her node.

Toggled off.

With an exhale, Soz lowered her jumbler.

"Gods almighty," one of the pirates muttered.

Doctor Carlon spoke, his voice easily carrying in the stunned silence. "She's a Jagernaut, asshole."

Soz looked around at the pirates. "And all of you," she said, "are under arrest."

Hypron sat on the edge of his bed in the dark, fully dressed, worn out but unable to lie down. Nothing could erase the images burned into his mind. He had killed today, and lived that death as if it were his own. Worse, he had felt that monster's pleasure in murdering Oxim.

After the battle, he had said nothing. He felt as if amber encased him. While Soz and the others had guarded the pirates, he had worked on repairing the mesh circuitry in the backup EI. When the racer returned with patrol authorities from the mainland, the officers asked for his statement, and Hypron had somehow given it, his voice numb. He had watched them take away the surviving pirates and the remains of the frigate captain. The ashes. No one arrested Hypron. No one condemned him. Self-defence, they said. He couldn't respond. Too much had happened, too much loss, pain, grief, violence. It seared his mind.

The door creaked, and an invisible cloak of calm spread over his thoughts. Soz.

Hypron closed his eyes. He didn't understand how her mind could be so luminous given what she lived through in battle, experiencing the injuries of her enemies, their pain, fear, cruelty, whatever they felt. Their *deaths*. He knew now, from Soz, what to call himself. Empath. Perhaps even a telepath. How could she survive it? ISC was even worse than he had thought, sending empaths into combat, even technologically enhancing their abilities, all so they could become better killers. He was surprised Jagernauts didn't all commit suicide.

"Hypron." Her voice was soft in the dark. The bed rustled as she sat next to him. She laid her hand on his shoulder, but he didn't move. He couldn't accept comfort, not after what he had done. She stroked his cheek, until finally his resolve crumbled and he pulled her close, resting his cheek on the top of her head.

"It's all right," she whispered. "You'll be all right, I swear."

"Soz—" His voice cracked. Nothing would ever be right again.

She touched his chin with her fingers and turned his face towards hers. Her lips were warm as she kissed him. He knew he shouldn't hold her, that making love wouldn't fix anything, but gods, he needed the refuge. He was breaking inside. He pulled her close, and she drew him onto the bed, caressing him.

As they came together in the deep, quiet places of the night, his mind blended with hers. She wrapped her legs around his waist, and he moved within her, strong and steady, until he finally lost all thought in the oblivion of a healing as old as the human race.

Hypron was drowsily aware of Soz turning over in bed. He lay on his back, one arm thrown over his head, the other feeling cold as she moved away. He wondered if she would leave.

"Not unless you want," she mumbled, her voice deepened by sleep.

"Stay," he murmured. She was shielding her mind somehow, but he picked up her contentment. After a moment, he added, "How can you hear what I think?"

She rolled over and nestled against his side. "I can't that much, only if the thought is intense and on the surface of your mind."

"I've never met anyone like me." He put his arm around her, settling her head against his shoulder. "Someone who feels moods." The closest he had known was with Oxim. Hard on the heels of that memory came a sharp pang of grief.

"You must have loved him a lot," Soz said. Then she muttered, "Gods, that sounded trite."

"It's fine," he said softly, leaning his head against hers. "I'm glad you stayed tonight."

"It's been a long time. I mean, since, you know." She slid her hand across his chest. "Since I've done this."

He hadn't expected that from so sensuous a woman. He knew little about Jagernauts, though. It wouldn't surprise him if they had trouble with the softer aspects of life given what they endured in battle.

"Why with me?" As soon as the question came out, he wished he had kept his mouth shut. He had no desire to know if she had slept with him out of pity.

Soz just said, "It seemed right." She shifted against him, slight movements, but erotic. "Such a sexy man."

Sexy? Good gods. Her brain was fried.

"You really have no idea, do you?" Her voice trailed off, sleepy and warm. "Foolish women here. Their loss ... my gain."

He didn't know what to make of that, but he liked it. He was less comfortable with her hearing his thoughts. He imagined a shroud over his mind. Then he thought, *You have green tufts of fur on your ears*. He smiled, imagining her reaction.

After a moment, when nothing happened, he thought, *I wish you weren't leaving*.

Nothing.

He imagined his thoughts forming *outside* his mental shroud. ***Did you catch that?***

She stirred against him. **Catch what?**

So. He *could* hide his thoughts. *I wondered how long you would be here*.

Until we finish the evacuation. Then she added, **We won't strand you, Hypron. We'll help you resettle.**

He closed his eyes, relieved. ***That's good to know***. Just those moments of exchanging thoughts made his temples ache. He mentally retreated, settling his shroud around his mind.

After a moment, Soz spoke. "Does it bother you that I have augmentation inside of me?"

He blinked, unsure how to answer. "It's different."

"The system is called a biomech web."

He supposed it should make him uncomfortable. She was probably the most dangerous human being he had ever met. But she felt so human, her body lithe and female against his. Even if this was only for one night, it was hard to believe a woman like her actually wanted him. Hell no, it didn't bother him.

"I'm all right with it," he said.

"I have an enhanced muscle system and skeleton," she said.

"Hydraulics, bioelectrodes, neurotrophic protections, bio-active threads, ear and optical implants, all that."

He wondered why she wanted him to know. "Sounds impressive."

"You're sure you're fine about this?"

"Really, it's no problem."

"Good." Then, in a perfectly normal voice, she shook his universe. "Because we can get the biomech for you. Not a weapons-grade system, but certainly the structural mech. So you can walk again."

Walk again? She was serious! His instant of euphoria died as fast as it had come. "I'm sure I can't afford that kind of treatment."

"Hell, yes, you can." Her voice was low, but none the less ominous for that. "Make a claim against Newland Corporation. I'll help you file. They owe you. *Big* time."

"Aren't you an ISC officer?" He wasn't sure, but he thought Jagernaut Secondary was a high rank in the military. "ISC helped Newland set up this colony."

"You're damn right. That means I know how to deal with the system. When I get back to HQ, there will be hell to pay. Newland might as well have given you colonists a death sentence."

"Oh." He hardly knew how to absorb her words. Then he wanted to kick himself. She was offering to give him back his life, and the best he could do was *Oh?* He was a dolt.

"Thank you." He wished he knew how to express how much it meant to him. "I don't have the words to say that right."

Her voice softened. "You don't need words. You shine inside. You must be an artist or something."

"My brother used to say that." He doubted he would ever again talk about his life without remembering Oxim. "I really don't know. I've been too busy trying to stay alive."

"We'll have to find out what you like when you don't have to worry about just surviving."

"It's hard to imagine." Nor had he missed what else she had said. "'We?'"

She tensed against him. "If, uh … you'd like that."

The night's quiet suddenly seemed thick. "You would want me, too?"

She spoke awkwardly. "Unless you don't like the idea."

Gods, she was serious. Of course he wanted her. "I do," he said. "Like the idea, I mean."

She exhaled, her body relaxing. They lay together in a silence after that, their limbs tangled together. An emotion came to him, one so rare it took a moment to sink in. He was glad to be alive. He had been dying inside for so long, he almost didn't recognize the lightness. Even if she left tomorrow and he never saw her again, she had given him a reason to pick up his life and learn to deal with his grief.

"I won't leave," she said. "You'll stay with me, yes? Let's see what happens. See if it works out."

He pressed his lips against her forehead. "Yes. Let's do that."

For the first time in years, Hypron drifted to sleep looking forward to the morning.